Advance Praise for *Familia*

"A masterfully woven tale of mystery,
reconciliation, and familial love."
—Abby Jimenez, *New York Times* **bestselling author**
of *Yours Truly*

"Lauren Rico's *Familia* has it all: An old crime, unsuspecting
victims, a genetic mystery that will explode a family, the
enormous tenderness of desperate parents. By page 30, I would
have walked on coals to finish reading this story."
—Jacquelyn Mitchard, *New York Times* **bestselling author**
of *The Deep End of the Ocean*

"*Familia* is an absolute delight. I couldn't stop turning the pages—
I needed to know what both the past and the future held for
these sisters and how they would put together the pieces of the
events that separated them to make their family whole again."
—KJ Dell'Antonia, *New York Times* **bestselling author**
of *The Chicken Sisters*

"A moving story about the bonds of sisterhood and unraveling
the mysteries of your past. I truly enjoyed going on this
journey with Isabella and Gabby. A wonderful debut!"
—Annette Chavez Macias, bestselling author
of *Big Chicas Don't Cry*

"A page-turning story of family lost and found, wrapped in the
tangled threads of an engaging mystery, and sprinkled with just a bit
of sazón, I loved everything about this modern yet timeless book."
—Ann Dávila Cardinal, author of *The Storyteller's Death*

"*Familia* is a compelling and emotional narrative that explores a
past wrapped in secrets, the bonds of sisterhood, and what it
means to be family. With twists that unfold in every chapter,
Lauren E. Rico crafts a compulsive story with engaging characters
that hooked me from the start. Gabby and Isabella will stay with
you long after you finish the last page. This is a must-read!"
—Kerry Lonsdale, *Wall Street Journal,* *Washington Post*
and Amazon Charts bestselling author

Familia is a novel of robust joy. The story spills off the page
in a rush of emotion that makes you feel like you've been
on the journey of a lifetime. Simply marvelous!"
—Amy T. Matthews, author of *Someone Else's Bucket List*

Dear Reader,

As I write this, my grandmother, Crucita, and grandfather, Mike, are in their early nineties, and as they gradually fade away so too do their memories. His childhood in a small mining town in Cuba during the years before World War II and Fidel Castro. Her recollections of tiny Ceiba, Puerto Rico, growing up the eighth of nine children raised by a single mother.

So many stories! Why didn't I listen all those times they told me about what their lives had been like? Why didn't I write down the recipes, make the family tree, or create the scrapbook? Mike and Crucita are the keepers of more family history than I could ever hope to reconstruct on some ancestry site. But, luckily for me, along with not looking back, I'm a staunch believer that it's *never* too late. Ever.

And so began *Familia,* a journey to rediscover my cultural heritage, to find my roots, so to speak. I could remain apathetic about my family history and miss out on so much richness, or I could jump in with both feet and just start swimming. I chose the latter . . . and here I am now. I did what my three-decade career as a broadcaster had taught me to do—I pulled out a microphone. When I asked my grandfather if he'd tell me his story, he looked at me and smiled. "I was wondering when you were finally going to ask," he said.

I listened intently at the kitchen table as he recounted his youth in Cuba, the tiny mining town that flourished then faded in the wake of World War II. He told me about his father coming ahead to the U.S. and sending for him to join him so they could work together and make the money to bring the rest of the family to New York. And they did. Not long after that, he met a pretty girl who had come from Puerto Rico. He took her out on dates, her mother happily serving as chaperone as he took them for nice meals, long walks, and the latest films. They were still teenagers when they got married and my mother was born. By the time I came along—their first grandchild—they weren't even forty years old yet. As of the time of this writing, they had just celebrated their seventy-fourth wedding anniversary.

My grandfather never returned to Cuba after Fidel Castro came to power, but he never stopped loving that tropical island lifestyle, so he and my grandmother moved back and forth to and from Puerto Rico several times. My two oldest cousins were born there, and their mother still lives on the island. It was and always has been a place they loved and found themselves pulled to again and again.

In my adult years, I visited them a handful of times, usually bringing along a friend or boyfriend, always seeing it through the eyes of a tourist. I took in the sights, soaked up the sun, drank the rum, and grumbled about what the humidity did to my hair. It wasn't until much later that I looked back on those times and that place wistfully, especially Guánica, the tiny fishing village on the southwest coast of the island where they'd lived an idyllic life. I will always remember the neat, pastel-colored concrete houses—neighbors up and down the blocks out on their porches, rocking, chatting, drinking, and listening to music. In this place, you had only to walk a couple of blocks to the baker, the doctor, and the beach. And the oceanfront boardwalk known simply as *El Malecón.* The heart of this little town, it always seemed to be bustling with music, dancing, and the town's signature *piragüeros*—vendors with little street carts offering various flavors of shaved ice known as *piraguas.* This is the Guánica I have written of in *Familia.*

In 2017, Hurricane Maria barreled through Puerto Rico, destroying nearly a thousand homes and buildings in tiny Guánica alone. Less than three years later, two earthquakes would hit one day apart, dealing the village a final blow. Now there are empty houses, once so bright and proud. I wonder now what will become of Guánica and the countless other little towns like it. Will they be resurrected? Will they simply fade away like the people who used to live there? Like my grandparents?

My husband and I recently returned to Puerto Rico—my first trip there since writing this book. Upon exiting the airport I was struck with a thought so powerful it nearly knocked me off my feet: "Oh, thank God, I can *breathe*!"

I was looking at the island with fresh, curious eyes, drinking it all in and embracing the culture, totally enthralled by everything around me: the water, the palm trees, the music, the food, the beaches, the artwork, the rum (yeah, some things never change!). Suddenly long-forgotten Spanish started to seep back into my brain, along with memories of local specialties my grandmother used to cook regularly. It was a week of romance for all three of us—me, my husband, and Puerto Rico! By the time we'd left, we knew we wanted to move there at least part-time in the not-so-distant future.

In *Familia*, Gabby comes to Puerto Rico skeptical about her connection to the island, but still with open eyes and an open heart. She takes it all in—the people, the places, the language, the food, the customs, savoring each and every experience, finding beauty and poetry every day. I thought about her—this person I'd created from the depths of my own subconscious—on every step of that trip. I looked and I listened, and I experienced, and it was the most fulfilling trip I've ever had in my life.

Fortuitously, it was during my most recent trip to Puerto Rico that the results of my own ancestry DNA test arrived, revealing to me sixty-nine generations of ancestors on the island dating back to the year 245 AD!

If there's anything I hope you take away from this book, it's a reminder to appreciate the culture and history we inherit with our DNA. At the same time, DNA is not what defines family. Family isn't just bound in blood or cemented by documentation. It doesn't live within the parameters of some paper "tree" filled with birth and death dates. It's not about who we share our DNA with so much as who we share our heart with. Throughout *Familia*, there are several minor but important characters who play a part in the ultimate resolution of the book. They're not related through genetic material or legal decree, yet as I wrote, I always considered them to be a sort of ad hoc family of their own—unified in their singular goal to do the right thing, their refusal to give up in the face of adversity, and their willingness to risk everything.

I hope that you will, unlike me, be brave enough to look back sooner rather than later so that you might see the complete picture of who you are and where you come from. I hope that you will find comfort in the knowledge that somewhere out there the universe, or God, or whatever "higher power" you believe in is conspiring on your behalf, weaving together the fragile gossamer threads that will eventually provide you with an unbreakable tether to this world and all that it holds for you—past, present, *and* future.

Go ahead and get out there . . . it's waiting for you.

Lauren E Rico

FAMILIA

LAUREN E. RICO

KENSINGTON
PUBLISHING CORP.

www.kensingtonbooks.com

KENSINGTON BOOKS are published by
Kensington Publishing Corp.
119 West 40th Street
New York, NY 10018

ISBN: 978-1-4967-4465-4 (ebook)

ISBN: 978-1-4967-4464-7

First Kensington Trade Paperback Printing: January 2024

10 9 8 7 6 5 4 3 2 1

Printed in the United States of America

For Mike and Crucita, the heartbeat of our familia

PROLOGUE

ALBERTO

That Day

Alberto never understood why people were afraid of the dark. Ever since he was a little boy, he'd welcomed the pitch black like an old friend. Whether the dark came of its own accord—like at the end of the day, or if he beckoned it with sleep, or booze, or drugs, it never failed to pull him into its open arms, wrapping him in black silky oblivion. It offered protection—if only for a few hours—from the brutal realities laid bare by the rising sun.

No, Alberto was not afraid of the dark, but the light scared the living shit out of him. And right now, the two seemed to be battling for control of his body. The daylight pulled him up briefly—just long enough for the pain to register. But then the tendrils of black unconsciousness coiled around his thoughts, pulling him back down into the deep end of oblivion. Sometime later, something beckoned him back up toward the surface. Something important. It was right there in front of him, but he was having trouble wresting himself from the blissful safety of the dark. Still, the daylight pulled at him, drawing him further and further out of himself and up toward the surface. And the closer he came, the more agonizing it was.

Every blink, every breath, every single twitch of movement sent searing pain rippling through his muscles, and he became aware of something digging into his face. Pebbles? He realized he must be lying facedown on the street. The thought was enough to make him open his eyes, which were immediately assaulted by the early morning sun. He closed them again more tightly this time, but it didn't matter. An aura of red shone through the delicate flesh of his lids, backlighting the tiny blood vessels and causing spots to float across his vision. There would be no more retreat into the black oblivion today.

It took a few long moments for his thoughts and his body to coordinate their efforts to drag him fully back to the present—and his current situation. He was splayed across a storm drain, his left cheek wedged into a deep fissure that split the asphalt.

"*Mierda,*" he murmured to himself. He pushed himself onto all fours, wincing and groaning in concert with his spasming muscles. "Okay, okay, okay."

Slowly, he lifted a hand to swipe at the tiny stones still embedded in his face. It felt good to be rid of them, but he felt the warm, wet tackiness of what could only be blood. This upped his alertness considerably. Had he fallen and hit his head? Been struck by a car? If it weren't for the fact that his limbs were intact, he'd have sworn he'd been hit by a train based on his pain level alone.

He pushed himself back onto his haunches. That's when he felt more blood, a tiny river washing down his face from somewhere along his hairline. Fat droplets of crimson splattered on the ground, disappearing against the tarry blackness. Alberto took a deep breath and, with every ounce of strength he could muster, straightened to his full five-feet-ten-inches. Around him were the backs of the faded, weatherbeaten houses.

It took a few seconds for him to place his whereabouts. He was at the end of the alley that ran behind his local dive bar, El Gallo Rojo, in the heart of Puerto Rico's La Perla. Only a stone's throw from the cobblestoned streets and quaint shops of Old San Juan, "The Pearl" loomed dull and bedraggled in comparison—a dark and dangerous neighborhood that tourists were cautioned to avoid before disembarking their fancy cruise ships. Not that they didn't find their way there regardless. Especially the ones looking for a little something "special" to take home. A little something that couldn't be found in the gift shops—but was easy enough to secure on most corners and back alleys of La Perla for the right price. Back alleys like this one.

Alberto pulled the filthy, sweat-drenched T-shirt off his back and held it against his head to stanch the flow of blood. He tried to piece together the events leading up to waking up here. There were drinks—lots of drinks. There were always lots of drinks since Rosaria had died seven months ago. It was the only way he could get through the day. Well, that and a little bit of that "something special" when things got really bad.

He forced himself to think back further until he could place himself at the bar, talking to Beatríz as he handed over the last bill in his pocket for one more beer. He'd needed to get out of the house—a tiny, concrete structure with faded blue paint. He'd promised Rosaria he'd paint it blue—her favorite color. He'd painted it for her after Isabellita was born. And they had been happy there. Right up until the night their second daughter was born. The night that everything went terribly, terribly wrong. The night that Alberto became a widower with a toddler and an infant. His girls. His Isabellita and his Marianna . . .

The instant her name sounded in his mind, an impulse shot through his alcohol- and grief-addled brain. He wasn't prepared for the sudden, overwhelming sensation of all his synapses erupting at once, and he had to reach out, steadying himself against a palm tree in order to keep from being knocked flat into the street again.

"Marianna," he whispered to himself as images of the child flooded his memory.

He was pushing her stroller down the street. He'd stepped into the bar to show Beatríz how big the girl was getting and accepted a beer "on the house." But, of course, it was never one beer, was it? And something had happened . . . someone had beat the shit out of him over . . . what? Something he couldn't remember.

But where was Marianna?

Alberto felt the bile rise hot at the back of his throat as he allowed his eyes to scan the area where he'd just been lying— almost afraid of what he might find. But there was no stroller. No baby.

"Por favor, Padre querido . . ." he murmured the instant he caught a flash of pink several feet away.

Please, dear Father . . .

He ignored the intense pain that came with each dread-filled step until he was looking down at the item.

Alberto Ruíz dropped to his knees, clutching the single, tiny pink sock to his chest as he looked upward, screaming his fear and his rage, shouting his pitiful pleas to the heavens. As usual, no reply came.

He couldn't remember what he'd done.

But whatever it was, it had cost him his baby.

CHAPTER 1

GABBY

Today

There's this misconception that truth is a fluid thing—that it morphs and changes, relative to the circumstances surrounding it. But that's not the case. Truth—the *real* truth—is as immovable as a mountain. Forget about "alternative facts" or "perceived reality." The truth is the *truth*, and no amount of spinning, bald-faced lying, or underhanded fuckery can change that. As Shakespeare once wrote: *The truth will out.* It's just a matter of time.

My job is to make sure it "outs" sooner, rather than later.

"How's the plagiarism piece coming, Gabby?"

At the mention of my name, I look up from the steno pad open on my lap where I've been half taking notes/half doodling. I sit up straighter in my chair—it's one of the ones lining the walls of the conference room, serving as overflow for the "grown-ups" table. *That's* where the editors, writers, photographers, and graphic designers sit. The rest of us mere mortals are relegated to the sidelines of the *Flux* magazine morning editorial meeting.

I clear my throat and reply to Max, our super-hot, super-British managing editor.

"Uh . . . yeah, it's going okay. I've been able to verify all of Lisa's quoted sources, and I've read the books involved—Jake

Finnegan's, as well as the three that he's been accused of lifting from. So, now I'm digging through Finnegan's backlist—I want to see if this is a one-off thing, or if he's been writing 'frankenbooks' all along and no one's noticed until now."

Everyone chuckles except for Lisa Mulberry, the author of the article in question. She wrinkles her cute little upturned nose at me. "Frankenbooks?" she echoes.

"Like Frankenstein?" I reply. She looks at me blankly. "You know, the monster—"

"I know who Frankenstein is," she tells me impatiently. "What I'd like to know is who asked you to go digging through the backlist? If I'd wanted you to do that, I'd have told you so."

Despite the fact that we've worked together for nearly three years, this woman seems to be under the impression that I'm an intern, there to serve her. I'm not. I'm a fact-checker, meaning it's my job to cover the magazine's collective ass by verifying that all the information written by divas like Lisa are legitimate and can be proven on demand. And, yeah, okay, I can be a pain in the ass—always nipping at the writers' heels requesting details about names, dates, and places—but they all love me when I can produce the proof needed to stave off a lawsuit.

I take a deep breath and do my best to sound pleasant, hoping she'll take the hint and do the same.

"Lisa, I'm just saying, it's not as straightforward as you might think. And this is a really serious accusation. We could destroy a man's reputation. His career. So, I want to be sure we've got it right."

"You mean *me*? You want to make sure *I've* got it right?" she spits back at me. "Do you really think I haven't vetted this story myself?"

So much for pleasant and professional.

Max pipes up from the head of the table, and the one-two punch of his lush accent and his soul-searchingly deep hazel eyes seems to smooth all Lisa's ruffled feathers in one fell swoop. Not to mention her ginormous ego.

"Oh, now, Lisa, you know that's not what Gabby was suggesting," he says coaxingly. "She's here to protect you."

Actually, I'm here to protect *Flux*. The fact that Lisa's ass happens to be covered in the process is purely incidental. Now, if I were the one writing this story . . . but, of course, I'm not. I'm never the one actually writing the story, a fact my colleague is only too happy to point out every chance she gets.

Clearly mesmerized by Max's easy, boyish smile, Lisa shuts up and nods her acquiescence.

Damn, this guy knows how to harness his hotness! It must be a British thing, because I can't think of a single American man who can turn a frown upside down faster than the Surrey-born Maxwell Taylor-Davies.

"All right then, let's continue, shall we?" he asks, not waiting for a response. "I'm excited to report that the results of our GeneTeam profiles are now available online. Kelly will be messaging each of you with a username and temporary password. If you volunteered for this assignment, please take some time this week to look over your results and put together a brief summary of the findings. I'd like to get this story up and running in the next week or two—"

"And what's the focus going to be, exactly?" asks Randy Greenblatt, another staff writer. He's considerably more talented and considerably less infuriating than Lisa.

Max shrugs and quirks an enigmatic eyebrow. "That remains to be seen. We've heard thousands of stories about families brought together—and torn apart—by the results of genealogical testing. I have a hunch we might just turn up something interesting among our staff. I'd love for us to be able to write a firsthand profile about that. But, barring the discovery of a little genetic 'skeleton in the closet,' we could also use the information to compare the different services based on our own little in-house test group. With everyone's permission, of course," he's quick to add.

This is a fairly standard practice for Max, who has this idea that there are unexpected, undiscovered stories all around us, just waiting to be uncovered and told. Since he arrived nine months ago, fresh off a stint at a London-based tabloid, he's solicited volunteers to visit psychics, attend seminars with A-list self-help gurus, and, as of three months ago, to spit into a little plastic tube to determine if one of us is related to Queen Elizabeth . . . or, better yet, Meghan Markle.

I normally pass on these extracurricular offers, but since my dad died last year, I've found myself missing that family connection. The only child of only children, I wasn't one to grow up with aunts and uncles and cousins—which might have been okay if I had a solid network of close friends. But I don't. Sure, there are a few girlfriends I see for drinks or lunch or a movie periodically, but the truth is that my parents and I were a very tight unit—just the three of us. No extended relatives, no close family friends. It was always just . . . us. And I liked it that way. Except now, it's just me. So, I'm hoping to strike a little DNA gold by tracking down a second cousin or great-aunt I don't know about.

"All right then, my friends," Max says, slapping his notebook closed on the table in front of him before uttering his standard end-of-meeting benediction. "Now go forth and engage the masses!"

I linger, finding a reason to dig through my bag—repeatedly—until most of the room has cleared. Then I mosey on over to my boss, who is scowling down at something on his phone. After a few moments, he looks up at me, smiling.

"Excellent work, Gabby. I love that you go above and beyond to get it right."

I fight off the urge to melt into a puddle on the floor. This is too important to get frozen in the tractor beam of his charm.

"Thank you, Max, I appreciate it. I was just . . . I was

wondering if you'd given any more thought to that proposal I sent you last week?"

For the briefest of moments, I see a cloud cross his face. He hasn't thought about it. He doesn't even remember it.

"The . . . uh . . . the pitch for the profile of that tiny town in Minnesota? The one where the cats all wear sweaters? And the wacky lady with her psychic pies . . ."

Now there's a spark of recognition in his eyes.

"Right! Right, right. What is it called? Maypole? Mayberry? Maytag . . . ?"

"Mayhem," I correct. "Mayhem, Minnesota. I thought it could be the first in an ongoing series about America's quirkiest towns."

He's nodding. Maybe I haven't given him enough credit. Maybe he did review it . . . but got busy with other projects in the interim. Maybe—

"Yes, yes, of course. Mayhem, Minnesota," he echoes. "I have to be honest with you, Gabby, everyone is pretty much locked into assignments for the next several months. I don't think I can free up a writer to tackle a multi-part series at the moment. But perhaps after the new year—"

"Me," I break in a little too abruptly. "I'd like to take a shot at writing it myself," I explain, certain that I was very clear about this part of the well-researched, well-thought-out proposal I sent him.

"Ah, yes. I see," he replies. "Well, here's the thing, Gabby. I'm sure you'd do an exceptional job with it, but you're just so valuable to us as a fact-checker at the moment." He perches on the edge of the table and leans in closer to me, dropping his voice as if he's telling me his deepest, darkest secrets. "Truthfully, you're the best I've ever worked with. And, when you think about it, your job makes you an essential part of *every* story we print. You might not get the byline, but there's no way these stories have a chance outside this room without your input."

I stare at him, determined not to say a word. Every article on negotiations I've read—including a few published in our own magazine—says you need to let the other person fill in the awkward pauses. If I rush in right now, I'll be letting him off the hook. And that's not what I want. Not this time. Hotty hot Brit or not, I want a chance to prove I'm more than the girl who confirms that it's Anne with an *e* or Sarah with an *h*. But I guess he's read those articles, too, because he just smiles at me, content to wait me out. Finally, it's his assistant, Kelly, who breaks our silent standoff.

"Max? They're asking to see you upstairs," she tells him as she sticks her head through the door. "Oh, I'm sorry, I didn't mean to interrupt . . ."

He holds up a hand, still smiling at me kindly. "Nope, all good, Kelly, thanks. I'll be right there."

When she's left again, Max looks at me closely. "Everything okay?"

"Yeah . . . I just . . . I feel as if I'm ready for the next step, Max."

"Look, I'll see if I can get you a bump in pay. God knows you're worth every penny," he offers with a reassuring smile, then looks down at his watch. "Listen, I really do need to go. Was there anything else?"

I shake my head, defeated. Again.

My boss gets to his feet and starts towards the door to the conference room. He stops and turns briefly. "Hey, don't forget to open your genetic testing results—you never know what might be lurking in your family history!"

"Right," is all I can manage as he walks out, leaving me standing in the wake of his five-hundred-dollar-an-ounce cologne.

Well, that didn't go exactly as planned. I'm getting a raise I don't need for doing a job I don't like. Not that I'm wealthy by any stretch, but my parents certainly left me in the enviable position of not having to worry about where the next paycheck is coming from. Thing is, I want my next paycheck to come from here—I just want it to be for checking my own facts, in my own article. I gather my things and go back to my cube, trying not to look as dejected as I feel—which isn't easy.

When I'm back at home in my third-floor brownstone apartment in Brooklyn, it takes several hours and a couple of glasses of chardonnay to work up the nerve to pop open the laptop and check the results of my GeneTeam report.

"Time to meet the relatives . . ." I murmur to myself as I enter the complex string of characters I've been given for a login.

A home page welcomes me and offers me the option to "take a tour" of the report and my personal results. I opt out, figuring I can manage to find what I'm looking for without too much direction. I bypass the brightly colored world map that indicates where my ancestors are from—already knowing that I'll find some derivation of Mediterranean origin. I can hash that out later. No, what I want is the section titled simply *Relations*. I'm immediately prompted to check several boxes, allowing the company to display my matches. I know, of course, that this may not lead anywhere. It would require that someone—probably very distantly related to me—has gone through the same process, with the same company, and checked the same boxes that allow us to see one another's profile information. The odds are . . .

Before I can even finish the thought, the page populates with an elaborate family tree graphic, littered with close to a dozen pictures of other members.

"What the—?"

I set the wineglass down on the coffee table and start scanning faces I don't recognize, attached to names I don't know. Who the hell are these people? This has to be a mistake. I navigate back to the map, homing in on the pie chart that breaks down my ethnicity like so many slices of apple crumb à la mode.

64% European
21% African
15% Native Taino

I blink hard, as if that will somehow clear my vision and change the results. It doesn't. Native Taino? Doesn't that have something to do with the Caribbean? Cuba, Dominican Republic, Jamaica . . .

"Pfft. This is just too much," I mutter, snapping a picture of the screen with my phone before sending it hurtling westward through the ether to my best friend Franny.

Five seconds later, I've got a FaceTime call coming in.

"What am I looking at here?" she asks, blond brows scrunched over green eyes. They match the scrubs she's got on.

"Oh, jeez, I'm sorry—I didn't know you were working! You should've just let it go to voicemail and called me later . . ."

"Honey, there is no later. I'm *always* working," she informs me flatly. "I'm a resident. It's what I do. Now tell me what I'm looking at?"

"Supposedly, that's my genetic makeup."

"Bullshit!" she declares with an incredulous laugh—as if I'm pulling her leg.

"I swear—that's what I got back from GeneTeam."

"Seriously? Looks like somebody in the DNA lab was hungover when they processed your sample! You sure you didn't send it to the place that does doggie DNA?"

"Do you see 'terrier' listed anywhere on that pie chart?"

"Oh, yeah, like you'd be a terrier. With those dark curls, you'd be a black poodle."

"Not helpful."

"Right, sorry. Okay, so it's probably just an error. Maybe a contaminated sample."

"Does that happen?" I ask hopefully.

"No idea," she says, with a shrug. "Ask a doctor."

"You *are* a doctor," I point out.

"Yeah, an ER doctor. Not a geneticist. Now, need to know how to get a zucchini unstuck from your hooha? Yeah, I'm your girl. Or, like last week there was this guy with a—"

"Please don't!" I head her off before this devolves into a conversation about the latest thing she's had to fish out of someone's orifice.

"Sorry, sorry. Anyway, what's the big deal? Call the customer service number and ask them to send you a collection kit so they can repeat the test."

"It's not that easy," I begin. "I did this for work, and the results—even if they're bogus—are part of the story the magazine is researching."

She smacks her forehead dramatically. "Oh! Of course! How could I have forgotten? You did this for the boss. The hottie with the accent. What's his name again? Marshall? Mitchell?"

"Maxwell," I reply. "You know very well it's Maxwell. Max."

"Right, right. Maaaaax," she says, drawing out his name. "Now I remember. He's the guy who refuses to give you a chance to write an article of your own."

I never should have told her about my frustrations at work. Now she's like a dog with a bone. "It's a big magazine, and the bar is really high. I'm sure he'll let me know when he thinks I'm ready."

"I'm not. Seriously, Gabby, when are you going to learn? You've got so much talent, but you just stand around, waiting for things to happen to you. It doesn't work that way. The people who get ahead in this world are the ones who actively go after what they want. That's how the Lisas of this world get ahead—they step right on the backs of people like you who are too polite to ask for what they want."

"It's not like I've got a terrible job," I point out. "A lot of people would kill for my job."

My best friend snorts at me from the Pacific time zone. " '*I want to be a fact-checker when I grow up!*' said no one. Ever. In the history of everything. Just sayin'."

"Okay, okay, I appreciate your concern, but—"

"What's wrong?" Franny asks when I stop short, mouth still set to form the rest of the sentence.

She can see me staring at my laptop, but she can't see what it is that I'm looking at. Suddenly I wish she were here with me, in this room, helping me to sort through all this.

"Umm . . . it's an alert from GeneTeam. It says I have a genetic match."

"What, already? What does it say? Who's the match?"

"Hang on, hang on," I mutter as I point and click my way to the profile. "Um, she's very pretty—long dark hair, dark eyes, probably about our age. Her name is Isabella Ruíz, and it says here she's a fifty percent match." We're both silent for a long moment after I read the report out loud. Finally I ask the question that's now crowded everything else from my mind. "Wouldn't that make her . . ."

"A full sister? Yeah, it would," Franny says, sounding as bewildered as I feel.

"Okay, this is just . . . this has all gone too far. First the wrong ethnic breakdown, and now they want me to believe I have a *sister* that I don't know about? How would that even work? Did my parents have a baby when I wasn't looking and put her up for adoption or something? No, this is just—"

I stop when I see the alert pop up on my screen.

"What is it?" Franny asks from three thousand miles away.

"She just sent me a message."

"Who?"

"Isabella Ruíz. She just sent me a message—like right this second."

Then I stop talking, because all I can do is stare, lost in the words until Fran's voice comes to me through the phone.

"Gabby?"

I turn my attention back to my friend, who looks as concerned as she now sounds.

"The message . . . she says: '*I think you're my sister.*'"

"Wait, what? That's crazy! She must be a crackpot. If she even *is* a she! I'll bet it's some pervy old dude looking for a little cyber bootie . . ."

I shake my head.

"No, this is vetted. You can't just send a message to anyone. You have to have a DNA match."

"Shit," she murmurs. "What the hell does *that* mean?"

"I don't know," I whisper.

And that's the God's honest truth.

CHAPTER 2

ISABELLA

Today

I refresh my messages. Again. And again. And again.

"A watched pot never boils," comes the groggy voice from beside me.

"More like an anticipated email never arrives," I correct Matéo as I glance down at him. "Am I keeping you up with the phone?"

"Nope."

As if to prove his point, he's snoring only a few seconds later.

With a heavy sigh, I turn back to the screen I've been staring at for hours now. I'm waiting for a reply that may never come. But it wouldn't be the first time, and that's never stopped me before. I've been chasing ghosts for as long as I can remember. Well, one particular ghost, anyway. The ghost of a little sister I barely remember. If I'm honest with myself, I'm not even certain that I *do* remember her.

I've never mentioned this to Matéo, but I sometimes think that the vague images in my mind are a composite of the handful of photographs I've seen and bits and pieces of stories I've heard over the years. Pictures and stories about the little girl with the silky dark curls and eyes the color of the Caribbean Sea. Those I'm sure I *do* remember, because I was fascinated by them—so striking against her golden skin. Just like my mother's eyes. *Our* mother's eyes. Mine and Marianna's.

I used to look for her everywhere I went—every town I travelled through, every school I attended. Every church I was dragged to, every street fair, every beach. I would scrutinize every little girl who was the age that Marianna would have been at the time. Kindergarten, second grade, middle school, high school . . . I never stopped looking, though I became a little less obsessive about it—about her—as the years went by. Not because I'd forgotten about her, but because life happened to me.

We had a tiny, weathered bungalow in the heart of Santurce—now a haven for hipsters with money to burn, but when I was growing up, it was more of a haven for sex workers, drug dealers, and carjackers. Like every other house in the neighborhood, the view from each window was obstructed by bars. Bars meant to put a little distance between our family and the grittier, seedier elements living just outside our front door.

After Marianna was taken, I became terrified that I might disappear off the face of the earth, too—snatched up by some monster lurking in the shadows. But as time went on, I started to realize the monster wasn't a person at all. It was the cases of beer and the empty bottles of rum. It was the heroin, or the oxy, or the coke—whatever my father's drug of choice was at that moment. Because, in the end, that was the only way Alberto Ruíz could live with himself. He had to obliterate the man he was—the man he had been. The man who was my Papi.

It would have been so easy to follow him down that brutal, ugly path, but by some miracle I discovered a bright spot in my bleak little world—painting. I loved it. And I was good at it—though not in any traditional way. Unlike other artists, my passion wasn't born in some stuffy museum; it grew right out of the dirty, craggy streets lined with trash, broken-down cars, and broken-down people. Inspiration struck me right on the street where I lived, and by the time I hit my teens, I could be seen running around town at all hours, a rainbow of spray paint stuffed into an old army surplus rucksack. I'd set to work creating larger-than-life murals on the sides of the dirty and decaying buildings of the barrio—aka "the hood."

In the beginning, I was unnerved by the attention I was getting from the gang members who ran the streets and drug dealers who staked the corners. They'd watch me—first with suspicion and then with curiosity. As my audience looked on, I turned the cement wall of an abandoned building into a series of geometric blocks and lines that, when viewed from a distance, became a replica of La Perla with its pink, blue, and yellow houses, with their shutters and balconies, their street-level doorways shrouded in shadow.

Eventually I became a source of entertainment on the slower nights in the barrio. Soon small groups would gather to watch me work—even jumping in to help me move the ladder I dragged all over town. I stopped being anxious around them—ironically coming to feel more secure as they kept a watchful eye—making certain I made my way back home in the late, dark hours. Through all of this, my father took up residence at whichever local dive bar would have him. On more than one occasion, a gang member or dope dealer would be kind enough to help me scrape him off the sidewalk and deliver him to his bed so he could "sleep it off."

This was, incredibly, how I'd met Matéo, the man sleeping next to me. He'd been a petty thief well on his way to becoming a drug dealer. He says that I changed him. But the truth is that love did. It changed both of us. Today he helps kids like himself as a social worker specializing in at-risk youth.

He must sense that I'm thinking about him—as he often does in that uncanny way of his—because he rolls over and squints at me.

"*¿Todavía nada?*" he asks in Spanish.

"No, nothing yet," I echo in English.

He shifts up onto his elbow and quirks a dark, sexy brow in my direction. "Oh, so we're practicing our English now?" he asks, switching languages with me.

I shrug. "You never know. I might be needing it soon."

"You mean if she actually replies to your message?"

I flip the phone over and set it facedown on the nightstand, and then slip down into the bed so I'm lying next to him.

"I wish I could unsend it."

I can see his concern, even in the darkened room.

"Why? Isabella, *mi amor*, you've been waiting for this day as long as I've known you. And now it's here. You've found her! You've finally found your baby sister!"

My reply is considerably less enthusiastic than his.

"Yeah, but have I?" I ask, as if he might have the answer. "What if I'm wrong? What if she's not Marianna?"

"Who else could it possibly be with those genetic markers? Did Alberto and Rosaria have any other children you don't know about?"

"No, of course not . . ."

"Okay, well, that alert you got says this woman—*¿como se llama?*"

"Gabriella," I reply. "Her name is Gabriella DiMarco."

"Italian?" He scoffs. "She was kidnapped by the Italians?" he asks incredulously, as if this were the most preposterous thing he's ever heard.

I chuckle. I can't help it.

"Yes, Matéo, Pope John Paul II snatched her off the streets of Old San Juan and took her away in his little Popemobile."

"Pfft," he says, waving a dismissive hand at me. "That thing only does like ten miles an hour. Nobody's making a quick getaway in that thing."

I wag a finger at him. "No, it can go up to *a hundred and sixty* miles an hour."

"Really?"

I nod. "Really. I suppose he needs to be able to outrun the devil."

Chuckling, he pulls me into his arms so that my head is resting on his chest, and I can hear the dull, muted thump of his heart beating beneath me.

"*Dígame,*" he says softly.

He wants me to tell him about this woman I've probably scared away. I couldn't help it—after five years on GeneTeam and countless alerts every time one of my dozens of cousins turned up as a match, I had no reason to expect this time would be any different.

"I got the alert," I begin slowly, telling him the story for about the fourth time. "I figured it was Titi Annamaria, or my cousin Olivia—they both joined a few weeks ago. But then I couldn't believe my eyes when I saw the number—a *fifty* percent genetic match! I read it over and over again, just to be sure."

"And that means she's your full sibling, right?"

"Yes. And . . . according to her profile, she's twenty-five years old, which would be about right—but there was no birthdate given." I shake my head. "I don't know. These family DNA labs make mistakes sometimes, don't they?"

I feel his shrug. "I don't know. Not often, I don't think. And besides, they've never given you a bad match before, have they?"

"No."

"And . . . there was a picture?"

This I haven't told him. "Yes . . ."

"Okay, so . . . ?"

"I made it as big as I could without it distorting and, near as I can tell, the eyes are the right color. I think . . . it's hard to be sure in a picture. But I'd know if I met her, Matéo. I know I'd recognize her if I saw her in person."

Ugh. I sound desperate, even to myself. This is pathetic— I'm not trying to convince him; I'm trying to convince *myself.*

Matéo is quiet for a while as he stares up at the ceiling above us. Finally, he looks down at me with the expression he had the day I met him. The day I knew I'd marry him.

"Bueno, sólo hay una cosa que hacer," he says.

And he's right. There *is* only one thing to do.

I have got to meet her, or I'll never know the truth.

The question is, how interested is Gabriella DiMarco in knowing it?

CHAPTER 3

GABBY

Today

Max is sitting at his desk, scanning the printouts I've handed him. After a minute, he looks up at me, sitting in the chair across from his desk.

"Gabby, are you quite sure it's incorrect? I'd hate to have to throw out the entire team's findings because we've got a reliability issue . . ."

The company spent a good bit of cash to do this. And he's right; one misidentification screws the pooch for everyone. It means that, while we can report on the problem, we can't use any of our results. But I can't help that.

"Max, I'm telling you, it's got me all wrong. European, sure, but African and Taino? My dad's family is from Abruzzi, and my mom's is from Corfu."

"Really?" he asks, as if this takes him totally by surprise.

"Yes, really. Why?"

"I don't know . . ." He shrugs. "You know I'm not supposed to comment on it, but I must admit, I always just assumed you were Latina. Your features, your dark hair—"

"My last name is DiMarco," I remind him. "That's about as Italian as it gets."

"Well, that doesn't mean anything. For all I know, you were adopted. Or . . ."

"I'm not adopted," I assure him. "My parents were very open—no way they would have kept something like that from me."

"Right," he mutters, turning his attention to the message from Isabella Ruíz.

I watch as his eyes move top to bottom, left to right as he scans each and every bit of information I've brought him— not that there's much. I was up most of the night running targeted searches, scouring official databases, and trawling library and newspaper archives. Then I scanned my favorite true-crime threads, cold case podcasts and blogs, and sub-reddits, looking for chatter about a baby who went missing off the streets of San Juan so many years ago.

Max sets the last page facedown on the desk when he's done, his eyes meeting mine in the chair across from his. "There's not much . . ." he begins.

"I know," I agree quickly. "I can't tell if no one was report-ing on this story at the time, or if someone was . . . and there just aren't any digital files of those stories available."

"Yes. Perhaps something we can find out with a few phone calls . . ." He taps his pen on the stack of papers he's just perused before continuing. "Well, there's enough to confirm the event took place . . . you can see that with the pieces the paper did on the tenth, fifteenth, and twentieth anniversaries. The ones with the age-projection images—which are total and complete *shite*, by the way."

"I know, right? I swear to God, it's like they didn't want anyone to recognize that poor girl!" I quip, half amused, half horrified by what the police allowed to be released.

Max is looking at me now, head tilted slightly to one side.

"What?" I ask, feeling slightly uncomfortable by his at-tention.

"*You* could be that 'poor girl,' you know."

I scoff and wave a hand at him dismissively. "Please, Max.

I told you—I'm *not* adopted. Seriously, there's no way this isn't a mistake with the lab. No. Way."

"And you don't think she could be playing at something here? Trying to get something from you?"

I shake my head. "I considered that, as well. But, as you can see, Isabella Ruíz is a real person connected with a real—if obscure—case. I think it's safe to say she truly believes I'm her sister. Which is unfortunate . . . but not my fault."

My boss rubs a bit of scruff on his chin as he nods thoughtfully.

"And what are your instincts telling you about the potential for a story here?"

I shrug. "Yeah, I think so. GeneTeam, through their incompetence, has just resuscitated this woman's hope that her sister is still alive. How crushed will she be when she finds out it's a mistake? Talk about upending someone's life!"

He considers me.

"All right. In the interest of due diligence, you should go home, go through the family albums, pull out the marriage licenses and birth certificates . . . see if everything is as it should be. Is there anything missing? Does anything look a little off? Even something as insignificant as a typo could indicate—"

"Max—"

He holds up a palm to stop me before I can protest.

"You know how this goes as well as anyone else. More, even," he reminds me. "I cannot sanction a story without covering all the bases. You're most likely right—no skeletons in the DiMarco family closet. But I must be able to say that we at least opened the door and had a peek inside."

I give a heavy, resigned sigh. "Fine," I concede. "I'll go through everything I have tonight."

"Excellent!" he says with a smile that could melt the polar ice caps. "Let's plan on meeting at this time again tomorrow to go through it all." He shifts toward the laptop next to him on the desk and starts to type as he speaks. "Let me just get Lisa in the loop here to join us . . ."

"Lisa?"

He nods, still typing. "Yes. If this is what I think it might be, we'll have to clear her calendar for a bit. Maybe plan a trip down there . . ."

"Down where?"

He looks up at me now, grinning. "Puerto Rico! Where else would I send her to get the story?"

Oh, hell. I was really hoping I had another day or two before we had to have this conversation. But here it is.

"No." The word comes out tentatively. It's not exactly a question, but it's certainly not a statement.

"No what?" he asks, still with the teasing grin.

"No, I don't want Lisa to do this story." This time, I manage to inject my tone with a little less sponge and a little more steel.

The megawatt smile dims slightly. "Excuse me?"

"I don't want Lisa. Max, I want to do this story myself," I say, then continue quickly enough that he can't get a word in. "I'm ready. I've been ready. You know that. Besides, this is *my* story, isn't it? Literally! This woman thinks I'm her sister. It's not true, of course, but don't you think I should be the one to have that conversation with her? Don't you think *my* voice is the voice that should be telling this story?"

Now all traces of the smile are gone; Max's face is impassive as he considers me and what I've just said.

"I think . . ." he begins slowly, steepling his fingers on the desk, "that on the one hand, this could turn out to be one of those 'family reunited' stories that make people get all misty-eyed. On the other hand, it might turn into an exposé on the home genealogy industry and how it's turning people's lives upside down. There's no telling which direction it will go. I really think this needs to be handled by someone with experience. By a pro . . ."

"Max, I *am* a pro. If you'd just give me a chance . . ."

Even as I'm protesting, he's on his feet and moving around to my side of the desk. It only takes a few seconds before he's leaning up against it, looking down at me, sitting in the chair in front of him.

"Oh, come now," he coaxes, sounding like Matthew on *Downton Abbey*. Or maybe more like the butler, Mr. Carson. "You know I'm not trying to oust you from this, but there's a lot at stake. So why don't we just call Lisa in here and start hashing out a plan? Tell you what—I'll send both of you to Puerto Rico. You can go fact-gathering in the wild! Doesn't that sound like an amazing opportunity?"

Sure, except that's not how it'll go. Max will send me off to this place I've never been, where they speak a language I don't understand, to meet a woman I don't know. And as if that's not bad enough, he'll make me take Lisa along for the ride. Sounds like a little slice of hell right there.

I shake my head. "No, actually, it doesn't."

His brows knit together as he sizes me up, finally sighing loudly as he lifts his hands toward the ceiling.

"I'm sorry, Gabby, you'll just have to trust my judgment on this one," he says ruefully but firmly.

He's made up his mind, and my heart sinks. I was so sure I had him.

I'm about to open my mouth to acquiesce when, from somewhere in the depths of my memories, I hear Fran's voice in my head, telling me to demand my seat at the table.

"Right," I mutter to myself, though Max seems to think I'm agreeing with him.

His tea-drinking, crumpet-eating British ass better think again.

"Right," he agrees with a nod, the pleasant expression

firmly back in place as he returns to his seat on the other side
of the desk. He puts on his glasses and peers at the computer
screen. "Are you free to meet with Lisa here in my office tomorrow at say . . . two o'clock?"

"Hmm?" I murmur, lost in thought. "Oh . . . no. Sorry . . ."

He looks up at me. "All right, then . . . when is a good time
for you?" When I don't respond, he takes off his glasses and
tries one more time. "Gabby, please don't be like that . . ."

"I think I'm being perfectly reasonable."

"And what if it turns out she really *is* your sister? Hmm?
What then? That puts you in a very awkward position."

I shake my head resolutely. "Nope. Not possible."

He's starting to lose his cool, the voice getting a little
louder, a little less amiable. "Anything is possible, Gabby.
You're only looking at things from your own narrow per-
spective. But don't you see? Writers—veteran writers—look
at something from all the different angles and try to get past
their own personal opinions and inclinations. That's why
you're not quite ready . . ." He shakes his head firmly, as if
he's just convinced himself of the validity of his own point.
"No. I'm sorry. It's simply out of the question."

He's called my bluff. But then, bluffing doesn't mean you
don't have a good hand. And I do have a good hand. The best
hand, in fact, because I have the one thing Max wants—the
story. And that's worth everything.

"Fine," I begin in a calm, measured tone. "Then I'm taking leave—effective immediately."

The hazel eyes nearly bug out of his head. "Leave? You
want to take a leave . . . now?" he echoes incredulously.

"Yes. Three weeks should do nicely, thank you."

Max's fingers grip the front edge of his desk, causing his
knuckles to go white as he tries to gauge my commitment
to this stance. We're back to the bluff again—he thinks I'm
playing chicken with him now.

"Gabby, I'm sorry, but I can't allow you to do this on your own. If you don't want Lisa or Randy, we'll find someone else. Hell, I'll go with you if you want . . ."

You just want a fair shake—he owes you that much . . .

"Thanks for the offer, Max, but that won't be necessary. I've got this," I tell him, wishing that statement were true.

It isn't often that my boss looks anything other than affable. But then, it isn't often that I'm telling him—in a not-so-roundabout way—that he can take his offer and—

"Gabby . . ."

The single word has become a warning, a threat. He's using my own name against me, and it really pisses me off. I get to my feet so we can be eye-to-eye when I say this to him.

"My life, my story. *My* story. And if you don't want it enough to let me tell it—*my* way—then I'll go freelance with it. I can think of about a dozen other editors in this city who would be thrilled to take me up on the offer."

The alabaster skin beneath his oh-so-sexy stubble begins to warm and redden.

"Please do *not* make me do this," he says through gritted teeth.

"You're the editor, Max. You can do whatever you want," I remind him. "And if you give me a chance, I will *not* let you down. But if you can't see your way clear to do that, then I don't see how I have a future here at *Flux.*"

As soon as the words are out of my mouth, I know they're true. I close my eyes and wait for his decision. I don't have to wait long.

"Well, then, Gabby," he says very softly, "I'm afraid I'll have to let you go."

I open my eyes and nod as if I'd expected this all along. As if I'd known this conversation would end with me leaving *Flux*—which it does. As if I'd fully intended to walk away from the one thing I have left to lose—which I have.

CHAPTER 4

ISABELLA

Today

They used to call me *la pequeña madre*—the little mother—because I was obsessed with my baby dolls. I'd diaper them, dress them, give them bottles, and rock them in the same black wooden rocker my mother had rocked me in when I was an infant. The day my parents told me I was going to be a big sister, I was thrilled—it was like my prayers had been answered! I would get to be *la pequeña madre* for real—with an *actual* baby to love and care for.

I've spent a lot of long, sleepless nights staring up at the ceiling, thinking about that time in my life. And, near as I can tell, that's the cutoff point right there. That's the last time I was really, truly happy. If only I could have stopped the clock—frozen time. This was the exact moment before everything in my life turned to shit. One day I had happy, laughing, easygoing parents who adored me. We weren't rich—hell, we couldn't even be called "middle-class," but we had each other, and we had love. And it was more than enough.

Until it wasn't.

My mother's screams woke me in the middle of the night. She was in labor, but I knew something was very wrong—it was too soon. The next-door neighbor stayed with her while my father ran to find the midwife, who lived a few blocks away. I just stood there in the doorway watching helplessly, paralyzed by the noise, the tears, the blood.

My God, there was so much blood.

An hour later, I was still rooted in that same spot when the midwife bundled the tiny baby in a pillowcase and handed her to me. She had to—my father was in no state to take her. He was distraught, weeping over my mother, who lay motionless on the bed, her chalky skin a striking contrast against the deep red of the bloody sheets. I just looked down at the tiny creature in my arms, wriggling and fussing, then I looked over at my mother, silent and still.

My not-quite-five-year-old mind wasn't capable of processing everything that had just happened. This was not the way it was supposed to go. What my not-quite-five-year-old mind *was* capable of processing was the fact that life as I knew it had come to a very abrupt end. I was aware, without being told, that the woman I loved most in the world would not be coming back to hold me, or rock me, or comfort me when I cried in the night. She would never hold the infant I was holding at that moment—the one we'd all waited for so excitedly.

That's when it happened.

As long as I live, I'll never forget the moment I looked down at that baby and wished her away. Because, in my kindergarten-level reasoning, if she'd never been born, my mother never would have died.

Suddenly what had once been a pretend game about being grown-up enough to take care of a baby had become my reality—and there was nothing fun about it. This wasn't a game; it was real life. My life. It wasn't *quite* so bad in the first days—which says a lot about how much worse it got. The shock was a blessing—and of course, that first stage of grieving, denial. There were also family, neighbors, and friends. But when their presence started to interfere with my father's chosen methods of grieving—getting drunk and stoned off his ass—he sent everyone away with assurances that he'd made arrangements for the baby to be well cared for. And she was. She was cared for about as well as any five-year-old could care for an infant.

And my God, did she need caring for, but Alberto was nowhere to be found.

There was only me. And Marianna.

On the good nights, we'd sit together in that big black rocking chair where our mother had rocked me, and I'd sing to her the songs Rosaria had sung to me.

On the bad nights, there was no amount of rocking, singing, or soothing that could comfort the cries of a child whose mother had left her alone and defenseless in a cold, cruel world. Not my cries, not hers. On those nights, we clung to each other in that old rocker—the five-year-old and the five-week-old—both of us lost to the kind of heaving, shuddering sobs that leave your throat burning and raw, your body aching from the strain of the convulsions.

I wince at the memories that have resurfaced with full-on HD, technicolor, surround-sound clarity.

Or maybe it's the iced coffee that makes me wince. It's bitter and ashy on my tongue—like it's made of cigarette butts and milk over ice with whipped cream and a drizzle of caramel. But I keep sucking it through the straw as I sit in the parking lot behind the Cool Beans Coffeehouse, staring at the wall as if it were a drive-in screen.

Painted there, just to the left of a rusty, rickety fire escape and ladder, is the reason I come here once or twice a month—the barely discernible remnants of an unfinished mural. It's the face of a crying angel—battered and faded by the relentless sun until she's become this gaunt, faded specter just sort of floating up there, her tears having paled to a dull, rusty red-brown. The entire effect makes for a freaky ghost angel crying bloody tears that no one notices anymore. No one but me.

I glance at the clock on the dashboard. I need to get back

to work before I miss the afternoon rush. It turns out being a conventional artist doesn't pay the mortgage, so I've hung up my aerosol cans in favor of an airbrush. I rent a booth inside an arcade full of gift and souvenir shops that fill with *turistas* several times a week when the giant cruise ships dock. They flood the cobblestone streets searching for rum to drink, silver to wear, and commemorative nail art to show off back at home. Now I start the car, taking one last glance at my phone screen before I pull away. Still nothing. At least, still nothing from *her*.

In spite of my past experiences, I let a small part of myself think this would be easy—imagining that she'd see the DNA results, get my message, and be thrilled to have found this piece of her she hadn't even realized was missing. As if she'd see me and just know instinctively that we were connected—that we had the same blood running through our veins. Of course, that's the kind of bullshit you see on made-for-TV movies—the happy Christmas ones, not the creepy ones with the cheerleader-turned-psycho-stalker.

Unfortunately, happily-ever-afters are a little harder to come by out in the real world. Yesterday, some random woman woke up to the news that she wasn't who she thought she was. Of course she'd be skeptical—God knows I'd be! And of course she'd need a little time to sort through this information. Because at the end of the day, this isn't about finding a family she didn't know she had—it's about losing the only one she's ever known.

No matter how you slice it, the truth of one life turns the other into a lie.

CHAPTER 5

GABBY

Today

"What the hell was I thinking?" I lament for the hundredth time.

"You were thinking you'd finally had enough," Franny's floating head informs me from the computer screen. We've gone with Zoom this time, so I don't have to hold the phone as I pace the creaking hardwood floors and pull the hair out of my head.

"This whole thing was supposed to be an opportunity for me to move *up* at *Flux*—not out!" I say, ignoring her statement. Now that the adrenaline rush of self-righteous indignation has worn off, I'm left wondering how things could have gone downhill so fast. "I can't believe I let you talk me into this! I had an excellent job with a prestigious publication. It wasn't my dream job, but I'd have gotten there eventually if I had just been more patient. But no!" I throw up my hands and shake my head. "No, I let you convince me to push Max."

If my best friend feels guilty for getting me all worked up last night, she doesn't show it.

"You need to calm your ass down before you stroke out," she warns me calmly.

I stop pacing long enough to spin around and glare at her image on the screen, looking back at me placidly from her tiny apartment. I'd throw something at her if it didn't mean I'd crack my screen in the process.

"Calm my ass down?" I echo incredulously. "My career is over, and you want me to calm my ass down?"

She throws up her hands. "Dramatic much?"

I ignore her and continue with my wailing and gnashing of teeth. "God, I shouldn't have let my pride get in the way. I should've just . . ."

"What?" she demands. "What should you have done? Stood by and let Lisa hijack your story? Please. You're just scared because you're not someone who jumps without a net. But you had to. I know you, Gabs. If you had caved on this, you would have regretted it the rest of your career. It would have gnawed at your guts until you couldn't stand working there anymore." She softens her tone. "Don't you see? Max didn't leave you any choice. It was stand up to him right then and there or give in and hand over your power."

"Pfft. What power?"

"The power to decide what comes next. Is there a story here worth pursuing? How do you tell it? Where do you want to see it published? *Do* you want to see it published? Now, these choices are yours and nobody else's."

She's absolutely right. The price for remaining at *Flux* was allowing other people to take what, by rights, is mine. At the end of the day, Max and Lisa would have made all the decisions while I sat on my hands over at my desk, making sure she didn't misspell the names of the people I should have been talking to myself.

I sit down at the table where my laptop—and Franny's face—are perched, and I slump down, allowing my head to drop onto my forearms.

"God, I wish you were here," I groan from within my little tabletop cocoon.

She snorts. "Why? So I could make you crazy in person?"

I raise my head, so I can look at her looking at me through our respective camera lenses.

"So we could make my mom's chocolate chip cookies."

Her face turns serious, and she nods her agreement. "Yes, you're right. This is an occasion that definitely warrants the magical powers of Lucy's cookie recipe. And ice-cold milk, of course."

"Mmm, that does sound amazing," I agree, closing my eyes for just a moment and taking a deep breath, as if all I need to do is picture the cookies to conjure them.

If only.

"I miss you, Fran," I confess. "And I miss my parents. Everything's just gone to hell since you moved, and they died. I feel so alone."

Those last four words have been rattling around in my head for months, only now making their way to my tongue and out into the world.

"I'm *always* here for you, Gabs. Always. No matter where I am. No matter what I'm doing. You need me, and I'm on the next plane out of LAX." She pauses to reconsider her own reply. "Unless I've got my hands in some poor guy's chest or something . . . But you can bet your sweet ass the second they wheel him up to surgery—or he codes—I'm outta here and headed wherever you are. Wherever you need me to be."

I find myself smiling and laughing a little through my tears.

"I love you," I tell her.

"I know," she informs me smugly.

"Franny?"

"Hmm?"

"I think maybe I need to go to Puerto Rico," I tell her.

My best friend nods.

"Yes," she agrees, "you do. Now, go into the kitchen and grab that in-case-of-emergency box of Betty Crocker cookie mix you've got stashed up in the cabinet. You're going to need it."

An hour later, I'm sitting cross-legged on the couch with a bowl of half-eaten, uncooked, probably salmonella-laden cookie dough, and a table littered with the archaeological treasures of my childhood. One box holds the crayon drawings, award certificates, and excellent report cards my mom couldn't bear to toss. Another houses a tiny baby blanket with bunnies, as well as a lock of my baby hair, my first tooth, and a single pink baby sock.

And then there are the photo albums—a visual timeline of the DiMarco family from my parents' wedding pictures to my college graduation. I allow my index finger to trace the plastic-covered images of Mack and Lucy through the years—her a kindergarten teacher, him a cop. I was a little late coming to the party—their "little miracle" to hear my mom tell it. They'd given up on having a baby when I came along unexpectedly—spending the next twenty-plus years as part of a tight-knit threesome.

Closing the last book, I sigh. I miss Franny. This long-distance BFF crap isn't really working for me. A glance at the clock tells me I've totally lost track of time—it's after two in the morning. I guess I'll be sleeping in tomorrow, since I don't have any place to be . . .

One quick shower later, I'm under the covers, just drifting off to sleep, when I hear Max's voice in my head.

"*. . . Is there anything missing? Anything look a little off?*"

"Shut up and let me sleep!" I tell my subconscious sternly.

Because that's what this is—some deep-seated, unresolved nonsense that's chosen this moment to surface. Well, it can just wait until later, after I've gotten a little sleep. No sooner do I close my eyes again when I hear it again—I hear *him* again.

"*Is there anything missing?*"

I sit up and swing my feet over the side of the bed onto the floor.

"What? What *is* it?" I ask my empty bedroom.

I get up with an impatient huff. The moonlight streaming through the bedroom window provides more than enough light for me to find my way back to the living room. There, on the coffee table, the albums are precisely as I left them. I sit down on the arm of the couch and stare down at them, willing my subconscious to give me another clue. But clearly, it's gone back to sleep, where I should be.

"This is insane," I mutter to myself, and stand, reaching down to close the cover on one of the open albums.

The first image is baby me, face covered in crumbs and frosting from the cake I've tried to stuff in my mouth. It makes me chuckle—I've never been able to get enough cake. There's a big wax candle shaped like the number one in the center of the whipped cream–covered confection. I flip the cover closed on the page of pictures and am about to go back to bed when something occurs to me.

That cake—that first birthday cake. That's the very first picture in the very first album. That's our starting point. But where are the shots of me just home from the hospital, or in my mother's arms, fast asleep? Where are the images of me feeding from a bottle and sleeping in a crib? Knowing Mack and Lucy, my first twelve months probably took up an entire book of their own. But I handled every item in that house before it was sold—there was nothing left behind. Besides, in thinking about it now, I can't recall ever having seen pictures from that period of my life.

I look down at the page open in my hands right now. That first birthday party was also the first in our New York house. When I was still a baby, Mack left his job in Ohio for a better one here in New York.

Wait, wait, wait . . . an interstate move with an infant? I mean, how could you *not* lose something?

Big move plus little baby could easily equal lost photo album.

Sounds more than plausible to me—it sounds downright likely, all things considered.

Except . . .

I slam the book shut before my brain can go a single thought further down this path.

"No," I say out loud, shaking my head. But the word isn't nearly as emphatic coming out of my mouth as it is as it echoes in my mind.

I glance at my laptop, still open on the dining table. I don't know what the hell is going on, but I've got to find out. Sooner, rather than later. I sit in front of the screen, log in to the GeneTeam site, and navigate my way to the woman whose face I've now memorized. I start to type.

Dear Isabella . . .

CHAPTER 6

ISABELLA

Today

When the alarm goes off, I want to throw my phone across the room. It was another night of tossing and turning punctuated by short, unsatisfying bits of sleep. I'm taking a long, hot shower when Matéo brings me coffee in a big mug.

"So good," I murmur, turning so I can sip as the water rains down on my back. "Thank you."

He nods. "Maybe you should just close up shop today," he suggests. "You look like shit."

"Gee, thanks, honey!" I reply sarcastically.

"You know what I mean . . ."

"I know, I know," I concede. "But we can't afford for me to blow off an entire day's business. It's going to be busy down at the cruise ship docks today. Lots of tiny palm trees and hibiscus flowers to paint." I hold up my hand and wiggle my fingernails in his direction. He just rolls his eyes and shakes his head.

"So, I guess no emails overnight?" he asks carefully, trying to sound all casual so I won't get worked up again.

"I haven't checked yet," I tell him. "I needed to get a little coffee in me before I start another long day of waiting on pins and needles. For nothing."

He picks up my phone from the bathroom counter and holds it up.

"You want me to check for you?"

I shrug. "Pfft. Sure, why not." Maybe it'll be less disappointing coming from him.

I close my eyes, enjoying the feel of the water.

"*Dear Isabella*," he says.

My eyes fly open, and my brows draw together in irritation. "What? Stop teasing me, Matéo. It's not funny . . ."

My husband holds up his hands as if he's being robbed at gunpoint.

"I swear to God," he replies, waving the phone screen at me.

"Really?" I ask, hair dripping into the mug.

"Really," he assures me with a nod.

"Um, okay . . . read it, read it! No, wait, hang on . . ." I turn the shower off and step out onto the shaggy bath mat so I can grab my robe and throw it on over my soaking wet body. "Okay, go ahead. I'm ready."

He looks down at the tiny screen and clears his throat before pulling out his rusty English.

"Okay . . . em . . . '*Dear Isabella, thank you for reaching out. I have to be honest with you—I have no reason to believe that I am the person you are looking for. I'm sure this will come as a major disappointment to you, but I'm quite certain this was an unfortunate mix-up on the part of Gene-Team. However, as it turns out, I am a freelance journalist and, if you don't have any objections, I'd like to investigate this error a little more. I thought that, if you're willing to meet with me, I could come to Puerto Rico as early as the end of this week . . .*'"

He lowers the phone and looks at me as I shake my head in amazement, hand covering my mouth. A second later I hurl myself into his arms, laughing like a giddy little kid.

"Ugh!" Matéo grunts. "Isabella, you're getting me soaked!"

I ignore his complaint and take his face in my hands, planting a big, wet kiss on his lips.

"She's coming!" I whisper-shout. "She's really coming!"

"Well?" I press, unable to wait for another second, watching as he rereads the email at my request. "What do you think? About her, I mean? Can you tell anything from that?"

"Well . . . I think she's a little formal sounding for my taste . . ."

I slap his shoulder. "Stop it! You know what I mean . . ."

He shrugs. "Isabella, I'm not sure what you want me to say. She's telling you straight-up that she doesn't believe the results are legit."

"Yes, but she's coming anyway . . ." I point out quickly.

He sighs and puts his hands on my forearms, looking up at me.

"I know. I'm just afraid you're going to get your hopes up, and this woman will come here and disappoint you."

"She couldn't disappoint me any more than the psychic who told me my sister was living in a yurt somewhere in Turkey raising goats," I remind him.

He smiles and shakes his head. "Well, that's true . . ."

"Or more than the private detective I gave my entire savings account to . . . right before he ghosted me . . ."

"Yeah, he was a real piece of shit, that one . . ."

"Or more than the hundreds of phone calls I've made, letters I've written, emails I've sent, and doors I've knocked on, trying to find out what happened to Marianna."

He takes my hand in both of his, holding tight.

"Isabella, *mi amor*, I just don't want to see you get hurt again. This Gabby DiMarco may very well be Marianna . . . but she may not *want* to be Marianna. And, if that's the case, your search *is* finally over . . . except you have nothing to show for it but rejection."

He's right, of course. My head knows that. But my heart?

Well, it knows that, too. It just doesn't give a shit. It's been hurt so many times in so many different ways by the mother who died and left me, and then the father who *lived* and left me. Hell, even my *abuelita*—once a fierce ally in this search—has left me on my own as she slips further into the unreachable darkness of her mind.

"I'm tough," I tell him.

"I know."

"I can convince her."

"Can you?"

"Yes."

"And how do you plan to do that?"

I'm quiet for a long moment.

"I don't know, Matéo, but I'll figure it out."

He nods at me with the expression of a man who knows there's no point in debating anymore. He may have won the argument on logic, but I take the prize for determination. And maybe I know he's right—that this could break me once and for all. But I also know he'll be there to pick up the pieces and put me back together.

It wouldn't be the first time.

And, sadly, it won't be the last.

Of that much, I'm certain.

CHAPTER 7

GABBY

Today

Thanks to my parents, I've seen a lot of the world, including most of the fifty states and a great deal of Europe. In that time, I've seen the blue-gray waves of the Atlantic Ocean, and the pink-tinged swells of the Pacific. But nothing could have prepared me for the sight of the Caribbean Sea as my flight begins its final approach into San Juan. Mesmerized, I contort myself so that the lower half of my body is facing forward, while the upper half is twisted to the left. I hope my seatmates don't care to see the view, because they'll have to get around me to do it. And I'm not budging.

The vast swath of water below me transitions from azure to lapis, lapis to cerulean, cerulean to teal—each band of color as delicate and translucent as the finest Impressionist painting. The image is only accentuated by the white sand beach that serves as its canvas. I've got one palm on either side of the small, oval window, my forehead pressed against its inner plastic pane.

"First time?"

"Hmm?" I'm so transfixed that I hardly notice the person in the middle seat speaking to me.

"Is this your first time in Puerto Rico?" he asks again, and I turn to face the older gentleman who's had the misfortune of being stuck between myself and a very broad-shouldered young man on the aisle for the last four hours.

"It is," I admit. "I didn't realize . . . I mean, I had no idea how beautiful it would be. From up here, anyway."

He smiles. "Oh, it's even more beautiful down there," he informs me with a nod out the window. "But it's more than just beaches. It's the mountains and the valleys, the rain forest, the dry forest, the caves . . ."

"Really?" I should know this. I should know all of this. It is, after all, my job to know these kinds of facts. But I haven't been able to bring myself to do too much research on Puerto Rico beyond what little information I could find about the case of the missing little girl named Marianna.

When the man smiles at my surprise, I see the glow of pride on his face. If his accent is any indication, he lives on the island.

"Puerto Rico is only about ninety miles long and thirty miles wide," he says, spreading his hands to indicate the size right there in row 14. "Do yourself a favor—rent a car and drive around the island. You can circle the entire circumference in about five hours if you take the main roads. The interior is a little trickier because of the mountains, but well worth exploring, as well."

"I'll do that!" I say, even though I have no intention of staying more than a couple of days—just long enough to put this mistaken identity business to rest. But who knows? It's not like I'll ever come back here again—maybe I should build in an afternoon to see at least a little of the island, if not the whole thing. The rain forest sounds interesting . . .

"Are you here on business?" my companion asks me.

"Sort of . . ." I say. "I'm . . . I'm a writer," I announce—the first time in my life I've said that out loud. When I repeat it, it's with more confidence. "I'm a magazine writer researching a story."

"How exciting," he says, eyes lighting. "Is it a travel piece?"

"Oh . . . uh . . . no, not exactly . . . um, true crime, actually . . ."

I don't know what the hell makes me say that to this guy. The words are out of my mouth before I can consider the wisdom of uttering them. Ah, well, we will land in just a few minutes.

"Really?"

The one word is filled with such breathy awe that I know I've just made a huge mistake. Shit.

"Yes . . . but it's a cold case . . ."

"Which one?"

He's twisted toward me the same way I was just twisted toward the view, looking at me with the same kind of curiosity.

"Oh, I'm sure you've never heard of it. It was just a kidnapping. A little girl about twenty-five years back—"

He gasps. "Marianna? You're talking about *Marianna Ruíz*, aren't you?"

I pull back several inches when it appears he might come right over the armrest and land in my lap. Yikes.

"I'm sorry—did you say you're investigating the Marianna Ruíz case?"

The question comes from the young guy in the aisle seat. He's now prairie-dogging around my new friend.

Shit. Shit, shit, shit. There's no stuffing the genie back in the bottle now.

"Well, I wouldn't exactly say I'm investigating it . . ." I offer, trying to downplay my interest.

"My mother still talks about her," the younger man tells us. "I wasn't even born yet, but she never wanted to let me out of her sight when we were in Old San Juan. She was afraid I'd be snatched up and smuggled out on one of the cruise ships . . ."

"Is that . . . is that what they say happened?" I ask, my

panicky regret subsiding slightly. Maybe the locals have more information than I had access to while doing my research back home.

He nods. "Yes, they think maybe she was sold on the black market for babies . . ."

"No, no," our middle companion breaks in, disagreeing. "No, it was a ransom. I heard they wanted ten thousand dollars, and the father didn't have it . . ."

"I heard the father accidentally killed her and then reported her missing," comes the voice of the woman directly in front of me. She's trying to look at us from in between her seat and the one next to her, but all I can see is one dark eye lined in blue.

"Miss, please turn around and face forward in your seat, we're about to land," I hear the flight attendant say from several rows ahead of us, where he's strapped into the jump seat.

"Blue-eye" disappears.

"Sounds like everyone's got a different theory," I say, more to myself than anyone else.

"It's become a cautionary tale that parents use to keep their kids from misbehaving in public," the older man explains. "But I was living nearby when it happened. I knew the father, in fact—we were in school together before he dropped out. I followed the story closely, and the police bungled the whole thing from the very beginning."

I'm sucked in anew, listening intently as my new bestie catalogs a litany of missed clues, crooked cops, and incompetent politicians. Seriously, I found next to nothing about this story online. But here, among the locals, it's been elevated to urban legend status for some—and worst nightmare for others.

I have a feeling I know which category I'm about to fall into.

CHAPTER 8

ISABELLA

Today

The last time I laid eyes on Baby Marianna, my father was taking her out with him in her stroller. Then she disappeared—just like I wished for. My rational, adult mind knows that one thing has nothing to do with the other, but I spent a lot of years thinking they did. Now, at last, is the day I've been praying for—the day she comes back to me. My heart is beating so hard, I'd swear it's banging against the inside of my rib cage.

I'm going into this cold—Gabriella DiMarco made the decision to come quickly. And in the few days between our first contact and her arrival, she didn't respond to my suggestion we speak by phone—or trade some details of our lives via email at the very least. Then again, if she knew the whole sordid story of the family she was born into, she might just change her name and drop off the face of the earth forever.

One thing about her is clear: she has expensive tastes and, apparently, a budget to back them. I knew this as soon as she suggested we meet in the obscenely overpriced bar in the ridiculously overrated La Playa Blanca Resort, where she checked in earlier today.

I arrive a little early so I can grab a spot at a small, U-shaped booth in the back corner. It's flanked by large potted palms, giving us at least a little bit of privacy. Not a bad idea, considering I have no way of knowing how this little reunion is going to play out.

Once I'm seated, I let my eyes wander around the room, constructed almost entirely of pink marble with brass fixtures. It was built to accommodate the wealthy *turistas*. But that's not the only clue I have about Miss Gabby's financial status. I don't know what she does for a living, but whatever it is, she was apparently able to take vacation at a moment's notice. Maybe she doesn't work at all? Maybe she's married with children. Maybe she's a doctor. Maybe she won the Powerball. Maybe she . . .

My wild speculations come to a screeching halt when a petite woman with long, dark, wavy hair crosses the palm-flanked archway and stops to peer around the room, looking for someone. She's looking for *me*. Tentatively, I raise a hand so that, when her gaze sweeps in my direction, it stops. I find I'm holding my breath as she makes her way around the other tables to where I'm waiting for her in the back.

Fifty feet. Twenty feet. Ten . . .

"Umm . . . Isabella? Isabella Ruíz?" she asks tentatively.

I look her right in the eyes and, I swear to God, my heart stops for a split second. They confirm what I've known to be the truth all along—and it's a tremendous relief. There's no mistaking them—the colors that radiate outward in her iris in an ombre effect—teal at the center, blending to sky blue, morphing to denim, a fine ring of dark cobalt encircling the outermost rim.

They are Marianna's eyes. And, before her, they were our mother's.

"Uhhh . . . yes, umm, hi . . ." I manage to murmur absently as I stand, entranced by her. "Hi, Gabby," I say.

Would it be too weird of me to lean in and sniff her hair? Maybe run a finger along one of those long, loose curls? Seriously—I can still remember the smell of her hair and how it felt so silky in my hands. Would it still smell like that? If I reached out and touched one of those curls, would it feel like it did all those years ago when I held her in my arms and rocked her?

Even as the thoughts jumble through my mind, it's all I can do to keep my hands to myself. Because I don't just want to smell her hair or see how it feels to touch it. What I really want to do is jump onto this table and drag her up there with me so we can have ourselves a two-person dance party smack in the middle of this fancy bar.

"Are you . . . okay?" she asks with concern, making me wonder what she's seeing on my face.

"What? Oh, yes . . . I'm sorry—you just . . ." I pause for a moment so I can reset my thoughts and my expression. "I'm just really excited to meet you, Gabby," I tell her sincerely, then gesture to the booth next to us. "Let's sit down," I suggest, then I spot the waiter. "Would you like a drink?" I ask, hand already up to get his attention. "I'd like a drink . . ."

"Um . . . yeah, sure, I guess . . ." she says, glancing at her watch as she slips onto the bench across from me.

To his credit, the waiter is at our table in under ten seconds.

"Hello, ladies, I'm Javier," he says, eyeing my companion with some interest. "Today's drink specials are—"

"Just whiskey and coconut water for me, please." I cut Javier off before he could finish.

"Whiskey and coconut water," he repeats flatly, and I can tell he's already pegged me as a local. Gabby, on the other hand . . . "And for you, *señorita*?" he asks, ratcheting up the charm.

I don't even hide my eye roll. I've seen these guys a hundred times—they work the tourists in hopes of a tip . . . which may or may not be of the monetary variety.

"I'll have the house sauvignon blanc, please," she replies with a polite smile. He waits a beat, as if hoping she might throw in a wink or her room number or something. As if! I'm about to tell him to get lost when she takes care of it herself. "I'm sorry—did you need something else?" she asks. "My ID, maybe?"

I guess Javier is used to "getting the girl," or at least, getting a few eyelashes batted his way, because he seems a little flustered as he mumbles and leaves quickly. Not that I blame him for trying—Gabriella DiMarco is beautiful. Even *I* can't take my eyes off of her—drinking in every line, curve, contour, and arch. I'm memorizing the geography of her features but, more importantly, scouring her features for some microexpression that might indicate a spark of recognition.

This is, of course, ridiculous. Marianna was only seven months old when I saw her last. She couldn't have possibly retained anything from those days. Right? So why is there this twinge of disappointment in my gut? How come I'm hurt that she doesn't feel it, too? That instant and immediate connection. The magnetism between us.

We stare at one another awkwardly for a second and then decide to speak. At exactly the same moment.

"Right, so—"

"Yeah, so—"

We both stop, deferring to the other. And then we do it again.

"I was just going to say—"

"I was wondering how—"

She starts to giggle, and I can't help but join her. It's hard not to. Finally, I point to myself, indicating I'm about to speak. She nods her agreement.

"What do you do, Gabby? For work, I mean?"

She relaxes a little, probably grateful for a question with an easy answer.

"I, uh . . . I work for a magazine. *Flux*? Do you know it?"

"Sure," I reply, nodding enthusiastically. "I read it on the checkout line all the time. You write for them?" I ask, impressed.

There's the slightest beat of reluctance before she responds.

"No, not exactly. I'm a fact-checker . . ." She's a little too quick to follow this up. "But I hope to be writing at some point. This job was just a foot in the door for me."

"A fact-checker?" I don't think I've ever heard of such a thing. "What kind of facts do you check?"

She shrugs. "Oh, I make sure all the sources—the people quoted in an article or whose information we use to write it—are real and that their statements have been accurately portrayed. I verify dates and places, make sure people and locations match up. It's all about responsible journalism, you know? No fake news or alternative facts. Nothing that can get the magazine sued down the road . . ."

Her voice and explanation both peter out, as if she's thinking her job sounds lame. It doesn't.

"Wow, that's really important," I tell her and watch as she perks up a bit, so I press on with the topic. "I mean, there's so much questionable, biased reporting that it's hard to know what to believe sometimes. You check the facts, so readers don't have to—yeah, you know I never thought about it before, but that makes a lot of sense. You want readers to think of *Flux* as a trustworthy source of information. And that's all because of you."

Her cheeks color slightly, but I can't tell if that's good or not. Have I said something to offend or overstep? My insecurities are quashed when she speaks again.

"Right . . . thanks. Um . . . yeah. That's great, thanks," she repeats, then smiles a little shyly as she confides, "Most people don't get it. Like I said, the plan is to be a writer, but . . ."

"But this was a foot in the door," I answer for her with a solid nod of agreement. "A good plan, I think. A very good plan."

She lets herself drop back against the tufted leather booth, and I catch a sigh of relief. Good, she's feeling a little more comfortable with me. Comfortable enough to do a little digging of her own.

"And you?" she asks. "What do you do?"

"Me? Oh, I do nails."

"Nails? Like fingernails? Are you a nail tech then?"

I'm grateful not to hear any judgment in the question.

"Sort of. I specialize in airbrushing and hand-painted nail art. The tourists love it, and I get a lot of business whenever the cruise ships are docked at the port for an excursion."

I hold out my hands so she can see a sample of my work—an assortment of designs to show potential clients—pineapples, frogs, palm trees, even a piña colada with a tiny pink umbrella in it.

"Oh, wow!" she marvels, and when she takes hold of my hand for a closer look, I feel an unexpected surge of electricity through my entire body.

I think I see something pass across her features—like she might feel it, too. But, just as quickly, she clears her throat and lets my hand go abruptly.

"Umm . . . yeah . . . they're really beautiful . . ."

"Thanks."

"And you make a living doing that?" As soon as she hears her own question, her cheeks start to redden. "I'm sorry, Isabella, that's none of my business . . ."

"No, not at all," I assure her with a hand wave. It's not a surprising question. "I do all right. And it's not just me; Matéo—my husband—he's got a good job."

"Right. Well, that makes sense."

"And you?"

"Me? Oh, yeah. I do okay. By New York City standards, anyway . . ."

I shake my head. "No . . . I meant . . . I was wondering . . . do you have a partner?" I finally manage to ask.

"Oh, right," she says quickly. "No . . . no partner. I mean . . ."

Before she can complete the thought, Javier is back with a small tray.

"Ladies, I have your drinks," he murmurs as he sets down first the wine and then my two cocktails.

Thank. God.

This is excruciating. And thrilling. And terrifying. All at the same time. And liquor is one of the few things that will address all of those feelings, all at one time. And quickly.

So I grab one of the glasses and tip the amber-colored liquid back before he's even left the table. It hits the back of my throat with a delicious burn before wending its way downward—spreading a warmth through my chest, to my core, and back up to my face, causing my cheeks to grow flush. And then it hits my bloodstream.

"So, Gabby, I'm thinking you must have come across a red flag or two in your life—something that didn't add up or look right. I mean, twenty-five years is a long time to hide someone's true identity from them."

CHAPTER 9

GABBY

Today

I practically choke on my wine. It burns as soon as it hits the back of my throat and continues to do so the entire way down, causing me to cough and sputter. I put a cloth napkin to my mouth and hold up my other hand in the "hang on a second" gesture.

Damn, this girl doesn't waste any time getting to the punch, does she?

"*Señorita* . . ." Javier the waiter has rushed over with a tall glass of ice water.

I grab it gratefully and take a long sip. It has the dual effect of soothing the cough while buying me a few seconds' reprieve from Isabella's intense stare.

"Thank you, Javier," I croak out. "I'm fine. Really . . ." I assure him, though he doesn't look too convinced.

When he's gone, I clear my throat, drink a little more, and consider the woman across from me. I have to take a beat so I can look at this objectively because, if I don't keep my emotions in check, they could very easily get away from me.

There is definitely something between us—but what that is, exactly, I can't say. Could be we just have good chemistry. It's also entirely possible I'm reading too much into everything at the moment because I want this to be . . . something.

But what that something is, I'm not sure. A friendship? A compelling story for me to write? A family?

Nope. I immediately shut that thought down.

I have a family.

I *had* a family.

I cough a few more times before speaking again, my voice hoarse.

"Sorry about that. Now what were you saying?"

I'm hoping she's had time to rethink that question/statement.

"I was asking if you ever had any suspicions you might be someone else? Any clues? Anything that didn't add up or maybe paperwork that didn't seem right?"

She sounds like Max. But now that she's asking a second time, I get a better sense of where this is coming from. Isabella isn't being accusatory . . . she's just curious—and she's hoping maybe I'll bring a new clue to this mystery of the baby sister she lost all those years ago. One of us really needs to sue the idiots at GeneTeam for this shitshow.

I decide to skirt the question, diverting the conversation in a different direction.

"This is all so . . . crazy. The whole thing was a work assignment. We all did it. We all sent in the DNA sample . . . I only agreed to it because I hoped I'd find a long-lost cousin somewhere . . ."

"Oh, you've got plenty of those," she tells me with a smirk just before she knocks back another good-sized gulp of her drink. "Not to mention aunts, and uncles . . ."

I straighten up, strengthening my stance a bit. I want to seem compassionate—because I *am* compassionate—but I also need to be clear and firm on this point so as not to prolong her misconception that we're sisters. So I take a deep breath, lean in, and speak in as soft and gentle a voice as I can muster.

"Isabella, I'm really so sorry about your sister. What happened to Marianna was . . . well, tragic. And I cannot imagine the kind of hell you and your family have been through since that day. But . . ." *Spit it out, Gabby. Just say it already.* "But I'm not her. I can't be her. I've given it a lot of thought— I've looked for the kind of 'red flags' you're talking about but, I swear, there's just . . . there's nothing."

She quirks an eyebrow over the rim of her glass. "Oh, yeah? Well, the scientific community differs with you on that."

I was expecting shock, maybe disappointment. But snark? Not so much. I suspect it might have something to do with that second drink she's working on now.

"Mistakes happen," I inform her, trying to sound diplomatic. "It's not common, but it does happen."

"There's no mistake," she informs me, as if it were chiseled in stone somewhere. "I held you the second you were born. I looked into your eyes every day of your life until the day you disappeared. I knew you before *you* knew you. And whether or not you want to hear it, Gabby DiMarco, you were *born* Marianna Ruíz."

I feel the prickle of irritation in my spine.

"But you *don't* know me," I reply coolly. "If you did, you'd know my parents—Mack and Lucy DiMarco—were incapable of doing what you're suggesting. Because that's what you're suggesting, isn't it? That my parents—the people I loved more than anyone else in the world—were kidnappers?"

Now she's the one trying to even out her tone.

"Gabby, I understand how you might believe that—"

"Believe it?" I echo incredulously, my volume rising a little more than I'd intended. "It's *fact*. I have a birth certificate to prove it!"

She shrugs, not the least bit dissuaded. "Birth certificates can be faked. It happens all the time."

My palms go up toward the ceiling. "You're really not even

willing to *entertain* the possibility that this was a screwup with the lab?"

When she shakes her head, her long, dark hair swishes around her shoulders.

"No," she replies calmly. "I'm not. Not now that I've laid eyes on you. There's no one else you *could* be. Not with those eyes. They're her eyes."

"What are you talking about? Whose eyes?" I ask, growing more frustrated even as she seems to stay perfectly unaffected.

"Our mother's. You have the same eyes. She's dead, you know. She died giving birth to you . . ."

Oh, now this really is too much. I've got to stop this nonsense before she's got us in matching tattoos and #1 SISTER charms.

"I'm sorry," I whisper intensely. "I'm so sorry, Isabella, but I am *not* Marianna! I don't know how many ways I can say it! And my parents—my *real* parents—were not criminals. DNA or no DNA, there's *nothing* you can say that will ever convince me otherwise."

My words hang there between us for a very long moment. Then, to my surprise, Isabella sits back and smiles.

"So, you do admit the DNA profile could be accurate."

"No," I respond, matching her stare-for-stare.

"Then why come here?" she asks curiously, as if she wants to know why I prefer chocolate ice cream to vanilla.

I hadn't wanted to get into this immediately, but I guess I don't have any choice now.

"Okay, so I believe there's a story here—for the magazine. Well, for *a* magazine, anyway. I think GeneTeam screwed up big time, and now they've turned both our lives upside down with a simple error at the lab. And considering the history you've had with, you know, your sister and all, it seems especially reckless to me. Cruel, even."

I brace myself for the blowup . . . but it doesn't come. Instead, Isabella Ruíz just considers me from the other side of the booth.

"That's it? You just came here to interview me for some article you want to write?"

"Well, not an article, exactly. I want to tell your story . . ."

"It's your story, too," she points out. "Right or wrong, accurate or not, you've been sucked into this too, you know."

"Well, clearly. That's why I'm here."

She cocks her head to the side. "But is it?"

"What do you mean?"

"I mean, is that why you came? Because I think there's more to it than a chance to write an article for some big publication. What is it?"

I shrug. "I don't know. I still think it's possible they just messed up the percentages on the DNA—that maybe we're like distant cousins or something. And honestly, I'd really like to connect with any family I might have. So there's that . . ." She nods as if this makes perfect sense. "And . . . so . . . I'd like us to take another DNA test. Here."

There, I've said it out loud. Now I hold my breath and wait for her response. I don't have to wait very long as Isabella scowls slightly, and her eyes narrow.

"We *had* a DNA test," she reminds me, unable to hide the shadow or irritation that lingers in her words. "And you don't seem to believe it. So what difference would another one make?"

"No, we had a *genealogy* test that gave us a genetic match that may or may not be correct. So, I propose we have a real DNA test. Like at a lab here in Puerto Rico. Just you and me. They'll compare our samples and tell us the truth once and for all."

I study her carefully as she turns this over in her head. There *is* a physical similarity between us. But nothing so striking that I'd have stopped to stare if I'd seen her walking down Broadway. We both have dark hair and fair skin. But my eyes are blue, and hers are brown. And where I'm more on the petite side, she's taller and leggy. Studying her features carefully, I don't see anything even close to a genetic "smoking gun."

Finally, after a few long seconds of ogling one another, she shrugs.

"Fine. We'll find a lab—"

"I've already found one," I tell her quietly. "It's not far from here, actually. We can walk there."

The dark brows shoot up now.

"From where? Here?" She's pointing down at the tabletop with her index finger. "You mean like now? You want to go do this *now*?"

I pull a shrug of my own. "The sooner we do it, the sooner we'll know for certain."

"Oh, Gabby DiMarco," she murmurs on a soft sigh of resignation as she shakes her head. "You have no idea. But you will." Before I can respond to this, she lifts her glass in a one-sided toast. "To the truth," she says. "Which is never as black and white as you think it's going to be."

I lift my glass and surprise her by clinking it with hers. "I'll toast to that."

Greg the lab tech is more than happy to swab our cheeks, dropping the extralong Q-tips into the fluid-filled plastic test tubes once he's through. He prints labels and has us each sign off on our own samples. Isabella seems to have sobered up a bit after our brief walk through town to the tiny second-floor lab on one of the back blocks off the main drag.

I'm so glad I thought to find this place and check it out in advance of my trip. She had no time to find an excuse to avoid doing the test—which I'm fairly certain she would have done, given the chance. I don't know what it is that she's angling for, but the more time I spend with this woman, the more confident I am that there was a mix-up at the Gene-Team labs. I make a note to check the small print on their website when I'm back in the hotel room. I'm wondering if I signed anything to prevent me from suing for emotional distress. Because this is pretty damn emotionally distressing.

"All right then, ladies, that's all I need from you," Greg announces as he pushes the frames of his glasses back up the bridge of his nose.

"Great, thank you. What time can we pick up the results tomorrow? I'd like to catch an evening flight back home."

Isabella glances at me, surprised, but doesn't comment.

The small man's brows furrow in concern. "Oh, I'm sorry, Miss—this will take at least five days to process—perhaps a week . . ."

"What?" My turn to be surprised. And pissed. "Your website says you can have DNA results in less than twenty-four hours!"

He looks sheepish all of a sudden. "Ah, well, no one's updated our website in a while. Since that last hurricane, we send these out to a lab in Miami—"

"Miami?" I practically shriek. "Miami, *Florida?*"

"No, Ohio," Isabella mutters next to me.

"Really, I'm sorry. I mean, I can ask for a rush on these, but they're pretty backed up . . ."

"You have my cell phone number?" I ask.

"Yes—"

"Great. Please call me the second the results are available."

"Yes, yes, of course . . ."

From next to me, Isabella is snickering.

"What's so funny?" I snap at her.

She just smiles and shrugs, totally unconcerned about my rising ire.

"Nothing . . . just, you know, you do all this research and didn't bother to pick up the phone and confirm the procedure . . ."

I glare at her and start to stomp out of the lab and down the creaky brown steps leading back to the street.

"Oh, come on now, Gabby," she calls after me. "It could be worse. So what if you need to hang out a little longer. Puerto Rico is beautiful . . ."

"I can see that!" I spit back at her once we're back on the cobblestone drive. "I just hoped . . . I just wanted to put a period on this and get on with my life."

She looks perplexed. "Put a period? What's that supposed to mean?"

"You know, like at the end of a sentence? I want to move on."

"So, you can 'put a period' there in five to seven days," Isabella says. "What difference does it make? You're stuck in paradise for a few days, why not make the most of it?"

She's right. I need to see the results with my own two eyes—at the same time she does, just so I know there's no shenanigans going on down here. Of course, I know what the results are going to say. I'm not Marianna Ruíz; I couldn't be. Still, somewhere in the back of my mind, a part of me does hope we're related—just a little bit. I mean, she's not a totally unpleasant person or anything. We might have been friends under different circumstances. So, I've got two choices here, I can sit around on the beach and churn out an ulcer in my gut while I wait for the results to come back . . . or I can do what I do so well. What Franny suggested I do—collect the facts.

I stop and turn to her with a sweet smile. "You know what, Isabella? You're right. I *am* going to hang around for the rest of the week."

"That's great," she says, smiling. "Let me show you around the island then—"

She stops short when I shake my head.

"No, I'm afraid I won't have much time for sightseeing. I've got to do some legwork for this story—researching and conducting interviews with people who were involved."

"Involved with what?" she asks slowly.

"With your case. I'm going to see if I can figure out what happened to Marianna," I inform her. "The *actual* Marianna."

She looks at me as if I've sprouted a sparkly unicorn horn from my forehead.

"What? Are you for real?"

"I am. I'm going to do it for the story I'm writing . . . and I'm going to do it for you."

"Pfft. For me?" She holds up her palms and scoffs, chuckling a little as she does. "I don't need you to go play Sherlock Holmes on my account. I already know where Marianna is. She's standing right in front of me."

"Yeah, well, I'm sorry to say you've got your facts wrong. So I plan to go out and find the right facts. Because the facts always lead to the truth, Isabella."

And, like it or not, the truth *will* out.

CHAPTER 10

MIGUEL

That Day

Detective Miguel Alvarez considered the man in front of him, hunched and sobbing—a filthy wreck of a human being who reeked of stale cigarettes and cheap beer. Not that this was an unusual sight in La Perla on a Sunday morning. What *was* unusual was the fact that Miguel was there at all. The people who lived in this neighborhood went to great lengths to keep *la policía* out. In fact, there was a long-observed tacit understanding between La Perla's denizens and law enforcement—so long as no one messed with *las turistas*, the dealers were free to deal, the hookers were free to hook, and the robbers were free to rob. As long as it stayed on that side of La Muralla—the crumbling four-hundred-year-old wall separating the city of Old San Juan from La Perla.

Miguel knew there would come a point when this was no longer sustainable—it was just a matter of time before something happened that was so horrific that the entire island would demand some sort of martial action. And then there would be no going back. But, for now, they hadn't reached that threshold, so La Perla took care of itself.

The fact that he was sitting here in El Gallo Rojo—at the request of the owner, Beatríz Rodriguez—told him that this tiny, insular community had already taken every measure possible to track down the missing child and had come up short. This situation was dire enough to warrant inviting the enemy inside. And dire enough for the enemy to accept.

No one who lived here had taken little Marianna Ruíz—of that much he was certain. Because, while you could get away with a lot of shit in La Perla, harming a child was not one of them. If it *had* been someone who lived here—or even a regular customer of any given vice offered in the area—Miguel would be here investigating a homicide instead of a missing child.

"Okay, Alberto, let's try one more time. What do you remember from last night?"

The father had been unable to give him much useful information. Right now, he had his elbows on top of the bar, face buried in his hands, sobbing openly. Miguel was half tempted to give the guy a shot of whiskey to calm his nerves. A little "hair of the dog." Not to mention a sure cure for the tremors the man was experiencing.

Alberto mumbled something undistinguishable into his palms.

All Miguel had been able to piece together so far was that Alberto had come out last night—probably looking to score a little coke—with his seven-month-old daughter in a stroller. He should be scandalized by this, but he wasn't. The rules of decorum and decency were very different on this side of La Muralla. If anything, he actually thought higher of the man for not leaving the child at home unattended. The fact that he took her with him showed at least he had some concern for her well-being—as was the fact that he'd been sobbing his eyes out ever since Miguel arrived.

"He doesn't remember anything," Beatríz informed him grimly. "I can tell you he came in here with Marianna around eight last night—said he was supposed to meet someone."

"Did he say who?"

"No, but . . ." Her voice trailed off as she glanced in Alberto's direction. He seemed to be unaware of the conversation happening around him. "I'm pretty sure it has something to do with Santiago," she said, dropping her volume so only he could hear what she said.

He didn't need to have a last name; Miguel knew exactly who Santiago was. And he knew exactly what Santiago was capable of—especially when it came to the people who owed him money.

"Alberto," he said a little loudly, trying to break through the fog of grief and guilt. "Alberto, did you meet up with one of Santiago's guys last night?"

The man nodded miserably, not bothering to pull his head out of his hands.

"*Oye, amigo, mírame,*" Miguel commanded more sternly.

Alberto looked at him, as instructed. "*Mija esta desaparecida,*" he whispered to Miguel, who sighed and put a hand on the other man's back.

"I know. I know your daughter is missing. That's why I'm here. Alberto, do you owe Santiago money? Is that why you were down here last night?"

Alberto seemed to pause for a very long time before finally nodding.

"*Sí.* I owe him a lot of money . . . after my Rosaria died, I needed the money to bury her. And the baby needs so much. And I can't . . ." His voice choked off in a fresh round of sobs. "I can't get through the week without something to . . ."

He didn't finish the sentence, but once again, he didn't have to. Miguel had actually met Alberto earlier in the year—not that he'd remember. His own wife, Hilda, had attended school with Rosaria Ruíz back when she was Rosaria Chavez, and he'd escorted her to the young mother's funeral after she had died giving birth to their second child.

Back then, Alberto had looked dazed—like a man who woke up from a beautiful dream only to find that his life was a living nightmare. Seven months later, he was gaunt and pale with sunken eyes. They were the eyes of a man so desperate to escape the ghosts haunting him every hour of every day that he would do anything, say anything, give anything to be rid of them, if even for just a few hours.

Give anything.

Was he desperate enough to have given away his own child?

"Alberto . . ." Miguel began again slowly, softly. "Is it possible you . . . did something with Marianna? Something you can't remember now?"

Or maybe that you can *remember and are too afraid to say out loud?*

Alberto's eyes grew wider, his face paler. He pulled something from his pocket and placed it on the bar top. Then he pushed back so hard and so fast that the stool he'd been sitting on toppled and slid several feet across the sticky concrete floor. A moment later, Miguel could hear the man retching in the alley out back.

He glanced at the item on the bar—a tiny pink sock.

CHAPTER 11

ISABELLA

Today

Matéo picks up on the first ring.

"*¿Bueno?*" he asks expectantly. *Well?*

"Well, *what?*" I echo the question back to him with more irritation than I intend.

"Well, is it her?"

I snort derisively. "Not a doubt in *my* mind."

"Ah, but she's not convinced."

"Matéo, she insisted on her *own* DNA test—just the two of us. She had an appointment set up for us at a lab in San Juan before she even left home!"

"And did you do it?"

My husband isn't surprised that she demanded the test—he's surprised I agreed to take it.

"What the hell else was I supposed to do?" I hiss at him from inside my car—which is parked in front of the San Juan Police Department.

"Okay, okay," he says, and I can picture him holding up his palms in a conciliatory calm-your-ass-down-please gesture. "So, what's next?"

"Pfft. No clue. She said something about finding the facts—oh, yeah—because she's a 'fact-checker.' That's, like, her job."

"What do you mean she's a fat checker? Like at a Weight Watchers meeting or something?"

"Huh? No—not a fat checker. A *fact*-checker. Like she confirms the facts in magazine articles."

"*Ah, sí, claro*—of course. They do it for the politicians on the news all the time. To see who's spouting bullshit and who's telling the truth. Right, so she's a researcher. But Isabella, that's not a bad thing. The test results will come back and confirm what you already know—that she's your sister. But what they won't tell you is what happened that day. My advice? Let her do all the investigating she wants to do. Maybe she'll turn up something that no one else has found."

I consider this, wanting to remain pissy but knowing he's right.

"I just . . ." I sigh, my tone thawing from frustration to disappointment as I rub the bridge of my nose. "I wanted her to know. You understand? I wanted her to know the same way that I just . . . know. I wanted her to *feel* the connection, even if she couldn't actually remember it."

His voice softens when he speaks again. "I understand. But you have to remember—you've spent your entire life looking for someone who didn't even know she was lost. You can't expect her to be happy you showed up and told her the only parents she's ever known are felons. They were her *parents*. You're still just a stranger."

"But that's so wrong!" I whine like a disgruntled tween. "I'm her *blood!* She should be angry with those . . . those frauds for stealing her away from her real family!"

"Listen, baby, I know this is hard, but you've got to take it slow. She needs to come to the conclusion that she's Marianna Ruíz. On her own. That's the only way she's going to believe it. So let her do what she has to do. Help her if she'll let you. You know the truth, right?"

It takes a long moment to get there, but I eventually agree begrudgingly.

"Right," I admit huffily.

"Right. So, be patient and let her find her way. You've had a long time to come to terms with this. She's had like five minutes. Give her some space, and she'll get there."

"You really think so?" I ask, hearing the softening of my tone—and my anger.

"I do."

Suddenly I want to cry. Damn it! I've known this woman for less than ninety minutes, and I've already got emotional whiplash.

"It's just . . . I'm so excited," I admit quietly. "Matéo, she's right here, right in front of me after so many years! I just want to grab her and hold her and cry and do all that girly shit that sisters do. The stuff we never had the chance to do."

"Okay, yeah, I get that—but Isabella, it's not like you haven't had *any* of that. I know you didn't have a great childhood, but there *were* some good moments in there along with the shit ones," he reminds me. "You've got your cousins, your aunt and uncle, your grandmother . . ."

I sigh again, feeling my pulse slow slightly. No one can talk me off a ledge like Matéo.

"You're right."

"I know."

"I love you."

"I know that, too," he says matter-of-factly.

I'm about to comment when I see the glass door of the precinct swing open and a familiar dark, wavy head of hair pop out. She's looking around for something. Or someone.

"Oh! I think she's looking for me; I need to go," I tell him hurriedly.

"Right. Call me later."

"I will," I promise, disconnecting the call so I can get out of the car and wave toward Gabby.

She looks relieved to see me, if not exactly happy, and gestures for me to join her inside the police station. The one she asked me to leave not ten minutes ago. But that was ten minutes ago.

"Thank goodness—I thought maybe you'd left," she says when I'm climbing the steps.

"Why? What's going on?" I ask instead.

"He won't tell me anything." She pauses. "Because I'm not . . . you know . . . family."

I try not to smirk at the irony.

"And what do you want me to do about it?" I ask, pretending I have no idea on earth where she's going with this.

"The detective who handles the cold cases will only speak with an 'interested party.' *You're* an interested party," she informs me.

Hah! "Interested" is an understatement. I've been a thorn in Detective Miguel Alvarez's side for literally decades now.

She's holding the door open in hopes that I'll just nod and follow her inside. But I just can't resist busting her chops. Just a little.

"I'm sorry, but didn't you just tell me you *didn't* need me to come in with you? That, as a journalist, you're trained to handle sources, and I'd only get in the way?"

I expect to take some delight in her response but, when she rolls her eyes, I have the unsettling feeling that I'm looking at my expression—but on her face. And it's more than a little freaky.

"Look, Isabella, I'm sorry if I sounded a little . . . you know . . . dismissive. I'm just a little out of my element, you know? I'd be really grateful if you could help me out here."

I dismiss the strangeness—and her concern—with a shake of my head, reaching past her to open the tinted glass door.

"It's fine. Whatever."

"Right," she says, following behind me, "he's just behind the counter. And—*oof!*"

When I stop short, she crashes right into my back.

"Sorry . . ." I mutter, staring at the guy standing at the counter, tapping on a computer keyboard. "Where's Alvarez?" I ask her over my shoulder.

"Who?"

"Miguel Alvarez. The detective on this case . . ."

She looks confused as she moves up next to me so we're side by side in the lobby. "I'm sorry—I don't know who that is. That guy right there—he's the one they sent out to speak with me. He's the one who said I needed an interested party. I'm pretty sure he's the guy in charge—"

"Like hell, he is," I mutter, starting toward the familiar counter and the stranger standing at it. But Gabby grabs my arm before I can take more than a step.

"He thinks my name is Lucy Mack," she whispers.

"What? Why didn't you just tell him the truth? About the DNA test and why you're here?"

She shrugs sheepishly. "I don't know. There's just something about this guy that's a little . . . unnerving. I can't explain it; I just didn't feel comfortable giving him my real name. Not yet, anyway."

Great, she thinks she's some fact-finding superhero. A modern-day Sherlock Holmes. But instead of a magnifying glass and disguises, she's got spell-check and Google.

I stomp up to the counter, fueled by my irritation with her and my suspicion of him. When I'm standing in front of the man who's *not* Miguel Alvarez, I stare at him until he finally bothers to look up. But the first thing he does is focus on my companion, who's standing just behind me.

"Ah, you're back, Miss Mack," he acknowledges flatly, clearly not happy that she has boomeranged on him. "And, oh look, you've brought a friend with you," he notes with a healthy dose of snark.

"Detective Raña, this is Isabella Ruíz. She was—she *is* Marianna Ruíz's sister."

"I'm sorry, but we need to see Miguel Alvarez, please. Detective Miguel Alvarez," I tell him firmly before getting further into pleasantries.

"No."

"I'm sorry . . . no?" I confirm, thinking I've either misheard or misunderstood him.

"That's right; I said no. I'm sorry, but that's not possible. Detective Alvarez is gone. He retired nearly two years ago. I'm Detective David Raña, and I filled the position after he left."

"Wait, what?" My exclamation comes out loud enough for people to stop their conversations and look in our direction. "Miguel Alvarez *retired?* But he didn't—he never told me . . ." My voice trails off as I realize how ridiculous this must sound to other people.

"Do you . . . know him?" Raña asks, now peering at me curiously.

"Sort of. He was the person who kept me up to date on the case all these years. I'm just . . . I'm surprised he didn't just let me know it wouldn't be him anymore. It's been a long time . . ."

"Right." Raña's wheels are turning again. "Okay, well, look, Miss Ruíz, I feel I need to warn you—it's not the best idea to allow a member of the press access to any information I'm able to disclose to you—which isn't much, since this is still considered an ongoing investigation."

"Ongoing?" I can't help the incredulity that accompanies those syllables. "Are you serious? Ongoing? Like *active?* As far as I know, the cops haven't done jack in the last—oh, I don't know—fifteen years? Because the last thing I recall is the age progression poster that was put out for the tenth anniversary of my sister's disappearance."

He doesn't respond, but he does seem to take note of the curious looks we're getting from the other people in the lobby. He clears his throat and drops his voice.

"Why don't you ladies come back to my office."

Without awaiting a reply, he turns and starts to walk away, leaving the two of us to scurry behind him, trying to keep up as he leads us through a biometric security door and a long corridor that opens up into a large room with several cubicles in the middle and small offices lining the walls. Even though he is in a corner, the detective's office is windowless and dim.

When did he say he took over this job? A year ago? Two? It looks as if he's just moved in. The walls are empty, and his desk is piled high with stacks of binders. All along the walls are white cardboard file boxes with what I presume are case numbers. The only available seating is a pair of metal folding chairs, which Gabby and I take.

Raña closes the door behind us, then walks around to the back of his desk. He looks down at the floor, then bends to pick up one of the boxes there, setting it atop his desk and standing over it. I can't help but notice it's marked: R-22583 Ruíz, M.

When Gabby pulls out her phone to snap a picture of the box, the detective scowls at her. "No. Pictures. *Please.*"

"Sorry," she mumbles, putting up her hands in an "I surrender!" gesture and then setting the phone on her lap.

He opens the top of the box, pulls out a large binder, then reseats the cover to use it as a table while he scans the pages.

"I've been reviewing the evidence in this case," he tells us. Then, to me: "And despite what you might think, Miss Ruíz, I do believe that Detective Alvarez did everything in his power where your sister's case was concerned. He explored every lead, considered each piece of evidence. He questioned dozens of residents of La Perla and further questioned tourists who were in the area on that day. He was thorough, and I don't believe he missed anything."

I hold his gaze for a very long few moments, searching for something I don't quite understand—and noting that he's doing the exact same thing. He thinks I know something. Which makes me think *he* knows something.

"Okay, so . . . maybe you start by telling us what happened when the girl's father—Isabella's father—was interviewed?" Gabby asks, her question forcing Raña and me to disengage our staring contest.

"Um, well . . . apparently, he was quite . . . upset. And it was difficult to get much information out of him at the time. We know that he'd been there with little Marianna in her stroller at the bar the night before. We also confirmed he was confronted by the enforcer for a known loan shark. But Mr. Ruíz was very intoxicated and could not recollect any of that interaction or how he came to be unconscious in the alley behind El Gallo Rojo. Only that he woke up Sunday morning severely beaten, and the baby was gone. That's when the locals mounted a search of their own."

I'd heard about the search. It wasn't one that the officials would have sanctioned—with kicked-in doors, broken windows, and potential suspects rounded up and interrogated, vigilante-style. The police were only called in *after* the entirety of La Perla had been checked, house by house, for my missing sister.

"And none of your interviews with them—the locals, I mean—turned up any usable leads?" Another good question from Gabby.

Okay, maybe she's not too bad at the Sherlock thing. She's asking the same questions I'd be asking, too, were I still looking for Marianna. But I'm not looking anymore. I don't need to. She's sitting right next to me. Not that Raña knows that.

He shakes his head. "No. There were enough witnesses in the bar to verify most of Alberto's timeline, but no one saw anything that proved to be useful."

"I read that the stroller was recovered in a dumpster," Gabby says. "Was there any forensic evidence on it?"

"Let's just say that our forensic capabilities were . . . limited at that time. So, no. Fingerprints were collected, but they only matched the father's. Your father's," he repeats for my benefit.

"And—"

"And that's all that I'm able to share with you," he says sternly, before she can get another question out.

"What about the sock?"

I hadn't planned on asking about it, but an image of it just popped into my head, and then the question just popped out of my mouth. They both turn to stare at me. There's irritation on his face and confusion on hers.

"Sock?" she asks. "What sock?"

The detective is not happy with me, but he reaches into the box anyway, pulling out a clear baggie. Gabby and I both lean forward to get a better look. The single pink sock looks impossibly tiny now that I see it for the first time in years. Suddenly I'm blasted by a rush of images and emotions— a jumble of feelings, smells, sounds—that take me back to that chaotic, confusing time in my life. A time when I was overjoyed . . . and then devastated. And caught in the middle of it all was this perfect little girl—inextricably linked to the worst day of my life. Which, for the record, was not the day she was taken from us. It was the day she arrived . . . the day my *mother* was taken from us.

I find myself reaching out toward the baggie. I want to touch the sock, as if I can somehow reconjure the remnants of my childhood through the thin plastic that protects it. But Raña pulls it away before my fingers can make contact.

"I'm sorry, Miss Ruíz, but I can't have your prints turning up on the evidence bag," he tells me.

But he's not sorry. He's a douche.

I yank my hand back as if it had been scalded. "Right, of course. Sorry," I mutter.

But I'm not sorry. I'm pissed.

"Right, well, as I said, that's really all I can share with

you at this time. Of course, if anything new should—" He stops mid-sentence, his brows drawing together as he takes in something on Gabby's face.

I turn my head to see what he's seeing when he looks at her.

She's gone chalky white, and she's staring at the pink sock like it's a tarantula sunning itself on the desk.

"Something wrong, Miss Mack?" the detective asks, and I can't help but notice the question is laced with curiosity instead of concern. He's thinking her reaction is some sort of clue, though—of what, I have no idea.

"You okay?" I murmur.

She breaks her death stare and turns to me. "I think I'd like to go now . . ." Her voice is small and shaky.

"Miss Mack? Is there something about this sock that you'd like to tell me?" Raña asks, holding up the item in question.

She's already up and out of the chair as she shakes her head.

"No. No, thank you, Detective . . ." she calls out over her shoulder.

He and I stand there and watch her skirt her way around the cubes and out into the lobby toward the front door. Then he turns and looks down at me suspiciously.

"Who is she?" he asks me quietly. "To you, I mean."

I shrug and turn slightly to look at him.

"Just a journalist," I tell him flatly.

When he speaks to me again, there's something challenging in his tone.

"You know, Miss Ruíz, I've been through every inch of that file, and I can't recall you ever having done an interview. Not for television, or the newspaper—and certainly not for some fancy magazine. So why this woman? And why now?"

I match the challenge and raise it a decibel of volume and a shit ton of provocation.

"You're the detective. You figure it out." I walk away. I can feel his eyes on my back until the moment I'm through the door and out of his sight.

Outside, I find Gabby sitting on the concrete steps, head in hands. I sit next to her, close enough so our upper arms are touching.

"What is it?" I ask her quietly.

When she looks up, her face is blotchy and wet.

"That sock . . ."

I nod my understanding. "I know, it's so . . . tiny. There's just something about it. I would get upset every time some idiot put it on the cover of the newspaper . . ."

"No, you don't—you don't understand," she tells me, her voice tightening as a new wash of tears spills from the ocean of her eyes.

I feel my stomach clench a second before she says it.

"I have the other one."

CHAPTER 12

GABBY

Today

"More?" Isabella is holding up the bottle of wine. I glance down at my glass, which has, at some point, drained itself.

I nod and hold it out for her. "Yes, please."

"Are you feeling a little better?" she asks gingerly, as if I might burst into tears again.

I'm pretty sure my little meltdown on the police station steps freaked her out. I know it freaked me out enough that I didn't want to be alone this evening. So when she offered a dinner invitation, I accepted it on the spot. And it was the right call, I realize, as I sit in the living room of their tiny bungalow. It's painted a pale blue with a postage-stamp lawn and a big palm tree out front, flanked by some sort of lush-looking shrub with waxy green leaves edged in a dark pink.

Inside, the rooms are connected by a floor made of huge terra-cotta tiles. The rattan furniture is covered with floral patterned cushions, and ceiling fans hum in each of the rooms. It's modest but lovely and homey—and it makes my Brooklyn apartment seem cold and empty by comparison. Thanks to the open floor plan, I can see Matéo hustling around the small kitchen—chopping, stirring, boiling, frying. I don't know what he's making, but it smells amazing.

"I am feeling better," I assure her, then I use my non-wine

hand to gesture to our surroundings. "You have a beautiful home."

She offers a half-smile. "Well, we don't have a concierge, or room service, or an ocean view."

"Or a private beach," Matéo adds, bustling out of the kitchen to put some serving dishes out on the table. "Or a Michelin-star restaurant . . ."

"Okay, I got it. You think La Playa Blanca is a little over the top."

"Ah, we're just teasing," Matéo says, good-naturedly. "Come and sit. We'll eat and you two can figure this out together."

Isabella and I exchange glances. "Together" had most definitely not been part of my plan. But then, my plan—flimsy as it was—has already gone to hell.

I sit at the place they've set for me, directly across from Isabella, stealing brief glances at her as she adds a few final items to the table. Her face is a bit longer than mine—more oval to my heart shape. Behind her bangs is a forehead similar to mine, and the curve of her—

I stop myself abruptly and look down at my lap, fussing with the napkin I've placed there. What am I looking for, anyway? A resemblance between us? There isn't one. There can't be one, because we're not related. Even if we do turn out to be cousins, it'll be second or third degree.

But the sock. There's no good reason for my parents to have had that in their possession. None. I could argue that there are a million babies wearing a million pairs of pink socks at any given time, but I don't. Because a part of me knows the one I have at home and the one sitting in that evidence bag are a pair.

"I hope you like *arroz con pollo*," Matéo comments, breaking into my thoughts.

"Mmm!" I agree with a smile, taking a closer look at the colorful assortment of items laid out between us. Joining the *arroz con pollo* are a salad laced with avocado and marinated red pimiento peppers, a loaf of crusty bread, and one item I don't recognize.

"Can I ask what those are?" I point to a plate with what looks to be big, fat bananas, squashed flat and fried.

"*Tostones,*" Isabella says, taking a seat across from me. "Fried green plantains. They're very good. Here, try it," she instructs, putting one on my plate.

I push it around with my fork before cutting off a small piece and putting it in my mouth. I'm pleasantly surprised to find it's savory, not sweet. Not like a banana at all. It's been fried to perfection with just a few grains of coarse salt on top. When I bite into it, it's crispy on the outside but tender on the inside.

"Mm . . . oh, that's good," I murmur after a bite.

"We'll have to make you some *plátanos maduros,*" Matéo says with a knowing smile. "You use plantains that are so ripe the skin has turned black. Then you slice them longways and fry them. They come out so sweet and delicious!" He pats his stomach to accentuate the point.

I like this Matéo. He's tall and thin, with dark hair that's just a little too long and a pair of tortoiseshell glasses. He moves easily around Isabella—in a way that tells me they've been together a long time. I get the sense he's her rock, and probably has been for some time now.

My mouth starts to water as I become acutely aware that the last thing I ate was a protein bar in the cab from the airport.

"Oh, jeez, I can't remember the last time I had a meal this good," I murmur, tucking into the chicken with rice.

"You don't cook?" Isabella asks, and I'm grateful for the neutral topic.

"A little. Not much, really. I'm pretty happy if I've got a big bowl of Cheerios and a banana," I explain.

Matéo snickers, and Isabella shoots him a look. "Yeah,

that's about the extent of Isabella's cooking repertoire, too. Although she's more of a Rice Chex kinda girl," he explains, even as she swats him.

"Perfectly acceptable choice," I state with a nod to her. "I like to let them sit in the milk—"

"Until they're soggy. Like little pillows," Isabella finishes for me.

"Exactly," I agree without too much thought as I spear some salad with my fork. When I glance up again, Matéo is looking between us with some interest. "Everything okay?" I ask.

He shakes his head—not in disagreement so much as to dispel a thought from his head. "Yeah. I'm just . . . the two of you . . ."

His wife looks up at him. "What? The two of us what?"

He shrugs. "I don't know, you're just kind of . . . you're alike."

We both stare at him, then at one another, then back to him again.

"What, because we like the same cereal?" Isabella asks.

"Yeah. Well, no. Not exactly. There's just this thing between you . . . an easiness is the best way I can describe it."

Once again, she and I consider each other across the dinner plates. I want to chalk up his observation to wishful thinking. Isabella wants desperately for me to be Marianna, and Matéo wants desperately for Isabella to be happy. That being said, I think I understand what he's trying to say. While things are a little awkward at times between Isabella and me, we do generally seem to "get" one another. But I could say the same about any number of other women I have encountered in my life.

"An easiness? I don't know about that, exactly," I begin slowly, quietly. "But I do appreciate the fact that you did the DNA test that I sprang on you, Isabella. And that you had my back with that Detective Raña guy."

She looks at me for a long couple of seconds before settling on a reply. "Gabby, I'll give you whatever proof it takes for you to believe the truth."

"We don't know what the truth is," I point out. "Not yet, anyway."

"I do," she says matter-of-factly, not for the first time.

I take a long, measured breath, working to keep my face impassive. "Well, I guess we'll see soon enough."

"So, Gabby, Isabella tells me you live in Brooklyn—" Matéo begins in a very unsubtle attempt to divert the conversation. But his wife isn't having it.

"How do you explain the sock?" she asks, cutting him off.

I take a beat.

"I can't," I tell her. "You said you had no doubts after you saw me, right? Well, I had no doubts *until* I saw that thing in the evidence bag. I was a hundred percent certain the DNA test was wrong right up to that second—"

"Uh-huh!" she declares with a triumphant nod and a silverware-jangling slap of the table.

"*But,*" I say pointedly and forcefully, "it's not exactly a smoking gun, okay? I've been thinking about it, and thousands—probably *hundreds* of thousands—of babies wear pink socks like that. I'd have to compare the two side-by-side to be sure they're a set. And even then . . . Anyway, yeah, I'm a little shaky on the hundred percent thing. But I'm still like ninety-eight percent certain we're not sisters."

"Seriously?" she grumbles and rolls her eyes at me, clearly frustrated that I'm not seeing things her way. When Matéo puts a hand on her forearm, she shakes it off, tossing him a look that makes him hold up his hands in surrender. Then she turns back to me. "If it were *just* the DNA or *just* the sock, I might understand. But the two together?" She shakes her head defiantly, long dark layers swishing from side to side. "No. No way."

I feel my pulse pick up along with my blood pressure. My

God, this woman is stubborn! She cannot even allow for the possibility she might be wrong.

"No way what? You can't tell me how to feel about this," I tell her, losing my battle to stay calm and unaffected. "I'm a grown woman. I can consider the evidence and make a decision on my own, thank you very much. Cut me some slack, will you? This all came out of nowhere. No-where!" I stress. "I was lonely, all right? I was looking for a distant relative. I never expected . . ." I wave a hand between her and me. "I never expected this, whatever this is."

Matching red spots appear on her cheeks.

"Yeah? Well, I don't understand how you *can't* see. Jesus, how much proof do you need?"

"More!" I snap back. "More! You're talking about my *parents*—"

"They were *not* your parents," she hisses in a voice that stops me cold. "They were your kidnappers."

Suddenly it's as if all the air is sucked from my lungs. I gape at her, unable to breathe, let alone respond.

"Okay, okay, I think that's enough, Isabella," Matéo jumps in, his tone calm but firm. Then he turns to me. "Gabby, what my wife is trying to say—badly—is that it's clear the two of you are connected in some way. She wants desperately for you to be the sister she lost." Now he looks at her pointedly. "But she knows very well that may not be the case. And she's very grateful you came this far to meet her—and to try and sort this out. One. Way. Or. Another."

His emphasis at the end is a message for his wife. And she gets it.

Isabella draws in a long, slow sigh, giving a begrudging nod on the back end of it. I start to speak, but she holds up a hand to stop me.

"Um . . . so, I've been looking for Marianna for twenty-five years, not even knowing for sure if she was alive. And when you turned up on GeneTeam, I couldn't believe what I was seeing. I mean, just like that, after all this time, you—she—was maybe alive and well in New York City!" She pauses, leaning forward toward me, across the table. "Listen, I don't know how you came to be Gabriella DiMarco, but before you were her, you were my sister. You were Marianna Ruíz. I'd bet my life on it."

By the time she's finished speaking, her words are choked, and tears have spilled over her lashes, down her cheeks. She swipes at them impatiently, looking up at the ceiling and shaking her head. I see it now. She's not angry with me. She's not even angry with my dead parents. Isabella is angry at God, or the universe, or whichever "higher power" it is she believes to be screwing with her. And really, who could blame her, considering everything that's happened?

It occurs to me for the first time that I have no idea what happened to this woman after her sister disappeared. She was what? Five years old? Who took care of *her*? Who loved *her*? What kind of a home did she grow up in? And how did she survive living in the long, dark shadow of that single event?

"Isabella," I begin more gently, "I don't know what to think about my parents . . . or the sock. But, for what you're saying to be true, I'd have to believe Mack and Lucy would have—could have—*literally* stolen a baby off the street. They were good, decent people—humble people. And devout Catholics, to boot." I reach out and touch her hand with the tips of my fingers. "I'm sorry, Isabella, this isn't about not being able to believe that I'm your sister. It's about being able to believe I'm *not* their daughter. And I just . . . I can't."

We peer at one another thoughtfully across the table, now littered with empty plates and glasses.

She blows out a puff of air she must have been holding while I was speaking.

"I can understand that," she says at last. "I can respect that. But even if you're not her, you—or at least your parents—are connected somehow. There's just no way around that."

I take my hand back, folding it over its companion on the place mat in front of me. I study the two of them, the long, lean fingers, the pink polished nails. She's not wrong, I do see that. Much as I'd rather *not* see it. And were it not for the possibility that my parents might be a thread in this huge, knotty tangle of time, I'd be pretty excited to find myself smack at the center of this crazy story. The story that might just turn out to be the crazy story of my life.

Suddenly I see that there's only one way to set this right.

"I have to figure out what happened," I announce. "All of it. I need to track down as many people as I can from that time and talk to them. I need to go to where it happened. I have to *literally* follow the trail of facts to see where it leads me. That's the only way we'll know for sure what's real . . . and what's just coincidence."

It's Matéo who answers first. "I don't think that's necessarily a bad idea, but it's been a long time. Some of those facts may have been eaten up by the birds by now."

Isabella and I stare at him, uncomprehending.

"What are you talking about with the birds?" she asks him.

"You know—Hansel and Gretel? They put out the trail of breadcrumbs . . ."

"¡Ay, dios mio!" She groans a second before her head hits the table in faux frustration.

I'm happy to see she's not crying anymore, but this is where I lose them as Matéo starts speaking to her in rapid-fire Spanish. I know a handful of words, supplemented by my fluency in French, but this conversation goes by so fast I can't catch anything recognizable. It starts to get a little heated, too. He's suggesting something. She's adamant in her rejection of whatever it is. He pushes. She pushes back. He gestures toward me, speaking emphatically, and she . . . does nothing. She looks from him to me and back again, then sighs.

"Fine. Fine, fine, fine," she concedes at last, exasperated.

"Right, so," she begins, turning to face me full, steadying her tone, "Matéo and I, we . . . agree . . . that you should not be going all over the island by yourself asking questions. I . . . will go with you."

I stare at her.

"What? No. Oh, no. But . . . thanks . . . but yeah . . . no."

Her hands go up, and she looks at Matéo with a *See? I told you so!* look. He points at me but looks at her, speaking loudly once more.

"Okay, just stop it already!" My words come out loudly enough that I take them both by surprise. "I'm fine. I can take care of myself."

"This isn't New York City," he points out. "You can't just jump onto a subway to get around, you know?"

"I'll rent a car."

He's not satisfied.

"And how about the language? The people here in San Juan all speak English, but you might not find that when you get to the smaller towns where the tourists don't usually stay. How will you communicate?"

"I'll hire an interpreter."

"*¡Jesucristo! ¡Ella es* exactamente *como tú!*" he spits out, slapping the table in frustration.

"I am *not* just like her!" I declare indignantly, folding my arms across my chest.

They both turn to stare at me in unison.

I shrug.

"Some things defy language. But your point is taken. I'll take you with me, but only if you let me pay you, Isabella." She scoffs and waves a hand at me, about to protest, but I cut her off. "No, your job is all about being there for the tourists. You don't work, you don't get paid. You'd have to let me pay you for your time and cover the expenses—hotel, food, car, whatever. Otherwise, no deal."

The woman who may—or may not—be my sister sets her

mouth in a straight line as she examines me. Finally, seeing whatever it is she was looking for, she gives a single nod.

"*Bien entonces. Trato hecho.*"

"That's a bit beyond me . . ." I admit.

Matéo interprets.

"She said, in her usual charming way: 'Fine then, it's a deal.' "

I smile a little when I echo her words. "*Trato hecho.*"

CHAPTER 13

LUCY

That Day

Underneath Lucy's bare knees, the floor was cold and hard. She was suddenly sorry she chose to wear a skirt rather than slacks for this outing—but somehow it had seemed more appropriate, more deferential for the place and the purpose of her visit there. She'd already lit one of the small candles that flanked the sides of the altar, dropping a sizable check into the locked collection box when she was done.

After that, it wasn't hard to spot the thing she'd come so far to see. The tiny church was silent and empty around her. She'd been surprised by its size, having built it up in her mind to be some grand, majestic tabernacle teeming with desperate women such as herself. But there was no one. Just her . . . and the Madonna.

She stayed like that for a long moment, head bowed, eyes closed, feeling the silence settle around her. She couldn't help but notice that the crucifix was as understated and demure as the rest of this house of worship. It was nothing like the usual displays she'd come to expect in Catholic churches—all bloody thorns and gaping wounds. Upon entering, she had lowered her head and dipped her knee in genuflection reverentially, making the sign of the cross as she did. But the truth was that it was not the son of God Lucy had come all this way to see.

The statue of the Madonna sat on a marble pedestal outside of the communion rail and to the right of the altar—a delicate porcelain figure, no bigger than her favorite doll—dressed in a velvet robe in deep crimson. Now, as she sat at the base of the figure, too afraid to look up at it, she recalled the words of the first commandment:

Thou shalt have no other gods before me.

Surely, the Holy Mother must be an exception. Not that it mattered, because it was already too late. Lucy had been enthralled by the statue and all the hope, and power, and promise that it held for her.

The story of the weeping Madonna had found its way to her several years earlier—nothing more than a footnote in an article she read in the *Reader's Digest*. She hadn't thought much about the story at the time, because so-called "Miracle Madonnas" were a dime a dozen in those days—hoaxes meant to generate a little attention and a lot of cash before they could be debunked by the Church.

But there was something about the account of the barren woman who came here and knelt before Mary, praying her most fervent prayer for a child. It was said that the woman was so devout, her motivations so pure, and her heart so full of sorrow that tears began to flow down the statue's alabaster cheeks, falling onto the praying woman's hand.

The woman swore that when she looked up, she saw her pain reflected on the Madonna's face, and she knew right then and there that God had heard her prayer and would answer it. And He did. Less than a year later, she gave birth to twins after having been told her womb could not sustain one life—let alone two.

This wasn't anything Lucy had taken seriously. At least, not until she and Mack had had their own fertility troubles.

And, even then, it didn't have any immediate significance for her as week by week, month by month, she sank deeper into her depression. The miscarriages, the rounds of IVF, the failed adoption attempts all whirled in her mind.

And then she remembered "The Weeping Madonna of San Juan."

It hadn't been hard to convince Mack to take a cruise. And then it was just a matter of finding one that docked in Puerto Rico. She let her husband think she was killing time in the church while he went off in search of some Cuban cigars. But now that she was finally here, she found herself paralyzed, with no idea how to proceed.

Was there some special incantation she needed to utter? A bible verse or hymn she was meant to recite? Suddenly this all seemed ludicrous. She was nothing more than another housewife, desperate for something she would never have. Lucy loved her husband more than anything, and together they had dreamed of being a family. But she had failed him, and now she couldn't help but think she'd not only ruined her own happiness, but his, as well. She was a failure, unable to execute the one thing she was literally *built* to do: reproduce.

All at once, the frustration, the anger, the fear came rushing out of her in one great gush of emotion. She cried, then she sobbed, then she wept. She spewed her rage—then immediately begged for forgiveness, unable to reconcile the pain with the anger, the anger with the faith. She was bereft, mourning the loss of something she had never had. Something she would never have.

When she had no more tears to shed, Lucy pulled a tissue from her pocket and blotted her face. At last, she was ready to look up at the source of all this foolishness—the glorified doll that she'd convinced herself could do what the most brilliant doctors and most sophisticated medical procedures could not. She was a fool; she knew that now. Her only saving grace was that Mack had not been aware of her ridiculous plan.

Lucy raised her eyes to the figure positioned above her, and her heart stopped for a split second at the sight of its face, awash with tears. And even that she might have chalked up to some hokey display to bring in the tourists, were it not for the expression of sorrow that had not been there just a short while before. She gasped, recognizing the exact mirror image of her own pain and emptiness—her own heart, laid bare and exposed in the expression of the Madonna.

A profound sense of calm and peace settled over Lucy then, as the sorrow leached from her very soul, replaced by nothing less than the most certain, the most divine knowledge.

Lucy would have her child.

She had never been more sure of anything in her entire life.

CHAPTER 14

ISABELLA

Today

Turns out the rooms at La Playa Blanca Resort are even fancier than the bar and the lobby. Not that this qualifies as a single room. From the foyer, I can see across the living room and dining table to the jacuzzi that sits on the oceanfront balcony. A peek to my left allows me to see through the bedroom with the king-sized bed and its *en suite* bathroom. I'm pretty sure I spot an alcove rain shower in there. One of the ones with like four heads. It probably changes colors, too. And there's nothing mini about the free-standing wet bar and the very full-sized top-shelf bottles parked on the counter behind it with an array of sparkling glassware.

I give a soft, low whistle under my breath as I come inside, dropping my purse and sunglasses on the six-top dining table.

"This place is bigger than the entire house we lived in when I was a kid."

"I know, it's big, right?" Gabby says as I take in the place.

"Do you always stay in places like this?"

She shoots me a look that suggests I might just be a little bit insane.

"Seriously? I'm more of a Hilton Garden Inn kinda girl. I got one of those last-minute deals. I mean, it's more than I'd usually spend on a hotel, but I wanted to splurge a little. Still, I didn't expect it to be quite so . . ."

"Over-the-top?" I suggest.

She shrugs and smiles.

"Hey, gotta treat yourself every once in a while, you know what I mean?"

"Not really," I mumble, moving toward the far end of the room, where I've caught sight of something that doesn't quite fit the high-end, neutral, beachy décor.

At first, I think it must be some sort of room divider, but as I get closer, I see that it's a really big board on wheels—half dry-erase, half cork. The cork side has been turned into a full-on "murder board" like you see on television, with several photocopied articles and pictures tacked up, twine wrapped around the pushpins and strung between different items to create a connecting line between them. The center-piece is a map of the island. At the very top of the whiteboard side, she's written the word *Facts* and underlined it.

I drop my purse on a chair and go to get a closer look at this impressive display of office supplies. It's like I've just walked into an episode of *CSI: Back-to-School* edition.

"What *is* all this?"

Gabby comes to stand next to me, clearly admiring her handiwork.

"Oh, I thought I'd get a little head start on our brainstorm-ing. I was out at the library as soon as it opened this morning, copying every article about the case that they had stored on microfiche—there was so much more available here than I was able to find online. Of course, I'll need help translating a few, but I think there's enough here for us to work with."

There's nothing here that I haven't seen before—a collec-tion of articles about Marianna's disappearance, most dat-ing from that first month after it happened. A handful are follow-ups taking place around the milestone anniversary years. It's a lot to take in, and suddenly I'm wishing I'd had a second cup of coffee before driving over here. I'm not used to having to think so much in the morning—I can just go on autopilot when I'm doing nails.

"Okay, so look," she says, pointing at a spot on the map— an inset of San Juan and La Perla. "It starts at that bar, the rooster bar?"

"El Gallo Rojo," I supply. "The Red Rooster."

"Right, El Gallo Rojo," she echoes in a slow but not terrible facsimile. Then she points to a small red pushpin marking an unnamed alley on the map. "So, this is where they found the pink sock behind the bar. And there's mention of the bartender in a couple of places, but it's strange—she's not quoted in a single article. What's that all about? You *know* the police spoke with her. She was the one who called them in the first place! What did she have to say?" She takes a black dry-erase marker and writes the bar's name on the list, followed by the name *Beatrice*.

"Beatríz," I correct.

"Hmm?"

"Her name—it's not Beatrice, it's Beatríz. *Bay-ahh-TREES*." I say it slowly and phonetically, correcting the spelling on the whiteboard as I do.

"Right, sorry. Anyway, so there are a couple of facts for us—this begins at the bar, with—Beatríz?" She attempts the name and, once again, I'm impressed by her ability to catch the intonation and emphasis on the accent. I give her a nod and the thumbs-up. She smiles briefly and continues. "See, I think we need to go back to the beginning. We need to establish a timeline and look at any person who might have been involved—or who might have seen something . . . ughh, hang on . . ."

Gabby returns the marker to its ledge and fishes her phone out of the pocket of her khaki shorts. All over her head, wispy, curly tendrils of hair have escaped the bonds of the loose bun she's created. It makes her look soft—almost gauzy, as if I were seeing her through some special filter. She reminds me of one of Degas's ballerina paintings.

I drop into an armchair and watch as she smiles down at the screen before typing a brief reply text.

"Someone special?" I ask, wondering who might be able to put such a genuine, unguarded smile on her face. Up until now, I've only seen her "polite" smile. The one she probably saves for strangers. Like me.

"Hmm? Oh, yes, actually. My best friend, Franny. She's a doctor in Los Angeles."

"Oh, well, that must suck, her being so far away."

She nods. "Yeah, it really does. She's the closest thing I've had to family since my dad died last year . . ." Her voice peters out, and the thought hangs there awkwardly between us.

Well, Franny might have been the closest thing a few days ago, but not anymore. Actually, never. Because I've always been Gabby's sister—she just didn't know it.

But she will.

"You've been friends a long time?" I ask, hoping to get a little insight into what her childhood was like.

Gabby nods thoughtfully. "Since we were like . . . oh, twelve, thirteen maybe? She used to come over after school, and my mom would give us chocolate chip cookies right out of the oven with a big glass of ice-cold milk."

Holy Hallmark, Batman!

"Wow. That's very . . . sweet," I say, hoping I sound more sincere than I feel.

Cookies and milk served by some housewife in an apron and pearls is about as realistic to me as some lady alien beaming down to my shop for a little interplanetary artwork onto their long, green nails. I mean, yeah, I may be *that* good, but it's still a little far-fetched.

"It was sweet," she agrees, unaware of the saccharine taste her recollection has left in my mouth. "It's one of my favorite memories," she adds, sounding wistful.

Jesus Christ! What's wrong with me? Am I seriously jealous of a dead woman and her freaking *Chips Ahoy*? God, how pathetic am *I*?

Very, I guess. Because even my self-realization doesn't shake the envy out of me. I have got to get my head out of my own pathetic past and focus on what's happening now. And whatever it is that's going to happen later, once we get those test results back.

"And so your friend—Franny? What did she think of all this? Of you coming here?" I ask.

"Actually, she's the one who convinced me to do it," Gabby explains, leaving the Big Board o' Clues to join me on the couch. "Of course, she was also the one who convinced me to play hardball with my boss—which got me fired. But—"

"Hold on, hold on. You got fired? So does that mean you're *not* working for *Flux* magazine?"

Her cheeks pink up a bit. "Yes. I mean no. I mean . . ." She fumbles awkwardly before stopping, shaking her head, and trying again. "It's kind of complicated—it just happened, and I'm still trying to sort it all out myself. But let's just say that Franny was the one who convinced me I could do the story—on my own. And that I needed to come here and meet you in person to do that." She pauses for a second and eyes me carefully, as if she wants to gauge my response to whatever's coming next. "Like I said, she's a doctor. And she's the one who gave me the idea that we might actually be cousins. That the lab might have transposed the percentages numbers somehow . . . like, we're a point-zero-five percent match and not fifty percent."

I have to work hard to keep a neutral expression, but she must sense that I think the theory is total and complete bullshit, because she drops the thought and returns to her board.

"Anyway, we need to figure this out," she says, her back to me as she picks up the marker again.

But I've heard enough. And I've had enough. So I get up and join her in front of her twisty little web of facts, plucking it from her grasp.

"C'mon," I tell her. "What we're looking for isn't in this room."

She looks very concerned all of a sudden.

"Where do you want to go?"

"La Perla."

"Really? Now?"

"Gotta start somewhere, Sherlock," I tell her over my shoulder as I start for the door. "Might as well be the scene of the crime."

CHAPTER 15

GABBY

Today

You can't see La Perla until you're almost on top of it—literally on top of it. The three-quarter-mile neighborhood sits outside and just below the great stone wall surrounding the city of San Juan. Centuries ago, it was here that the slaughterhouse was located, and where slaves and other "undesirables" were sent to live.

We're standing just above La Perla, close enough that I could almost step right off the stone fortification and onto one of the many corrugated steel roofs in various conditions. Many of them are slanted, showing signs of rust and decay. There are a few that have been painted—one of them to look like a Puerto Rican flag with its blue triangle, inlaid with a single white star, set against red stripes. And then there are the houses with no roofs at all.

From where we're standing, I can look directly down and inside of the dwellings where signs of domestic life—a toppled fridge, part of a toilet tank, chunks of a once-painted concrete wall—are odd accents among the rubble and debris of recent hurricanes. It's not hard to see the losses sustained by this marginalized *(literally)* community—situated directly in the path of violent winds and an angry sea.

"Wow," is all I can manage to murmur as I take in the crowded rows of concrete houses.

They're mostly perched on a precarious angle at very steep pitch, each tier divided by the narrowest of roads and back alleyways. Cars and motorcycles are crammed in at odd angles wherever a few spare feet can be found to accommodate them.

"You probably read about the forts," Isabella says, gesturing between the two hulking structures connected by the wall.

"Yeah, a little, but they're much more impressive in person," I comment. "Especially when you look at them sitting at either end of La Perla."

She shoots me a surprised glance. "Right? I've thought that before, too. My friends think I'm crazy."

I shake my head. "No, I'm with you. They look . . . I don't know . . . a little surreal, I guess? Like they're out of place and time?"

"Exactly!" she says, nodding enthusiastically.

I don't delve too much further into my specific thoughts on this, because they'll probably come off as pretentious and over-thought. The truth is that when I look at the five-hundred-year-old forts, I can't help but see them as not just a historical juxtaposition, but also a philosophical one.

Here are two behemoth fortifications built to fend off an enemy who could be spotted on the horizon, arriving either by land or sea. An enemy who could be outmatched by brute force and outwitted by clever strategy. Fast-forward to the twenty-first century, when your enemies are much more insidious—disease, poverty, civil unrest, and humanity's ever-weakening moral center are the biggest threats to our modern existence. There isn't a fort on the planet that could protect us from that kind of destruction.

"Okay, let's get going," Isabella says with a nod toward the steep, two-floor staircase that will allow us to enter, as a big sign advertises:

Comunidad La Perla.

The community of La Perla.

I hold tight to the rail as we make our way down. Isabella seems much less concerned about falling and breaking a leg—or worse—than I am. And where the last step ends is where La Perla begins.

"Okay, so I want you to stay close to me," Isabella says, stopping to give me the unwritten neighborhood rules. "Do *not* go off on your own, okay? That's really important. And don't say anything to *anyone*. Let me do all the talking. I'm serious—no questions. Okay, Sherlock?"

I shoot her a look. I'm not nuts about this new nickname.

"Really? Is that going to stick now?"

She shrugs. "You'd prefer Nancy Drew?"

I shake my head. "Not really, no . . ."

Isabella moves closer and leans in so I can hear her when she drops her voice. "I just want to make sure you get that there's like a code of behavior here. Especially if you're not from the island."

I nod solemnly. "Do I . . . should I be worried?" I ask, wondering for the first time if maybe coming here wasn't the best idea. "I could go back and wait in the car," I offer. "Or if it's too dangerous, we could just—"

"What? Oh, no, no," she says, putting a reassuring hand on my arm. "No, no, sorry, I didn't mean to scare you. It's perfectly safe here—so long as you respect the people who live here. You might see some . . . you know . . . *business dealings* going down around us. Don't stare. You don't need to run away, but don't look too interested, either."

"Okaaaay," I agree reluctantly, hoping I'll recognize these "dealings" when I see them.

As I follow closely behind her, I notice her long, dark

hair fanned out across the back of her white cotton peasant blouse. There's something about Isabella that I find so appealing. She's got this effortless confidence that I really admire . . . and envy. Something tells me *she* would've found a way to stand her ground at work without getting herself fired in the process. That being said, there's also a razor-sharp edge that comes with her particular brand of self-assuredness. It's the kind of hardness that you find in people who are street-savvy—the ones used to fending for themselves. I can't say I envy that.

"Careful," she calls back to me over her shoulder.

We pick our way along narrow passageways that run between houses—some of them in shambles. It seems as if every few feet, I'm peering directly into what was once someone's home, through doors and windows that no longer exist.

But then, in another bizarre and incongruous twist, we're standing in front of the most beautiful basketball court I've ever seen. It's painted in checkerboard fashion with bright orange, yellow, green, and blue squares, the words La Perla written center court in front of purple concrete bleachers. Right now, a group of teenage boys are playing—laughing, joking. I don't understand what they're saying, but I think it's safe to assume they're trash-talking one another as they move back and forth across the squares. I snap a quick picture with my phone.

"*Ven*, Gabby," Isabella calls once she notices I've lagged behind.

I assume, from the context, that *ven* means *come*, and I scramble to catch up with her, dodging some rogue chickens and a crowing rooster along the way. Several other sights catch my eye, including what looks to be a steep concrete pool painted in bright color patches. There are some younger kids fearlessly executing some truly terrifying stunts on skateboards. They launch off the edge of one end, plummet down to the bottom, only to pop up on the other side—often with a twist or twirl in the process.

"This is the Bowl of La Perla," Isabella explains. "On the weekends, they fill it with water, and it becomes a swimming pool."

"What a great idea!" I exclaim, grabbing yet another quick snap before we hit the very bottom of the incline.

Here, where the earth gives way to the ocean, there's a concrete boardwalk lined with a handful of businesses, including a bar, a walk-up food window, and a few shops. The sound of live music spills out of darkened doorways, mingling with the sound of the ocean just below us. We take a moment to pause and lean against the guardrail, looking out at the jagged rocks and thin slice of sand. This isn't like the expansive, white-sanded beaches we flew over on the way into San Juan. This is a craggy, sharp bit of coast that seems to suit the neighborhood perfectly. A little rough. A little scary. Far enough away to be safe, but still a little too close for comfort.

"Okay, here we are," she says, with a nod in the direction of a squat, putty-colored structure. There's a big red rooster painted on one of its walls.

El Gallo Rojo.

The Red Rooster.

Inside, it's dark—there are no windows to speak of, the only light coming from some neon signs advertising assorted brands of beer, and some strands of bare bulbs strung across the ceiling, crisscrossing from corner to corner. There are several wooden tables, outfitted with mismatched chairs of the folding, ladder-back, and resin varieties.

A long, wooden bar runs most of the length of the rear wall. Any lacquered coating that it once had must have worn away some time ago, causing it to look more like the counter in a butcher's shop than a bar top. I don't understand the lyrics of the music playing, but I recognize the overall sound as a modern one rather than something with an old-timey vibe to it. I make a mental note to do a little research into the LatinX pop scene.

When I feel my phone vibrate in my pocket, I pull it out.

"Hey, I'm going to go check with the manager—see if he can give me any information about anyone we're looking for," Isabella says, leaving me alone to check my messages.

There's a voicemail from Max. Tentatively, I push the play arrow and put the phone to my ear, holding it tight against the ambient noise surrounding me.

"Gabby, this is Max. Please call me back when you get this; I want to talk to you before you run off to Puerto Rico on your own . . ."

"Too late," I mutter, stopping the message before it's finished. I have nothing to say to him.

I turn around to survey the area around me. It's barely eleven in the morning, but there are already several occupied tables—not to mention several empty bottles littering those tables. Someone is smoking. I guess the anti-cigarette lobby hasn't got quite the stronghold here that it does back home. The smell makes me think of my dad, Mack, who tried for years to quit. The patch, pills, gum, hypnosis—he tried everything. But nothing seemed to get the job done. He wasn't a nervous man by nature, but clearly there was something about the habit that he found soothing.

For a split second, I wonder if that's because he had some deep, dark, secret hidden under that easy, affable nature. Was he hiding the truth about . . . me?

What the hell am I even considering here?

I'd have to believe that the people I loved most in this world could have *kidnapped* me and raised me as their own. But I can't. Because to believe that would mean that my whole life was a lie. And that, I do *not* believe.

"Nope. No."

I don't even realize I've spoken aloud until I feel Isabella's touch on my shoulder.

"Hey, Gabby, you okay?"

"Hmm? Oh, yeah . . . yes. Yeah, I'm fine. Find out anything?"

She holds up a matchbook with a phone number written inside the cover.

"Someone try to pick you up?" I tease.

"All the time." She plays along with a grin. "But that's beside the point. I got a phone number for Beatríz—she's living in Ponce now. A couple hours from here. I think we need to pay her a visit in the next day or two."

"Wow! Our first lead," I declare.

Isabella peers at me a little more closely.

"You okay? You look a little . . . I don't know, pale maybe?"

I start to deny it but then stop myself. "Yeah, you know, I'm not real comfortable in this place. Do you mind if we get going?"

"Nope, that's fine," she says, and I'm grateful she doesn't ask any questions.

I can't exactly explain my discomfort at being here, other than to say that it's like a mini, Puerto Rican version of the Overlook Hotel in *The Shining.*

Too many ghosts here—none of the friendly variety.

CHAPTER 16

ISABELLA

Today

When Gabby takes out her phone to snap a picture, all she can see is the mural—a spray-paint reproduction of the Mona Lisa draped in a Puerto Rican flag. All I can see are the two guys standing just out of frame, conducting a little street-side retail. They haven't noticed her yet, but if she hangs out here much longer, they will.

"C'mon, Gabby . . ." I coax, making a move to walk away.

"Hang on—just a couple more—my God, this thing is spectacular! I could do a whole article on the street art here alone . . ." she murmurs, excitedly—and obliviously.

"Yes, it is," I agree, continuing with a little more urgency. "But, seriously, you need to stop. Like *right now*. If those two guys over there think you're a narc, we're gonna be in a world of shit."

Thankfully, that's all she needs to hear. Gabby stops abruptly, tossing the phone into her bag and pretending to be deeply intrigued by something in the other direction. It's almost comical, and if I were painting her, I'd add a thought bubble right over her head:

Drug deal? What drug deal? I haven't seen any drug deals . . .

When we've safely left the "danger zone," I relax a bit and soften my tone.

"Listen, I'm sorry, I didn't mean to scare you back there. I think it's so great that you appreciate the street art. You just have to be careful about catching someone's, you know—*business*—in a picture."

One of her dark eyebrows arches up. Just the one. And I nearly stop in my tracks, because I happen to know that just twenty-four percent of the population can raise a single eyebrow. My mother could. I can. And now I know Gabby DiMarco can, too. I guess she's not the only one collecting clues.

"Right, right. I'm sorry. I just get so excited when I see things like that—so vibrant and . . . alive. And right smack in the middle of . . ."

I can tell she's looking for a word that won't offend. But she's in La Perla and, proud as its residents are, it is what it is.

"The barrio," I offer. It's a word that works in both Spanish and English.

She gives me a sideways glance. "Can I ask you a question?"

"Yeah, sure. Of course," I reply as we walk through an area hit particularly hard by the last hurricane.

"This is some pretty primo real estate right here—overlooking the ocean like this. And I'm guessing the properties on the other side of the wall—the inside of the city—they're probably worth a small fortune . . ."

"So how come La Perla hasn't been turned into some high-rise, luxury condos?" I supply.

"Well, yeah, exactly. I guess I'm so used to Manhattan, where the lower-income areas have been gentrified. Is that not a thing here?"

I shrug. "Sure, in other areas. But not here. Not in La Perla. These folks are proud to live here—for a lot of them, it's part of their family history. I can't tell you how many times big land developers have tried to buy up this property.

But over and over again, they refuse. La Perla is their home, and no one's going to take it from them."

Suddenly the pathway we're on narrows considerably, and we have to shift single file toward the green house on the far end of La Perla. Gabby stumbles slightly, reaching out to steady herself on my shoulder.

"Sorry," she mumbles from behind me. "Bad choice of footwear, I guess."

I glance over my shoulder and down at the strappy little sandals she's got going on. I've seen them in the mall and admired them myself. But their three-figure price tag definitely cooled my attraction to them.

"Your pedicure is shit," I point out. "I'll have to fix that for you later."

"Oh, I know! I couldn't get in at my regular place before I left. Are you sure you don't mind?"

"Well, I can't be seen in the company of someone with poorly tended toes. It's not good for business."

Gabby giggles at this, and the sound gives me an unexpected smile. It's like listening to tiny little bubbles floating up into the air, all light and free.

"Oh! Here we go," I say, catching sight of our destination.

According to Matéo, whose office isn't too far from here, the person we need to speak with is a man known simply as *El Viejo*—literally, "the old guy." I don't know him personally, but I know who he is. Everyone who spends any time over here does. Not that anyone can remember what his given name is. El Viejo was born here, grew up here, fell in love and married here, raised his kids here, and buried his wife here. Few people have seen the kinds of changes he has—which is why we're coming to see him.

I've never actually lived in La Perla, proper, but I've been down here enough times that it felt like it—especially when I was younger, and my father would bring me along to score some drugs or have a drink at one of the local dives. When I was older, the same dealers and bartenders had my number in their phones so they could call me to come take his passed-out ass home.

When we get to El Viejo's residence, I'm surprised to find the man is a lot less *viejo* than I remembered. It's been some time since we've crossed paths, and I was expecting some frail ninety-year-old with no teeth and a cane. Not this guy. Sure, the hair under his beige "pork pie" fedora is more salt than pepper, but that's really the only outward sign of his age that I can find at first glance. He's neat and trim, wearing a *guayabera*—the traditional men's summer shirt with two vertical bands of tightly sewn pleats running the length of the front and back of the shirt—and a pair of khaki shorts. He completes the outfit with a pair of brown slides with a braided leather upper covering his instep.

He's sitting, one leg crossed over the other, on a wrought-iron rocking chair on his tiny, wood-planked porch—newspaper in one hand, cup of coffee in the other. There's a small radio on the windowsill behind him, and I recognize the tune as a Tito Puente classic from the sixties that my grandmother loves—"Oye Cómo Va." El Viejo is tapping his foot and nodding his head in time to the bongos.

I feel a sudden pang in my gut. This guy looks happy. Really, truly happy. It makes me think, for just a second, that this could have so easily been my father's life, too. If he'd made different choices. But he didn't. And so here we are.

"Hola, Señor. ¿Cómo está hoy?" I call out to him from the gate. He lowers his paper, offering us a broad smile.

"¡Muy bien, gracias a Dios!"

"What did he say? Something about God?" Gabby whispers from behind me.

"I asked him how he was, and he said: 'Very well, thank God.'"

She nods as if this is exactly what she suspected all along.

"Ah! You speak the English?" the old man asks excitedly when he catches our exchange. "I speak the English, too! Come, come!" He crooks a finger at us to join him, pulling two more chairs from the corner of the porch and setting them out near his own.

"Can we talk with you for a moment?" I ask.

When he squints as if he's trying to work out the translation, I realize his idea of "speaking the English" might be a few phrases here and there, so I repeat the question in my native language—and his.

"*¿Podemos hablar con usted por un momento?*" I ask. "*Somos reporteros.*"

Okay, maybe we're not reporters, but close enough. And it's not likely he's going to ask for some identification.

"*¡Sí!* Yes, of course!" he agrees, immediately followed up by an offer of *café con leche*. I accept for both of us, having been desperate for a cup of coffee and warm, steamed milk for hours now. I don't bother asking Gabby if she wants it. If she doesn't, I'll take hers, too.

He disappears for a few minutes, returning with a tray stacked with a French press, two large coffee cups, and the pitcher of milk. There's also a little sugar bowl. In under sixty seconds, he's set us up with the perfect pour. I let my nose sit close to the brim so I can inhale the moist, rich aroma.

"*Gracias, señor.*" To my surprise, the perfectly pronounced thanks comes from Gabby.

"*¡De nada!*" he replies jovially. "Is nice to have company— and to practice the English. *Dígame*—tell me, what I can do for you?"

"*Señor,*" Gabby pipes up, "I'm looking for some information about Marianna Ruíz. Do you remember? It was a long time ago . . ."

Suddenly the affable smile fades from El Viejo's face, and I notice his involuntary intake of a long, measured breath.

"Marianna," he murmurs, reaching up to scratch his neck,

suddenly a thousand miles away. I don't press him, just wait patiently until he's ready to say something more on the subject. Finally, his eyes refocus on mine. "Yes, yes, *el bebé,*" he recalls. The baby.

We're both nodding.

"Were you here that day?" she asks, pointing toward the ground.

He nods again. "*Sí.* Yes, I was here when *la policía* were looking for Marianna," he explains, using his index finger like a lasso above his head, meant to encompass the entire neighborhood. "They ask questions from all of us who live here. But I don't see anything."

"*Señor,* what do people here believe happened to Marianna?" I ask in between sips of coffee. He may not have seen anything, but I'd put money on El Viejo knowing all the gossip in La Perla.

He's quiet for what feels like a very long moment, and I can tell he's considering what to tell us—if anything. All these years later, and there's still a code of silence on this topic in La Perla. On most topics, actually.

"*Ah, bueno . . .*" He sighs now, sitting back to study our faces. When he finally speaks again, he's lowered his voice—in both pitch and volume. "Most peoples, they believe she taken by Santiago and *Los Soldados Salvajes.*"

Gabby's face immediately swings to me for clarification.

"The Savage Soldiers," I explain. "They were a local gang. Very powerful here in the nineties. Santiago's the guy who ran the gang." Then, to him: "But why would they want a baby?"

He shrugs. "Maybe to sell? Maybe to . . ." He raises his brows and shrugs slightly, letting the second thought trail off, unsaid.

It's a familiar gesture all these years later—people being unable to verbalize the worst of the worst-case scenarios in this case—child sex trafficking. Which is not looking likely—

thank Christ—considering the woman sitting next to me is Marianna. That's what I'm betting on, anyway.

When I steal a glance in her direction, she doesn't seem to be disturbed by anything she's hearing. In fact, it's like she's cataloging the information as it comes in. It's kind of interesting, actually, to see the way her mind works—the kind of woman she's grown to be. I feel an irrational twinge of pride at what my *probably-sister* has accomplished, in spite of her genetics.

"And what about this guy—what's his name? Santana?" she asks after a few seconds.

"Santiago," I correct.

"Is that his first name or last name?"

I shrug. "Nobody really knows. Alberto owed him money, and someone from his gang went to collect it. They beat the shit out of him, and when he came to, the baby was gone."

"But someone *must* have seen something," Gabby insists. "Or heard something about it. I mean, this is such a tiny community!"

"I'm sure you're right. I'll bet more than a few people saw something suspicious that night. Something important. But Santiago wasn't the kind of guy you could point a finger at. Not unless you wanted them to find pieces of you washing up on the beach for the next month."

She sighs heavily at the same time she scrunches up her brows . . . and I totally get what she's feeling. Even I find it a lot to take in, and I've had a quarter-century to become acquainted with all the details of the case—and all the rumors surrounding it.

"Okay," Gabby says on a resigned sigh. "So what happened to Santiago, then? Is he around? In jail?" When El Viejo shakes his head, she tries again. "What about one of this gang's members, maybe?"

"No, *mija*," he says with a dismissive wave of his hand. "No. Soon after Marianna, *la policía* came, and they arrest many people. They go through our houses, break down our doors." As he tells us this last part, he gestures to the house behind him and the porch we're sitting on.

Gabby looks to me to fill in the blanks.

"So . . . not long after all this happened, Puerto Rico got a new governor," I explain. "Up until then, there'd been this 'live and let live' attitude the police had about the gang activity in La Perla. So long as they kept their dealings in that one area and didn't mess with any of the tourists, then the cops would look the other way. But the new governor? She was over it. So, she staged this all-out raid—a hundred cops storming the neighborhood, kicking down doors and pulling junkies out of crack houses. They busted sex workers and dealers and went after the gangs hard."

"Holy shit," she murmurs. "What happened? Did it work?"

I shrug. "Yes . . . and no. I mean, there were plenty of decent people living here." I tilt my head in the direction of our host. "And then along come the cops, trashing their houses and scaring the hell out of them. So, yeah, it was kind of a shitshow here for a while . . . but crime rates dropped after that."

El Viejo nods his agreement. "Yes, yes, is true. Many of the gang members, they go away to other parts of the island."

"And Santiago?" she asks tentatively, sounding like she's not really sure she wants to know.

"Ah, well, there've been all kinds of rumors about what happened to him. Some people say he went into witness protection; others are certain he was murdered by a rival gang—or maybe even one of his own gang. There are even people who are convinced the guy went to Cuba to start a whole new syndicate there. But it's all rumors. No one knows for sure. Or, if they do, no one's saying."

"Unbelievable," Gabby murmurs, shaking her head incredulously. "It's like the plot of some crazy whodunit. Everyone's got a theory."

Her comment makes my brain light up with an idea.

"Señor . . ." I begin slowly, having the sense that I'm finally about to ask the right person the right question, "what do *you* think happened to Marianna Ruíz?"

The expression on his face—a half-smile and raised brows—tells me I've just hit the jackpot.

"I think," he begins deliberately, "I think that she was taken by *Piegrande*."

I blink and stare at him, thinking I must have misheard or misunderstood. Or maybe he misspoke.

"Umm, Señor . . ." I begin tentatively. "*¿Piegrande?*"

He nods, still smiling.

"What?" Gabby asks quietly from next to me. "What did he say? Why do you look so surprised?"

"He, um . . . he says he knows who took the baby . . ."

My voice trails off as I look to El Viejo one more time for clarification. He doesn't bat an eyelash.

"Who?" she demands, growing frustrated by the delay in my translation.

I clear my throat. "He, uh . . . he says . . . it was Bigfoot."

CHAPTER 17

YETI

That Day

He'd chosen the moniker *Yeti* because he was a big guy, and it made him sound menacing. He liked the idea of being named after some huge, scary dude who hid out in the woods stalking the shit out of people. Unfortunately, he hadn't realized when he picked it that Yeti are in the cold climates. Really, Sasquatch, or *Piegrande*—Bigfoot—would have been more appropriate. Luckily, most of the guys he ran with either didn't know or didn't care enough to give him shit about it.

Besides, it beat the hell out of his real name, Elano—which they would have absolutely given him shit about. What his mother failed to consider when she gave him this name was that it very easily became *"el ano."*

The anus.

Not a very dignified name for a gangbanger—especially one who was trying to move up the ladder. These days, nobody knew his real name. Nobody except for his mother, who, last he'd heard, was with husband number four somewhere in South Florida.

Not even Santiago knew his real name, and Santiago knew everything about everyone he employed. Or so he thought. Yeti felt the older man couldn't see all his potential—how much he had to offer. He wanted to be thought of as more than just an enforcer, more than a glorified thug who collected debts and meted out street justice.

Yeti considered himself an idea man, and he had to make Santiago see that.

Finally, the opportunity had presented itself early this morning, when he tracked down Alberto Ruíz. The deadbeat owed Santiago, and he was late making the payment. At first, Santiago had cut him a little slack, because the money was to bury the guy's wife and feed his two kids. But when word got back to him that Alberto was spending money in El Gallo Rojo instead of on diapers and formula, Santiago sent Yeti to deliver a message.

And hell, yeah, he'd delivered it—not just to Alberto, but to *anyone* in La Perla who even *thought* about crossing *Los Soldados Salvajes*—The Savage Soldiers. Yeti was proud of himself. He'd showed ingenuity and initiative. Surely Santiago would appreciate this and reward him accordingly.

The thought of it made him smile as he darted up the stairs to their safe house in Santurce—really just a dusty old apartment above an empanada shop where some of them crashed sometimes. The real center of their operations was at Santiago's estate up in the mountains nearby, though it was rare he'd allow anyone to go there. But this might just change all that. Yeti had visions of becoming Number Two, being groomed by Santiago to take over one day. He imagined them sitting out on his huge, marble porch, sipping rum and strategizing the future of *Los Soldados*.

Of course, he wouldn't mention how close he'd come to getting caught. Yeti had been careless, taking too much time to get the hell out of *el barrio*—the hood. To be fair, he was toting a little extra baggage. Baggage that needed sorting out.

He wasn't sure who called the police—maybe that *puta* from the bar, Beatríz. She was a shit-stirrer, that one. A fact he'd brought to Santiago's attention on more than one occasion. But there was some history there—something that kept

Santiago from teaching that bitch a lesson. Something that prohibited any of them from touching her. Yeah, well maybe now Santiago would decide it was finally time to do something about her. Because someone was going to get a beatdown, that was for sure.

Today the cardinal sin had been committed. You *never* invite *la policía* to La Perla. Never. There was an unwritten but long-standing agreement between the police and the residents of the area—so long as their "business" was conducted outside of the city wall, away from *las turistas*, the cops wouldn't come looking for reasons to bust them.

But if *la policía* were *called* there? And then they just happened to come across something illegal? Well, that was a whole other situation entirely. All bets were off—just as they were today. The place was crawling with cops shaking down his homeboys, not to mention the local crackheads—even the old guy who collected cans got his cart tossed.

Of course, Yeti knew no one would have the *cojones* to finger him, but he still couldn't risk being detained by the cops. Getting busted could easily earn him a one-way trip to the prison in Guayamon—where his gang members were a minority and the target of every rival organization. He'd known way too many *soldados* who'd been found shanked, or strangled, or hanging from bedsheets, and he wasn't about to become one of them.

So Yeti had moved as fast as he could, considering his size. It helped that he'd grown up in the area and knew every back alley and shortcut in a five-mile radius. He was several blocks away from the scene before anyone even realized there'd been a crime. With the added weight of the duffel, it took him close to an hour to reach the apartment, and he breathed a long sigh of relief. Here, he could relax a little, melting into the bigger, busier community.

Now he knocked three times on the apartment door, counted to three, and knocked twice more. When it was the new kid, Coquí, who answered, Yeti was a little disappointed. He'd hoped to find someone higher up the food chain here— someone with whom he could share the story of his idea and who might help him figure out what the next steps were. Still, it could be worse. At least the kid was smart; plus, he knew how to keep his mouth shut and take orders.

He noticed a pillow and sheet lying rumpled on the ratty old couch where the kid must be sleeping these days. He really was a kid—sixteen, maybe seventeen—and Yeti knew he had no place to go, no people of his own. Well, gang life wasn't easy—but at least you were never alone. Someone always had a couch for you to crash on and a meal to share. And, most importantly, someone always had your back. Because to be one of the Savage Soldiers was to pledge absolute obedience and loyalty. Anything less would be grounds for expulsion. And, by expulsion, he meant death.

"*¿Qué pasó?*" Coquí asked in a voice still thick with sleep. *What happened?*

"La Perla is crawling with cops," Yeti explained, setting the duffel bag on the card table. "I had to haul ass out of there before someone could see me."

As predicted, Coquí refrained from asking too many questions. That trait would go a long way to keeping him in Santiago's good graces. Lucky for him, because if there was one place you did *not* want to be, it was on Santiago's shit list. Might as well put a bullet in your own head—it'd be faster and a hell of a lot less painful than what he'd have in mind for you.

"What can I do?" he asked.

Another excellent quality, Yeti thought. The first thing he wants to know is how he can help.

"I need you to help me with something—maybe come with me to find Santiago," he explained in Spanish.

Coquí nodded and came closer to the table while Yeti un- zipped the duffel bag. But when he saw what was inside, he took an involuntary step backwards, as if he'd just seen a snake preparing to strike. In his haste, Coquí tripped over a chair and landed hard on his ass.

Yeti laughed at the kid's expression—like something right out of a cartoon. He looked dazed, disgusted, and terrified all at once.

As well he should be.

CHAPTER 18

ISABELLA

Today

Matéo strokes his chin thoughtfully as he listens to the person on the other end of the phone line. His office is the size of a broom closet, and Gabby and I are practically in each other's laps as we sit across from him, staring hopefully, waiting impatiently. I called him from La Perla, and he promised to do a little legwork in exchange for bringing him a little lunch.

His job as a social worker gives him access to files and databases that the rest of us don't have. It's not exactly ethical . . . and I'm thinking it could definitely cost him his job. But then, my husband has always been a big believer of the expression *"Es más fácil pedir perdón que pedir permiso."* It's easier to beg forgiveness than ask permission.

It also doesn't hurt that my Matéo is that irresistible combination of hot, heroic, and humble. He's the guy that women love and men respect.

"Yeah," he says to the other person on the line. "Uh-huh. Yeah, yeah, yeah." Now he's nodding, concentrating hard on what he's hearing. He opens his mouth to speak again—going so far as to actually allow his mouth to form the words—and then stops when another tidbit comes down the line, causing his eyebrows to shoot all the way up to his hairline. "Yes. Okay. *Bueno*, thanks, man," he says, finally disconnecting.

He shakes his head slowly and lets out a long, slow column of air.

"Okay, so, according to my buddy in the central records office, Alvarez has retired to Yauco—not far from where your aunt lives, Isabella. I've got his address. Unfortunately, without knowing Santiago's first or last name—whichever it is that's missing—it's hard to know exactly what happened to him."

"Yeah, but he was so well-known down here. I can't believe the police wouldn't have some sort of a file on him, even if it was just under his alias or whatever," I counter, dismissing the idea that Santiago flew totally under the radar.

He pauses for a second, as if debating whether or not to tell us the next bit. "Yeah, well . . . my guy agrees with you on that. He seems to think that maybe, at some point, someone made Santiago's file . . . you know . . . disappear . . ."

"Disappear? How does *that* happen?" I demand incredulously. I may not have always liked the way the police handled Marianna's disappearance, but I'd hardly call them incompetent. Not then, and not now.

"It was someone on the inside."

I turn in my chair to stare at Gabby.

"How the hell would you know that?"

She shrugs. "It's the only answer that makes sense. You have to have access to that kind of information, and you have to have *high-level* access to be able to alter that kind of information. Or to make it disappear altogether."

Matéo is nodding. "Exactly."

"Okay," I say slowly after a few seconds. "Then what about our Bigfoot? You gonna tell me he's gone missing, too?"

He smiles and chuckles a little while shaking his head. "Oh, no, there have been plenty of Bigfoot sightings . . ." my husband replies. But when I glare at him, unamused, he clears his throat and tries again, seriously this time. "Right. Yeah, so your guy isn't Bigfoot, he's actually *Yeti*—which, by the way, should have been Sasquatch. The Yeti aren't tropical. In fact, they're related to the Abominable Snowman . . ."

I glare at him. "Seriously? Now? You're going to geek out on me now?"

He waves a dismissive hand at himself and gets back on track. "Right. Doesn't matter. Anyway, far as anyone can tell, he was well on his way to becoming Santiago's right-hand man in the Savage Soldiers. And that was a pretty big deal for the day. It would have given him some serious clout—not just with other gang members, but also in the eyes of rival gangs."

I shrug. "Okay, he was on his way up to gang superstardom. So what happened? Sounds like he never made it."

His mouth tightens at the corners. I know my guy well enough to know he's about to give us some bad news.

"Yeah, Isabella, he actually *is* MIA . . . and has been for, well, the last twenty-five years."

"Him, too? So you're telling me *no* one knows what happened to him."

Matéo leans forward, resting his forearms on his desk. "No, not exactly. There's some evidence that he left Puerto Rico—possibly for the Dominican. But there are no more references to him after that."

When I notice Gabby tilting her head next to me, I have the strangest sense that I'm looking at myself—that I'm peering into a mirror. It's yet another similarity between us. So far, nature has racked up more points than nurture. But, of course, it ain't over yet.

"Do you think the two are related?" she asks. "Yeti's disappearance and the kidnapping?"

Matéo considers the question.

"Well . . . yeah, I'd say it's certainly possible. I mean, up till this point, he was doing great. He was a trusted member of the organization, he had his boss's ear, and he was involved in some pretty high-profile shit. If he really was the one sent out to teach Alberto a lesson, then he'd have been the last person to see the baby. But then, out of nowhere, he up and disappears." He pauses for a second, taking a deep breath and exhaling slowly. "I've got to tell you—it makes sense to me that this guy would have been involved. Santiago didn't do this job personally, and Yeti would have been the most likely one to have been sent. But . . ."

"But what?" I press.

"But don't you think it's strange that this is the first you're hearing about this guy? Think about it, Isabella, there's been zero mention of him in any of the articles or reports we've read—and we've read them all. We knew Santiago sent someone out to collect from Alberto—but we didn't know exactly who that was. How come this is the first time we've come across this guy's name? I could see if there was very little information . . . but there's absolutely nothing. And maybe you could chalk it up as 'one of those things' . . . except then there's the missing Santiago file. A little too much of a coincidence, you know? Kinda supports the idea that maybe someone *was* trying to bury something."

Gabby and I exchange concerned glances.

"Shit," I mutter softly. "It really *is* starting to look like someone on the police force was involved."

"Look," Matéo says, "Working here, I get a good look at how the system works. And it's not always strictly by the book, if you know what I mean. There are cops who will go out of their way to tip someone off if it benefits them— maybe the person is well-connected and a good source of intel for them. Occasionally, they'll even do us a solid and look the other way when a basically good kid makes some stupid mistake. But during the time frame we're talking about, it was like the Wild West out there. You wouldn't *believe* the shit you could get away with if you knew the right people."

We all let this statement settle for a moment, the room going quiet, save for the sounds of a basketball bouncing somewhere down the hall. The noise makes him glance at the clock on the wall over my head.

"Oh, man, I have to go," he says, gathering the remnants of his lunch and tossing them into the trash can. "I'm coaching the basketball team this afternoon. We've got the big match tomorrow."

Gabby and I get to our feet, and I lean across the desk to kiss his cheek. "Right—thank you, honey."

He raises his index finger at me. "Ahh . . . don't be so quick to thank me," he warns sheepishly.

"Why is that?" I ask, straightening up to get a good look at his face. His very guilty-looking face.

"Well . . . your Titi Annamaria called . . ."

Oh, hell.

"And . . . ?"

"It's Olivia's *quinceañera* tomorrow night."

I smack my own forehead.

"Oh, shit! I totally forgot to RSVP no for us! Oh, God, she's going to kill me . . ."

"Yeah, well, she took your 'no reply' to mean we accepted the invitation."

My eyes narrow, and my voice drops. "What. Did you. Do?" I demand in my best soft-but-deadly tone.

"What the hell *could* I do? I just yessed her the whole time. So she might think we're going to be there . . ." He spits the words out quickly, then closes his eyes and braces, as if I'm going to hit him.

"What?" I howl incredulously. "You did . . . what? Well, you're just going to have to call her and cancel. Tell her . . ." I search for a believable excuse to blow off a major family celebration. When I notice Gabby watching us curiously, I flash on the answer. "Tell her I have a friend visiting from out of town. Yeah, that should do it. Annamaria is nothing if not polite. She'd never want me to leave a guest sitting at home alone . . ."

I stop when my husband's guilty expression doesn't shift. "Okay, so, I *might* have told her that . . . and she *might* have said to bring her along . . ."

"Are you *kidding* me?"

"Isabella, I'm sorry, I just . . . you know how your aunt can be . . . she just will *not* take no for an answer."

"She does when I'm the one giving it!"

Now he crosses his arms over his chest and smirks. "Then maybe *you* should have answered one of the dozen messages she's been leaving you for the last two weeks," he counters.

"A *quinceañera*?" Gabby asks from next to me. "Isn't that like a sweet sixteen?"

"Yes, but bigger. Think wedding meets coronation," Matéo explains.

"Oh . . . I'd actually *love* to see that!" she says.

Of course, she would. I can see the journalistic wheels turning in her little head.

"How are you even going to manage?" I ask my husband. "Didn't you just tell us your kids have a big basketball game tomorrow?"

He shrugs. "I'll meet you there. I can take a shower in the locker room and go directly from there. I'll miss the mass, but I should be able to make it in time for the party."

"The mass? Oh, no. I'm not going to any mass," I declare, throwing my hands up toward the ceiling. "Fine, I'll go to the stupid party, but I'm not setting *foot* in the church."

"Okay, so it's settled," he agrees, smacking his hands together and rubbing his palms like some cartoon villain.

"You're enjoying this," I accuse him.

"Who, me?" He looks sheepish. "I would never take pleasure in your misery! Now, if you ladies will excuse me . . ."

"Sure," I mutter, "lob that Molotov cocktail, then run away."

He comes around his desk and drops to his haunches so we're face-to-face; then he puts his hands on my shoulders, leaning in close.

"It's going to be fine," he murmurs in my ear. "It will mean the world to Olivia that you're there. Besides, Annamaria will string you up like a piñata if you're a no-show." He presses a kiss to my cheek. "I'll see you at home later."

He gives Gabby a smile and a nod as he walks out of the room without so much as a glance backwards.

"Ughhhhh!" I moan, dropping my head into my hands on the desk.

"What? Why are you so upset? This sounds like it'll be fun!"

"Hah!" I let out with a sharp, short laugh.

"But aren't you happy to see your aunt and cousins and everyone? Or do you not get along?" she asks, testing the waters around the subject of my family.

I wonder if she's thinking they might be *her* family, too?

I shrug. "I'm not unhappy to see them. I just . . . they can be a bit much, you know? It's a big, extended family on that side, and I'm going to get a lot of questions about when we're going to have a baby, blah, blah, blah."

"Oh. Is that a thing? I mean, I don't want to pry . . ."

"We will. Probably. Someday. I've got time; I've just never felt ready. But who knows? Maybe once this is resolved . . ." I gesture between her and myself.

And it's not a lie. This business with Marianna has consumed me for so long, it's been hard to think about anything else. I barely have enough bandwidth for my marriage and my work.

"Well," Gabby says matter-of-factly, "I'm excited to see something so special."

"Pfft. You say that now. Wait until you're drowning in glitter and tiaras. It's like walking in on a fairy princess massacre."

Gabby can't seem to decide whether she should laugh at the image or be horrified by it. I point at her.

"Yeah, exactly. *That's* what it's like to go to a *quinceañera*."

CHAPTER 19

BEATRÍZ

That Day

Beatríz was exhausted by the time she arrived at Santiago's apartment in town. Between the all-nighter at the bar and then dealing with a despondent Alberto—not to mention the cops crawling all over La Perla—she was ready to fall over. Her plan was to cook him breakfast, maybe fool around if he was up for it—which he always was—and then try to get a few hours' sleep. But that plan went out the window the second she walked through the front door.

For as long as she could remember, Beatríz had been drawn to the bad boys. Who wanted to go to bed with dull and deferential when you could have dark and dangerous? And Santiago was nothing if not dark and dangerous. And sexy as hell. Most importantly, he loved her—not that he ever said the words. He didn't have to. The way he kissed her told her everything she needed to know.

That's not to say that she was blind, or deaf, or dumb. Beatríz was well aware of the kinds of things that went on in Santiago's world—and she did her best to steer clear of it. Still, every once in a while, she found herself at odds with how he conducted his business. She'd never say so, because above all else, Santiago valued his reputation. As a result, he would not allow anyone to undermine his absolute authority when it came to his business dealings. No one was above punishment for such an infraction, not even Alberto.

The fact that his wife, Rosaria, had died earlier in the year was of no consequence to Santiago. It couldn't be. Everyone in La Perla had a tragic story. And, while it made Beatríz sad to see the poor widower fall deeper into debt and depression, she had every intention of steering clear of his dealings with Santiago. But as she knew only too well, all the intentions in the world do not equal a single action. What you *intend* to do and what you *actually* do are two entirely separate things.

All hell had already broken loose by the time she arrived. The normally cool and controlled Santiago was totally off the rails—his face a deep red, bordering on purple as he yelled. She could actually see his pulse thumping at his temple while the sinewy cords of his neck strained against his skin. She had never seen him this angry before, and it was terrifying.

"*Santiago, mi amor,*" she exclaimed, dropping her bag to rush to his side. She put a gentle hand on his shoulder, which he immediately shook off. "*Por favor, cálmate,*" she begged, but he had no interest in calming down.

In fact, he seemed to be just getting started, and Beatríz had only to look a few feet away to know who was responsible for whatever this shitshow was. It was that sociopath-in-the-making, Yeti. He was always the one stirring up the shit in a never-ending quest to climb the ladder and curry favor with Santiago.

Yeti hated her; she could see it in the way he narrowed his eyes whenever he looked her way. He'd never tried to hide it—at least, not from her. Of course, in front of his boss, he was all sweetness and sunshine. Yeah, well, that was about to stop.

"What the hell did you do?" she demanded.

Yeti didn't dignify her question with a response, but his

lip curled up in a menacing snarl. Like the rabid dog he was, she thought.

"This . . . this imbecile has put everything I've worked so hard to build at risk with one incredibly bad decision," Santiago spat. "How could you have been so stupid?"

For his part, Yeti looked equally furious, except he was smart enough to keep his mouth shut. Still, when his eyes landed on Beatríz, she saw the warning in his gaze. Oh, yeah? She levelled a little glare of her own, telegraphing her own message right back to him:

Bring it, you piece of shit. I know who you are—I know what you are.

Her thoughts drifted to her pistol then, under the nightstand, tucked away in the back against the wall. Just as her Papi had taught her years ago, she envisioned the chamber—it was loaded. She envisioned the safety—it was off. She knew where to aim if she wanted to bring a man to his knees. And she knew exactly where to aim to bring a man to his grave. There was no question which scenario it would be in this instance.

She pivoted slightly, about to head toward her bedroom, when she caught a fleeting glimpse of a third person, standing in the shadows several feet away, obviously hoping to steer clear of Santiago's sights—and his wrath. Beatríz knew the kid called Coquí from the bar. He'd become a courier of sorts—delivering Santiago's messages to her and her clientele, picking up packages and occasionally moving cash and other valuable commodities back and forth. He was tall and skinny, still a teenager, she imagined. He was good at avoiding trouble by keeping his ears open and his mouth shut—a skill more of the Savage Soldiers would do well to learn.

She'd already walked several feet past him when her mind processed what it was her eyes had picked up in the millisecond-long glance she'd cast his way. She stopped and then turned—very slowly—until she was face-to-face with the young man holding a baby tightly to his shoulder. The child's chubby little hand was wrapped around his necklace as he gently patted her back.

Oh, sweet Jesus. She'd just left the police scouring La Perla in search of this child—Marianna Ruíz. Alberto's little girl.

"W-what . . . what is *that*?" she gasped, spinning around to stare at her lover.

"*That*," Santiago hissed, "is going to take down everything I've worked so hard to build! *That* is a one-way ticket to federal prison!"

Beatríz beckoned for Coquí to pass her the child, but when he tried to pull the little girl from his shoulder, the baby began to wail. Similarly, the moment he returned her to her former position, she calmed instantly.

Shit. Shit, shit, shit. She knew she had to do something here. Before things got any more out of hand.

"Okay, let me talk to Alberto—"

"No!" Santiago roared. "No one talks to anyone! This. Never. Happened."

And how exactly was that supposed to work? She wondered but didn't dare ask.

"*Jefe*," Yeti began, "this sends a message. No one will ever screw with you again. They'll pay with their money—or they'll pay with their family."

Beatríz held her tongue—which wasn't easy. She could not, under any circumstances, do something that would make Santiago look weak in the eyes of his men. She had to let him keep control of this situation, at all costs.

Santiago took a few steps toward the man. And then a few more. Until they were toe-to-toe. Yeti did not budge an inch. They were matched for height, so he didn't have to look up at him, either. But they were so close that Beatríz could see the spittle from Santiago's mouth when he spoke again.

"I am not in the business of taking children. And now you

have pulled me into your stupid little scheme . . . for what? Do you think Alberto is going to suddenly come up with the money he owes me? He doesn't have a pot to piss in! So even if I wanted to be merciful, I can't. Because I cannot allow a debt to remain unpaid. So now what, you idiot? What do you propose we do with the baby?"

Yeti shrugged. "We'll just sell her. There's a black market for babies. And if we can't find a couple willing to pay for her, we'll sell her to *los pervertidos*. They'd pay good money for a little girl like—"

Before he could get the rest of that sentence out, Santiago had Yeti by the throat. He pushed him clear across the room, slamming him against the concrete wall so hard, they could all hear the crack of his skull.

"You listen to me, *Yeti*," Santiago sneered, mocking the young man's chosen name. "I expect you to take care of this—of her. I don't *ever* want to see her face again. I don't *ever* want to hear of her existence again. You will make her disappear—permanently. And you will make certain it's done with as little trauma as possible. Quick. Painless. And far, far away from me. Do I make myself clear?"

Yeti, whose eyes were starting to bulge, nodded as best he could with a large hand squeezing his throat. Santiago leaned in closer.

"If you screw this up, there will be no mercy. No second chance. Do you understand what I'm telling you?"

Another nod from Yeti, this one smaller and tighter. All signs of his bravado had disappeared, erased by the fear.

Beatríz dared a glance in the direction of Coquí and the child and, for a split second, their gazes locked.

When she looked back on that moment, she wouldn't be able to put words to what it was that had passed between them. All she knew for certain was that an unspoken understanding—an alliance—had been forged in less time than it took her to inhale a single breath.

She turned back toward Santiago, trying desperately to keep her voice soft and submissive.

"*Santiago, por favor* . . . please, my love, there's no reason to harm the child. Surely there's another way—"

He dropped Yeti, spun around, and stalked to her in under two seconds, this time walking her backwards until she hit the kitchen bar behind her. Then he lowered his mouth to her ear so only she could hear him.

"Beatríz, my love, I adore you. But stop now before you do or say something we'll both regret. It would break my heart to lose you, but I won't sacrifice myself for anyone. Not that baby. Not even you."

He didn't have to ask her if she understood.

The way he looked at her told her everything she needed to know.

CHAPTER 20

GABBY

Today

We're on our way to Guanica, a town on the southwestern part of the island where Isabella spent some time living with her mother's side of the family.

My side of the family?

The thought goes flying from my head—not because I don't want to contemplate it, but because my chauffeur takes a hairpin turn at breakneck pace, sending me slamming into the passenger side door, the armrest digging into my ribs. That's when I get a good look out the window. Big mistake. Beyond the guardrail is a very steep, very scary-looking drop of about, oh, say, sixty thousand feet. Not really. But it sure as hell seems that way. I force myself to face forward and focus on the horizon ahead of us.

"My God! Who taught *you* how to drive?" I ask a little too loudly.

She just shrugs and grins proudly. "I taught myself. I can drive a stick shift, a tractor, a boat, and a semi, too."

I shake my head. "Is there anything you haven't taught yourself to do?"

The smile fades a bit. "Uhhh . . . well, let's see. My dad taught me how to drink a shot, and he also showed me how to roll a joint. And the best way to treat a hangover . . . so, there's that . . ."

I gawk at her profile as she continues to concentrate on the road ahead of us—which is a good thing. This stretch of the Expreso Luis A. Ferré takes us through some mountainous twists and turns.

"Well, that's some great parenting right there," I mutter under my breath, bracing myself against the glove box when we have to stop short for an unexpected traffic backup.

"We'll be out of the mountains soon," she reassures, clearly sensing my anxiety. "Then it's a straight shot. We'll be in Guanica in less than an hour. But I'll need to stop for gas soon."

I nod, and we ride along in silence for a few minutes before I speak again. "Mack—my dad? He taught me to drive," I say after a little while, a hint of reluctance to my statement. Isabella has some very strong feelings about my parents, and I've decided the less I mention them, the better.

She nods and quirks an eyebrow, seemingly interested in this new little tidbit about me. "And what about your writing? Did you get that from him?"

The idea of this makes me laugh. "What? No. He hated writing anything. I just kind of started doing that on my own."

Not that I've been doing much of it in the last couple of days. I feel as if we've been playing some bizarro live-action version of Clue.

"To be honest, I don't know what to make of that. Of him . . . of them."

I sigh and glance out my window again, noting that we seem to be on the decline now, making our way out of the mountains and, thankfully, lessening our chances of plummeting to our deaths. There are several long minutes when the only sound in the little car is the staticky sound of the radio as we move out of range of the station. That's when the phone rings. I silence it immediately, but it's definitely caught Isabella's attention. I see it when she glances first at me, then down at the phone in my hand, then back at me again.

"Max," I answer without bothering to wait for the question that I know is coming.

"Max?"

"My ex-boss. The one who fired me."

"If he's your *ex*-boss, why is he still calling and texting you?"

"I told you before, it's complicated."

"And he fired you." She confirms.

"Yes," I reply, then reconsider. "Well, yes and no . . . that's even more complicated."

Suddenly there's a dramatic gasp from the driver's seat, and Isabella slaps the steering wheel.

"Ahh! You slept with him, didn't you?" she accuses.

"What? No! Why would you think that?" I demand, unsure of why I'm having such a strong reaction.

A slow, sly smile starts to cross her face. "Why would you ask me why I think that? A little quick to protest there, aren't we?"

"I am *not* sleeping with Max."

She gives an exasperated huff and rolls her eyes at me. "I can't believe how sensitive you are. Fine, fine. So then what is the deal with this guy? Did you have feelings for him or something?"

I want to end the Max-centric conversation, but I also recognize this to be an opportunity. Sometimes it's easier to talk about these kinds of things with someone you don't know.

"I'm attracted to him," I admit, and cringe, waiting for her to use the admission against me.

"Okay, that's a good place to start," she says, without the teasing. "And do you think he might be attracted to you? I

mean, you are seriously hot." The last part takes me by surprise, and apparently it's written all over my face. "What?"
Isabella asks, her head moving back and forth between me
and the road.

"Please don't get us killed," I say. "And . . . thanks. That's
really sweet. I think maybe? He's a little hard to read. But
yeah, I've caught him watching me a few times. His office is
all glass, and he's got a direct view of my desk."

"But he's never asked you out?"

"No. And I'm not sure he can. The whole sexual harass-
ment thing is a big deal nowadays. He's probably not supposed
to have personal relationships with people he supervises."

She seems to consider this. "Well, you could ask him out."

"You know, I'm just not . . . I don't really date . . ."

"I get it."

"You do?"

"Sure, I've been there. Sometimes it's easier to just lay low
and hide out at home. There was a long time when I felt the
same way. And then Matéo . . . well, let's just say he's not the
kind of guy who lets you get away with that for very long."

I smile a little. I can totally see that. "Yeah, Franny is like
that, too. But now that she's moved . . . well, it's just harder.
I'm sure I'm a little depressed since she left, which doesn't
help. Whatever it is, I can't seem to make myself go out."

"So you don't have many friends," she surmises.

"Nope."

"And you're not feeling comfortable asking Max—or
anyone—out on a date."

"Yup."

She's quiet for a long moment before she speaks again.

"Okay, you know what? Let's come back to that—to the
relationship thing. Tell me why you're not working for *Flux*—
and Max—anymore."

I sigh. "He wanted to do this story."

She looks confused. "Which story?"

"*This* story," I repeat, now gesturing between the two of us. "Our story. Yours . . . and mine."

I go on to give her a brief explanation of how I came to be on the GeneTeam site in the first place and Max's grand plan for a riveting story of a family torn apart, reunited, and put back together again. The perfect cover story to get the soccer moms to toss *Flux* onto the conveyor belt at the checkout line.

"So, what? You didn't want them to do the story?" she concludes.

"Not exactly. I didn't mind the magazine having the story—it's just . . . *I* wanted to be the one to write it."

She nods. "Okay, sounds reasonable, considering it's happening to you."

I feel buoyed by her understanding of the situation and her agreement.

"I know, right? But Max doesn't think I'm ready for that."

"I don't understand."

"What don't you understand?"

"I mean, I know your job is as a fact-checker, but you're really a writer . . . yes?"

"Well, yeah . . . I mean, I think so . . ."

She shakes her head. "No, it doesn't work like that. If you write, you're a writer. If you paint, you're a painter. If you sing, you're a singer. You may be a total shit writer, or painter, or singer—but that doesn't make you any less of one."

Well, since she put it like that . . .

"Yeah, okay, I'm a writer," I agree.

Now she nods, keeping her eyes on the road ahead of us.

"Right. So what's stopping you from writing this story? Why do you need his permission?"

"If I want it published in *Flux,* I need his permission."

"Are you telling me that if you write an amazing, in-depth, insightful, kick-ass story, he's going to reject it because he doesn't think you're ready? And what does that mean anyway? *Ready?* What's the metric he's using? How will he decide when you're finally good enough to do something like this?" She shakes her head and gives me a quick sideways glance. "I don't know, Gabby, it all sounds pretty arbitrary to me. And this Max guy? What's up with firing you—or letting you quit, whichever—and now blowing up your phone? I think he screwed up, and now he knows it."

I think my mouth is actually hanging open.

I've known this woman for five minutes, and she's just given some of the best, most powerful advice I've ever gotten in my life.

"I'm sorry . . ." she begins, sparing me a quick glance, "was that too much? Matéo says I have a habit of being dismissive of other people's problems—of simplifying them. I wasn't trying to—"

"No!" I cut her off abruptly. "No, no . . . I think . . . I think I never thought of it that way. I've been just sort of . . . waiting for permission. But you're right; I don't need it."

"You don't need it," she echoes firmly. "So find your facts, Gabby DiMarco. Do all that Sherlock shit you do so well and then write your story—whatever it turns out to be."

There's something about the way she tosses out those last few words, as if she's got something on her mind she's not saying.

"Meaning?"

I don't need to clarify what I'm asking about—she knows.

"Meaning you should be prepared—the story you think you're writing might just turn out to be a different one entirely."

"Not if I write the truth. Facts are facts. The truth is not a fluid thing."

Isabella scoffs and shoots me another glance, this one incredulous.

"What planet do *you* live on?" she snarks. "Yes, of course facts are facts. But facts and truth aren't the same thing, are they?" She continues before I have a chance to even think about responding. "Isn't the truth about perception? My truth may not be the same as your truth—but they might still be . . . the truth."

"That makes absolutely no sense," I counter. "If that were . . . you know . . . *true* . . . then murderers would get off all the time. Oh, and those nutty conspiracy theorists would—"

"Would what?" She cuts me off. "What would they do, Gabby? Those people already believe they know the truth and everyone else is just wrong, or stupid, or evil. And as for murderers, that's where the facts come in. If the facts support someone committing a crime, then they've committed the crime. The only variable there is how they're sentenced. If the guy's 'truth' involves voices in his head telling him to kill people, he'll likely get psychiatric help. But if his truth is that an entire subset of society is unfit to live, and he sends them to the gas chambers by the tens of thousands . . . yeah, well, that's a whole other thing. Either way, facts are what can be proven. Truth is what you choose to believe—with or without the facts to back it up."

I open my mouth to debate this, but then stop. She's not wrong, and I can't believe I never looked at it like that. I think back to my Shakespeare . . .

The truth will out . . .

I'm sure it will. The question now is, *whose* truth will that be?

CHAPTER 21

YETI

That Day

Yeti cursed aloud the entire way there—over an hour. He cursed at Santiago for leaving him holding the bag—literally. He cursed at Beatríz for showing up and ruining his plan—as if she had any right to question him! Well, at least now he knew the truth—she was fucking Santiago. And he'd make sure every member of *Los Soldados Salvajes* knew about it before this was all over.

More than a few people would be questioning their loyalty to a man who got led around by his dick. He even cursed himself for leaving his car behind in La Perla so that they had to walk. The least Santiago could have done was offer them a ride. What would have taken twenty minutes by car was taking over an hour as they skirted the main roads in an attempt to avoid being seen or caught on some security camera somewhere.

At least the walk had given him some time to work out the details. He'd decided along the way that strangulation was the best option. It was clean and fast. Or perhaps he'd break its neck instead. Either way, the small, dilapidated shack he'd chosen would serve his purpose perfectly. It had been abandoned after the last big hurricane ripped much of the roof clean off, leaving the structure listing to one side.

Between its remote location and its exposure to the elements, there wouldn't be much of a body left by the time someone stumbled on it—let alone any kind of evidence that could implicate him.

His stomach was grumbling loudly by the time they finally got there, reminding him it had been hours since he'd eaten anything. He wanted to get this shit over with so he could go find a plate of hot empanadas and a bottle of cold beer and put this clusterfuck of a day behind him.

"Okay," he began, turning to Coquí, who was holding the baby—bouncing it up and down in his arms. *"Dámelo."*

Give it to me.

Coquí stopped bouncing the child, but other than that, didn't make a move. He just stared back at Yeti, who was getting more irritated by the second. He didn't have time for this bullshit.

"Give. It. To. Me."

When, again, Coquí didn't immediately follow his order, Yeti stomped over so they were toe-to-toe. He was bigger than Coquí. He was stronger and meaner than Coquí. And, unlike Coquí, he couldn't give a shit about anything or anyone.

"Now! I will *not* tell you again!"

Instead of just doing it, the kid looked away from him, up at the sky where the roof had once been, as if contemplating the secrets of the universe. At the same time, he transferred the child from both of his arms to just his right, tucking it up against his shoulder like it was a football.

Yeti was done. He reached out to yank the baby from Coquí's grasp, but before his fingers could even graze the child's flesh, Yeti felt the air in his lungs come rushing out in a hot, violent wave. It was the only warning he got an instant before the blinding pain in his groin dropped him onto his knees. *Pendejo* Coquí had kicked him squarely in the *cojones* and was over him now, pushing him onto his back. Suddenly he was on top of Yeti—straddling his rib cage. Then, with one arm still supporting the baby, Coquí leaned forward, wrapped his other hand around Yeti's neck . . . and shifted all his weight to bear down on him.

He could have easily fought him off had he not already been immobilized by the agony radiating from his crotch. As it was, he struggled between losing breakfast and finding air—clawing at Coquí's hand around his neck. He was *not* going to die like this—at the hands of a pussy kid. He had to do something, and fast.

He tried to claw at Coquí's face, but the son of a bitch turned his head, and Yeti only succeeded in grabbing the medal around his neck, breaking the chain, and sending San Cristóbal flying somewhere onto the filthy floor. With his lungs burning from the lack of oxygen, Yeti cast his hands out onto the floor as far as they would reach, desperately searching for something—anything—to use as a weapon. When his fingers swept across something hard and wooden—a stick or dowel of some sort—he didn't know exactly what it was he'd grabbed until he swung it toward the other man's head. It was a broken chair leg with a nice, jagged point. Yeti summoned every last bit of energy he could find in his fading body and, while he wasn't quite strong enough to actually stab his attacker with it, he did manage to connect with Coquí's temple forcefully enough to catch him off guard. Coquí loosened his grip for just an instant—but Yeti was ready, and it was enough. Because of the way Coquí had distributed all of his weight to the one arm, he was off balance when the blow hit, knocking him backwards off of Yeti and onto the floor.

A small trickle of blood ran down Coquí's face, and he paused just long enough to wipe at it before it dripped down onto the child, who was still in his arms and, miraculously, totally unfazed by this violent turn of events.

Yeti managed to drag his aching body back into a standing position while Coquí scrambled backwards. After putting some distance between them, he, too, managed to stand. And then they were facing each other, both bloody and breathing heavily, already exhausted from the effort of fighting.

"You're a dead man," Yeti spat at him.

"Maybe so," Coquí said impassively. "But you're still not getting this baby."

Yeti snarled like a wild animal. "Then you'd better hope to God you can kill me."

"No hoping about it," Coquí replied with a shrug that made Yeti's blood boil.

How dare this little *pendejo* think he could take him on!

And then, in one white-hot, blinding flash of rage, everything that had been lying down in the depths of Yeti's psyche surfaced, bursting up and into the air, the daylight, the present. His frustration with Santiago, his disdain for Beatríz, his annoyance at Alberto and the little brat for causing him so much aggravation.

Hunching slightly, he launched himself forward without warning and, with the strength of a madman, he hurled himself right into Coquí, causing him to fly backwards with the momentum, trip, and land hard on his ass. All the while holding the child upward, so it would not hit the ground with him.

Without thought, Yeti dropped the broken chair leg so he could snatch it right out of Coquí's arms. Then he straightened up, a triumphant growl escaping his lips as he held it—now wailing—over his head. But Coquí wasn't done. With surprising agility, he recovered the broken chair leg and lunged directly at Yeti's core, left exposed as he held the child aloft. They hit the ground together—the three of them, Yeti immediately positioning the child in between them like a makeshift shield, grinning with satisfaction.

Coquí had tipped his hand—he'd shown Yeti that the baby was his weakness, and Yeti planned to use that against him starting right now. If Coquí wanted to gut him, he'd have to go through the screeching little snotball to do it. And, just to hedge his bets, he wrapped one of his mammoth hands around the baby's throat and he squeezed, just the way Coquí had done to him not two minutes earlier.

"Go ahead!" he hissed, kicking back to put more distance between them and Coquí, who looked as if he wanted to pounce—and then pound his head into what was left of the shack's wood floorboards. "Go ahead and see how fast I snap this little neck. The bones are soft. They'll crumple in my hand."

Yeti watched with satisfaction as Coquí's face grew red with rage. Son of a bitch wasn't shrugging now! But he did still have a hold of the only weapon in the room.

"Throw it here," he instructed, but Coquí didn't make a move. "*Now!*" Yeti added for effect, even as he tightened his grip around the child, whose deafening wails grew even louder. He couldn't wait to smother the thing just so it would shut the fuck up!

There was undisguised hatred in Coquí's eyes as they moved from Yeti to the child, and then back again. Finally, he tossed the jagged wooden leg toward him. It was just far enough that Yeti had to stretch a few inches to grab it.

He realized his mistake a second too late.

The second in which Coquí was upon him.

But Yeti had no intention of going down. Not today. Not any day.

He grasped the makeshift spike, and he struck.

CHAPTER 22

ISABELLA

Today

My aunt and uncle have somehow managed to transform the local Knights of Columbus hall into a dreamy wonderland to rival even the grandest grand ballroom on the island. Gauzy panels of material edged with strings of tiny, twinkling lights are draped from the middle of the ceiling, radiating outward like spokes on a wheel. And there are flowers everywhere. So many flowers—huge bunches wrapped in blue ribbon and set around the room in big, galvanized buckets, with smaller versions on each table.

"Are *all* of these people your family?" Gabby asks, craning her head so she can do a visual sweep of the tables. The place is filled to capacity, and you can hardly hear over the chatter, which is periodically punctuated by a scream of delight or a roar of laughter.

"Most of them," I say, resisting the urge to point out that they're her family, too, whether she believes it or not.

There are friends and neighbors there, too; I recognize several of them from the years I spent living in this town with Titi Annamaria and Tío Tomás, sharing a bedroom with two of their four older daughters. My aunt was pregnant with Olivia the night I realized I had to leave them—to go back to San Juan . . . and Alberto.

*   *   *

While my two roommates slept soundly, I tossed and turned, having trouble falling asleep. When I heard voices from down the hall, I knew my aunt and uncle were still up and in the kitchen, so I decided to get up for a glass of water or maybe a cup of my Titi Annamaria's herbal tea. She and Tío Tomás didn't hear me coming down the hall, so I was able to overhear a little of their conversation as I got closer.

"Annamaria," my uncle was saying regretfully, "I love her, too, but I just don't see how we can keep doing it. Now that they've cut my hours back at work. And with the baby coming . . ." His voice was soft enough that I wouldn't have heard him had I not been just outside of their sightline.

I knew immediately they were talking about me.

At this point, I'd been living with them for a couple of years, like just another daughter—they had four in their teens, and she was heavily pregnant with Olivia. I went to school with them, did my homework with them, laughed and joked and talked boys with them. There was always food in the fridge and someone to kiss me goodnight. It was the most stable I'd been in my life . . . and the happiest.

"Tomás, I am not going to send my sister's child back to that . . . that pathetic excuse for a father. He can't take care of himself; how can he possibly take care of her? She's at an age where she needs support and love—"

"She's at an age when she costs a lot more money. New uniforms for high school, new shoes, and supplies. And what about the extras? Are we supposed to keep her at home while we buy the other girls pretty new dresses and tickets to the school dance? Who's going to pay for the field trip to Vieques next month? And what about the baby?"

"What about the baby?"

"She needs everything—a crib, diapers, clothing, car seat. Then there are the doctor visits, the formula—"

"*Stop it,*" *my aunt said quietly but firmly.* "*Just . . . stop, Tomás. We'll get by. We did it with the other children.*"

"*With the other children, we already had everything we needed. But we got rid of it all once we decided four children was enough. No one expected we'd be doing this again after thirteen years . . .*"

"*Oh, so this is my fault?*" *my aunt countered with some irritation.* "*Because I seem to recall you being there, too . . .*"

"*No! No, no, of course not! I'm just saying, it's different this time. And it's not fair to her or to our girls, Annamaria. And I think you know that.*"

I held my breath for what felt like a very long time, waiting for my aunt's response.

"*Maybe Alberto can come up with a little cash to help out . . .*"

But her words rang hollow—the eleventh-hour appeal of a condemned man . . . or woman. Except I hadn't even realized I'd been on trial. I thought everything was fine. But now I knew better.

Without warning, a wave of nausea hit so hard, so fast that I bolted past the kitchen, hurling myself onto the floor of the bathroom just in time. A cold sweat broke out across my entire body, and I was shaking visibly.

"*¡Dios mío!*" *Titi Annamaria exclaimed when she found me like that, curled up in a ball on the cold tile.* "*Isabellita, what is it, my love? Are you sick?*"

I could only nod, because I knew if I opened my mouth, the words would come tumbling out whether I wanted them to or not. My instinct for self-preservation would win out over my pride, causing me to admit what I'd heard and beg her not to send me away. So I kept my goddammed mouth shut and pretended my dinner hadn't agreed with me.

The next day, I told them I'd heard from my father—he'd gotten a job working the cruise ship docks and wanted me to

*come back to San Juan so we could be together. I could see
that Tío Tomás was relieved bordering on thrilled. He didn't
have to make the call. He didn't have to be the bad guy. Nor
did he have to make himself crazy figuring out how to make
the numbers work. Titi Annamaria looked as if she wanted
to press the matter further—like she didn't quite believe me.
But in the end, she never asked, and I never offered—neither
of us even vaguely aware of how this single decision would
impact the rest of my life.*

These days, things are much better for their little family—
all four of the older girls are out of the house, two of them
married with children of their own. In the meantime, Olivia
came along and grew into an extraordinary young woman—
smart, sweet, kind, and beautiful. She is beloved by everyone
whose life she touches. And now, fifteen years later, her parents have the means to do a bit more for her big day than they
were able to do for her sisters.

I glance at my watch now. We've been through the cocktails and the sit-down dinner. The waitstaff are scurrying
from table to table, collecting stray plates and silverware.

"Well, Gabby, you're about to get quite a show," I tell her.

"Really? Is there a candle ceremony like they do at a sweet
sixteen? Oh, how about the daddy-daughter dance?" she
asks.

"No on the candles," Matéo replies. "But yes on the dance.
Plus, there are shoes . . . and a doll."

"A *doll*?" she echoes.

Before I can explain, all the lights dim, save for the ones in
the front center of the hall, where a large peacock chair has
been adorned in ribbons and flowers to create a throne.

"Here we go," I murmur.

I've built a good side hustle for myself doing nails for events
like this one, bringing the nail bling to many a *quinceañera*
and her court. Over the years, I've seen everything from lav-

ish, black-tie affairs to casual backyard barbecues. Some are crazy over-the-top—and, let me tell you, Bridezilla ain't got *nothing* on Quinzilla. You haven't lived until you've seen a full-grown fifteen-year-old literally throw herself down on the floor in a thousand-dollar dress, beating her fists and feet while screeching because someone had the nerve to wear *her* color. So much for entering the realm of womanhood.

But now, as the double doors at the back of the hall swing open, I gasp along with everyone else in the room. Even my cold, jaded heart cannot help but thaw and swell for the little girl who once snuffled in my arms. She was the first baby I could bring myself to hold after Marianna—her tiny head covered in wild, downy black hair and smelling of talcum. I was as mesmerized by her then as I am right now as she seems to float across the room.

It's like witnessing something magical—an ethereal creature made of spun sugar and gossamer, sprinkled with a generous coating of fairy dust. The bright lights catch the aquamarine sequins on her dress at just the right angle so they twinkle like a sky full of tiny stars. Her hair, still that same shade of black/brown, hangs long down her back, a cascade of dark, silky curls.

"Oh, my God," Gabby murmurs, awestruck, as the entire room around us erupts in applause. "She's just . . . *stunning!*"

We all watch, rapt, as she takes her throne and my aunt gingerly removes the simple white flower crown that adorns her youngest daughter's head, replacing it with an intricately filigreed tiara made of crystals.

Now she is a princess in the eyes of God.

After this, she is presented with *la última muñeca*—the last doll—fashioned to look like her, right down to the aquamarine dress and long dark curls. Later on, she will give it away to one of the little girls who are here tonight.

Now she has put aside her childish things.

The big moment arrives in a clear plastic box, which Titi

Annamaria presents to Tío Tomás. He kneels down before his daughter and, with shaking hands, removes the ballet flats she's been wearing, replacing them with a pair of high heels.

Now she steps into the shoes of a woman.

A slow waltz has started to play, and Olivia slips into the waiting arms of her father. She rests her cheek against his shoulder, unable to see the expression on his face above her— a bittersweet combination of regret and pride. He clings to her tightly, as if he can somehow hang on to his baby girl for just a little longer. But, of course, it's too late for that now. The child was gone long before this make-believe world of glittery shoes and fancy dolls.

"Hey, baby, are you okay?" Matéo asks, leaning down to whisper in my ear. His face is full of concern.

That's when I realize I've been crying—not something I like to do in public. I nod, snatching a linen napkin from the table so I can wipe my face.

"I'm just . . . I'm so happy for her," I lie, twisting my mouth into something resembling a smile.

It must be convincing enough, because he just wraps an arm around my waist and pulls me up against him. Here I take a long, slow breath, willing myself not to lose my shit.

This—this right here—is why I hate God. It's why I will *never* set foot in a church again. It's why I do not pray, or genuflect, or even say "God bless you!" when someone sneezes.

I try to blink back the resentful tears gathering just behind my lashes. I never wanted this for myself, so how could I possibly be envious?

Maybe because my entrée into womanhood wasn't anything to be celebrated, cherished, or captured for posterity. Maybe because if I were given a chance to live that time again, things would be different. I wouldn't need a big fancy party—just an opportunity to avoid the achingly lonely, painful journey that it turned out to be.

But, then again, aren't these the events that shape who we become? And would I ever trade that—even if I could? My life, my husband, the person I am today?

It is, of course, a ridiculous thought to entertain, considering no one's managed to crack the whole time travel thing yet. Still, I indulge myself for a single heartbeat, imagining that *I'm* the one standing up there, safe and surrounded by people who love me.

But then the heartbeat passes, and I'm just . . . me . . . again.

So I fake applaud. And I fake smile. Then I for real cry.

CHAPTER 23

GABBY

Today

I spent my fifteenth birthday in Paris, shopping, and eating, and shopping some more. I was totally onboard when my parents offered to take me on a spring break trip abroad instead of a party. Then, when we showed up at the airport, and they had Franny waiting to surprise me at the gate, I nearly lost my mind with excitement. It was probably the best birthday I ever had.

Still, standing here now at this *quinceañera*, I can't help but wonder—if I had a big family like this one, would I have felt differently? Olivia has taken her first tentative steps into womanhood this very night—borne out not by the sentimental traditions, but by the presence of so many people who surround her and support her, joyously celebrating the day she was born onto this earth. All these people—parents, siblings, aunts, uncles, cousins—have gathered here as part of an unspoken promise. So long as even one person in this room is alive, Olivia will never be alone.

I have the sudden, irrational sense that I've been cheated out of something I never even knew existed. All at once, the warm, fuzzy glow of the night has turned to a hard, frigid iceberg in my gut and, for a brief second, I think I'm going to hurl right here, all over Tío Javier, Doña Alma, and the other unsuspecting denizens of table eleven. My hands shake as I grab and down a goblet of ice water in one long swig.

What the hell am I even doing here? How could I be so disloyal to the memory of my parents? They gave me a fantastic life, and yet, here I am, running around a strange island with a strange woman, playing a game of hide-and-go-seek with the truth. Or maybe it's that I'm playing house—pretending that I can start over with a new family, in a new place. For God's sake! The fact that I even got on the plane to come here suggests that I believe Isabella's claim that I am her sister Marianna. And, if I *am* Marianna, then it's true that somehow, somewhere, someone snatched me away from the family I was *meant* to have—delivering me right into the arms of the one I did have. It's also true that the exact same thing is happening in reverse right now—pulling me away from Mack and Lucy only to deposit me here in this strange place with these strange people.

They can't both be true. The truth of one life makes the other one a lie.

But which is which? And which one do I *want* to be the truth?

"Hey, are you okay?"

Matéo's voice brings me back to the here and now—to the passenger seat of his SUV. Isabella will stay at her aunt's house tonight so she can pay her Detective Alvarez a visit in the morning. Matéo has been charged with seeing me back to the resort. Not that I mind; he's a good guy, as evidenced by the concern in his tone and on his face right now.

"Hmm? Oh, yeah . . . just a little . . . I guess it's all this family stuff. It makes me miss my parents, is all."

"I'll bet. I'm sorry you're alone, Gabby," he offers quietly.

"Do you think it's true?" I blurt without thought.

He seems to know exactly what I'm asking, and he's not at all flummoxed by the question.

"Yes, I do."

The three words are calm and simple and decisive.

"But why? How? You've only known me for a couple of days."

"I didn't say I *know*," he corrects, giving me a quick sideways glance. "You asked me if I, personally, believe it, and I do. I could be wrong. But . . . I don't think I am. Not now that I've met you in person. You can't see it, but the similarities between you and Isabella—they're striking."

I scoff. "She's tall; I'm short. I have the blue eyes; hers are brown—my build is slight; hers is—"

Matéo stops my comparison with a wave of his hand. "I don't mean physically, though I can absolutely see the resemblance between the two of you—it's more in your expressions than your features."

I shake my head, rejecting the notion, but he continues.

"You have the same impulses, the same ridiculous cut-off-your-nose stubbornness. You feel deeply, but you don't trust easily. And you jump right in with both feet, thinking you've got it all figured out—only to get really pissed when you realize you don't."

"Yeah, I'll own that," I agree. "But those aren't exactly rare traits. They hardly prove I'm Marianna."

"You're right. And really, we can all speculate on whatever we want, but we won't know for sure—one way or the other—until the results of that DNA profile come back."

We ride in silence for a couple of minutes, and I can't help but notice I'm a lot less stressed now that Isabella isn't behind the wheel.

"You know, you're a much better driver than your wife," I tell him after he negotiates a particularly sharp curve.

He snort-laughs. "Everybody's a better driver than Isabella!"

"She told me about how she had to teach herself because her father didn't."

He glances at me for just a second before returning his eyes to the road ahead. "No, Alberto didn't teach her much of anything. Except for where to score drugs and how many beers you can have before you black out." I'm not sure how to respond to that, so I don't. And after a moment, he shoots me a wry smile. "What can I say? He was hardly 'Father of the Year' material."

Something occurs to me . . . something dark that I'd have trouble asking Isabella directly. But it's different with her husband.

"Did he . . . was he ever . . . you know . . . did he ever hit her? Or anything else . . . ?"

He shakes his head. "No, nothing like that. He would have had to notice her to abuse her physically."

"What do you mean 'notice her'? How do you not notice your own daughter?"

"Gabby, Alberto was *totally* checked out. Isabella was pulling him out of bars by the time she was twelve, staying up all night to make sure he didn't choke on his own vomit. She made her meals, got herself to school, and ran around in the streets late at night painting buildings whenever she could get away with it."

"Wait . . . what? I thought she lived with her aunt and cousins!"

"Mainly when she was younger. But once Olivia was born, there wasn't a lot of space—or money—to go around, so she went back to San Juan. To Alberto."

I consider how it must have felt for her, going from the stability, structure, and security of one home to the chaos, disarray, and—let's face it—danger of the other one.

"Sounds like Alberto Ruíz was a real piece of work," I mutter, more to myself than him.

"Still is," he replies, matching my tone.

Whoa . . . did I just mishear him? Or maybe misunderstand him?

"Umm . . . Matéo, I'm sorry, but did you just refer to him in the present tense? Like today? I mean, isn't he . . . dead?"

He turns to look at me so quickly that the wheel jerks with his motion, sending us pants-peeingly close to the guardrail for a few moments before he regains control. But there's hardly time to let out a sigh of relief.

"*¡Jesucristo!*" he gasps.

"Oh, God! I'm so sorry!" I offer quickly. "Really—I didn't mean to distract you, but I swear I thought he was dead!"

"What? No! Why would you think that?"

"Because Isabella only talks about him in the past tense—like, you know, like he's dead!"

He opens his mouth to say something, closes it, then changes his mind and opens it again.

"Gabby, Alberto is not dead. He lives like a hermit in the house he grew up in—about forty-five minutes from San Juan. We see him once a year—maybe. And that's usually by accident when we run into him somewhere. He never asks to see Isabella. He never calls her. Hell, he didn't come to his own daughter's wedding. So, yeah, he's a dick, but he's a living, breathing dick."

And just like that, everything changes.

CHAPTER 24

ISABELLA

Today

I spent my fifteenth birthday in the hospital, crying and sleeping, and crying some more. Alberto promised me he'd come home for dinner. We didn't have money for a *quinceañera*, but at least we could do that much to celebrate. I even scraped together enough cash to buy a small cake from *la panadería* down the block. Señora Ortega wrote my name on it in pretty pink frosting and threw in a pack of candles for free. But by nine-thirty, it was clear my father would not be attending my two-person party.

Determined not to feel sorry for myself, I did what I did best—I lost myself in my art. I'd had my eye on a blank wall on the back side of a closed pharmacy. It was perfect—there was just enough light spilling in from the street that ran along the front of the building but angled in such a way that the police were unlikely to spot me working and bust me. Again. Because, by then, I'd been hauled in for vandalism and destruction of private property at least a half-dozen times. Each time, I'd gotten off with a stern warning, thanks to the intervention of one Detective Alvarez. Though he'd been clear that if it happened again, I'd be on my own.

It was a risk I was willing to take, not that I thought much about that as I scaled the ladder leading up the second- and third-floor fire escapes. It took close to two hours for me to get the angel roughed in. Her face battered and bruised, she looked upward toward heaven. There were tears streaming from her eyes. In need of a break, I figured I'd climb down and stretch a bit, maybe smoke the joint in my bag. Then I'd go back up for round two, adding more details and shading. I was pretty sure if I left it overnight, no one would bother the partially finished mural, and then I could return with my tall ladder tomorrow night to do the background—an outline of the San Juan skyline but made to look all sharp and jagged.

It wasn't until my feet were back down on the asphalt of the parking lot that I realized I had company. The two men— probably in their early twenties—stepped out of the shadows and approached, startling the hell out of me. One was big and beefy with a shock of red hair. The other had scraggly blond hair. They didn't look like locals.

"Hey, y'all are pretty good," the tall blond one drawled at me with a goofy smile.

They didn't sound like locals, either.

"Thanks," I muttered, making a move to grab my bag.

Just like that, the privacy of this spot—the very thing I'd liked about it—turned into a very big liability. Because if no one could see me painting, then no one could see me cornered by these two *turistas* who were inching closer to me.

"You're not leaving already, are you?" asked the redhead. "We was just gettin' ready to have us a little party."

I forced myself to smile as I considered the odds that someone would be out on the street, close enough to hear me if I screamed. They weren't good. Not here in this commercial area. Not at this hour.

"Yeah, sorry, guys," I replied, trying to sound casual and relaxed—not at all concerned about their presence. It took a lot of effort. "It's late. And my father'll be here to pick me up any second now."

Suddenly I wished it were true—that, somehow, against all odds, Alberto had sensed that I was in trouble and pulled himself off the barstool so he could come out and find me—save me. So that, for once in my short life, he could be there when I needed him. But, of course, it was a lie—all of it. He wasn't coming. And he never would.

That harsh realization jarred me into action. I chucked the bag of paint at them even as I was scaling the ladder again. If I could get up high and attract some attention . . . but it turned out Blondie was fast. And strong. I was dragged down by the ankle, kicking and screaming until the instant my head hit the concrete curb stop, exploding with the kind of pain that takes you out of yourself.

I remember them working together to flip me over—I'd stopped fighting by then, the blood running freely down my face, pooling in my ears, and covering my lips. The metallic tang filled my mouth, and I remember looking up to see the angel—except from that angle, she appeared to be crying bloody tears.

After that, everything went dark.

Thank God.

After the *quinceañera*, there's a smaller after-party thrown by one of Olivia's older sisters. I beg off, deciding to take advantage of the fact that my aunt and uncle's house is empty and quiet. I'm just drifting off when the buzzing of my phone jerks me awake again. I swipe to accept the call and give him my best sleepy-seductive voice.

"Calling to tuck me in?"

"No," he replies flatly. "I'm calling to ask you why you told Gabby that Alberto's dead."

I sit up straight.

"What the hell are you talking about? I never told her he's dead!"

"Yeah, well, she was under the impression that was the

case. How could it not have come up? How could *he* not have come up while you've been together this whole time?"

"Okay, well, first of all, 'this whole time' has been like five minutes, so cut the melodrama. And of course he's come up! We've been retracing his steps!"

"Have you been referring to him in the present tense?"

The question takes me by surprise.

"Have I what?"

"Present tense. You know—'my father *is* a good-for-nothing jackass.' As opposed to the past tense. 'My father *didn't* give a shit about anything but his coke and his booze.'"

"I know the difference between present and past tense," I hiss back at him. "And when speaking about him . . . in the past . . . I used past tense. I don't think we've spoken at all about him today. So, yeah, I can see how she might draw that conclusion, but I certainly didn't try to mislead her about it. Why would I?"

"That's what *I'm* trying to figure out."

"Is she upset?"

"Well, she thinks you lied to her."

"Why? Why the hell would I lie about something like that?"

"I don't know, Isabella—"

I cut him off. "Look, believe me, don't believe me . . . whatever, Matéo. I'm dead tired and all I want to do is sleep before I have to see Alvarez in the morning. And that's future tense, for your information."

It's not often that I get pissed at my husband. Good and pissed, anyway. We've had our tiffs, our spats, and our squabbles—as any couple who's been together as long as we have would. What's very rare are the nights when neither of us is willing to concede the stupid argument and call a truce. It's the old "don't go to bed angry" chestnut—and I'm about to violate it.

He's quiet for a long beat, and when he speaks again, his tone is considerably softer.

"I believe you. Of course I believe you. I guess I just wondered if maybe some part of you *wanted* her to think Alberto was dead."

"Why? What purpose would that possibly serve?" I demand with undisguised irritation.

"Because if Gabby knew Alberto was alive . . . she might want to meet him."

Everything seems to stop for just a second. A second that I use to hold my breath, close my eyes, and take a quick look deep down in the depths of my subconscious. And there it is, waving back at me. I'll be damned.

I exhale and adjust my own voice.

"Yeah . . . I think maybe you're right. But I didn't do it intentionally—I swear to God—"

"No, no, no—of course you didn't!" he jumps in right away.

"Well, you weren't so sure about that when you called me," I counter.

"I'm sorry. I guess I felt bad for Gabby finding out like that—that her real father isn't dead. And I sort of . . . yeah, I was pissed that I was the one who had to tell her."

Right. Matéo likes to be the good guy. Give him runaways, teen gang members, and underaged criminals, and my husband is right at home. But stick him in a car with a crying woman? Gabby's lucky he didn't drive the two of them over the guardrail just to avoid the entire situation.

"Honey, get some sleep," I tell him quietly. "I'll call you in the morning before I see Alvarez, okay?"

He sighs deeply. "Yeah. Just . . . maybe call Gabby in the morning, too, okay?"

"I will," I promise him. "I love you."

"I love you, too," he says.

And he does—I can hear it in his voice. It's just the first time I can ever remember having to listen for it.

CHAPTER 25

BEATRÍZ

That Day

Beatríz drove the car slowly, inching along the back roads until she found what she was looking for—the unmarked turnoff. It wasn't a road, exactly—more like a rocky dirt path carved out amongst the overgrowth, barely wide enough for a car. The only reason she even knew where this place was located was because Santiago had asked her to meet him here one night with a bag of supplies. Considering the list included rags, buckets, bleach, tarps, and duct tape, she didn't ask what it was for—it was one of those things she was better off not knowing.

No sooner had Yeti and Coquí left than Santiago had grabbed his keys and phone. At first she thought he meant to follow them, but he told her he was going to tend to some business at a small private bank several towns away. That's when she realized he was putting some distance between himself and the task he'd given to Yeti. He was establishing an alibi for himself. Banks had people. Banks had security who would be making note of those people as they came and went. And banks had security cameras, which Santiago would, undoubtedly, find a way to stay within sight of at all times. If there was anything Beatríz's man was adept at, it was protecting himself and his growing empire.

Once she spotted the turnoff several yards away, she took
a quick glance in all the mirrors, just to be sure no one else
happened to be driving, walking, or biking down this deso-
late road at the moment. She'd been smart enough to bor-
row her sister's nondescript Corolla. It wouldn't do to have
someone making note of her white BMW—the one Santiago
had given her for her birthday last year. But it turned out not
to matter in the end, as she was very much alone and unobserved as she made the turn and disappeared down the path.

Her teeth rattled in her head as the car bounced and
bucked down the steep decline leading to the beat-up little
shack by the water. It had once been someone's home—more
years ago than she could remember. A sweet little bungalow on a craggy swath of waterfront. But somewhere along
the way, it had been abandoned, the small dwelling falling
into disrepair, the property becoming overgrown with bushes
and thicket. It was miraculous that the dilapidated structure
hadn't been totally leveled and blown out to sea during the
hurricane.

She wasn't sure what she was going to see when the car
finally emerged into the clearing at the base of the hill. Honestly, she'd been too afraid to even think about it. Most
certainly *someone* would be dead. Perhaps more than one
someone. If the baby were dead, then Coquí would be, too—
Beatríz was certain of that. She needed to prepare herself for
the possibility of that gruesome scene, as well as the possibility of meeting up with Yeti.

Just then, her car pushed past the last of the brush, and
she found herself on the remains of what had once been a
concrete slab. She put the vehicle into park, got out, and approached the shack slowly, hand resting lightly on the pistol
in her bag. If Yeti was there, she wasn't about to let him take
her down, too.

She finally got up the nerve to open the creaky, splintered
front door—nudging it with the barrel of her gun and then

stepping to the side immediately, in case he was there already, waiting to pounce. But when nothing happened, she took a deep breath, hastily made the sign of the cross, and inched her head just far enough so she could peer inside.

Beatríz pulled back immediately, flattening her back against the exterior of the shack, and slapped a hand to her mouth to keep from screaming . . . or maybe crying. Maybe both. She stood there for what felt like an eternity, trembling as she tried to process what she'd glimpsed inside. She couldn't be sure exactly what she'd seen beyond the blood. It was everywhere.

When she felt in control again, she removed her hand, steeled herself for what was coming, and slowly pivoted so her entire body stood in the door frame, light spilling in from behind her, casting the edges of the single room in shadow while bathing the center in bright late-morning sun.

"¡Jesucristo!" she whispered under her breath as she took in the scene.

The source of the crimson appeared to be the body lying crumpled in the middle of the floor. Was it Coquí? Yeti? When she tried to conjure images of either man, her mind went completely blank—short, tall, big, small—she couldn't have described either of them if her life had depended on it. If that was Coquí dead there on the wooden planks, then Yeti could still be here somewhere. And the little girl . . . or the little girl's body.

Unless, of course, her first instinct had been right, and Santiago really had followed them here to see to it the job was completed. In which case, she was as good as dead herself. He had warned her to stay out of it, yet here she was, smack in the middle of it all—and with a car full of post-crime cleaning supplies. She couldn't be sure either way. But leaving wasn't an option—not until she knew for sure the child wasn't in there somewhere, alive and in need of help. She wouldn't be able to live with herself.

It was the thought of Marianna that gave Beatríz all the

resolve she needed to take that first tentative step across the threshold, pistol clutched in her trembling hand, raised just enough to facilitate shooting. If she had to.

It only took a few steps until she was standing over the body. She could see the source of all the blood now—a thick wooden stick of some sort—a chair leg? Whatever the hell it was, the thing had been driven into this guy with enough force that she could see the bulge of it underneath the back of his shirt. He'd been gored. One of the men whose images she couldn't recall thirty seconds ago was now burned into her memory for the rest of her life. His face was grotesque—a stark white, mouth frozen partially open in a grimace, his unseeing eyes gazing upward.

Stuffing the gun back into her bag, she made the sign of the cross once more before bowing her head. A rapid stream of words poured from her heart, taking wing on her breath, and spilling past her lips—the most fervent of pleas made to a God she wasn't even sure she believed in anymore.

A quiet shuffle from the darkest corner of the room yanked Beatríz back to the moment, sending her pulse into an even more frantic and erratic rhythm.

"H-hello . . . ?" Her voice quavered with fear.

And then he separated himself from the shadows, stepping out and directly into a bright shaft of sunlight that spilled in from the roof. The bloody sight of him stole the very breath from her lungs.

CHAPTER 26

GABBY

Today

"Wow. So this guy—this Alberto guy—is alive?" Franny asks from nearly twenty-five hundred miles away in the comfort of her living room.

It's a rare night off for my friend, and she's opted to spend it at home in her jammies with a glass of wine rather than out clubbing like we did when we were in college.

"Apparently so," I tell her one-dimensional image.

"Are you going to go see him?"

"No, no. What good would that do? There's no point."

It's strange how, while I've opened my mind to the possibility that Isabella and I might be more closely related than I wanted to believe initially, I'm unwilling—or unable—to extrapolate that to Alberto. A sister is one thing; a father is another. I've had one of those before and, for me, there will never be another one. Not that this keeps me from being curious about him.

There's a *ping* from my laptop to indicate a new email has just come in.

"Oh, here we go," I tell her. "These must be the pictures Matéo promised to scan and send."

"Oh! I wanna see!" Franny declares excitedly, putting down the wineglass and drying her hands on her pajamas, as if I'm planning to reach right through the screen and hand them to her.

"Okay, I'm just going to forward the whole email," I tell her as I hit send. Ten seconds later, we're both staring at images of a man who has been nothing more than some faceless, shadowy figure who pops up from time to time as a character in the narrative I'm trying to establish.

There aren't many of them, Alberto apparently not being one for family pictures. Included are a group shot at someone's birthday party where he's holding up a bottle of beer, as if mid-toast. In another, he's sitting in a recliner, head tilted back, with an infant Isabella perched against his chest. They're both fast asleep.

And then there's his mugshot. I wonder what it was he did to warrant this, but Matéo hasn't included any details. Judging by the man's disheveled, glassy-eyed, heavy-lidded appearance, I assume it had something to do with public intoxication or, more likely, some sort of disturbance. It's not the greatest assortment or representation of the man, but it's enough to give me an idea. As I study the images one by one, I scrutinize every inch of his face, his features, his expressions, looking for something—anything—familiar. Anything that might signal he and I are connected somehow.

"Well?" I hear Franny ask, glancing up to see her watching me through the lens of my own computer camera as I peer curiously at the eclectic array.

"I don't know. He looks like any other guy." Something occurs to me, and my eyes shoot up to meet hers. "You don't . . . do you see a resemblance between us? Between him and me?" I ask her, afraid of the answer I might get.

She takes a few seconds to peer at the part of her screen where the pictures must be open. Then she looks to me once more shaking her head—much to my relief.

"No. Not particularly. I mean, maybe if I saw him in person, it'd be different, but not in these pictures."

"Do you—" My thought is cut off by the sound of my phone ringing. "What the . . . ? It's after one in the morning! Who's calling me at this hour?"

"What does the caller ID say?"

"Blocked. It's a blocked number . . . oh! You know what? I'll bet it's Matéo checking to see if I got the pictures. Let me get this, Franny. Check in tomorrow?"

"You better!" she admonishes with a wagging finger. "This shit's better than *The Real Housewives*!"

"Right. Love you, Fran."

"You too, Gabs."

We offer a couple of mutual virtual kisses and log off. I immediately answer the cell before Matéo gets sent to voice-mail.

"I got the pictures, thanks," I say. "The mugshot was particularly impressive." There's a long pause on the other end. Shit, maybe I've offended him. "Matéo?"

"No, afraid not," replies the British accent.

Oh, hell. Seriously?

"Max, why are you calling me in the middle of the night? And what's with the blocked number?"

"Well, I've tried calling in the middle of the morning, the middle of the afternoon, and the middle of the evening—with no response. I thought I might as well try now—and without using my own number. And apparently, I was right."

There's something in his tone that's different—an edge of irritation.

What has *he* got to be irritated about?

"What is it, Max? I need to go . . ."

"Waiting for *Matéo* to come over?" he asks, taking special care to wrap his name in disdain.

Holy shit. Is he . . . ? Is it possible . . . ? Could Maxwell Taylor-Davies be drunk-dialing me? And is that . . . *jealousy* I hear in his tone?

"I don't see how Matéo—or anyone else I see—is any of

your business," I reply, doing nothing to correct his perception. "What do you want? Why do you keep calling and texting? You fired me, remember? I don't work for you anymore."

He seems taken aback for a second, and I hear his breath pick up as he starts to move around—probably getting out of bed.

"This was a bad idea. We should have this conversation another time . . ."

I make a snap decision. Time to stop this ridiculous back-and-forth between us. It's like watching a set at Wimbledon, only without William and Kate hanging about.

"I won't pick up the phone again, so I suggest you say whatever it is you have to say now."

"Gabby, I practically begged you not to quit . . ."

"I didn't quit. You fired me."

"I don't see it that way . . ."

"I really couldn't give a flying fig how you see it, Max. If memory serves, you said, *'Well then, Gabby, I'm afraid I'm going to have to let you go.'* Sounds like a firing to me."

"I didn't want you to go . . ."

"No, I'm sure you didn't. Not once you realized that I took the story with me. *My* story, Max. Literally."

"It's true, I think we can do a brilliant job with it . . ."

"You mean you think *Lisa* can do a brilliant job with it."

He doesn't correct my correction.

"Come back. I'll mentor you. We'll work on your Minnesota story. And then when the time is right . . . when you're ready . . ."

Suddenly I'm back in the car with Isabella this afternoon, remembering her words. They made so much sense, the way they just cut through all the double-talk and mansplaining.

"Max, I'm a writer. I write. That's what I do. If you want to hire me back, you can offer me a job as a staff writer. But I'm sorry, I'm not coming back as a fact-checker. That part of my career is done. From here on out, the only facts I check are my own."

There's a long pause on his end before he finally speaks again.

"Gabby . . ."

It's all he has to say. The way he utters my name tells me everything I need to know.

"No," I say and then hang up before he can squeeze in another syllable.

Knowing he's going to call back in a matter of moments, I decide to just turn the phone off altogether.

"Go to voicemail," I mutter to myself as the screen goes blank. "Go directly to voicemail. Do *not* pass GO. Do *not* collect two hundred dollars . . ."

Five minutes later, I'm parked at the desk in front of the laptop. Isabella's words from earlier today stick in my mind. She's right, the only thing I need to do to be a writer is write.

So that's what I do.

CHAPTER 27

MIGUEL

That Day

By the time Miguel Alvarez arrived on the scene, it was already looking like a three-ring circus. News vans lined the normally deserted back road, several cameramen and a few daring reporters already perching atop the vehicles in hopes of catching an unobstructed view of the property below. He parked and made his way down the footpath that had been cordoned off for police to use. The forensics team was already taking pictures and measuring tire tracks on the main path of egress—a narrow dirt road.

Alvarez was no stranger to death. Over the years, he'd been called out to investigate shootings, stabbings, suicides, overdoses, drownings, and suspicious accidents. The ones he dreaded most—the burnt bodies—were the ones that came up least—thankfully. Unfortunately, today just happened to be one of those rare occasions. And, as much as he'd rather be in La Perla managing the Marianna Ruíz kidnapping, he had to at least come and check this out in case the two were related.

As he approached the still-smoldering shack, he tried to recall the last time anyone had actually lived here. Before Hurricane Bertha, for sure. No actual tenants had resided there for years. He seemed to recall it had gone to the bank in foreclosure at some point and was never resold. Or maintained. At one point, it had been a crack den, but regular patrols by the uniformed cops had curtailed that practice. Now? He wasn't sure.

"*Dígame,*" he said when he finally located the junior detective waiting for him on site.

Magda, a serious young woman in her late twenties, exhaled long and slow, her dark brows arching as she did.

"*Jefe,* a jogger saw the smoke and called nine-one-one," she explained.

On a normal day, a jogger might or might not bother calling in suspicious smoke in an area like this. But then, this wasn't a normal day, and everyone within a five-mile radius of La Perla knew that from word of mouth alone. By tonight, that reach would extend considerably with the help of the media outlets. News of a missing child always got people's attention.

News of a dead child always kept it.

Not that they knew . . . not for sure, anyway.

Magda led him around to the other side of what was left of the shack, where a small group of officers was busy taking pictures, jotting down notes, and looking generally distressed. He got it because he felt the same; it was hot as hell without standing next to the remains of a fire, and the sweat was literally pouring off everyone near the site. But the worst of it—the thing that made his stomach lurch—was the sickly sweet smell that hung in the air. No mistaking the scent of burning muscle, hair, and fat tissue.

"Okay, tell me what I'm looking at," he instructed his subordinate. He didn't have time to try and decipher the twisted mess in front of him.

"Right," she began. "Well, it was a pretty small structure to begin with, and there wasn't much of it standing at the time of the fire. It'd pretty much burned itself out—right down to the concrete slab—by the time the fire department arrived. They gave it a good soaking, and some of their guys are still here, but the consensus from the fire marshal seems to be arson."

"Arson," he repeated to himself.

"Yes, sir. There are signs an accelerant was used, and they've found what they believe to be bits of a gas can that exploded. We've got our people checking with local gas stations to collect security footage. Maybe we'll get lucky and find someone filling up a gas can."

Uh-huh. And maybe he'd win the Powerball.

"Anything from the neighbors?" he asked.

She nodded. "They told us the shack was used for gang activity in the last year or two—which makes sense considering how remote it is, even in an urban area."

"And what makes them think that?" he wondered aloud.

"Cars coming and going at odd hours—sometimes expensive cars. And they . . . uh . . . they reported sometimes hearing screams."

Miguel looked down at the junior officer. "Right. Not that any of them bothered to report it at the time."

Magda grimaced. "No, sir. I'm sure they were afraid of retaliation . . ."

And afraid of ending up in the shack themselves. It must have been one of the spots Santiago used to "encourage" people to do what he wanted them to do or tell him what he wanted to know. Whatever the purpose, something had gotten out of hand this morning—badly enough that someone felt they needed to set fire to the place to cover it up.

"And the body?"

She pointed toward one of the men working in the charred, wet rubble. "That's the skull right there; see it under that sheet of metal? We think that was part of the roof."

Miguel followed Magda's finger as it traced the outline of the corpse for him. This was a grown man for sure. An adult. But who? The medical examiner would have to see what he could do with DNA and possibly dental records—assuming whoever this was had a reason to be in the system.

He turned back to Magda with a sigh. "All right, then, Detective, you were the one who made the call—what makes you think this has some connection to my Marianna Ruíz investigation?"

That's when Magda beckoned him to a spot about six feet away from where they were standing. Another officer was taking, logging, tagging, and securing any items that might be of evidentiary value. Magda had a word with the guy, who nodded, reached into his box of tricks, and produced an evidence baggie just big enough for the tuna salad sandwich his wife usually packed for him.

"What *is* that?" he muttered to himself and squinted.

When Magda held the bag up against the afternoon sky, he had a much better time making out what appeared to be a small swatch of white fabric with tiny pink hearts.

"We think that as it burned, this bit of cloth separated from the rest of the garment and got caught on the breeze before it could be completely incinerated. Then it lodged against the rocks over here."

Miguel pulled the slim notebook out of his jacket pocket and flipped back to the description of Marianna that he'd taken only that morning. The last thing she'd been seen wearing was a pair of pink pants, pink socks, and a white shirt with tiny pink hearts. He spun around again and walked quickly back to the ruins of the shack, circling it as he peered inside . . . looking for something he hoped he wouldn't find.

Marianna had been there. But was she still in there . . . somewhere? Would a child's small, soft bones be consumed more easily than the skeleton of a grown man? He had no idea because, thank God, he'd never had to look for a child's body at the scene of a fire. Until now.

"Please," he muttered under his breath, unsure if he was asking to find something . . . or to *not* find something. Neither was an appealing outcome at this particular time and place. It was out of his hands regardless.

"¡*Jefe!* Here! Here, I've got something . . ." one of the investigators called out excitedly.

Miguel took a deep breath and closed his eyes for just a moment, aware of the fact that this might very well be the last time he walked this earth without a particularly horrific image burned into his memory. One that he would never be able to un-see. Then, he steadied his nerves, exhaled, and turned to face whatever it was that waited for him on the other side.

When he reached the spot where the other man was sifting through debris, he dropped down onto his haunches to get a better look at what—or who—had been discovered. The investigator used a small stick to lift a piece of tin so he could get a look at what was underneath.

After staring for a long moment, he stood up and faced Magda again, a grim expression on his face.

"I'm going to need a pair of gloves."

CHAPTER 28

ISABELLA

Today

Miguel Alvarez does not look happy to see me peering at him through the bars of the gate that secures his patio. Well, the feeling is mutual.

I'm nursing a wicked headache after last night's festivities, and I'd give just about anything to be home in my own bed under the covers.

"Isabella," he says warily. "What can I do for you?"

"I have to talk to you."

"About what?" he asks, his tone mirroring the irritation on his face.

"Are you really going to make me stand out here?" I ask, quirking a brow at him.

Another heavy sigh as he turns the deadbolt and the door swings outward.

"Come in," he says, gesturing toward a pair of shiny wrought-iron rockers on the tiled porch. One for him, one for his wife. What's her name? Hilda. But if the single sedan in the carport is any indication, she doesn't appear to be home at the moment. "All right, Isabella, what's going on?" he asks once we're both seated.

So much for small talk. Fine. He wants to cut to the chase? We'll cut to the chase.

"Yeti."

The single word comes out of my mouth with the kind of reverence you hear from *los locos* who actually *do* believe in Sasquatch, flying saucers, and the Bermuda Triangle.

"What about him?" he asks without batting an eyelash.

I'm relieved that he doesn't insult me by playing dumb. But I'm also pissed that he knows exactly what I'm talking about—and probably has for years now.

"Who *is* he? And how was he involved? And why the hell haven't I ever heard about him before now?"

He starts to rock in his chair, back and forth, back and forth, casting his gaze out to his small, perfectly manicured lawn.

"You know that banana tree was dead when I moved here?" he tells me, gesturing to a very healthy-looking tree with a full bunch of bananas hanging off the stem and a lovely deep purple flower cascading off the bottom. The fruit is still green, but it probably won't be more than a week or two before he starts to see the faint yellow tint appearing, signaling its maturity. "The previous owners even threw me some extra cash to have it removed and replaced with a new one. But I decided to give this one a chance. So, I pruned it down to almost nothing and kept the roots nice and moist. And with a little help from the sun, it came back stronger than ever in record time."

When I came to in the hospital that horrific night, it was Miguel's voice that cut through the fog of pain and drugs. It was his hand that I reached for when I woke up screaming—the only time I allowed another human being to touch me in those first days . . . after. And when drugs finally made it possible for me to sleep uninterrupted by nightmares—I could sense him in the room with me. His strong, paternal presence wrapped around me and comforted me. I rested safe and secure knowing—even in my unconsciousness—that I wasn't alone. *He* wasn't on a barstool somewhere drunk, or in an alley stoned out of his mind. *He* was the one who showed up—not in his capacity as a detective, but as a father to a girl the same age as me.

But we don't talk about that time, or its aftermath. At least, not openly. This little banana story is a metaphor—or is it an analogy?—for me. For my life. He's reminding me that I was once nearly dead, and I, too, came back stronger and healthier. It's sweet. But it's not what I need right now.

"Miguel . . . what about Yeti?" I ask again.

He doesn't miss a beat in his reply, as if the bizarre little banana reverie had never happened. "We have reason to believe the man known as Yeti fled the island shortly after your sister went missing."

Okay, this fits with the info Matéo was able to find.

I blink hard. "And how long have you had this information?"

"A long time."

"How long?" I repeat, needing to know.

"Pretty much since the beginning," he tells me calmly. "Yeti was the last person to see Alberto. He was always a suspect—the enforcer, the one who beat the shit out of him. The last person we know for a fact had access to the baby. Think about it, Isabella, you always knew he existed, you just never put a name to him. For God's sake, you were only five when it happened. And you didn't start this insane quest until you were in your twenties—"

"No. No, no, no. Don't even try that shit on me, Alvarez. You of all people know I have *never* stopped looking for her. And if I never heard the name Yeti, it's because you never mentioned it. All this time I've been led to believe that it was Santiago who was the prime suspect."

"Yeti worked *for* Santiago. He was the one sent out to collect the debt. So, yes, all roads lead back to Santiago. But it was Yeti who most likely *took* Marianna. And what he did with her . . . well, you know as well as I do that we can only speculate."

Actually, that's not quite true anymore. I don't need to speculate on *what* happened to Marianna—only *how* it happened.

"All this time," I mutter. "All this time I could have been trying to figure out what happened to this Yeti guy. Instead, I was looking for a needle in a haystack—because nobody else was interested in helping me find my sister."

He holds up his palms defensively.

"Whoa, whoa, whoa," he protests. "That's not true—and it's not fair. You *know* I've spent the last twenty-something years trying to solve this case. And then I finally had to retire, leaving it unsolved. Not exactly an auspicious end to my career, you know?"

"Yeah, about that," I say, hurling myself through the door he's just opened before he can slam it shut on me. "You retired."

"I did."

"And you didn't tell me."

"No, you're right. I didn't tell you," he agrees flatly.

"Well, what the hell's with that?" I demand.

He blinks a few times before giving me one of his snarky non-answers.

"I'm terribly sorry, I totally forgot I was supposed to report all my life events to you. Should I have alerted you to the fact that my daughter had a baby last summer? Or that the doctor is treating me for gout? Or that my colonoscopy came back clear? Or that—"

I hold up my palms in surrender. He had me at colonoscopy. Yuck!

"Hey, don't be a dick, okay? I mean, let's put aside the fact that it would have been the professional, courteous thing to do—let me know that someone else was taking over the case. But you and me, we've got history, Alvarez. We've been through a lot together . . ."

"No, *you've* been through a lot. I just happened to be there when it happened," he corrects me, not unkindly.

"It was more than that, and you know it," I counter, my voice coming out in a low, husky whisper, as if I'm afraid someone might overhear.

"I appreciate that you feel that way—"

"No!" I say, now speaking too loudly. I readjust my volume before trying again. "No. I'm not gonna let you pretend we don't have a . . . a relationship—that you didn't go out of your way to look out for me my *entire* life. Like when I got busted for vandalism and you got the charges dropped. Or when I needed someone to stand next to me at my wedding. Or . . . you know . . . through that whole ordeal . . ." A huge lump in my throat is starting to make it difficult to speak— my voice growing more brittle with every word. "So, yeah, Miguel, I won't lie. It hurt me a lot that you left and didn't even bother to tell me you were going."

Oh, hell. The tears have started. I *hate* the tears. I work so hard *not* to have the tears, and this is like the second time today they've made an appearance. That maybe-sister of mine is starting to rub off on me with all her "feels." Alvarez considers me and then sighs deeply before getting to his feet and pulling me to him in an embrace. Instinctively, I wrap both arms around his waist and I hold on tight.

"You're right, Isabella," I hear him say softly from above my head. "I do care for you very much. I always have—ever since you were a little girl. Ever since Marianna went missing. It's like she was gone, but you were the one who was lost. Right there, in the middle of all those people and no one could see you, except for me. I swear you stole a piece of my heart right then and there."

"Yeah, well, I'm good at that—stealing things, I mean," I mutter into his gut.

He chuckles. "I don't know about that. The three times you got hauled in for shoplifting would suggest otherwise." He pauses, and when he speaks again, his tone is somber and sincere. "But listen to me, no one is giving up on Marianna. I may be retired but David Raña is there, and he'll help you now."

I look up at him incredulously, stepping out of his embrace as I do.

"And why the hell should I believe that?" I demand, the shared intimacy of just a moment ago chilling considerably. "I never laid eyes on the guy until the other day when I just stumbled into him. He never once bothered to reach out after he took over for you. What kind of cold case expert is he, anyway, if he doesn't even interview the family, huh? Sorry, Alvarez, but I don't see anything there *to* trust. Raña's just another asshole who couldn't give a shit about me or my sister."

He sits back down in his rocker hard and when he speaks again, there's an edge to his voice that wasn't there before.

"Look, Isabella, David Raña may not be as warm and fuzzy as I am—"

"Pfft." I interrupt him with a snort/scoff combo and get a warning eyebrow raise.

"*But*," he continues, intentionally stressing the word, "I hand-picked him as my successor. When it comes to these cases, Raña is like a dog with a bone. It doesn't matter how long it's been—how cold the trail has gone—once he's picked up a file, he will not rest until it's closed . . . one way or another. You know, he's not a cold case detective. That's not his official title, anyway. It's just something he does after-hours when he's not working on current cases. I've never seen someone so devoted to giving families closure. So, no, he's not going to win any congeniality awards anytime soon. But he's the detective—the *only* detective—I would entrust your case to."

Funny how his intense defense of Raña has totally sucked the air out of my intense offense of him. I want to dispute his assessment, but I know anything else I say about the man now is only going to make me sound like a sullen teenager.

"I should have heard about all of this from you," I say instead, but it still makes me sound like a sullen teenager. "You should have told me about Yeti when you knew about him."

"How did you find out, anyway?" Alvarez asks.

"El Viejo."

He looks impressed now. "That's smart. If ever there was anyone with institutional memory about La Perla, it's him. But, Isabella, listen to me. I didn't see any point in discussing Yeti with you. He was gone. And you were finally getting on with your life. You and Matéo—who is an exceptional man, by the way. You needed to move forward. You couldn't keep living in the past . . . in the shadow of tragedy."

I shrug and shake my head, unable to tell him he's wrong and unwilling to admit to him that he's right.

"What's going on with the art?" he asks when I don't comment on his comment.

I shrug and look down at my hands in my lap. "Not much."

"What happened to that residency you were offered in Detroit? The one working for the Urban Housing Coalition?"

"It wasn't right for me," I tell him.

"Really? Why's that? Because it seems to me you thought it was right up your alley when you applied . . ."

"I . . . I thought I'd like it. But then when they offered, I realized . . . Michigan is so far . . . too far."

He sighs deeply from next to me, then sits back in his chair and rocks for a good thirty seconds before finally responding.

"Isabella, you know you don't have to feel afraid—"

"Afraid of what? I am *not* afraid!" I snap back. "I'm just fine and dandy, thank you very much."

"Are you? Sarcasm aside, *are* you fine?" he asks, not rising to the bait. "Maybe you're due for another visit with your doctor. You know, there's no cure for PTSD—it doesn't just go away on its own. Ever. It's something you have to deal with your whole life. You might go years with . . . nothing—not so much as a blip on the radar. And then, one day, you catch a whiff of something that just takes you right back to the moment, as if it were yesterday . . ."

"Right. Well, thanks for that rosy outlook on my future," I grumble at him. "Nice to know you expect me to live shittily-ever-after."

"That is *not* what I mean, and you know it—"

"I don't need help," I interject firmly. We've had this conversation a thousand times over the years. "I've gotten along just fine so far. I don't need to be unpacking all my baggage for some overeducated overachiever who thinks they can fix me."

"I wish you'd just trust me on this. I know what I'm talking about."

"Trust you? Why should I trust you?" I ask, my mood darkening with my frustration. "You hid this whole Yeti thing from me. And then you retired—you like actually left town—without so much as a goodbye!"

"Okay, now, that's enough," he says with enough force to surprise us both. "I didn't move to China, I moved to Yauco—literally right down the road from where your family is! If you'd bothered to call anytime in the last three years, you'd have known. I wasn't going to interrupt your life by showing up and reminding you of all the baggage we share. Not when you had finally reached a point where you could go a week, a month—a year—without calling me to check on Marianna's case. I wanted to leave well enough alone—maybe give you a little peace. So, sue me." The frustration and hurt in his voice are unmistakable.

It's taken a frying pan to the head, but I realize, at last, that he's telling me the truth. He wasn't trying to avoid me. He was trying to avoid bringing all the memories to me.

"I'm sorry, Miguel," I say softly.

He grumbles something vaguely resembling an acceptance. I wait a few more seconds before I try my luck.

"Hey, can I . . . can I ask you something?" I ask tentatively. "Your daughter—it's Miriam, right? Did she have a boy or a girl?"

The smile that fills his grumpy, craggy, serious face is absolutely brilliant. "A little boy," he tells me proudly. "She named him Miguel."

Yeah, that seems right. I smile back at him.

"Congratulations, *Abuelo*."

CHAPTER 29

GABBY

Today

When I answer the door, I find Isabella standing there with a bag of cookies in one hand and a half-gallon of milk in the other.

"A peace offering," she says, holding them up for me to see. "They're not homemade, but like Matéo said, I'm not a cook. Still, you'll notice I did spring for the Pepperidge Farm ones."

As she says this, she waggles her eyebrows up and down.

"Isabella—"

"Listen, Gabby, I know they're not your mom's, but I thought maybe a little something to remind you of her might make a difference in how you're feeling."

"Isabella—" I try again, but she holds up a hand to stop me again.

"Just give me a second. I need to get this all out." I fold my arms across my chest and watch her take a deep breath as if gathering her courage. Then she speaks again. "It's a lot to take in, and I haven't done a great job of giving you the time and space to process it all. And I'm sorry about that. And I'm really sorry about the confusion over Alberto's . . . *status*. May I please come inside?"

I throw the door open so she can walk past me into the living area of the suite. "That's what I've been trying to get you to do, but you wouldn't shut up."

Once she's inside, she drops the cookies and milk on the table and turns to face me. "Listen, I'm sorry, I really had no idea you thought Alberto was dead. And, in all fairness, you didn't ask—you just kind of assumed."

I throw up my hands. "What was I supposed to think? You rarely mention him and, when you do, it's always in the past tense."

Her eyes are glued to mine. "There's a lot of baggage there. More than I can unpack right now. But I promise I'll tell you more about it later. For now, we really need to get on the road."

"What? Where?"

"To Ponce. I was able to get in touch with Beatríz, and she's willing to meet us this afternoon, but we need to get moving if we're going to make it on time. You in?"

Am I? Well, I've come this far . . .

"Depends. Are there any more un-dead relatives I need to know about?"

She shakes her head. "Nope. He's the only one."

"Ugh, fine," I huff in exasperation. Then I grab my purse and sunglasses and start toward the door. Isabella puts the cookies on the counter and is about to stick the milk in the fridge when I stop her. "Hey! That comes with us," I command.

She puts her hands up in surrender, milk jug still looped around her thumb. Her smile a mixture of amusement and relief.

"You got it, boss. Hey, do you mind if we make a stop on the way? It won't take long, I promise."

"Whatever," I reply with overly dramatic indifference, rolling my eyes as I pluck the cookies off the counter.

*   *   *

"You're sure you'll be okay out here for a little while?" she asks me, even as she's got one leg out of the car already. "I promise—we'll get lunch right after this . . ."

"Isabella, I'll be fine," I assure her. "It's a beautiful afternoon; I'll probably take a walk if you think that's okay."

She nods and gets out, only to reappear when she opens the back seat and leans in to grab a small cardboard box off the floor behind her seat. It's stuffed with favors and mementos from Olivia's *quinceañera*. She's meant to deliver them to her grandmother here at the nursing home where she resides. Once Isabella is gone inside, I start to wander around the side of the building, where there are a number of trees laden with heavy, hanging fruit. Mangos! I pick one easily and bring it to my nose for a sniff. Oh, yes. Most definitely mango. Its skin is still warm from the sun when I slip it into my bag.

As I come around the back of the property, I stop dead in my tracks, staring at one of the most beautiful gardens I've ever seen—bursting with hibiscus, birds-of-paradise, and a number of equally gorgeous species I don't recognize. They blaze in shades of red, orange, pink, and yellow, nestled against a backdrop of waxy green leaves—some variegated, some dappled. It's like watching the sun set against the horizon of the ocean, and it takes my breath away.

But the most impressive thing about this botanical wonder? It's not even real.

I'm standing in awe of a work that has been masterfully painted on the canvas of a high concrete wall surrounding the retirement home.

"Well, hello, beautiful!" I murmur, putting a single palm on the hard surface, warm from the afternoon sun.

Now, at second look, there's something about this faux flora that feels familiar. The color choice, design, and character of the images all bring to mind the mural we saw in La Perla—the one with the Mona Lisa draped in the Puerto

Rican flag. And now that I've made this connection mentally, there's no unlinking the two pieces in my mind—no mistaking this artist's distinctive mix of realism and whimsy.

I turn around and consider the windows that face this direction. It must have certainly been an improvement over the previous view—a plain concrete wall. Not much to find inspirational or stimulating there. No, this was created specifically for the enjoyment of the residents of the nursing home. And it's something very special.

In fact, this entire place is something special. *Hogar Nuestra Señora de la Paz*—which, Google tells me, translates to *Our Lady of Peace Home*—is painted in a sunny shade of yellow, with crisp white trim around the windows, doors, and ironwork. A long terra-cotta patio runs the entire rear width of the building, a broad portico providing protection from the sun and occasional rain. Beyond that lies a lush carpet of Bermuda grass, dotted with four-top tables under big canvas umbrellas, and a wide paved path allowing for easy navigation either on foot, or with a wheelchair or walker.

Only one of the tables is in use at the moment—a quartet of men laughing and talking as they shuffle a mass of dominoes in concentric circles between them. There's a bucket of iced beer next to them and a small radio is playing a tune with a wailing brass line and thumping bass. Looks to me like life is pretty good here at Our Lady of Peace.

When one of them, a thin Black man in a baseball cap, notices me noticing them, he waves me over.

"*¡Ven, ven, señorita!*" he calls out.

I point to myself with a questioning expression which is, of course, ridiculous. I'm the only *señorita* in sight at the moment. But he nods, beckoning me toward their table with a broad smile.

"*No hablo español*," I blurt before anyone can ask me anything I don't understand.

"*¿Hablas inglés?*" asks another gentleman, this one bald with a neatly trimmed, white goatee.

Okay, that much I understand. So far, so good.

"*Sí,*" I agree. "Yes, I speak English."

"What your name?" the Black man asks in slow, halting English.

"Gabriella," I tell him, deciding that my full name would probably be one that's more familiar to them.

They all nod, as if I've just revealed some great, universal truth.

"I Enrique," he explains, tapping his own chest. Then he points to his goateed friend. "He is Juan." After that, he adds Jaime and Renaldo to their merry little band.

"*¡Mucho gusto!*" I say, feeling brave all of a sudden.

They all grin and nod approvingly at my ability to say I'm pleased to meet them. Okay . . . maybe I'm going to be better at this Spanish stuff than I thought! Is it possible I have an aptitude for languages that I never knew about?

Jaime gestures toward me as he says something to Enrique who, in turn, tries to translate.

"Emm . . . from where you come?"

Ooh! I know this! I was studying some verbs on my phone last night, and this was actually one of the practice conversation questions.

"*Soy de Nueva York,*" I declare proudly.

This effort wins me a round of applause from my new friends.

"*Hace mucho frío en Nueva York, ¿no?*" he asks slowly and deliberately so I can catch the words.

Frío is cold . . . and New York . . .

He's asking me if it's cold in New York. Oh, I have *so* got this.

"*Sí, hace frío en Nueva York.*"

Again, with the smiles and the nods of approval.

Hah! Wait till Isabella hears me in action! Or *acción* as we say *en español!*

Emboldened by my linguistical success, I wade out a little further into the weather conversation. Just as *frío* means cold, I know *caliente* means hot. So, digging deep, I assemble something vaguely resembling a coherent statement.

"En Puerto Rico, estoy muy caliente."

I'm so proud of myself that I can't hold back the grin that runs from ear to ear. Seriously—how good am I? Not only have I confirmed that it is, indeed, cold in New York, but I've also managed to convey that I, personally, find it hot here in Puerto Rico. *Go me!*

Except, when I look around at the four faces, they seem to be perplexed. No, more than that—shocked. I feel my smile falter. What the hell? I've somehow managed to scandalize four senior citizens with my atmospheric declaration. Maybe they're hard of hearing? It looks like Enrique might be sporting a tiny hearing aid, so I try again.

"Estoy muy caliente," I repeat.

Same bewildered response, except now they're muttering among themselves.

"Nosotros somos muy viejos . . ." Jaime says, pointing to the group of them. Then he tries to translate his point. "Emm . . . we old. You . . . young."

They're too old? For what? I'm about to try and sort this out when I hear Isabella behind me.

"There you are! I've been looking all over for you . . ." Her voice trails off when she catches the expressions on my new friends' faces. "What happened?" she asks me in a lowered voice. "Why are they looking at you like that?"

"I don't know!" I hiss under my breath. "First they told me it was cold in New York. I agreed. Then I told them that I've been hot here in Puerto Rico, and I got . . . that . . . look," I explain, gesturing in their general direction. "Then one of them told me they're too old."

Isabella frowns.

"Too old for what?"

"I have no idea!"

She lets out an exasperated sigh.

"Okay, what, *exactly,* did you say?"

"I said, 'I'm hot here in Puerto Rico.'"

Isabella rolls her eyes. "In *Spanish*, please."

"Oh, right, sorry! All I said was *Estoy muy caliente,*" I explain.

She's quiet for a moment, and I think she's probably as confused by their reaction as I am. But an instant later, she throws back her head and laughs. And laughs. And laughs until she's bent over, holding her sides.

"What?" I demand indignantly, sensing this is at my expense. "What *is* it? What did I do?"

When she can finally stop cackling long enough to breathe, she looks at me glowering down at her and starts all over again. Finally, I throw up my hands and stomp away, back to the sanctuary of my concrete wall garden.

"Hey, Gabby," she says, joining me after a minute, her voice hoarse from the laughter. "Hey, don't be pissed. You just . . . you got your 'hots' wrong, that's all," she explains.

I cross my arms in front of my chest and glare.

"Yeah, and what's so funny about that? Like they couldn't figure out what I was trying to say? I mean, *caliente* is *caliente*, right? And we'd just been talking about the weather in New York . . ."

She's shaking her head. "No, *caliente* is an adjective, and you use it when you're talking about *things*—like hot food or hot coffee. When you're talking temperature, you say *calor,* which is a noun. In that instance, you're talking about heat. So what you *should* have said was *tengo calor*—literally, 'I have heat.' That being said . . . *caliente* has an alternate meaning."

"Okay . . . so what do they *think* I said?"

"Oh, no thinking about it," she blurts with a snort. "There was no mistaking what you said to them."

"For God's sake, Isabella—"

The headache is starting to amplify again, and I'm in no mood to play word games with her.

Her palms go up in surrender. "Okay, okay, okay, I'm sorry. You said"—she has to fight back a snicker before finally managing to choke out the sentence—"you—you told them you're *horny*. Very horny, to be specific."

I stare at her, trying to process this. I'm about to call bullshit, but when I glance toward the four men at the table, I decide to keep my mouth shut. Renaldo is wiggling his eyebrows up and down at me and tilting his head slightly in the direction of the main house. I guess he's rethinking the whole "too old" thing.

Nope. She's not bullshitting. I just came on to a table of octogenarians. I pull a facepalm.

"Oh . . . oh, God, I'm so embarrassed!" Then to Isabella, "How do I say that? Is it *estoy embarazada*?" I guess.

"What? No! No, no!" She's holding up her palms again, shaking them. "Don't say that—that means you're *pregnant*!"

I gape at her. Horny. And pregnant.

In less time than it takes me to blink, we're both howling, tears streaming down our cheeks. At one point, I have to cross my ankles and hop up and down to keep from wetting myself. I'm not sure how long we do this for—it must be for some time, because I'm actually getting a stitch in my side. But then something strange happens. I sense someone watching me—but it's not the men. I straighten up, wiping my damp face with the backs of my hands, and turn toward the source of my unease.

The old woman is small and slightly hunched. A long silver braid hangs down her back, and she's wearing a housecoat with tiny red cherries on it; there are slippers on her feet. When our eyes meet, her face—bronzed by the sun and weathered by time—fills with emotion. Literally expands with a depth of feelings that come off her small frame in waves. Before I can think to move, she's hurled herself at me, pulling me to her chest with a force that's surely impossible in a woman of her age and stature. Except, it's not. Not right here, right now, anyway.

"*¡Rosaria! ¡Ay, mija, Rosaria! Mi amor, has vuelto a mí . . .*"

She is weeping as she runs her hand over my hair and face again and again.

"Abuelita! That's not Rosaria!" Isabella is saying as she tries to pry the surprisingly strong grip from my head.

When, at last, she's successful, the woman, still crying, reaches up and puts a warm, soft hand on each cheek, holding my face in her hands and murmuring softly as she does.

"*Rosaria, mija . . . Rosaria . . .*"

I shoot a side glance at Isabella.

"Who's Rosaria?" I whisper, afraid if I speak too loudly, I'll agitate the woman further.

Isabella, who's been splitting her dumbfounded stare between the two of us, looks me in the eyes and replies flatly.

"She's your mother."

CHAPTER 30

ISABELLA

Today

Watching Gabby at *Plaza las Delicias* is like setting a kid loose in a candy store. Okay, maybe if the kid liked to savor each piece of candy before moving on to the next—because she's definitely not a gobble-it-all-up kinda girl. But she's definitely got that over-the-top excited vibe as we get out of the car, and I set her free to explore. She moves from statue to statue, examining each thoroughly before carefully reading its placard and then examining it once again. By the time she's done there, she's covered pretty much every politician, poet, and composer who is immortalized in this spot.

I suppose this is what she does . . . this is who she is—a fact collector.

I leave her to make a quick trip to the empanada stand across the street, and by the time I return, she's already made her way past the two fountains and crossed the perfectly manicured lawn along a path of mosaic tiles. I take a seat on a nearby bench and watch her at *Parque de Bomba*. With its vivid black-and-red-striped exterior, the old two-story fire station is featured on many a postcard and in glossy-paged guidebooks. Over the years, it's been converted into a museum of firefighting, complete with an old-time truck on display right at the front entrance. I consider walking over to take the pictures for her, but a glance at my watch reminds me that Beatríz will be here any minute. I wave her over.

"Wow, what a lovely little town!" Gabby exclaims when she finally joins me. "Ponce," she murmurs to herself, allowing the name to roll around on her tongue.

"Here," I say, handing her a small, oil-stained paper bag. Her nose twitches and her brows go up.

"Ohhh, what's this? It smells yummy!"

"Lunch."

She reaches in and gingerly pulls out a small, savory meat pie. Once she's got it in her hand, she seems to recognize it.

"Oh! Are these empanadas? I've read about these!"

I look at her in amazement.

"Seriously? Gabby, you live in New York City—you can get any food you want. You telling me you haven't had an empanada before? Like in your whole life?" I ask incredulously—and with a little more edge in my voice than I'd intended. It's reflected back in her startled expression. "I'm sorry," I offer quickly. "I didn't mean to snap at you—and over something so stupid. I guess I'm still a little rattled about what happened. Back at the nursing home with my *abuela*? I haven't seen her get that emotional in a long time. She was so . . . overjoyed . . . to see you."

When she nudges her shoulder against mine, I know I've been forgiven.

"Yeah, that was a little . . . intense," she admits softly.

"I appreciate you being so kind with her—so gentle," I offer. She could have pulled away or corrected the old woman. Instead, Gabby just smiled as my *abuela* stroked her face adoringly again and again.

She shrugs. "Well, *she* certainly seems to think I'm related to you."

I nod. "Yes, she does."

We leave it like that—neither of us disclosing our own thoughts on the matter. My opinion hasn't wavered. Not a single bit. Just the opposite, in fact. My grandmother's reaction was further proof in my mind. But as to what Gabby is thinking and feeling about all of this . . . she hasn't really said. And I haven't really asked.

"Well," she begins now, holding up her partially eaten empanada, "I promise you I'll never pass up one of these again. They're so good!"

I chuckle when a little juice from the ground beef drips down her chin. I'm just handing her a napkin when I spot the woman we've been waiting for coming toward us. She's a bit older, for sure, but still the dark auburn beauty who owned El Gallo Rojo until just about twenty-five years ago. She recognizes me the moment our eyes meet.

"*¿Isabella?*" she calls out when she spots me, stopping to put her hands on her hips and cock her head to the side. "*¿Isabellita Ruíz? Eres tú?*"

"*Sí, Señora Rodriguez, soy Isabella,*" I respond, confirming that it's me.

"*¡Ay, qué hermosa eres!*" she murmurs when she finally reaches me.

I thank her for the compliment, though I don't feel especially beautiful. Not today . . . not for some time now. And seeing Beatríz brings a pang to my gut that I hadn't anticipated. Something wistful about the past.

"*Gracias, Señora,*" I reply.

At Gabby's request, I keep up with her alias, introducing her as my friend Lucy from New York. Still, I watch the older woman's face carefully, looking for the slightest sign she might recognize her as Marianna. But I don't catch so much as a flicker. Clearly, she has no idea who Gabby may or may not be.

God, am I really the only person who could spot those eyes a mile away?

"I am so happy to see you!" she begins, switching to perfect English for my companion's sake. "How have you been?

I heard you married Matéo Salazar—such a nice young man. I always knew he'd get his act together and do something good."

She is, of course, referring to my husband's formative years when he got in with a bad crowd. It wasn't a gang so much as a group of bored, rowdy teenagers with way too much time on their hands.

"Yes, it's been about eight years now. And he's doing an amazing job with the kids. I'm very proud of him."

As Beatríz beams at me, I'm struck by the fact that, twenty-five years ago, she would have been close to the same age I am now. For some reason, I hadn't made this connection until right now, and now I'm looking at her—and myself—differently.

She *was* me. I could have been her.

Not really, of course—our life experiences were so different. Still, I can look back at her as she was then and, knowing what I know now, imagine what it had been like for her.

She must sense my internal contemplation, because she's looking at me a little too closely now, her eyes narrowed slightly, and her head tilted to one side quizzically.

"*Dime*," she says softly. "Tell me—what is it that I can do for you?"

I haven't given this much thought—how to approach her, figuring I'd know what to do when the time came. But here it is, and here I am, and now I'm not so certain.

"I . . . uh . . ." When I pause, she puts a hand on my leg.

"What is it, Isabellita?"

"Marianna," I say at last. The name comes out as a whisper. Beatríz nods slowly. "Okay . . . what about her, my love?"

I take a quick, deep breath and rip the Band-Aid off.

"I'm wondering about that day—the day she disappeared. You were there that day . . ."

"*Sí*," she agrees. "Yes, I found your father sobbing and yelling in the alley behind the bar that morning."

"Beatríz, I need to know what happened to her . . . and I think you can help me with that."

Her expression is totally neutral as she considers what I've just said. "*Mija*," she replies at last, "why do you concern yourself with things that happened so long ago?"

"It's me," Gabby pipes up, redirecting some of this awkward, intense conversation her way. "I'm researching a story about that day."

Beatríz clucks her tongue and shakes her head. "A story? Like for television?"

"No . . ." Gabby starts, then stops herself. "I mean, maybe . . . I don't really know yet."

Now the other woman gives Gabby the side-eye before bringing her attention back to me.

"*¿Confías en esta chica?*"

She asks the question in Spanish with a not-so-subtle tip of her head in my companion's direction.

"Yes," I reply in English. "Yes, I do trust her."

If Beatríz is embarrassed for asking, she doesn't show it. Just the opposite, in fact, she doubles down. "Hmm. And who do you work for?" she asks Gabby.

"I'm a freelance writer," she explains. "Isabella and I met . . . online . . . through a website. And I offered to help her track down some answers about what happened that day. I'm kind of good at that—finding the answers to things."

"Oh, yes?" Beatríz's tone has definitely taken a turn for the frostier. "And what story will you tell?" she wants to know. "Will you be like those other jackals who sniffed around La Perla for years, writing about what a dangerous place it was? Like the ones who nearly killed off all the business down there when the *turistas* were afraid to come? When everyone thought babies were being snatched right off the street?"

Clearly, Beatríz was one of the owners whose businesses suffered post-Marianna—during that brief period when my sister's disappearance made national news.

"I'll tell the story that Isabella and I agree on," Gabby replies calmly. "It is not my intention to exploit anyone."

I don't know why this comes as a surprise to me. We haven't really discussed in any detail exactly what she would write. And, while I didn't expect her to go full-on tabloid sensationalism with the story, I'm not sure I expected her deference to my feelings, either. At the end of the day, I don't give a damn about the story. I only want her. I only want Marianna.

"Hmm," Beatríz repeats, as if she's not convinced. Still, she continues. "What do you want to know?"

"I was hoping you'd tell us a little about Santiago . . ." Gabby begins, testing the waters.

"Yes? What about him?" she asks guardedly.

"You were together a long time."

Beatríz nods. "Yes, many years."

"When did you leave La Perla to move here to Ponce?"

The older woman seems to consider this. "Oh . . . pfft . . . perhaps twenty years ago?"

"Can I ask why? You had a thriving business there."

"I wanted to be closer to my daughter and her family. And, yes, El Gallo Rojo was doing very well, which is why I was able to get such a handsome price for it. Then we came here and bought some commercial properties—office buildings, a medical complex, that sort of thing."

"Wow, that must have been quite a change," I can't help but comment. "After all those years behind the bar, always interacting with other people. Did you miss it?"

Her face softens when she looks at me.

"No, *mija*. I wasn't sorry to be done with that part of my life. Too much history. I saw too many things. This way was better."

"And . . . Santiago didn't mind?" Gabby asks. "From what I've heard, he was very . . . active . . . in the area at that time."

"You can say it," Beatríz replies bluntly. "I know who he

was—what he was. Isabellita, you must remember when the police raided La Perla?"

"A little," I admit. "I was pretty young. I remember people talking about someone going on television and taunting the police . . ."

"*¡Ay, esos cabrones!*" she spits out in Spanish. Then, just to cover her bases in English, "Those little shits bragging to a television crew that the police had no authority there . . . that they could sell drugs openly, to anyone. *Idiotas* . . ." She shakes her head as if it happened yesterday rather than over two decades ago.

"That affected your business?" Gabby inquires.

She shrugs. "It affected Santiago's business, and *that* affected my business."

"Because people stopped coming?" Gabby follows up.

"No, because when Santiago was unhappy, everyone was unhappy."

The sentence hangs there between us. Beatríz has just "opened the door" to a very sticky subject.

"He was a dangerous man," I note quietly. No question mark there—just a statement of fact.

"He was," she agrees without argument.

"Did that . . . you know . . . did that bother you, Beatríz? Like you said, you saw a lot. You must have heard a lot over the years, too."

She nods curtly at my observance. "*Claro.* Of course."

"How do you love a man like that?"

The question could have been offensive, but the way Gabby couches it makes her sound genuinely interested—genuinely curious to know how their relationship worked.

Beatríz raises a hand and waves it, as if she's shooing a gnat.

"You young girls," she says with a sour expression. "You think you have forever. You think you will be young, and pretty, and sexy for your whole life. So, you waste half your lives waiting for your *¿cómo se dice Príncipe Azul?*"

She turns to me for a translation.

"Prince Charming," I provide.

"*¡Ah, sí, sí!* Yes, you wait for your Prince Charming to come along—that perfect man . . . so handsome, so brave. But there is no such man. *No* man is perfect. Not Santiago, not Alberto, not your Matéo, Isabella. No man. So, you have to decide how much imperfection you are willing to live with."

I let out a long stream of air that's been slowly collecting in my lungs—the result of gradually holding my breath over the course of several minutes. I can't decide who's more deluded here—Beatríz for believing Santiago was an "imperfect" man, or me for not wanting to call her out on it. In the end, it doesn't matter, because Gabby takes the matter into her own hands . . . and it's spectacular.

"I'm sorry, but . . . *imperfection?* Seriously?" Gabby demands incredulously. "That man ran an entire crime syndicate! He controlled the drug trade in La Perla and ran a loan shark operation. He ordered Yeti to beat the shit out of Alberto, which was—incidentally—the last time anyone saw that baby alive! Near as I can tell, Santiago was a violent gangbanger drug overlord at best, a cold-blooded baby-killer at worst! So, yeah, I think I'll take my chances waiting for Prince Charming, thank you very much—because I'm not willing to live with quite as much imperfection as you are, Beatríz."

Holy. Shit.

Did geeky, academic little Sherlock just bitch-slap big, bad Beatríz Rodriguez? I didn't see that one coming! And, apparently, neither did Gabby herself, judging by the speed with which the blood is draining from her face. Not that I can blame her—considering the *mal de ojo* she's getting from

Beatríz at this moment. Still, I'm proud of her for what was a gutsy, if stupid, move, as she's about to find out.

"*Oye,*" Beatríz hisses in Spanish, then remembers to switch back to English so Gabby will understand every word she spews. "Listen, there will come a time when you look back on your life and you see things may not have turned out the way you wanted them to . . . but they've turned out the way they were meant to."

"I don't know what that has to do with anything—" Gabby tries to break in, but gets cut off by a menacing index finger way too close to her face.

"It means that I loved a very complicated man. A good man who didn't realize he was a good man. But that's what I did for thirty years. I reminded him. I helped him to see the difference between right . . . and wrong. And let me tell you," she continues, poking the air with the finger for emphasis as she delivers each word. "Back then, down there—it wasn't always so clear who was good and who was bad. Not that it matters—sometimes good people do bad things. And sometimes bad people do good things." I'm not prepared for the moment she twists so she—and that finger—are facing me. "Isn't that right, *Isabella?*"

I gape, unable to do anything other than nod dumbly. On the other side of Beatríz, Gabby's forehead is creased with confusion. She has no idea what this woman is talking about. But I do. And in the span of a few seconds, she's confirmed a suspicion I've held for a decade and a half.

Within twenty-four hours of my attack, police were called to a gruesome scene at a seedy little hotel on the outskirts of the San Juan tourist district. It was a favorite spot for the spring break crowd, and the police were always there for something or other. But on this particular morning, housekeeping staff walked in to find two men in their early twenties—one blond and one redhead—dead in their hotel room. It appeared to have been a drug deal gone wrong.

But was it?

That's what the papers reported and the conclusion the police came to. But it felt off to me—the security cameras had gone offline during the night, and there was no video surveillance available. There were plenty of interviews, but no arrests were ever made in the case, and it eventually just faded away, despite the protests of the victims' families. In the end, no one was ever charged.

The day it happened, Alvarez came to the hospital with a photo lineup for me to look at and, with a shaking hand, I'd pointed out the two men who had attacked me. He had nodded, folded the photocopied images, and stepped out to make a phone call in the hallway. Next thing I knew, it was over. There was no one for me to press charges against. Case closed. No trial. No testimony. And, while I was relieved, something about it all never sat right with me. Those guys had been savagely beaten and then shot, execution style—a familiar signature for the Savage Soldiers. But even if the two had tried to stiff one of the gang's dealers, that level of violence was usually reserved for rival gangs and honor killings. Not for a couple of rapists on holiday from America's Heartland. Which always made me wonder.

Was it just an incredible stroke of coincidence that Santiago's crew had a fatal run-in with the two guys who just happened to have attacked me? Or did someone tip someone else off—maybe make a case for "sending a message" to the *turistas* about messing with the locals? And, if that were the case, then who?

Because no one knew exactly what had happened to me, or who exactly had done it. Except for me. And Miguel.

Of course, this had all been just speculation on my part . . . until now, when I'm sitting across from Santiago's longtime lover. Beatríz has been watching the past unfold across my face, patiently waiting for me to get to the end of the story. She nods now, as if recognizing my understanding.

"Listen, *mija*," she says, taking my hand. "All I'm saying is that nothing is ever black and white. Not for you, not for me, not for Santiago."

I look at Beatríz for what feels like a very long time, remembering all the times she made sure there was a hot meal waiting for me at El Gallo Rojo, all the times she slipped me a little cash to buy a new pair of shoes, or school supplies, or to put some food in the refrigerator. I remember and, in my mind's eye, I can see what must have happened on that day—that *other* day, twenty-five years ago.

"Did he order Yeti to take my sister?" I ask quietly, directly.

The woman sitting next to me sighs. It's a long and resigned sigh—the sigh of a woman who's seen too much and can only now, in retrospect, begin to make sense of it all.

"No," she says softly. "No, Santiago did not tell Yeti to take Marianna . . . Yeti did that all on his own. And then he brought her to Santiago, expecting he'd . . . I don't know . . . do *something* with her. But my Santiago never once touched that child. I know this for a fact because I was there that morning. I saw her. And I saw him."

I catch sight of Gabby's expression over Beatríz's shoulder, and there I recognize the same conflicting emotions that are playing out in my own head and heart right now. At last, we are finally able to place the baby in Yeti's hands . . . and in Santiago's home. But we're missing something.

"Beatríz, if what you're saying is true—if Santiago never planned on taking Marianna in the first place, and it was just something that this Yeti guy did on the spur of the moment—then why wasn't she just returned home? Or left somewhere she'd have been discovered? It makes no sense."

Something sad crosses the older woman's features.

"Oh, Isabellita, I wish it had been so easy," she tells me ruefully. "You have to understand—Santiago was a very powerful man. And men at that level, in that business, have a target on their back at all times. So, it was *crucial* he be respected by everyone—either out of loyalty or out of fear. In that world, a man who is not respected is a weak man. And a weak man is a dead man. If he showed the least bit of leniency, it would have been perceived as weakness. Yeti forced Santiago's hand by taking the child and put him in an impossible position. So, he did the only thing he could do."

Oh, God.

"So . . . you're saying Yeti took it upon himself to take the baby?" Gabby clarifies, her tone dripping with incredulity. "That he showed up with her as a sort of what . . . an offering to his boss? And Santiago—who you say would never hurt a child himself—instead ordered Yeti to do it? Are you seriously saying that he had to *kill* Marianna instead of just admitting there had been a mistake?"

Somewhere in that assessment, Gabby DiMarco has lost sight of the fact that she may very well be Marianna Ruíz. That, in the end, the baby wasn't killed. She survived—*thrived*, in fact, in the arms of a loving family nearly three thousand miles away.

Beatríz does not try to defend Santiago anymore. She just looks down at her hands in her lap and shakes her head, clearly recognizing the ridiculousness of this conundrum her man was in—that he put himself in. The obscenity of it, really. Because we all know a good man never would have been in this position in the first place. A good man never would have valued his own reputation over the life of an innocent child. A good man never would have sent a child to her death in order to spare himself a little embarrassment. He could have found another way, and she knows it.

And it's with that thought that everything shifts, and I can see how it must have gone down.

"You tried to talk him out of it," I say. "But he wouldn't listen."

When Beatríz brings her eyes up to meet mine once more,

she looks so much older than she did when she arrived here to meet us not thirty minutes ago. It's all right there on her face—I just couldn't see it before. How she spent what should have been the best, the happiest years of her life struggling to save a man in whom she saw a flicker of goodness—despite every heinous thing he'd ever done.

Beatríz Rodriguez loved Santiago. And she hated herself for it. Part of her *still* hates herself for it.

"I don't know what happened after they left with the baby," she tells us. "Only that I never saw any of them again."

Wait. Wait, wait, wait . . .

"I thought you said Santiago didn't touch the baby," I point out.

She looks confused for a moment. "He—he didn't. He stayed behind with me. Back at the house . . ."

Alarm bells are going off, and red flags are popping up. I close my eyes and concentrate on her words . . .

". . . *after* they *left with the baby.*"

They.

Oh, my God. There was someone else!

"Who?" I demand a little too loudly.

She looks at me, furrowing her brows in confusion.

"Who . . . ?" she echoes, uncomprehending.

"Who was with them?" I say more slowly, but no less emphatically. "With Yeti . . . and Marianna? If Santiago stayed behind with you . . . who was the 'they' you were talking about? Who else was there, Beatríz?"

The expression on her face tells me she's kicking herself for the tiny detail. I half expect her to backpedal and tell us she was mistaken but, amazingly enough, she keeps pedaling forward instead.

"Coquí," she whispers. "It was Coquí."

And just like that, I've got a piece of the puzzle I didn't even know I was missing.

CHAPTER 31

COQUÍ

That Day

Now he was a murderer.

Coquí had always known this day would come, though he never imagined it would be under these circumstances. In his mind—in his fantasies—it had always been that *mamabicho* stepfather of his. And somewhere in the middle of this mess, the realization hit him over the head like one of those anvils that falls from the sky in a cartoon. If he actually *had* killed the cocksucker, his mother would still be alive now. But Coquí hadn't stopped him when he had the chance, and he'd lived with that guilt every moment of every day ever since.

Until this day. Because today he had finally found the courage to stand up to the devil. A different devil, to be sure, but in some ways, a worse devil. He knew as surely as he breathed that if Yeti had walked out of that shack, he would have killed again. And again. And again. Because a man who had no qualms taking the life of an innocent child had no boundaries. There was nothing he wouldn't do, no line he wouldn't cross, to get what he wanted.

What Coquí had never anticipated was the guardian angel who'd been dispatched to aid him. Back at their house, Beatríz had made it clear she did not approve of Santiago's plan—but he never imagined she'd go so far as to thwart them. Showing up at the shack like she did—with a gun in her hand and a gallon of gas in her trunk—was tantamount to Russian roulette as far as he was concerned. There would be no mercy if her lover found out what she'd done . . . what she was doing.

Coquí didn't ask what she'd planned to do had it been Yeti standing there in the middle of the shack, covered in blood when she arrived. He didn't want to know. It was enough that she shook him out of his stupor, having him strip to his boxers so his clothing could be burned along with the wooden chair leg and everything else in that shack that might carry his fingerprints, or a strand of hair, or a droplet of his DNA-laden sweat.

Right now, he was hunched down in the back of the car, below the window line, while Beatríz purchased some supplies for the little girl and some non-bloody clothing for him. The child snuggled comfortably in his arms, cooing and smiling and babbling happily, totally unfazed by the bloody, gory violence of the last hour. Because it had been bloody. And it had been gory. And God knew it had been violent. It was a single misstep—nothing more than a tiny stumble, really—that had tipped the scales in his favor.

Things weren't looking good for him as an enraged Yeti stomped toward him, mouth twisted in that "mad dog" snarl he had. Coquí locked the baby against his body with his left arm, unwilling to put her down, even if it meant fighting one-handed for the duration. Yeti had both hands free, and one of them was holding the only thing close to a weapon.

Coquí saw the determination on Yeti's face as he made what was meant to be his final assault on him and the baby . . . and he braced himself for whatever would come next. Not that he could have ever anticipated what would come next. Yeti's foot landed on a small piece of debris from the collapsed roof— just enough that he wobbled slightly. One instant more, and he'd have simply lifted his foot and placed it back on level ground. And that would have been that. But then something extraordinary happened—time literally stood still. Actually, it was more like it slipped into that frame-by-frame slow motion you could create when watching a DVD.

Whether it was some otherworldly intervention on his behalf, or a simple trick of his own mind, Coquí watched in awe as each second spooled out into a series of milliseconds, giving him ample time to see, and think, and react even as the events were unfolding around him. He saw the moment Yeti stepped on the debris, the mild surprise that registered on his face, and the start of the motion to shift his stance and rebalance himself.

It was just that single frame of time when Yeti was vulnerable, foot too high to touch the ground and too low to step and extend. Coquí knew instinctively that this would be the moment Yeti's grip would be the most slack. As bizarre and surreal as it seemed to him, he didn't waste this tiny sliver of an opportunity questioning what it was or how it had come to be. He simply reached out and plucked the makeshift weapon from his nemesis's grip.

And then he drove the splintered, jagged end of the chair leg right into Yeti's gut with every ounce of strength he had left in him. It sank so far into his flesh that Coquí's knuckles grazed the fabric of Yeti's T-shirt, and it pushed right out the other side of the man's body—effectively goring him. That was when time, sound, and space all flooded back in one deafening *whoosh*, so powerful that Coquí was sent stumbling backwards until he hit the wall and slid to the wood planks below him, baby still pinned to his chest with his left hand.

Once Coquí regained his equilibrium and his senses, his eyes found Yeti on the floor several feet away from him, gurgling and gasping, his head trained upwards toward the sky

210 *Lauren E. Rico*

where the roof had once been. A shaft of sunlight streamed down on him, illuminating the crimson droplets that spluttered from his gaping mouth.

He had no idea how long he sat there like that, watching Yeti die. It wasn't until he heard the sound of the car approaching that he dragged his battered, bloody body up to a standing position and slipped into the shadows along the back wall of the shack. If it had been anyone other than Beatríz . . .

Coquí jumped at the sound of the car door locks popping up. He heard Beatríz open the trunk and then slam it shut before sliding into the front seat and locking the doors behind her. She was careful to face forward as she spoke, just in case someone recognized her and reported back to Santiago that there had been someone in the back of her car. It was unlikely, but the simple precaution outweighed the risk. No sense in all three of them being in Santiago's sights.

"Are you okay?" she asked.

"*Sí*," he replied.

"All right, then. I'm going to take us someplace where you can wash up and change—where you'll be safe."

He didn't reply, even though he knew there was no safe place. Not for him. Not ever again.

CHAPTER 32

ISABELLA

Today

"What are you making for dinner?" I ask Matéo, watching him scurry around the kitchen via FaceTime.

He looks over his shoulder at me before grabbing some adobo from the pantry. "*Carne asada*," he says.

I can almost taste the marinated, grilled strips of steak. Oh, and the way he makes his *arroz* . . .

"You'd better save me some," I warn him with a wagging finger.

He returns to the counter where his phone is propped up so he's facing me again. "You know I always do, baby. I'd planned on you being back for dinner . . ."

"I know. But this Beatríz thing . . . my God, Matéo, this shitshow just keeps getting bigger and bigger."

"Well, I think it's a good idea, the two of you spending the night out there. I'd rather you do that than drive home in the dark. Especially the way *you* drive!"

I wave a dismissive hand at him. "Pfft. You worry too much."

"No, actually, I don't," he informs me. "Now, tell me more about what happened at the nursing home. How did Gabby react to your *abuelita* going all prodigal son on her?"

I consider this for a second before answering him.

"You know, it's weird, Matéo; she didn't really want to talk about it. If it were me? Hell, I'd be asking a million questions, looking at photographs—I'd want to know everything. I'd be looking for that connection."

"Well, you're not Gabby. And remember, she might not *want* to find a connection. We've had this discussion before, Isabella. She might feel that accepting your family means betraying hers. Just let her process it. I'm sure she'll let you know when she's ready to dig deeper. Give her a little time to get there."

This is why I love my husband. He doesn't just talk you off the ledge; he climbs out there with you, takes you by the hand, and leads you back to safety. Then he nails the window shut so you don't climb out there again.

"I know, I know. You're right. I'm just . . . I don't want to wait. I've waited long enough. Now I want it all to happen quickly; to be resolved quickly. I'm just impatient, I guess."

"Who, you? Never!" he quips, his words dripping with sarcasm.

I roll my eyes and shake my head. "Okay, okay. You can stop now, *Señor Smartypants*."

He chuckles, then turns more serious. "So, what's next?"

I sigh heavily, sitting back hard against the driver's seat of my car.

"Well, I'm here in the parking lot of Walmart, waiting for Gabby. She booked us a room at some little place nearby, and she wanted to stop and pick up a few essentials. Of course, her idea of essential is toothpaste, deodorant. I'm thinking more like a cocktail. Or three. Anything in the rum family will do quite nicely, thank you very much. And now that you've mentioned *carne asada*, I'm thinking dinner would be good, too . . ."

He quirks one of his dark eyebrows, and my knees wobble a little. He's so damn sexy when he does that, and he knows it.

"The eyebrow, huh? You're lucky I don't haul ass right back home and jump you right now, mister. It's been that kind of a day . . . I could really stand to work off a little anxiety."

Now he adds a smirk to the brow.

"Dude, you're killing me!" I whine. "Stop being so damn irresistible, will you?"

When he speaks again, his voice is lower—both in pitch and volume. He's doing his best "sexy times" voice.

"Well now, if you'd like to unbutton that blouse a little, I'm sure we could work at least some of it out for you . . ."

But the reaction I have isn't the one he was looking for.

I smirk. "Hah! Have you forgotten the *last* time you wanted to try that?"

Matéo throws up his hands, all pretense of sexy gone now.

"How many times do we have to go through this? You said you had something 'very special' for me, and I should be prepared to 'go all night long.' What was I *supposed* to think?"

"Well—"

"I'll tell you what I was *not* supposed to think," he interrupts, holding up a finger for emphasis, "I was *not* supposed to think that you were going to drag your computer to a place at the dinner table and include me in your crazy-ass family's crazy-ass Christmas Eve celebration!"

I don't even try to hide the chuckle. In fact, I just give up and bow my head down, laughing at the memory of his face when we connected the call.

"Not funny!" he's saying loudly down the line. "So not funny! Your cousins, your aunts—oh, God, your grandmother! They all saw me *naked,* Isabella!"

I force myself to stop laughing long enough to correct him.

"Oh, but you weren't *totally* naked," I remind him, my voice shooting up in pitch as I try to hold back more howls. "You *were* wearing that bow . . ."

"Isabella . . ." he says, warning me to stop.

"And it was so pretty, too—all red and shiny! Abuelita

was so impressed that you could even tie a bow that straight and pretty. Especially on your—"

"Okay, okay, okay! I give up," he says loudly, throwing his hands up in defeat. "Whatever it is, I'll do it! Just please, for the love of all that is holy, do *not* bring that up again! Your cousin has only now *just* stopped sending me screenshots—and it's been three years! God, and that meme . . ."

I pull myself together, still snickering as I wipe the tears from my face.

"Okay, honey, okay. I'm sorry . . . I won't go there again," I promise, even though we both know I will. Multiple times.

"What happens next in your little investigation?" he asks, trying to steer our conversation away from his penis and the fact that my entire family has seen it—literally wrapped up in a bow.

"Ahh . . ." I begin, my voice ragged from the laughter. I'm still wiping the moisture from under my eyes as I consider the question. "Well, I'm not really sure. This Coquí guy adds a whole new layer to this mess. Nobody's mentioned him before."

"Is it possible that Beatríz could be lying? You know, just to protect Santiago? Maybe deflect the attention from him?"

I shrug. "I don't see why . . . I mean, she was honest enough about the kind of man he was. And about how much she was willing to overlook to protect him."

"I'm not sure if that's being loyal, or being an accessory after the fact," he muses.

"A little of both, I suppose."

"And, well, if the baby really was killed . . . then you know Gabby can't be her."

"You'd think, right? But my grandmother sure seems to think Marianna is alive and well and walking around in Gabby DiMarco's body. The only thing I know with any certainty is that we're missing something—something big. And

I feel like every time we move forward in one direction, we step back in another. We're just throwing shit at the wall now to see what sticks."

He shrugs. "Well, that's what detectives do, isn't it? Sure, you chase the facts like your buddy Sherlock there, but you also have to try on different theories for size, don't you? The thing is, it's like you're peeking through a keyhole. You can only see so much—and then you've got to figure out the whole picture based on this tiny little glimpse you've got. And even then, what you're looking at? It might be the critical bit—or it might not."

His analogy makes perfect sense. "You're right. What I really need is someone with the key to the door."

"You could always go back to the new guy on the case— what's his name? Raña? You might be able to get more from him if you go without Gabby."

"Pfft." I shake my head. "I don't know. He's kind of a dick. All uptight and by-the-book."

"You mean like a professional?" Matéo offers with a smirk. "You're just used to the kind of relationship you've had with Alvarez."

When I hear the segue, I jump on it.

"So, about Alvarez . . ." I begin, with a change in tone that indicates I'm done playing and back to being serious.

"Yeah?"

"There's this thing Beatríz said. I don't know. I might have misunderstood . . . but I don't think so. I think she was telling me something . . ."

All traces of kidding leave his face as he sobers up. "Okay. Tell me and I'll help you sort it out."

Yes, he will. He always does.

"She kind of confirmed what I always suspected . . . that Santiago had something to do with . . . you know . . . the deaths of the two guys . . ."

I don't need to go into any more detail; he knows exactly what, where, when, and to whom I'm referring, and he lets out a long, slow breath.

"Really? Are you positive that's what she was telling you? Because we don't know for sure, not really. We've thought maybe so, but it could have been like the police said, it could have just been a drug deal gone bad—"

"No, I'm sure," I say, my voice reflecting my own growing certainty. "That's the only thing she could have been telling me."

"Okay, so what does that have to do with Miguel Alvarez?"

"Well, the way I see it, if what Beatríz said was true . . . then someone would have had to have told Santiago what happened to me. And they'd had to have known who it was that did it . . ."

"Yes," he agrees thoughtfully. "Yes, that's exactly what it would mean. And you think that person was Miguel?"

"I think it has to be. He was the only person who knew."

"Sweetheart, this is a pretty serious accusation. Take a breath and think back for a second. Are you absolutely positive you didn't give those details to anyone at the hospital? Remember, you were sedated a lot of the time. You may not even know half of what you said, or to who."

I shake my head.

"No. Miguel was there when I woke up for the first time. He was the only one I told everything to. He was the one who brought me the pictures to look at—like a lineup—from my hospital bed. I didn't actually know their names until later on. There *was* no one else."

There's a long beat of silence as he takes this in.

"Okay, so . . . if you're right, then that means Detective Miguel Alvarez disclosed confidential information about your assault to a known criminal, who then tracked down the bastards, beat them to a bloody pulp—killing them both in the process—and then set it up to look like a botched drug deal. Have I got that right, Isabella? Because that's a big deal. A very *illegal* big deal. Some people might even say that constitutes murder-for-hire."

His voice is as somber and serious as I've ever heard it. He wants me to think this theory through to the very end. Because it has serious consequences if it ever goes beyond the two of us. Which it won't. Ever.

"Yes, that's what we're saying."

I watch on the tiny screen as he raises his arms above him, clasping his hands behind his neck. Then he lets out a low whistle while shaking his head.

"I don't know if that makes me like him more now . . . or less." He pauses for a moment and then nods more definitively. "More, I think. Yes, definitely more."

I feel the corners of my mouth tip upward into a slight smile.

"I'm not sure what to think," I admit. "God knows I wished them dead. But it's not something I'd have asked him—or anyone—to do for me. But when I think about what it would have been like to go through a trial back then . . ." My voice trails off.

I can't go there. Not now. Maybe not ever.

"You've been dredging up a whole lot of memories lately—most of them bad," Matéo reminds me. "It was just a matter of time before this one surfaced, too. In fact, it wouldn't surprise me if you've got some suppressed mother memories floating around in there, too," he says, tapping his temple with his forefinger.

"Great. More PTSD fun to look forward to," I mutter and roll my eyes.

"You know, you could always go back to that therapist you liked," he reminds me. "What's her name? Dr. Davis? It's been a while. Might be time to make an appointment—you know, just to check in."

"Miguel suggested the same thing."

"Oh, yeah. My opinion of that man is definitely on an upswing."

I spot Gabby coming out of the store, hauling so many bags that she's tripping over them.

"You have got to be kidding me," I mutter to myself.

"What? What's going on?"

"Gabby. I think she just bought out half of Walmart. And not the regular one, either. I'm talking about the Super Walmart."

My husband chuckles. "So much for a few essentials!"

"Right? Ugh. I'd better go help her. Call me before you go to bed?"

He nods. "Absolutely. Hey, Isabella, you want me to sniff around? See if maybe I can find out anything about this Coquí guy?"

I have the overwhelming urge to kiss this man who's been with me long enough to know that I'll take a little down-and-dirty intel over hearts, flowers, and candy any day. Oh, yeah, I *so* married the right guy.

"That . . . would be amazing. Thank you."

"What do you think your next step is?" he asks curiously.

I shrug.

"I don't know. Maybe you're right—maybe I'll go see Detective Raña. I'll talk it over with Gabby and see what she thinks."

"Excellent idea," he agrees. "Okay, then, I'll call you later—"

"*¿Oye, Matéo?*"

"*¿Sí?*"

"*Te quiero.*"

He smiles. Not the sexy smile or the sweet one. Not even the million-dollar smile. It's the one he saves just for me. It's *our* smile. Mine and his.

"I love you too, baby."

*   *   *

"You said it was a 'little place' you found online. *Little* place! I'm thinking it's some motel—maybe a little B and B . . ." I say—again. Because it bears repeating.

Gabby has booked us into one of the most exclusive couples' resorts on the island, *Isla de los Sueños,* Isle of Dreams. And it *is* an isle of dreams—for honeymooners, maybe. Not for two women who hardly know each other. There are flowers everywhere, a bottle of champagne, rose petals on the bed, chocolate-covered strawberries, and a jacuzzi tub for two—complete with an array of "love oils" in assorted, edible flavors.

"Jesus," I mumble, picking up the passionfruit gel for a sniff. "I'm not sure I'd be comfortable bringing Matéo here, and we've been married for more than eight years!"

"We lucked out," she tells me with a grin, laying out her new Walmart purchases on our shared king-sized, four-poster bed. "They had a last-minute cancellation and could take us. I figured room service and a private splash pool were so worth the upgrade."

By upgrade, she means the ridiculous price tag.

I know we agreed she would cover the expenses, but this is insane. A couple of nights at this place run about as much as my mortgage payment. Easily.

"Okay, just so you know, everyone in this place thinks we're a couple," I inform her as I move over to the dresser and pick up the room service menu for a perusal. "I know that's what *I'd* be thinking."

"Here, look at this bathing suit I got you," Gabby says excitedly, ignoring my comment.

When she turns around to face me, she's holding a hot pink bikini, wiggling it from side to side, making it dance on its plastic hanger.

I try to curb the reflex to wince. "Yeah . . . you know, I don't really do bikinis," I explain, trying to sound casual.

She looks puzzled by this statement. "Why on earth not? Isabella, you've got an amazing body!"

I feel myself shrink a little deeper into my jeans and T-shirt.

"What else did you get?" I ask, changing the subject as quickly as possible. I'm grateful when she drops the bikini banter in favor of her other purchases.

She rummages through more bags. "Oh! Look at this—I got us matching pajamas!"

She's holding up two sets of shorts and tanks, both with pink hearts imprinted all over them. They're followed by pink toothbrushes, a pale pink shirt dress for me, and darker pink sundress for her. Even the pack of panties she bought for us to split comes in different shades of pink. Well, she's certainly in touch with her inner fourteen-year-old.

"Where's the remote?" I ask, looking around. "I wouldn't mind watching a little TV . . ."

"Oh, there's no TV," she says. "No Wi-Fi, either. This is one of those 'get away from it all' places."

"What?" I mutter incredulously as my glance swings all the way around the spacious room. She's pulling my leg, right? She must be. All this high-end décor . . . surely there's a hidden flat-screen just waiting to slide out of a dresser or down from the ceiling or something. But no, she's right. Not a Sony, Samsung, or Sanyo to be found. This only solidifies my belief that the people who stay at the *Isla de los Sueños* are only here for one reason. The fact that she's oblivious to this makes me wonder . . .

"Gabby, when was the last time you got laid?"

She stops folding the new panties into teeny, tiny little squares and turns to face me, still holding one in her hands.

"Excuse me?"

"I'm sorry—what I'm getting at is when was the last time you were in a relationship with someone? I mean, you've only mentioned this Max guy—and you don't really know what that is—if anything."

She glances up at me briefly, then returns her attention to the pink panties she's dividing and folding. "There was a guy. It's been a while, though . . . maybe three years? Yeah, three years. Because my mother was sick then. But we were pretty serious."

At last, a glance into who Gabriella DiMarco is and what her life has been like. I pat the bed next to me, hoping she'll stop folding and join me sitting up at the top of the bed, back against the headboard. She does.

"Yeah? What was his name?"

"Joel," she says a little distractedly, as if she's conjuring his image in her mind. "Joel Bradley."

"And what happened to Joel Bradley?"

She gives me a rueful smile. "What happens so often when you leave mid-semester to take care of your dying mother. One of my so-called friends was kind enough to console him in the wake of my devastating absence."

"*¡Ese cabrón, hijo de puta, lambón!*" I hiss loudly. Gabby glances at me, perplexed, so I translate. "Uhhh . . . something like an asshole-son-of-a-bitch-bootlicker. More or less . . ."

Her brows go up, and she nods, impressed. "Can we work on that one later? I'd *really* like to add that to my vocabulary."

I grin. "Yeah, you bet. I'll write it out for you phonetically just to make sure people understand you."

She grins for a second.

"Excellent idea. But, yeah, I've dated plenty of guys—lots of first dates that didn't go anywhere. The occasional relationship that lasted a month or two. I'm just . . . I have a very specific personality, and I'm not everyone's cup of tea, you know? I've resigned myself to the idea that there just may not be anyone out there for me . . . not for anything serious, anyway."

There's something about the way she tells me this—a sadness underneath it all that tells me it bothers her more than she's saying.

"Ah, well, you're not the only one. Matéo says my mood changes so drastically and so quickly that he gets whiplash sometimes."

"I can see that. Maybe just a little . . ." she says with a grin, holding her thumb and forefinger a slight distance apart to indicate a small amount.

I shrug. "Yeah, well, let's just say I've got a lot of baggage—and not all of it Marianna-related. Before I met Matéo, I'd sworn off men. No dates. No sex. Nothing. I shot down every guy who tried. Not because I thought I was too good for them or anything like that . . . but because I was . . . well, I'd been burned before. I just . . . I didn't—I *couldn't* trust anyone."

She shifts a little closer, angling her body slightly so she's facing me.

"So what changed?" she asks. "What made you finally trust Matéo?"

"Um, well, one night I got a call to go and get Alberto . . . my father . . . from El Gallo Rojo. The bartender told me I'd better come get him quick—that he was totally hammered and about to get the shit kicked out of him. When I got there, he was totally out of control—staggering around, yelling and cursing. He wouldn't listen to me . . . or anyone else, for that matter. All I knew was I had to get him out of there before the police—or someone worse—came to get him out *for* me. And . . . as it happened, Matéo was there that night. He saw what was going on, and he stepped in—it was amazing the way he got my father to calm down. Next thing I knew, this guy was helping me get him back to the house. I was nervous, because I didn't know him, you know? I was anxious about letting him inside, but there was no way I could manage on my own.

"He must've just sensed it, because once we got my father to bed, Matéo suggested we sit outside on the front porch—where the neighbors were coming and going all night. Lots of people and nosy *abuelitas* around. The next night, he showed up with dinner—which we ate out front on a card table. The night after that, he showed up with a DVD player and pulled our TV outside so we could watch movies out there. And it went like that all summer long. It's like he made his way into my life one inch at a time. By fall, we were hanging out in the living room, and come Christmas, he'd moved into my bedroom. We were married out there on that porch," I murmur, remembering the beautiful day, the simple, cream-colored dress my grandmother made for me, and Matéo in his suit. Nothing fancy, nothing flashy.

"Wow, that's some story," Gabby murmurs, looking totally enchanted.

"Um, yeah, I guess. Beatríz was right, though. If I'd waited for some rich Prince Charming to sweep me off my feet, I'd still be single. I opted for the average guy. The decent guy."

She looks at me like I'm insane.

"I can't believe you," she says, shaking her head.

"What?" I demand. "What's that supposed to mean?"

She groans in frustration. "Isabella, for such a smart, savvy woman, you can be so dense!" She laughs and knocks her shoulder against mine. "Don't you see?" she says softly. "You *did* hold out for Prince Charming—except, he's even better than the guy in the fairy tales! You never hear about *that* guy cleaning up vomit and turning the front porch into a movie theater, do you? He just rides in on the white horse and lets the servants do all the hard work. Yeah, seems to me Prince Charming is *exactly* who you got, Isabella."

I'd never once thought of it that way, but she's absolutely right. I nudge her shoulder back, and it feels good.

CHAPTER 33

BLANCA

That Day

At first Sister Blanca had been disappointed with her posting at the tiny little church—really no more than a chapel—tucked away on the back streets of Old San Juan. It had neither the history nor the grandeur of the cathedral in the square. Celebrities did not flock there to be married; tourists did not come to light candles and make contributions. Truth be told, very few stopped there at all—mainly just a handful of devoted elderly parishioners and the occasional tourist who wandered in off the street looking for a cool respite on a hot day. There wasn't even a full-time priest assigned here, just one who split his time between this parish and two others farther out on the island.

What *Nuestra Señora de los Milagros*—Our Lady of Miracles—did have was a legend, albeit one that most had forgotten over the decades. The story of the woman who brought her hopeless prayers for a child to the feet of their Blessed Mother statue, only to have her weep. And to have the woman become pregnant against all odds.

Blanca didn't know how she felt about this. The events had never been authenticated by the Church, nor had they been repeated. So, little by little, as the years had passed, fewer and fewer desperate women showed up here looking for a miracle. It had been more than two years when the American woman showed up there that afternoon, dropping to her knees and bowing her head.

Blanca had considered approaching the woman but didn't want to startle her or interrupt her prayers—which looked rather intense. So, she lingered in the background, waiting for an opportune moment to offer her comfort and perhaps guide her in a rosary. Clearly, the woman was suffering, and that had been Blanca's solemn vow as a nun—to help ease the pain of those people whom God brought into her life. And this morning, He had brought her the American . . . and a miracle.

She hadn't been there more than five minutes when Blanca noticed the woman look up into the face of the statue . . . and gasp. Something she saw scared her. Silently, the nun had slipped through a side door only to reappear closer to the altar—where she could get a better view of the Madonna. Which appeared to be . . . weeping.

It was just as the legend had told.

Blanca had always chalked it up to condensation—it was incredibly humid here this time of the year. And she might have done the same on this day, had she not witnessed the actual streaming of the tears. This wasn't beaded precipitate forming and dripping. This was a mother crying in empathy for her heartbroken child. Blanca saw it. She felt it. She knew it to be true. And she dropped to her knees right there on the cold slate floor, head bowed in recognition of what she was witnessing.

She had no idea how long she stayed like that, but when Blanca looked up from her own reverie, the woman was gone. And Mary continued to weep.

Blanca spent the rest of that morning in prayerful, tearful contemplation of the inexplicable events. She had been meant to witness this miracle—of that much she was certain. But to what end? What role was she meant to play in God's plan?

"*Por favor, Señor, muéstrame el camino,*" she recited in her mind over and over again. *Please, Lord, show me the way* . . .

Hours later, she was still kneeling at the altar in prayer when the heavy wooden door flew open and banged against the plaster wall, making her jump. She got to her feet and turned to find Beatríz standing there. They hadn't spoken for many years now. Before Blanca had become the bride of Christ. Before Beatríz had become the whore of Satan.

Blanca still prayed for her, asking the Lord to help her escape the seductive lure of that evil man, Santiago; to find her way back to the Church, and back to their friendship. But it had been years since they'd even laid eyes upon each other—despite the fact El Gallo Rojo was less than a ten-minute walk from the church.

"Blanca, is that you?" Beatríz whispered into the empty sanctuary.

"Yes, it's me," Blanca assured her, moving into the light so she was easier to see.

That's when she noticed the boy with Beatríz. Well, not a boy exactly, but not quite a man yet, either. His dark eyes were huge and haunted, anguish written across his features. Fresh, bright red blood splattered his T-shirt, and he clutched a duffel bag to his chest as if he were carrying his own heart in his hands.

Something told Blanca that was exactly what he was doing. Just as something told her to hold out her own hands and relieve him of his burden.

"*Dámelo,*" she instructed.

But he shook his head slowly. He didn't want to give it to her. Beatríz touched his arm gently and spoke to him softly, as if trying to soothe a skittish woodland creature.

"It's okay," she assured him. "She's a friend. You can trust her."

The statement surprised the nun. Yes, it was true, she could be trusted. But the fact that Beatríz would refer to her as a friend after all this time—after all the hateful things she'd said to Blanca over the years. Putting the thought aside, the nun drew closer—slowly and carefully, until she was close enough to reach out and take his upper arms in her hands. She stared directly into his coal-black eyes and there found the answer to her prayer of only minutes ago. God was illuminating the path she was meant to take.

Clearly, Beatríz had been meant to bring the boy to Blanca. And now it was Blanca's turn to see him on the next leg of his journey—whatever it might be.

"I'm here to help you," she explained gently in Spanish.

The moment the weight of the bag left his own strong hands, it was if a great burden had been lifted from his slim shoulders, as well. The boy wept—wet, shuddering gasps of relief. Beatríz pulled the young man into her arms, patting his back and murmuring comforting words. When Blanca peered into the bag, she nearly dropped it. Her eyes flew up to meet Beatríz's. A moment later, they were all in tears.

CHAPTER 34

GABBY

Today

I lift my leg out of the bubbling hot tub so I can get another look at my toenails and the perfect little pineapple on each of them. They're so adorable that I wonder how I've lived without them for so long.

"They're beautiful," I tell Isabella, who's sitting across from me, a piña colada in one hand. "Really, Isabella—just gorgeous! I've never seen anything like it. You've got a gift!"

She scoffs. "Oh, yeah. I've got *quite* the future ahead of me!" she snarks. "Now that I've nailed the palm trees and the pineapples, I'm moving on to the piña coladas with teeny tiny little umbrellas."

I snort with rum-induced laughter, pointing at her. "Ahh! I see what you did there!" She looks confused. "*Nailed*? You *nailed* the palm trees and the pineapples? And you do nails . . ."

Isabella rolls her eyes and shakes her head while grinning. "Holy *hell*, but you're a goofy drunk!"

"Hey, I am *not* drunk," I protest. "*Maaaybe* a little tipsy . . . but I know a good thing when I see it. And you are a-ma-zing," I declare, stretching the single word out over three syllables. "Did you always want to do nails?"

"Uhhh . . . no," she says slowly. "I went to art school for a while. The nails were just a side hustle when we were saving for the deposit on the house. But when I rented a space in a shop that gets a lot of tourist traffic, it really took off, so it just made sense that it became my main gig."

"Wait, you were an art major? That makes *so* much sense! Oh, of course you were! What do you . . . are you a painter? Sculptor? What?"

"I'm a painter," she replies, looking a little suspicious. "Have you really not figured it out yet?"

Maybe it's the rum, but I have no idea what she's talking about.

"Figured what out? Why are you being so mysterious all of a sudden?"

She shakes her head and offers the hint of a smile. "Give me your phone," she instructs, holding out the palm of her hand.

I pass it to her with a questioning look, which she ignores as she helps herself in pushing, swiping, and pinching until she finds what she's looking for. When she turns it around, so the screen is facing me, I see the mural in La Perla—the Mona Lisa wrapped in the Puerto Rican flag. I reach to take the phone from her, but she shakes her head and holds up her index finger, telling me to wait a second. Then she's back at it again, swiping until she can show me one of the pictures I took of the "wall garden" at the nursing home.

"Oh. My. God." I murmur, totally gobsmacked. "Isabella . . . those were you? *You're* the artist?"

She nods with a faint smile. "Yup. They're mine. Also, some other ones that we didn't walk by. I must have four or five of them down in La Perla now—I was part of an artists' collaborative that went in after the last big hurricane. You saw how bad it is now; can you imagine what it was like before? All the rubble and destruction. That community lost so much. So . . . a bunch of us went in and tried to give back some of the identity they'd lost. Now you see musicians playing live along the boardwalk on the weekends, and little food kiosks have popped up. It's a whole different vibe."

"I can't believe I didn't know this about you," I say, more to myself than to her. But then, why would I know this? We've only known each other for a few days—which is like five minutes, relatively speaking. "But, Isabella, why aren't you doing *that* full-time?"

She gives me a wan smile and shakes her head.

"Nah. I don't really do much painting anymore."

"Why not? I've seen so much street art in New York, and there isn't anything that compares with what you've done . . . everything you create is so vivid and nuanced! You'd think you were working with acrylics on canvas! There *must* be a grant or some arts organization . . . some angel investor looking to support the beautification of the island?"

"You know, I'm just . . . I'm in a different place right now. Maybe later on, but I haven't wanted to paint in a while."

Just as I open my mouth to press for more details, my phone rings in my hand, obscuring one of the mural pictures with Max's face.

"You should answer that," she says, giving me the distinct impression she really wants out of this conversation.

So I swipe and put the phone to my ear.

"What do you want, Max?" I ask coolly.

"Gabby? Oh, thank God you picked up!"

The desperation in his tone makes me set my own drink down on the ledge and sit up a little straighter. I have to force myself to focus through the rum cloud that's settled around my head.

"What is it? What's wrong?"

"It's Lisa," he says. "I was out of the office yesterday, and I left Randy in charge. Big mistake . . ."

I think hard, conjuring my colleague's face in my head. He's a responsible guy. No reason not to leave him in charge.

The only issue he has is with that Lisa. She tends to steamroll him . . .

Uh-ohh . . .

"What did she do?"

"Ah, where to begin? For starters, she took advantage of him—and my absence—to swap out her final copy. Then she lied to the production department, telling them she had editorial approval—which she most certainly did not."

"Oh . . . oh, hell . . ." That's bad. That's really, really bad.

He offers a bitter laugh. "Oh, but wait, there's more— she sent an advance copy to that author—what's his name? Finneran?"

"Finnegan," I offer. "Jake Finnegan. The one we were investigating for plagiarizing other authors?"

"That would be the one. She calls his most recent release a 'frankenbook,' and he's threatening to sue if we allow it onto the newsstands."

"Frankenbook?" I echo incredulously. "She used that word? The word I used at the editorial meeting last week?"

"Yes."

I'm torn between humor and indignation.

"Okay, well, that's not great. She should have chosen her words better. But I suppose if she can prove plagiarism—"

"She can't."

I'm thinking I must have misheard him. Even she could not be *that* arrogant, entitled, and stupid. "Wait, what?"

"She told his people to back off, that it's already been fact-checked."

"Fact-checked by whom? Who did you get in to cover for me when I left?"

Silence.

"You did get someone in to cover for me, didn't you, Max?"

His reply comes in the form of more silence.

"She's claiming you did it—"

"She's *what*?" I exclaim loudly, startling Isabella enough that her hand jerks and her drink sloshes over the rim of the glass and down her arm.

"*¡Hijo de puta!*" she mutters, across from me in the hot tub, but I'm too enraged to comment.

"That's total and utter bullshit! I mean, I don't know—maybe he did plagiarize, but I left before I could get through his backlist. I didn't sign off on anything . . ."

"Which is why we're looking down the barrel of a multimillion-dollar defamation lawsuit. Assuming she's wrong, that is . . ."

He leaves that thought dangling out there. And I realize what it is that he wants—why he was so desperate to get in touch with me.

"No. Absolutely not. No way." The words spill out of my mouth even as I shake my head adamantly.

"Gabby, please . . . I'd be so grateful if you could come back here. I know you're in the middle of something . . ."

"What? What does he want?" Isabella demands in what she mistakenly thinks is a whisper.

"Max, you can't possibly think I'd come back now—"

"What? Oh, hell no!" She's abandoned all pretext of keeping her voice down at this point.

"Who *is* that?" Max asks.

"It's . . ." I pause, not quite sure what to say because I'm not quite sure what the answer to that question is.

Sister? Maybe. Friend? Possibly. Badass? Absolutely.

"It's Isabella Ruíz," I say, bypassing the relationship conundrum altogether.

Before I can say another word, Isabella reaches across the hot tub, plucking the phone right out of my hand, almost dropping it in the water that's bubbling all around us.

"Hey!" I protest, but she waves me away with her tropical-themed manicure.

"Hello? Is this *Maxwell*?" she asks, putting an unnatural emphasis on his name.

Shit! Shit, shit, shit!

"Isabella, give me that phone!" I hiss.

She ignores me.

"Maxwell, this is Isabella Ruíz. You know, the one whose story you want so bad. Listen, dude, what the hell? Maybe you British boys don't know much about us Latina girls, but let me just tell you, unless you're Hugh Grant, nobody's got time to listen to you be all coy and stuttery and shit. We're busy playing detective down here, Maxwell, so take out your own trash and stop bothering her!"

With that, she hits the big, red button that sends him hurtling back out into the ether.

I gawk.

"What did you just do?" I demand, incredulous. "Isabella, what were you thinking? He's my—"

"Boss? No, actually, he's not."

"Yes, but he and I are—"

"Nothing. You're *nothing*. You're not colleagues, you're not friends, and you're sure as hell not lovers," she informs me, smacking my phone against the palm of her hand for emphasis. Then she points it at me and does this thing that I can only describe as a brow lift/half-shrug/eye-roll combo . . . with just a hint of chicken neck for emphasis. "You don't owe him a damn thing," she informs me. "That man doesn't want you as a writer . . . but he wants you to pick up after them? Pfft. No. People do to you what you let them do to you, Gabby. My *abuelita* taught me that."

Suddenly I'm back in my kitchen up in Westchester County, my father giving me a pep talk on standing up for myself at school. I hear him clear as a bell.

"You stand tall and hold tight, Gabby girl. People can only do to you what you allow them to do to you."

I'll. Be. Damned.

In the course of about thirty seconds, I experience anger, frustration, embarrassment, amusement, relief, gratitude, and awe. And it's exhausting. Because being around Isabella is like being on a roller coaster—terrifying and exhilarating at the same time. You close your eyes and pray and hold on for dear life the entire time you're on the stupid ride, only to jump right back on the line to do it all over again.

CHAPTER 35

COQUÍ

That Day

He recognized the tiny church at the top of the hill right away. His mother had often come here to pray to the Holy Mother for intercession—for mercy from her abusive husband. But her prayers had not been answered. After she was murdered, Coquí had never set foot in that—or any—church. Until today.

At Beatríz's insistence, Coquí explained everything to the nun. She just sat there next to him on the pew, listening and nodding, occasionally reaching out to pat his hand or back in a gesture of comfort. It had been a very long time since anyone had touched him like that—with affection and comfort. Then, when she promised him God's grace, he'd started to weep—long, desperate wails of rage and grief for everything he'd lost then, and now. That's when the miracle occurred.

Sitting there, between the nun and the barmaid, the image of Jesus hanging from the cross in front of them, peace washed over him. It was such a strong sense of well-being that it was almost euphoric. He couldn't remember a single moment in his short life when he'd ever felt more safe, more loved, or more clear about the part he was meant to play going forward.

So now, hours later—exhausted and in pain—he slipped

through the narrow, back alleyways the same way he had when he was younger. Even in his current state, carrying the extra weight of the child, Coquí knew how to make himself invisible, how to melt into the shadows and hide in plain sight. His heart was pounding so hard, he was certain he'd be able to see it thumping through his shirt if he took a second to look down. But he didn't have a second to spare as he followed the nun's instructions.

All the while, images of Yeti at the shack flickered in and out of his mind like the trailer for some bloody film. Before he died, Yeti had called him an *hombre muerto*. And he had been absolutely right. He *was* a dead man. While Coquí hadn't been in the gang very long, he'd been there long enough to know how ruthless Santiago was—and how proud. He was well aware of the fact that he was unlikely to come out of this alive by the time it was all over.

He shook the bloody thoughts from his head, knowing he had to concentrate on the task at hand. He'd only have one shot at it. The American woman had left a check at the church, and Beatríz was able to work her connections to find out which ship they were on. Meanwhile, Hermana Blanca had used her connections at the foundling home, putting into place the other details needed to see the child safely delivered to the other side of the Atlantic.

She was strapped to him right now, in a backpack meant to transport a small dog with a mesh window for air and extra padding. They'd given her a drop of cough medicine in hopes it would keep the child drowsy and quiet long enough for him to get her settled without detection. And it was a good thing, too, because *they* were watching. Everywhere he went, he spotted uniformed and undercover *policía* trolling the docks in search of the missing Marianna Ruíz. Some of them would be on Santiago's payroll, as well—all the more reason to keep his head down under the baseball cap. He slumped to look smaller, a pair of headphones affixed to his head and a pair of aviator sunglasses. He didn't look anything like himself.

As he'd arranged earlier, Danny was waiting for him, smoking a cigarette behind the pallets of trash offloaded from the ship he worked on—the same ship the American couple were booked on. They had been friends since the "before" times, playing basketball together as children. Coquí trusted Danny as much as he trusted anyone. He slipped his friend a fifty-dollar bill Beatríz had sent along for his trouble, and Danny helped him change quickly into the spare uniform he'd brought for him. Coquí was a little bit taller, and the pants sat too high above the too-small shoes he had on, but it would have to do. With much of the crew on dinner break, the two of them were able to slip unnoticed to the ship's huge laundry, where a housekeeping trolley was waiting. They set the backpack carefully on the lower shelf, camouflaging it with some towels, and then Danny took him as far as the freight elevator, giving him the key card and directions to the deck and room he was looking for.

Fifteen minutes later, it was done. Twenty-five minutes later, he was back on the dock in his street clothes, unnoticed as he slipped into the shadows once again and started back toward the church.

As he walked, it occurred to him they were a very unlikely trio—Coquí, Beatríz, and Hermana Blanca—brought together under an unlikely set of circumstances. Now they were the only ones who could set this wrong right. At least, as right as it could be. And that would have to be enough.

CHAPTER 36

ISABELLA

Today

I can't say exactly how much liquor I had over the course of the night—but it must have been substantial, considering the size of my hangover this morning. Holy shit, I haven't gotten that hammered in a long time. Probably because I've usually got Matéo in my ear telling me that rum is not my friend. But that's not exactly true. My relationship with rum is a compli-cated one . . . it *was* my friend for several years throughout my late teens and early twenties. Rum was my *only* friend, in fact. And I'm not one to just toss aside a friendship like that. Still, right now, I wish I had the energy to kick rum's ass.

My head is pounding, and my tongue feels like I drizzled it in honey and licked an entire shag carpet—an old green one. Like from the seventies. With lots of cigarette smoke and dog hair embedded in it.

Gabby, on the other hand, appears to be fresh as a daisy when she comes out of the bathroom showered and sporting her new pink sundress. She twirls it around for me, making the skirt billow.

"What do you think?" she asks.

"That I'm going to barf if you do that again," I groan. "Do you mind holding still for a little while? Or, at least, moving a little more slowly?"

"You know, you should've followed your own advice. I drank a glass of water for every cocktail I had last night. And you were right! I feel so much better this morning! Almost like it never happened!"

"Oh, it happened," I mumble, swinging my legs out of the bed and onto the tile floor with some difficulty.

"Well, don't worry, your tea and toast is already on the way. Oh, and I picked up a bottle of Tylenol from Walmart yesterday . . . just in case."

"Well, aren't you the little Girl Scout," I snark.

She ignores the tone and smiles at me. "I was, actually! I sold the most cookies three years in a row! My mom helped, of course."

I can't decide which I find more offensive right now—the thought of cookies or the thought that she had another mom after her *actual* mother died giving birth to her. Either way, I opt not to say anything. I'm in a foul, foul mood, and I know from personal experience that I'm better off just keeping my mouth shut.

"What are you thinking for today? Do we go back to San Juan? Or did you want to take another run at Detective Alvarez—see if he knows anything about this Cokie guy?"

"Coquí," I correct grumpily.

"Hmm?"

"Like ko-KEE, not KO-kee."

She nods and holds up an *okay, I got this* pointer finger. "Coquí," she parrots, nailing it this time.

I have to give her props for the effort. Most *turistas* who come here don't bother trying to pick up any Spanish.

"Perfect," I tell her.

"What does it mean?"

"What does what mean?"

"The name *Coquí*. Does it mean something?"

"I'm surprised you haven't come across it in your research, Sherlock. The *Coquí* is a little tree frog that croaks exactly the way its name sounds—co-KEE, co-KEE, co-KEE," I imitate. "It's like the national mascot of Puerto Rico—on every damn T-shirt, towel, mug, and postcard. It's a pretty popular request at my nail stand, too." I wiggle my left index finger, and she leans in to get a closer look.

"Oh, so cute!"

"Yeah, until you get a bunch of them together in one place, and then they're obnoxiously loud."

"Really? I mean, how loud could a bunch of frogs be?" she wonders.

"*Deafening*. Don't worry, I'm sure you'll hear them before you leave."

Before she leaves. It feels strange to think about her not being around anymore—about resuming my life the way it was before. She hasn't been here long, and yet I feel as if I've known her forever. It makes me wonder how things will change once we have the DNA results back—which should be any time now. I already know what they'll say, but she needs to see it in black and white from an "official" lab.

"Okay, now that we've got my vocabulary lesson out of the way, what do you want to do today?" she asks.

"Well, as much as I'd like to stay here and lay out in the sun all day, I really should get back to work at some point."

"Oh."

The single syllable is dripping with disappointment, and for some reason, that irritates me.

"Oh . . . what?"

She shrugs. "I don't know . . . I guess I was hoping we could get out there and dig around some more. We're so close—I feel it."

"Well, Matéo promised to look into Coquí. I'll check in with him. But I really can't afford to miss the cruise ships that'll be docking this weekend. That's a big chunk of cash for me."

Her expression relaxes as she waves a dismissive hand in my direction. "Oh, is that all? The money? Don't worry about that, I told you I'd cover everything and compensate you for your time. That was the deal."

She's right, that was the deal. Only now, it feels wrong. It feels condescending and offensive. And it pisses me off.

Everything pisses me off this morning—and I *know* this doesn't bode well for us.

At this very second, I'm standing at a crossroads . . . I have the opportunity to head off a potential disaster, if only I just excuse myself to the fancy bathroom and call my husband so he can talk me off the ledge. I *know* this. And yet . . .

"I love how it's so easy for you to say that."

And there it is. I've just fired the shot across the bow— which I regret almost immediately. Not that I do anything to take it back.

Gabby looks at me from under her long, dark lashes. "You're in a really foul mood," she observes coolly. "Maybe you should take a couple Tylenol and go back to bed for a bit, see if you wake up feeling better."

"Thanks, but I like my foul mood," I reply petulantly.

And I'm not lying. I know exactly what I'm doing; I just can't seem to stop myself.

I don't know exactly when it happened, or why, but somewhere between the time we arrived at this place till now, I've come to see that I'm in a very dangerous position. I'm already in way too deep. We're getting too close—too friendly. Gabby's kindness is like a hair shirt on my back, a tortuous reminder of my failings as a sister and as a human being. To accept it would be a signal that I think I deserve it.

I don't. Not from her. Not now—maybe not ever.

"You know, when I used to get into a nasty mood, my mother would say—"

"Oh, here we go with the mother talk," I interject nastily.

She stops, all traces of helpfulness erased from her expression.

"What the hell is *that* supposed to mean?"

"Just that I'm about to be regaled with another moralistic tale about St. Lucy."

Gabby's eyes narrow to slits, and her lips pull into a hard line across her face—a damn near perfectly straight line, the artist in me notes.

"Isabella, I think you should stop talking. Now. Before you say something you can't take back."

"Oh-ho!" I declare with enough gusto to make my head throb even more. Not that I give a shit about that right now. "Did I hit a sore spot? C'mon, Gabby, you cannot possibly expect me to believe old Lucy and Mack were as perfect as you make them out to be." I switch my tone to a poor imitation of her. "*They were such wonderful people,*" I coo exaggeratedly. "*So humble and pure. Just a schoolteacher and a cop . . .*"

"Stop it. Right. Now." The warning is soft but fierce.

"A cop!" I echo myself and start to laugh. And laugh. And laugh.

"What?" she demands, losing her cool. "What's so funny about that?"

It takes a few seconds for me to catch my breath, and by then, there are tears streaming down my face.

"It's just so . . . so . . . ironic!"

"What the hell is wrong with you, Isabella? What are you talking about? How is that ironic?"

I gasp and wheeze and gasp some more, then I grab a tissue from the nightstand and give my nose a big honking blow.

"You know," I reply, still clutching the tissue as I splay my arms out and up toward the ceiling. "He was a *cop.*" When she glares without response, I continue. "His job—his actual career—was upholding the law, catching criminals, and bringing them to justice . . ."

"I'm pretty sure that's the general job description . . ." she reminds me with shrill irritation.

"But he committed one of the most serious crimes there is!"

The stare I'm getting from Gabby is positively murderous now. I've passed the point of no return. There isn't a hint of anything kind or sympathetic on her face now—only the cold, hard ice that so often precedes the red hot magma of sheer rage. Talk about ironic . . .

"My father," she begins in a thin, quiet voice, "was not a criminal. Neither was my mother. And you'd do well to get that fact straight."

"Right, the facts," I echo thoughtfully. Not that I'm the least bit thoughtful. If I were, I'd retreat right now, apologize, and do my best to smooth things over. But I don't do any of those things. Instead, I just plow right on. "Well, let's look at the facts, shall we? A seven-month-old child is snatched right out of her stroller. She disappears for a quarter-century, only to resurface as a successful, well-adjusted young woman who was raised in Utopia, USA, by Mom and Pop Perfect. They even kept a souvenir of her abduction—the single pink sock. So, if I've got this right—and I'm pretty sure I do—we're talking kidnapping, transporting across state lines, falsifying documents . . ."

"Isabella," Gabby warns in a low-pitched growl.

"Hardly the sort of behavior you'd expect from a law enforcement professional . . ."

"You need to shut up. Like right now."

I hear the steel in her voice. I just don't care. That's when I realize this has been building for a while now. Since before I ever even met her.

"Of course, I can see why you'd want to pretend it never happened. Look how well it turned out for you! Braces and Girl Scouts, horseback riding, elite private school, family trips abroad . . ." I'm vaguely aware of the fact that I crossed the line some time ago. At this point, I'm so far over that it's easier to just keep going rather than turn back. "Yeah, I think I might be able to overlook the fact that the people raising me were felons, too, if I got to live a life like that."

I expect her to scream, curse, maybe throw something at me. What I don't expect is the slap. It comes so fast and so hard that it takes me a full three seconds to associate the sudden stinging sensation on my cheek with the crimson-faced woman in front of me. My first instinct is to throw her petite little ass down on the floor and kick the shit out of it. Instead, I do something worse. I grin.

"Wow. Maybe not such a perfect little girl after all," I observe, voice dripping with sarcasm. "I doubt Mack and Lucy would approve of slapping someone, Gabby. Maybe there's more Ruíz in you than you'd like to admit—"

This time, when she raises her hand to hit me again, I catch her by the wrist and hold her.

"Let me go!" she grits out between clenched teeth.

"Why? So you can slap me again? No, I don't think so. Use your words, Gabby. Because if you touch me again, I'm going to pound that pretty face of yours into the ground. And we both know I'll do it."

She's breathing heavily and her nostrils are flaring, but she manages to yank free of my grasp before taking a wobbly step backwards.

"You have no right—"

"To what? Criticize your parents? Oh, I think I have every right, considering what they stole from me . . ."

Now *she's* the one smiling, shaking her head so that her long, dark curls swish from side to side with the motion.

"No, no, I see you. I see what's really going on here. You're not mad at them for taking me. You're mad at them for *not* taking you!"

My retort—all teed up and ready to go—curdles right there on my tongue, leaving an acrid film of bile in my mouth.

"You have no idea what you're talking about," I hiss back at her.

"Don't I?" Her hands land on her hips, and she tips her head to one side. "Admit it, Isabella. You're just jealous because I had a stable home and parents who were there all the time. Someone worried about me—where I was, what I was doing, who I was with. Someone cared whether I lived or died. Someone actually *loved* me."

There's this point right before a tsunami slams into the shore that the ocean actually sucks back the tide from the beach—harnessing the power of each and every molecule of H_2O that it can draw toward itself, allowing it to grow bigger, stronger, and more deadly by the second. But in that instant when the sea is literally swept away, there is nothing. Without any water, the sand of the ocean floor glistens in the glorious sunlight, leaving people to stand and marvel dumbly even as the hundred-foot wall of sea bears down on them.

We are there right now, Gabby DiMarco and I, both mesmerized and paralyzed by the immense power swirling around us at this moment. We are a split second away from total and complete devastation. What remains to be seen, though, is which one of us will be pulled in to become part of the deadly force . . . and which of us will be swept away by it.

CHAPTER 37

MACK

That Day

Mack was exhausted, and his bum knee was bothering him after a long day walking cobblestoned streets in search of tchotchkes with images of tree frogs, palm trees, and ancient forts. It wasn't that he disliked the island. Quite the opposite—Puerto Rico was, by far, his favorite stop on this ten-day floating tour of hell. If he thought Lucy would agree, he'd suggest they stay on here and spend a few more days exploring the island rather than continuing on to Jamaica and the Bahamas.

It wasn't the ports of call that Mack hated so much as the boat itself. He hated that feeling of being trapped somewhere out in the middle of the ocean with no land in sight for days at a time. He hated the throngs of people pushing and shoving their way through buffet lines, elbowing their way to the best seats, and parking their fat asses on the best lounge chairs all day while their insufferable brat children peed in the pool and drenched everyone in a twelve-foot radius of them.

That was the worst of it, really. The kids. Not so much for himself, but for Lucy. They never spoke about it, but it was always there between them wherever they went. It was hard at the best of times, when they were alone or in the company of adults only, but everything changed when there was a child in their orbit. It didn't matter how old, or what gender. He watched his wife watching them, knowing exactly what was going through her head, feeling another tiny piece of her heart break off and fall away. He worried that she would, eventually, run out of pieces and there would be nothing left but a shell of the woman he'd married.

But here, in Old San Juan, something had shifted between them. She'd been so anxious to get off the boat and get moving as soon as they were permitted. Then she'd promptly sent him off on some wild goose chase in search of illegal Cuban cigars that he didn't even want. Figuring she needed a little time to herself, he indulged her, perusing the storefronts a little before finally finding himself a beautiful waterfront park where he could sit with a cup of coffee and an American newspaper he'd picked up in one of the shops.

When Lucy met up with him later for lunch, she was all smiles, chatting excitedly about the beautiful church she'd stumbled across and how much better she felt about "things" after taking some time there to pray and reflect. He was a devout Catholic and believed in the power of God to heal broken hearts and broken dreams, filling them with other things—more rewarding, fulfilling things. After all, he knew from experience that God worked in mysterious ways. You just had to trust Him to show you the path. And then you had to be brave enough to follow that path—wherever it might lead.

As they inched forward on the line to reboard the boat, he wrapped an arm around Lucy's waist and pulled her closer to him. She looked up and smiled as she leaned into him. It had been so long since they'd been truly happy.

First, they couldn't conceive. Then, joyously, they did. Except that began the cycle of miscarriages—four in total. They went three rounds of IVF, each one failing to produce a viable pregnancy. He'd watched his wife wilt and fade a little with each and every thwarted effort.

When adoption agencies told them there was a years-long waitlist, and that at their age, they were unlikely to be approved to take on an infant, he'd consulted an adoption attorney. The guy was considered "the best" in baby-deprived circles, but Mack had found him slick and untrustworthy. He was telling them—without telling them—what would be required to purchase a child.

That was when Mack had called it quits. He would not risk her life for what was clearly not meant to be. The decision had sent Lucy spiraling into a depression that lasted months. Until one day, out of nowhere, she presented him with the brochure for this Caribbean cruise. It wasn't his idea of a vacation, but if she was willing to exert the effort to get out of bed, pack a bag, and board a mammoth boat, he'd follow her to freaking Timbuktu.

"I thought we might try the steakhouse tonight," she said. "Doesn't that sound good? A nice juicy steak and baked potato?"

"Um . . . well, yeah, it sounds great, honey," he replied, trying not to sound too startled that she wanted to dine outside of their cabin.

When they reached the front of the line, they presented their identifications and waited patiently as one of the white-uniformed employees checked them back in before smiling and welcoming them back aboard whatever the hell the name of this thing was—The Mystic Mandible? The Musty Mariner? He couldn't keep it straight. He didn't care to.

"Home again, home again," he muttered, slipping the key-card into the slot on the lock of their incredibly overpriced, undersized stateroom, and then held the door for her.

When he went to pull the card out, it got jammed and took several tugs before he could finally extricate the thing.

"Good Lord, I thought I was going to have to call the concierge in with the Jaws of Life!" he grumbled, finally entering the room, letting the door swing shut behind him as he did. He didn't see her at first, expecting her to have kicked off her shoes and dropped onto the couch already. "Lucy?"

"Mack, over here."

Her whisper came from the other side of the room, on the far side of the bed. But she wasn't on it, she was next to it, kneeling on the floor.

"Luce, what are you doing? And why are you whispering?"

"Shhh!" she hissed at him. "Keep your voice down, or you'll wake her!"

It wasn't until he walked closer to the bed that he saw what his wife was talking about. Or, rather, who his wife was talking about.

There, in the middle of the bed, lay a child. He couldn't say how old—six months, maybe? She was sound asleep, thumb in her mouth, pillows lining the perimeter of the bed so she couldn't accidentally roll off.

"What the hell?"

"Mack!" his wife clucked, and his first instinct was to apologize for cursing in front of the child.

Then he realized how insane that thought was and stomped closer to stand behind Lucy, peering down over her shoulder at the strange little creature in their bed. That's when he noticed the diaper bag sitting on the floor in front of the end table. Picking it up, he carried it to the dresser and started to paw through it. There were diapers, bottles, cans of formula, a few changes of clothes, and assorted baby accoutrements, which he didn't recognize but knew to be associated with the inner workings of an infant.

He spotted a manila envelope in the front pocket and pulled it out—Lucy too busy cooing over the child to even notice him or what he was doing. Inside the envelope, he found an official-looking document printed on heavy paper.

Across the top, in embossed letters, was written *Certificado de Nacimiento*. Birth certificate. Then the child's name, Gabriella—

He stopped reading, closed his eyes, opened his eyes, and looked again. But it hadn't changed. It still said the child's name was Gabriella DiMarco. Listed for *Padre* was his own name, Mack DiMarco, and printed on the *Madre* line was Lucy DiMarco. He looked incredulously between the document and the baby and back again.

"No, no, this is . . . wrong," he said.

"No, Mack," Lucy informed him, her voice full of tears as she brushed some stray curls from the little girl's forehead. "Everything is exactly right."

CHAPTER 38

GABBY

Today

We'd all like to believe that we're good people. And I think most of the time, we are. But there are moments when even the kindest, most forgiving person can be pushed too far. When even they cannot find the strength to quell the rage and hold a civil tongue. This is one of those moments for me.

When I hurl the words at Isabella, they are calibrated to do the maximum amount of damage. And I hit my target dead-on.

"Screw you," she whispers, eyes narrowed and lips pursed. "Screw you and your perfect life. What did it get you, huh, Gabby? Maybe mommy and daddy did love you—enough to steal you, anyway. But where are you now? You're alone. You're lonely. You're desperate . . ."

"I am *not* desperate!" I bellow back at her.

"Aren't you? You hopped on the first plane here, didn't you? And why were you doing that genealogy test, anyway? Hoping to dig up some long-lost cousin?"

That's exactly what I was doing, but I'll be damned if I'm going to admit that to her. Not after she's made it sound so . . . pathetic.

"It was for work. It was all for work," I maintain.

"Oh, right! The big job! The big career that you say you're so determined to have!"

"What the hell is *that* supposed to mean?" I demand, bristling.

"I don't know . . . you tell me! How long have you wanted to be an actual writer—the one telling the stories? And how many times have you let yourself be put off by some editor—Max, the guy before Max, the woman before the guy before Max—hmm? No, really, Gabby, I want to know. Because, as far as I can tell, all your little facts aren't worth shit except to make sure other people look good. I mean, it's not like I've seen you write a single word since you got here. At least not one that wasn't on your precious whiteboard."

My face is so hot at this point, I'm sure I must be beet red.

"I wouldn't be so quick to judge," I hiss back at her. "It's not like you're living the dream either. How badly could you possibly want it when you let some second-rate professor shame you into dropping out of art school? And now, here you are, doing nails for all those rich *turistas* you have so much disdain for! What's stopping *you*, Isabella? And don't give me that bullshit about there not being any opportunities. I've spoken to Matéo. I know about the grants and the interest from that advertising agency. So don't you dare stand there and talk to me about being too afraid to put myself out there!"

"Yeah, well, not everybody scored a shit ton of insurance money from their dead parents," she spits at me.

I stand there and stare at her. I blink hard.

"Is that what this is all about? Are you . . . jealous of the money? Were you thinking you'd somehow hit the jackpot when you found me? All your financial problems are over. Is that what you thought, Isabella?"

Even as I hurl the accusation, I know it's unfounded and absolutely untrue. The woman in front of me is fiercely proud of her independence. Which is how I know it will hurt.

"Of course your mind would go there, considering how much money you throw around all day every day. See, I tend

to think that's more about you than me. I think you're trying to buy yourself a new family. Maybe some new friends.
Because that's what it is now, Gabby, isn't it? You *did* have
it all—the perfect life, the big house, the private school, and
the fancy trips abroad. But now? Now you've got nothing.
Nothing but memories—and stolen ones, at that!" She sneers
at me now, shaking her head. "And you've got it all wrong.
I *am* loved—by my husband. By my cousins, and aunts, and
uncles. Which is more than you can say."

My fingers are itching to pick up one of the very tasteful,
very heavy sculptures placed around the room. I was wrong;
she's just as good at this as I am. Maybe better. Maybe the
same. Because maybe *we* are the same. But I can't think about
that right now.

"Why did you even bother to look?"

When I ask the question, she appears genuinely taken
aback.

"What? What are you talking about?"

"Why did you even bother looking for me, or Marianna,
or whoever your sister is? Because, clearly, you don't want to
find her. Were you just hoping to find a little company in your
misery, Isabella? Maybe you wanted your sister around so
you wouldn't be the only one feeling abandoned by Alberto?
Maybe you—"

"I wish you'd never been born."

The words are all the more harsh because they're not spit,
or hurled, or yelled. They're whispered—but with enough hatred to ensure they will carry across the room and right to
my gut.

"What did you just say to me?"

"You heard me. If you hadn't been born, my mother would
still be alive. I'd have had a good life, a family—I wouldn't
have been . . ."

"Oh, please! Will you just stop already? You *would* have,
you *should* have, you *could* have. You act like you're so tough,

like you're not afraid of anything, or anyone. But that's all a show, isn't it? That's all just an act . . . a big, elaborate lie. Just stop feeling sorry for yourself. Mothers die, Isabella. Sisters go missing; fathers turn into addicts. It sucks, but it happens."

She's quiet and still for a long moment; then, she just gathers her purse and her keys and walks to the door.

"Oh, yeah, right. Just leave now. Run away . . ."

She stops, hand on the knob, and tilts her head back toward me. It's not a complete turn—I can only see part of her profile when she speaks again.

I brace myself for the next hateful thing that's coming my way.

"You missed one," she says quietly. "Mothers die, people go missing, fathers become addicts . . . and fifteen-year-old girls get raped."

It is hateful—it's just not what I'm expecting. And it's not intended for me. At least, it's not intended to wound me.

"Isabella—"

But she doesn't stay long enough for me to finish that sentence. Not that I know what the rest of that sentence would have been.

I'm still standing there, staring at the door, when I hear the Yaris pull away.

CHAPTER 39

BLANCA

That Day

Blanca was on the kneeler, deep in prayer, waiting for the deep, throaty sound of the cruise ship horn. One long blast followed by three short ones to signal its departure from port. When the sound finally came, she felt a rush of relief that nearly brought her to tears. The baby was on her way to a new life. A safe life. A happy life. She made the sign of the cross, thanking Jesus Christ for his mercy and wisdom.

That was when she heard the knock at the chapel door, which she'd bolted shut an hour earlier. Her eyes flew to Beatríz, who'd been sitting in the back pew as they waited for the boy to return. He knew to use the back entrance. This was someone else.

"Hurry, go downstairs," Blanca hissed, motioning her toward a small, discreet door just beyond the altar.

Even as Beatríz hustled through the pews, the knock came again, followed by a woman's muffled voice.

"Hello? Is someone there? Please let us in—please . . ."

"Just a moment," she called out, waiting until Beatríz was out of sight before going to the heavy wooden door. She closed her eyes, said a silent prayer, and slowly opened the door. Standing on the other side was the woman. The woman who had been there that morning. The woman who should have been on the ship that just left port. In her arms was the child they'd just gone to such great lengths to get on that ship with her. And standing at her side was a tall, burly man who looked less than pleased.

Blanca's heart sank.

"May we come in, Sister?" he asked in a deep, deliberate voice. "I think there's something we need to talk about."

With a sigh of resignation, she nodded and pushed the door open all the way so they might join her inside the chapel. She bolted it behind them.

"W-what can I do for you?" she asked softly, pretending to have no idea who they were.

He glanced down at the woman.

"I understand my wife was here this morning. And she seems to believe she had some sort of . . . mystical experience. Next thing I know, this child is in our stateroom, along with falsified documents . . . with *our* names on them. I can't help but think this all has something to do with this place," he said, gesturing around the small space.

For a brief moment, she considered denying all knowledge of the situation, but then the couple might bring the child to the authorities, and all this would have been for nothing. Well, this hadn't been part of the plan—her plan, anyway. But clearly it was part of *God's* plan. And her only job was to serve as His instrument in executing whatever that plan turned out to be.

"Please, come and sit," she murmured, leading them to the first pew.

"This is that little girl, isn't it?" he asked suspiciously. "The one everyone's been talking about all day."

Blanca took a seat next to them and considered him for a moment. She didn't feel any fear in his presence. To the contrary, there was something about him—about them—that felt right. Yes, they were meant to be here, she was sure of it now. And so she began.

"Please, let me start at the beginning. I was here when your wife came this morning. She didn't see me, but I saw her. And I saw the virgin . . ."

"I told you!" Lucy interjected, elbowing her husband. "You thought I was crazy! But it happened, Mack. That statue right over there." She leveled a finger at the figure. "I prayed, and she wept! She heard my prayer . . ."

"Lucy," her husband said, shaking his head in disbelief. "You know as well as I do that there's no way—" He stopped short when the nun put a hand on his forearm.

"She is right, señor. I had never seen it before—only heard stories from years ago. But then I witnessed it with my own eyes. And perhaps I would have talked myself out of believing that later . . . had this child not arrived here a short time after your wife left this church . . ."

She watched as the wife clung to the child, now sleeping peacefully against her shoulder.

"You are her mother now," Blanca said softly.

Lucy nodded reverentially. "Yes, I know."

Mack, however, was not convinced. He ran a meaty hand through his salt-and-pepper hair, clearly having a hard time sorting this bizarre turn of events.

"This . . . Sister, what you're proposing is kidnapping. I heard all the chatter in town this morning. This girl has a family. This isn't just illegal, it's immoral."

"How can it be immoral when she was given to us by the Holy Mother herself?" Lucy asked softly so as not to disturb the child, but with a certainty that far outweighed her husband's doubt.

Mack's face held both anguish and resolution.

"Lucy, I'm so, so sorry. I'd give anything to be able to say we'll take her . . . but, without the parent's consent? We'd be sentencing them to a life of agony, wondering what had become of her—is she dead or alive? Is she safe? Is she happy? Or . . . you know what can happen to beautiful, innocent, little children, Lucy—the kind of monsters who prey on them. Do you want them wondering, somewhere in the back of his mind, if he'd inadvertently sent her to a hell that we can't even conceive? No, sweetheart. I couldn't live with myself."

Lucy remained calm, unmoved by her husband's declaration.

"She's ours, Mack. You'll see." She nodded toward the crucifix hanging in front of them—Jesus's anguished face turned upward toward heaven, waiting for the deliverance He knew would come . . . eventually. But even the Son of God had had to endure unthinkable suffering before He was delivered.

Blanca closed her eyes for a moment and silently spoke the words inside her heart. *Lord, hear my prayer. Jesus, hear my prayer. Holy Mary, Mother of God, hear my prayer . . .*

"You're the only ones who can help the little girl." The voice came from the far side of the chapel, where Beatríz had reappeared.

"She says you're the only ones who can help the little girl—" Blanca started to translate but stopped abruptly when Mack stood and walked toward the other woman.

"Dime," Mack said, stunning everyone except for his wife. *"Dime por qué."*

Tell me. Tell me why.

Beatríz told him.

CHAPTER 40

GABBY

Today

I secure a rental car with the help of the concierge and settle the staggeringly high bar bill. I can't stop thinking about what Isabella said—all of it, but especially the last thing she threw my way before walking out of the door and, possibly, my life. It explains so much about her—the tough exterior that doesn't quite go all the way to her core, her reluctance to put herself "out there"—both literally and figuratively. And, sweet Jesus, the trauma she's probably endured every day since it happened.

How had it all gone south so fast? As I replay it all in my mind over and over again—every ugly word of it—I'm still not sure what I did to set her off so quickly and so drastically. A lot of it must have been simmering just under the surface for a while now, considering how targeted her jabs were . . . and, let's face it, how accurate.

It's true that I've been throwing money around ever since I got off the plane—and it's not as if I'm like that at home. It's not as if I was raised that way. She also wasn't wrong when she accused me of just playing the part of a journalist. I've barely written a word. And I can't ignore her comments about me being lonely. I had it all. Emphasis on *had*. Now what have I got? No job, no friends, no story, no sister— though I'm not sure that last one was ever going to happen.

"Damn it!" I yell, smacking the steering wheel.

I'm just so done. As soon as I get back to the hotel, I'm going to pack my bags and get my ass back to Brooklyn. Maybe I'll adopt a cat. Or five.

The GPS says I'm still an hour from San Juan when Max's face pops up on my screen.

"What?" I demand harshly. "What do you want now, Max?"

There's a long pause.

"Well, I wanted to apologize for before—for bothering you and making an unreasonable request."

I sigh. "That's okay. I can understand why you were so panicked. What's going on with Lisa and the lawsuit?"

"Oh, well, after pulling an all-nighter, four of us managed to plow through Finnegan's backlist, and I'll be damned if he hasn't been stealing material for more than a decade!"

"Seriously? So Lisa was right . . ."

"Well, yes . . . and no. Legal tells us that he was very shrewd—changed things just enough to ride that plagiarism line. There's no doubt of his intentions when you compare his material to other writers', but he knew exactly how to protect himself. A judge may or may not rule against him. But that's not our problem. The authors whose work he so liberally 'borrowed' from will no doubt be consulting their attorneys."

"Oh, shit. So, what does that mean for the magazine's liability?"

And Lisa's ass?

"I had a very frank conversation with Finnegan's agent, and I think we've come to an understanding. I told him no way in hell we'll settle and pointed out how a long, drawn-out trial will only keep her client in the spotlight. Guilty or not, it'll be rehashed over and over again. We might get a fine and a slap on the wrist, but Finnegan's career will be over."

"Holy shit," I murmur, stunned by the turn of events. "So . . . what's next? For *Flux*, I mean?"

"Ah, well, we've pulled the article from the web, and we'll write a statement for the back matter of the next edition. Not a full-on retraction, per se, but a very small note that pretty much puts the blame on Lisa for incomplete reporting and defying editorial guidance."

"Oh. Oh, wow, Max . . . Lisa must be out of her mind!"

"I wouldn't know," he tells me coolly. "She doesn't work for me anymore."

"What? You fired her?" I'm incredulous. She's always managed to walk away unscathed, but I guess she finally crossed one line too many.

"I did."

"That's . . . just . . . wow, Max. Good for you."

"Well, I just wanted to let you know how it all worked out. I'll leave you to your great adventure . . ."

I'm overwhelmed by a sudden wave of homesickness. His voice, his laugh, his sense of humor—it's all so wonderfully familiar. And safe. And I can't think of anything more appealing right now.

"Listen, Max, I'm coming home tomorrow—tonight, if I can find a flight. Do you think we could have coffee or something?"

"Um, yes, sure. Of course," he replies. I've caught him off guard. "So you're done? Does that mean it was a cockup at the lab, and you're *not* related?"

I sigh. "No. Actually, it means that I give up. All I want to do right now is go home."

"I don't understand. What happened?"

"Isabella and I had a horrific fight. Just . . . just awful. She said so many hurtful, hateful things—and I just lobbed them right back at her. It was ugly, Max. Really, really ugly. I don't see how we can come back from this to work together."

He's quiet for a few long seconds.

"Okay . . . tell me something, Gabby, where are you in your fact-finding at this point?"

"I, uh . . . well, we were kind of stumped, and then this woman mentioned a name we hadn't heard before. But I don't know if that's anything . . ."

"So you got a whole new lead?"

"I suppose . . . yeah . . . maybe . . ."

"And, what, you think you can wrap that all up tonight or tomorrow?"

"Huh? No, no. I just . . . I didn't see much point in moving forward with the story. Not without Isabella . . ."

My voice peters out as his disapproving silence makes its way down the East Coast and across the Atlantic.

And then he utters the five words that every *Flux* writer and editor dreads hearing during our editorial meetings. The phrase that means evisceration is imminent. Thankfully, they've never been leveled at me. Until right now.

"Let me get this straight . . ." *Shit.* "You flew all the way to Puerto Rico—a place you've never been—to meet a woman claiming to be your sister. You drive all over the island together chasing facts and put together what looks to be a very promising story—not to mention the truth about your personal history—and now you're going to hang it all up because of a little spat?"

"I wouldn't call it a spat—"

"Whatever. Clearly you've come to care about this Isabella—"

"I wouldn't say—"

"Wouldn't you?" he counters before I can even get the whole protest out. "Because it seems to me you're acting more like a third-grader than a reporter. Your bestie hurt your feelings, and now you're going to take your toys and go home?"

I'm stunned. He's never been this harsh with me, and it's more than a little jarring. All I can do is stammer in response. "I . . . are you . . . I can't . . ."

"Oh, don't sound so gobsmacked, Gabby, you're a big girl—and know that I'm saying this to you as your friend, not your former boss . . . if you want to be a professional, act like one. Put the personal feelings aside and go after the story—wherever it leads. Here you are with a big, juicy clue, and you want to hop on the first plane home? Hmm. Maybe you don't want to be a professional writer as much as you thought you did."

My blood boils, and the "screw you" dies right there on my tongue before I can fling it at him and hang up. Because Max is a lot of things, but a liar isn't one of them.

"You're right," I manage in a small voice after a long pause.

"Yes! Now *that* is a professional move right there," he tells me enthusiastically.

"What? Doing what you tell me to do?"

"No! You need to be strong enough to push back when you know you're right. And you have to be smart enough to accept when you're wrong, get over it, and move on. Are you going to move on, Gabby?"

I think about Isabella and Marianna. I think about the DNA and about my parents. If I stop now, I'll never know the truth about any of them. I'll never know the truth about myself.

I've got one more fact to follow.

"I am."

CHAPTER 41

MIGUEL

That Day

Miguel was standing dockside when the enormous ship sounded its departure blasts. He scowled, still not happy he hadn't been able to get permission to search all the ships before they departed San Juan. But that had come down as a hard *no* from the brass, stating they had no reason to disrupt the ship's schedule or disturb the passengers, who brought so much in tourism dollars to their community. Besides, he was told, they had a stringent security protocol in place. There was no way anyone could have boarded with a kidnapped child in tow.

The detective was about to turn around and head home to his wife for the night when a movement caught his eyes. Even as the ship was reversing, a dark-clad figure jumped from a side cargo door, just managing to catch the end of the dock without hitting the water below. Behind him, someone else— a crewmember, it looked like—stuck his head out and looked around, offering a brief wave once he confirmed the other man had landed safely on the dock. The jumper returned the wave and slipped into the shadows while the crewmember disappeared behind the cargo door.

"What the hell . . . ?" he muttered under his breath, his eyes following the man, who was carrying a backpack and wearing a baseball cap with sunglasses, even though it was nearly dark out.

Miguel had a good gut—a gut that had never once failed him. So, when it started throwing up alarms and red flags, he hurried to catch up, keeping far enough back so as not to attract attention. The two of them moved in tandem like that, up the steep cobblestoned streets, slipping down narrow alleyways, and cutting through various abandoned or closed properties until emerging behind the tiny, little-used church on the hill.

Miguel stepped into a dark doorway just as the other man glanced around, checking for people like him—people following him. Believing himself to be unobserved, he pulled off the baseball cap and glasses and stepped to the door, knocking twice. When it opened, the light inside the church spilled out onto him, and Miguel got a good look before the young man disappeared inside, the sound of the door locking behind him audible.

Miguel knew him. He was sure of it. The detective rarely forgot a face, especially one involving a case he'd worked. He closed his eyes for a moment and indexed his memories until coming up with the name. Jaime, maybe? No, Jacinto. Jacinto Nuñez. Yes, that was correct. Only he'd been much younger—much smaller when Alvarez had been called to the scene where the boy's mother had been shot and killed by his stepfather before the cowardly son-of-a-bitch had turned the gun on himself. Last he'd heard, the boy had run away from foster care several times before turning seventeen and leaving once and for all to become a member of Santiago's *Soldados Salvajes*.

Shit. His gut was screeching at him now.

There was no way this didn't have something to do with the Ruíz baby.

But there was only one way to silence the deafening noise in his head—and to find out what this was about.

Miguel stepped out of the shadows.

He went to the back door and knocked twice.

CHAPTER 42

ISABELLA

Today

Matéo is pacing a hole in the carpet at the foot of the bed, raking his right hand through his thick hair. He sighs, starts to say something, stops, and begins pacing once more. I've finally confessed everything that happened this morning—the real "everything," not the glossed-over version I gave him when I first got home. The version he didn't believe—and so picked at, bit by bit, until it collapsed under the weight of its lies. Now, thirty minutes later, he knows everything—every awful word that was said.

And he is *not* happy with me.

"Matéo, please . . ." I groan from my side of the bed, where I've been since I got home, hoping to sleep off the last of this wicked hangover.

No such luck.

"I just—I can't understand, Isabella. Why? Why did you do it?"

"Do what? I told you, she started it—"

"Do you even *hear* yourself?"

My husband isn't a loud man. And he's not the kind of guy who loses his temper or his patience easily. So, for him to come to this place is very unusual for him—and very disconcerting for me.

"What do you want me to say?"

"I don't want you to say anything—I want you to *do* something. I want you to face your demons once and for all. The only thing you've ever wanted—for as long as I've known you—is to find your sister. And now that it looks like you have, you blow it all to hell! Why, Isabella? To what end? Where does that leave you now?"

My eyes are closed, and I can just *feel* his hard gaze on me, even if I can't see it. After a time, he comes closer and closer until he's standing right next to me. Then he drops down onto his haunches and rests a hand on my forearm.

"Isabella, please look at me," he says in a whisper. I do, and I see that his eyes have softened a little. "I love you so much. There is nothing I wouldn't do for you. But there are times . . . there are times when I get so frustrated, because the only thing standing in the way of your happiness is you. It's as if you're determined to stay that angry, lonely, distrusting girl I met all those years ago."

He pauses, takes a deep breath, and searches my face for some understanding before he continues.

"If you live back there—back in the past—you'll never get over the things that have happened to you. And if you live in the future—always imagining the perfect sister, or job, or family—you'll never appreciate everything that's right in front of you." I watch as he takes a deep breath, steeling himself to say whatever it is that's going to come out of his mouth next. And I prepare myself for the worst. As I always do.

"If we're going to stay together, you have to live right here with me. Today. Because I can't . . . I *won't* see you destroy yourself over and over and over again out of some twisted sense of guilt. Isabella, you can only outrun the tide for so long. It might take years—decades even—but eventually, you will drop from exhaustion, and it will catch up with you. And by then, it'll be too late. You won't have the strength to fight it. By then, you'll be too broken."

I think of the tsunami again, sucking in the tide to fuel itself for the impending destruction. "Matéo, I don't know what to do anymore," I say, hearing tears choking my words but unable to stop them. "I don't know who I am anymore."

My husband nods, as if this is what he's suspected all along; then he gives me a wry smile. "I know. It's ironic, isn't it? For all these years, you've been looking for Marianna . . . and somewhere along the way, you lost Isabella."

It's as profound and as accurate a statement as I've ever heard him utter.

"How do I come back?" I wonder out loud, not quite sure who it is that I'm asking.

He shrugs. "I don't know the answer to that. What I know for sure is that there is something inside of you—something holding you back. Something that will *not* allow you to be happy—truly happy—for any length of time." He looks away from me for just a moment before looking back. I recognize it for what it is—a break in the intensity between us so he can say what has to be said without being swayed by our mutual attraction. "Isabella . . . if you don't figure this out soon, then I don't know if I'll be able to stay in this relationship with you. I can't live my life like that. I won't live my like that."

Time stands still for a moment—and I can see the wall of water that's about to sweep me away. It would be so easy to just . . . let go. It would be so easy to spend the rest of my days suspended in the salty, murky depths of despair. But Matéo is throwing me a life ring. Only, to grasp it requires a brutal fight against forces so much bigger and stronger than me. It's not impossible, but it'll be bloody, and it'll be painful.

"I understand," I tell him.

He shakes his head. "No, I'm not sure you do." He sighs as he looks down at his feet for a few seconds; then he meets my eyes again. "I'm going to go spend the night at my parents' house—"

"No, wait, Matéo—" I sit up too quickly and grab the headboard, waiting for the vertigo to pass.

He sits down on the side of the bed and takes my free hand.

"I'm just taking a night, that's all. This doesn't mean anything other than I think we both need a little space to calm down and to think through things." Now his warm hand finds my face, and I lean into it.

"I'm coming back," he assures me firmly. "Just take the evening to rest. I think when you've had some sleep, things will make more sense to you, okay?"

I nod, feeling the tears brimming.

He bends down to kiss my forehead.

"I love you," I tell him.

"And I love you," he replies. "But sometimes that's just not enough."

I don't dream of my mother very often. And even when I do, she's just a fuzzy, vague blob—like some generic avatar in my subconscious labeled MOTHER. But this time is different. This time, I see her with perfect clarity.

"Ven, Isabella, mi amor," she calls to me from the kneeling rail set out in front of a bank of memorial candles.

I enter my own dream, watching myself join her there on my knees. I can't be much more than four or five—the age I was when she died. My small fingers immediately set to work tracing the cracks in the burgundy vinyl that covers the rail cushion—I know them by heart, making my way around to the raised lines of piping and dipping underneath to find where the material has been stapled into the wood. The pine is smooth, save for a small divot on its surface where a knot has fallen out. The entire thing is just so . . . surreal. But I can't say it's unpleasant.

Slowly, she makes the sign of the cross, showing the child version of me each movement so I can copy her. And when I do, I'm rewarded with that brilliant smile—always lined in red lipstick. Not that bright, garish shade, but a darker, softer hue. One that makes her look as if she's just stepped out of a World War II movie. Coupled with the dark curls framing her face and those striking blue ombre eyes, she is simply stunning.

And my *God*, she's young! But then, she would be, wouldn't she? She's been preserved—frozen in time for all these years, even as the world has continued to spin on its axis. Even as I have grown older, now a full five years older than she was the day she died.

As she bows her head in silent prayer, I stare at her, drinking in every detail of the woman kneeling next to me—every curve, and line, and shadow of her face, memorizing her profile so I can bring it back with me after I wake up.

What is she praying for?

She lifts her head and turns to me, as if she's heard the question I haven't uttered. When she speaks, the sound of her voice takes my breath away—overwhelmed by the sense of familiarity that goes back to my time in the womb.

"I light a candle in memory of the people who have left us for heaven," she explains softly. "To show that we still love them, and they have not been forgotten." Now she puts her hand to her belly, which I notice for the first time is swollen. "And I light a candle for this little one who has not yet come to us—your little sister, Marianna. I light a candle and say a prayer that she will come into this world healthy and have a happy life. And you must pray for her too, Isabellita. Because when you have a sister, you are never alone in this world. She is the only person who will be with you for your entire life, *mija. De la cuna a la tuma.*" *From the cradle to the grave.*

"Please don't leave me, *Mami*," I beg my mother's apparition.

"But, my love," she says gently with a reassuring smile, "I have never left you! I've always been right here." Now she touches her hand to her heart before repeating the gesture on me. "*Somos familia ahora y siempre.*" *We are family now and always.*

I don't know what it is that sucks me back into the real world, but it does so without warning, literally ripping me out of my mother's arms. I sit bolt upright, eyes jerking around the room wildly, my breath coming fast and ragged.

"Oh, my God," I murmur to myself. "It was a dream . . . it was just a dream . . ." I put a hand to my face only to find that it's damp with tears.

It was so real, I've been crying in my sleep.

"Matéo—" I begin, twisting toward his side of the bed.

But it's empty. And the room is silent. Because the house is empty. Because Matéo is gone for the night.

A quick glance at the clock tells me it's close to nine. I've slept away the entire afternoon and the evening.

"He's not leaving me," I tell myself. Then, more firmly, "He is *not* leaving me."

I get up and go to the bathroom, hoping a splash of cold water on my face will help me to wake up and calm down. No such luck. For less time than it takes to blink, it's my mother's reflection looking back at me in the mirror. It takes a moment to realize it's not another dream, nor is it some apparition.

After all this time and all the fuzzy, faded memories in my mind, I've had a clear, sharp look at my mother in her twenties. And for that first moment, I was startled by just how much of her is in me. For all these years, I've been trying to conjure her accurately in my mind—and on canvas—when she was right there in front of me all this time.

I grab a towel, drying my face as I walk out to the carport and flip on the light, making my way to the back, where a tarped canvas rests against the concrete wall. When I peel back the cover, I find my mother staring back at me—at least, my last attempt to capture my mother's image. With the dream still fresh in my mind, I realize that, while I've done a fair enough job of capturing her physical attributes, I've done a shit job of capturing her spirit. The tender eyes, the soft smile, the concerned forehead . . . I missed them all, and they are all the things that made her who she was. I reach out and touch the canvas. It's all wrong, and there's no fixing it. I'll have to start over . . . because I have to do it justice—do *her* justice. It has to mean something—to her, and to me. That's when Matéo's words come back to me . . .

"*I want you to face your demons once and for all.*"

But my mother isn't a demon. To the contrary, she is an angel—an ethereal creature who has somehow managed to send me a message. I wonder how many of them I've missed? It took that dream—like a frying pan to the head—for me to hear what she was trying to tell me about Marianna . . . and myself.

So I guess that just leaves Alberto as the demon to be faced. Unless . . .

A hand goes to my mouth, and I shake my head, still staring at the canvas.

"No. Uh-uh. I can't . . ." I tell the object, shaking my head.

But even as I say the words, I know they're a lie.

I can.

More importantly, I have to.

Because there is simply no other way.

CHAPTER 43

MIGUEL

That Day

"*¿Sí?*" the nun asked, peering out at him in the darkness of the alley.

"Excuse me, Sister, I need to speak with the young man who just came in here," Miguel informed her in Spanish, already pushing past her.

"*¡Espere! ¡Espere!*" she called after him, but it was too late. He wasn't going to wait. Not when he could hear the raucous sounds taking place out in the sanctuary.

Miguel stopped short, totally unprepared for the sight in front of him. Every member of the small, eclectic group was speaking loudly, excitedly. So loudly and excitedly that they never heard him come in or approach them. The only person who tracked his approach, aside from the nun scurrying behind him, was the child. She looked about seven months old and was peering at him over the shoulder of the woman holding her. Her hair was dark and curly, her placid gaze the deepest blue he'd ever seen.

"This is insane!" hissed a large, beefy man—a *turista* for sure, based on his accent. Northeast somewhere? New Jersey, maybe? New York? "We can't just come back from vacation with . . . with a baby!"

"Mack," said the woman holding the baby. "I don't think we have a choice . . ."

That's when the younger man spotted him approaching. His eyes grew large, and he leaned down to whisper in a petite woman's ear—he immediately recognized her as Beatríz from El Gallo Rojo. Her eyes flew to Alvarez, causing the others to turn in response.

"*Buenas noches*," Alvarez said. "Good evening. My name is Detective Miguel Alvarez with the San Juan Police Department." Everyone froze. Still, the only one unaffected was the little girl, who now offered him a shy smile before burying her face in the woman's shoulder. He looked at her for a long moment. "And that," he continued, never taking his eyes from her, "is Marianna Ruíz."

It was the American man who stepped forward first. He nodded at Miguel and offered a big hand. "Detective, I'm Mack DiMarco—I'm a detective myself, with the NYPD."

Alvarez shook the man's hand and returned the nod of his fellow cop. "I wonder if someone might explain what's going on—and how the little girl came to be here?"

Now their eyes darted back and forth amongst themselves. He watched carefully. Finally, the nun spoke.

"Detective, I am Hermana Blanca, and I have offered this young man and this baby sanctuary here in the church. Their lives are in danger . . ."

Okay, he'd get to that part soon enough.

"And how do *Los DiMarcos* figure into that plan?" he asked, his tone still very calm and businesslike.

"We got back on our cruise ship and found her in our stateroom," Mack supplied. "It was quite a surprise . . ."

"No, no, it was not a surprise," the wife interjected. "I knew she'd be there."

Oh, now this was getting very interesting. Was she about to admit to being involved in the child's disappearance?

"I was here earlier today, and I prayed to the Holy Mother,"

she explained, pointing to a statue on the far side of the sanctuary. "I prayed that Mack and I would have a child of our
own. And when I looked up, she was weeping! For *me*! I
knew right in that moment, without a doubt, that the Lord
would act on my prayers. And He did! When we got back to
the boat, she was there, waiting for us. It was a miracle." Her
volume dropped drastically on that last word.

Okay, not exactly an admission of guilt. This wasn't the
first he'd heard of the "weeping Madonna." Several years
back, when he was a uniformed officer, it had created a
frenzy of visitors to the small house of worship and an influx
of *turistas* looking for the answer to their own baby prayers.

Miguel turned to the young man he'd recognized in the
dark.

"*Eres Jacinto Núñez,*" he said.

"*Fue. Pero ahora mi nombre es Coquí,*" he explained.

That had been his name, but now it was Coquí.

"Are you the one who put the child on the boat?" Alvarez
asked him in Spanish and received a slow nod in return.

But somehow, he doubted it was Coquí who had orches-
trated this whole thing.

"All right," Miguel said, switching to accented English,
"how about you all have a seat here in the front pew, and you
can tell me what's going on here."

"Okay, okay, okay," Miguel said loudly in an attempt to
get everyone to stop talking at one time. He was finally feeling as if he had a clear—or at least a *clearer*—picture of what
had transpired. He pointed at the baby. "Marianna is taken
from Alberto in lieu of payment by the enforcer named Yeti.
Santiago wants nothing to do with it, but decides the child
has to be killed to avoid the perception he's weak."

He swung his finger around to Beatríz and Coquí, seated
together at the far end of the first pew. "Coquí, with the
help of Beatríz, manages to snatch the baby from Yeti. They

bring her here, where Sister Blanca has the idea to give her to Mrs. DiMarco, who by some miracle, had made the statue weep and just happened to leave a check with her name and address in the collection box. Have I got this right so far?" Miguel asked, pausing to allow any corrections or additions. When no one spoke up, he continued. "That's when Beatríz works some contacts to locate the exact ship and room of the couple named DiMarco, while Sister Blanca uses *her* contacts to acquire a fake birth certificate for the child. Then this young man," he said, swinging back in the direction of Coquí, "delivers the baby and the documents to their stateroom on the cruise. After Mrs. DiMarco tells her husband about her trip to the church, Mr. DiMarco decides he does not want them to risk being party to a kidnapping scheme, so they get off the boat with the baby and come here." Alvarez sighed, his brows high as he rubbed his hands together. "And so here we are."

He'd always wanted to deliver one of those grand, Holmesian monologues wrapping up an entire crime. But now that he had, he discovered it wasn't nearly as satisfying as he'd imagined. Mainly because he knew there were pieces of the puzzle missing here—most of them having to do with the man called Yeti, who was conspicuously absent.

Miguel had heard his name mentioned before by the gang unit and knew he was an up-and-comer in the Savage Soldiers. But that was about all he—or anyone else—had been able to put together on him so far. There was no trace of his real name or any family connections. The police didn't even have a clear photograph of him. Apparently, he'd just risen out of the rank-and-file, determined to make his way to the top. And fast.

"What happens next?" the nun asked.

Miguel considered this question. "I know what I should do. I should return that child to her father and I should have the rest of you questioned as part of the investigation into her kidnapping. That's what I *should* do."

The words came out harsher than he'd meant for them to sound . . . but the truth was the truth.

"It was something you *should* have done about forty minutes ago," Mack DiMarco pointed out.

As a fellow member of the law enforcement community, he understood Miguel's predicament in a way the others could not.

"You're right, yes," Miguel conceded.

"But . . . it's not as clear-cut as you'd like," Mack concluded.

"Again, Mr. DiMarco, you are correct. Do you have any other observations you'd care to share?"

He wasn't being sarcastic. Alvarez really did want to know what Mack would do.

"I think . . ." Mack began slowly, "that no matter how you slice it—legally speaking—your hands are tied. The law is very clear on the course of action you are to take."

"No, you don't understand," Beatríz insisted, shaking her head vehemently. "You don't know Santiago. I *sleep* with this man. He's ruthless when it comes to preserving his reputation. If he knows that baby is alive . . . she won't be for very long."

Mack looked at the child sleeping in his wife's arms when he spoke again. "Then again, Detective Alvarez, you know as well as I do that the legal thing is not always the right thing. Or even the safest thing. I've known a few 'Santiagos' in my time, too. And it wouldn't surprise me if, like back in my own police precinct, he had managed to find . . . *friends* on the inside. Officers—who were either afraid of him or on his payroll—willing to tip him off to the details of this case."

Miguel was grateful to have someone who understood the

intricacies of his position. Not that it made his decision any easier.

"She has a father," he said at last. "He can't spend his life thinking she was stolen . . . or worse." And that had to be the deciding factor. "No, I'm sorry. I just don't see how this can work—"

"No, wait, please!" the nun interrupted before he could declare the matter closed. She leaned forward to touch the shoulder of Coquí, seated in the pew directly in front of her. "There's something else you need to know before you make this decision. Please . . . please just . . . just listen for a minute, okay?" Then she put her mouth close to the young man's ear. *"Dile,"* she urged quietly.

"Tell me what?" Alvarez asked.

Coquí had trouble meeting anyone's eyes, choosing instead to look between the floor, the door, and the crucifix hanging in front of them. His voice was soft, and they all had to lean in closer as he told his story from the moment the man called Yeti showed up at the door of the apartment.

He explained his horror at the plan to kill the baby, but his fear of disobeying Santiago. He told him about the long walk to the shack in the middle of nowhere, and the ensuing fight with Yeti. When he reached the last part of the story, he looked tentatively at Hermana Blanca. She nodded solemnly.

With a faltering voice, he explained how he'd intended to hurt Yeti, knock him unconscious. How he had just wanted to give himself a little time to leave with the child and get somewhere safe. But Yeti had been like a mad dog, making it clear that he intended to kill Coquí and then the baby. He'd done what he had to do in order to ensure the child would live. When he'd finished telling them everything, they were all quiet for a long minute.

"I realize there are laws to uphold," the nun said to no one in particular. "But I think we can all agree that this boy should not have to face charges for protecting a baby. Not because the law wouldn't give him a fair chance . . . but because he'd likely be dead before he could even defend himself in court."

Her words hung in the air for a long, uncomfortable moment within which no one made a move to disagree with her.

Finally it was Mack who broke the silence. "Okay—so, just to be clear—because we *must* be absolutely clear on this—we are talking about doing something with serious consequences for everyone in this room. Let's all take a few seconds to consider the potential ramifications. Because—and correct me if I'm wrong here, Detective Alvarez—we're talking fraud at best and kidnapping—possibly even murder, at worst."

Miguel looked at Mack DiMarco, admiring his directness and wishing he'd had a boss like him. Someone smart, with a moral compass, and a sense of empathy and compassion. This man "got it" in a way that very few did. Police work was not black and white because crimes—and the people who committed them—were never black and white. There was almost always a mitigating circumstance to consider.

"This is true," Miguel agreed. "So . . . let's speak theoretically, shall we? Say we work out some sort of . . . alternate plan. In the event that it came to light, Sister Blanca and Beatríz could be arrested for assisting in a kidnapping. Also, there is no statute of limitations on murder. At any time, Coquí could be tried and convicted of killing Yeti—who, if I'm not mistaken, is sitting in the morgue after he was pulled out of a burnt-out shack this afternoon. Now, should Santiago discover Coquí's role in all this . . . we all know what he'll do. And then, of course, there are the DiMarcos . . ." Miguel turned to face Mack and Lucy. "There is the possibility that you might raise this child as your own, only to have the news break at some point. The lies could tear your family apart—even if the courts did not. And they just might. You could lose her. You could lose everything."

"If the father's in, we're in," Mack said quietly but firmly, taking Lucy's hand as she nodded her agreement.

"And so am I," Sister Blanca echoed.

They waited while Beatríz carefully explained everything to Coquí in Spanish as he listened attentively, nodding occasionally. When she'd finished, he looked directly at Miguel.

"I don't care what happens to me. Just please help the little girl."

They all nodded.

They all swore.

The decision was made. Now they just had to figure out how to pull it off.

CHAPTER 44

GABBY

Today

Finding La Perla again isn't difficult. Finding my way *around* La Perla is a whole different thing. You'd think it'd be hard to get lost in an area less than seven hundred yards around. Apparently not. At least, not for me. So I roam the narrow streets and alleyways, making my way in the general direction I think I should be headed. After my conversation with Max, I took a little time to regroup and rethink the story. He was right; I have a lead that has to be followed up on, with or without Isabella. And there's only one source I can think of to look for that information.

When El Viejo sees me, his eyes light up with recognition.

"Ah, good afternoon, *Señorita Reportera*!" he calls out, already beckoning me with one hand as he turns down the volume with the other.

That's right, he thinks I'm a reporter. Well, I kind of am now, right?

Absolutely. I stand up straighter, smile brighter, and join him on the wood plank porch. "Señor, may I speak with you for a few minutes?"

"*¡Claro, claro!* Of course! Come," he replies. A moment later, he's pulling a chair from the corner of the porch so that I can sit next to him. "Would you like coffee?"

As yummy as the last cup he made me was, it's getting to be late, and I don't want to be trying to navigate my way out of here after dark.

"No, thank you."

He returns to his seat, leaning forward. "What I can do for you?" he asks in his slightly askew English.

"I was hoping you could help me with something . . ."

"Yes, yes," he agrees with an enthusiastic nod.

"I was wondering if you've ever heard of someone called Coquí?" I ask, careful to get the name just right.

The man steeples his hands under his chin, looking off into the distance as he searches his memory. I see it the moment he latches onto that particular fragment of the past.

"Yes . . . Coquí . . . *yo recuerdo* . . ." It takes a moment for him to realize he's slipped into Spanish. "Sorry, yes, I remember. It was a long time ago . . ."

"You do? What can you tell me about him?"

He sits back in his rocker, his gaze periodically returning to some distant point only he can see. "His name was Jacinto. Jacinto Nuñez and he was . . . oh, let me see . . . he had maybe fifteen or sixteen years? It was very sad. His . . . how you say? The husband of his mother?"

I think for a second and then it comes to me. "Oh! His stepfather?"

He nods emphatically. "Yes! Yes, his stepfather was bad, bad man. He hit Jacinto's mother all the time. Then one day . . ." his voice trails off, leaving me hanging.

"What?" I ask, unable and unwilling to guess what terrible fate befell this family. Because, judging by his tone, it was pretty bad.

"One day they fight bad and the . . . the stepfather . . . he shoot the mother, then he shoot his self."

I gasp. "What? Oh, no! What happened to Jacinto?" I ask.

"Ah, well, then it was no good for the . . . emmm . . . the people who help the children?"

He throws out the clue as if we're playing a game of Taboo.

I think for a second. "Child protective services? Social workers?"

"Aha!" he exclaims, pointing at me. "Yes, the social workers they try to find him a new home, but he keep leaving . . ."

"He ran away? From foster homes?" I guess.

"Uh-huh, yes. Then he joining *Los Soldados Salvaje* and becoming 'Coquí'."

He doesn't need to translate that one for me; I've heard it often enough at this point. "The gang," I say, and he confirms with a nod. "Wow, that is sad . . ."

"Oh, no, no—is not all that happened."

"Oh, okay, what else?" I ask, thinking this should be the plot of a novel.

"He die."

"He . . . die? Who, Coquí?"

"*Ay, sí.*" The words come out on a regretful sigh. "They find his body in a building that burned. They think that maybe he make Santiago angry . . ."

I've been leaning forward this whole time, literally on the edge of my seat. But now I drop against the back of the chair with a thud, feeling dejected—not just by the loss of the lead in our little saga, but also for the loss of a young man I never knew. A young man who never stood a chance.

In the end, I agree to the cup of café Americano when El Viejo offers it again. I need a little time to digest all of this and decide what—if anything—it has to do with that day. If Coquí was dead in the fire—was he murdered and then the fire set to destroy the evidence? And what happened to Yeti? The baby?

I still can't wrap my head around the fact that the baby in question could very well be me. Not that it would clarify any of this mess. In fact, it only complicates things. How could Mack and Lucy have become involved in this? How had they managed to keep it a secret from me all these years? And . . .

why? Did they really think I could love them less if I knew the truth?

These are the questions rolling around in my head as I finally give the old man a hug and exit his gate out into La Perla. It's getting dark now, and the alleyways between buildings are cast in shadow that wasn't there before. I reverse navigate as best I can; still, I manage to get myself turned around enough to be nervous when I take a turn onto a stretch that's totally deserted. The handful of ramshackle houses here—if you can even call them that—have been reduced to partial floors and half-rooms filled with the rubble of crumbling walls and collapsing ceilings. It's a harsh reminder of just how precariously this community is situated should another major storm come this way. And it's creepy as hell.

I can hear people in the distance and try to maneuver myself in their general direction, but a couple of bad turns have me standing on a street that dead-ends at the wall that surrounds the city. When I look, the stone is all I can see for more than a hundred feet.

"Shiiit," I mumble under my breath, turning around so I can head back in the direction I came.

I pull out my phone to see if I can get a map up to help me find my way. But I have exactly zero bars, and there's no Wi-Fi network to be found in range. I stuff it back into my pocket and spot an alley on the other side of one of the skeletal dwellings. Without much thought, I step over the threshold and pick my way around piles of debris of what must have been a first-floor living room. It's not as straightforward as I thought, though, and when I realize there's a huge hole in the floor, I consider going back out the way I came. Except when I turn to look, the shadows are so long and so dark that it's hard to make out the details of the twenty-five or so feet I've just climbed through. Until a figure separates itself from one of those shadows.

My heart jumps into my throat as, in an instant, I think

about Isabella . . . everything she told me about being careful down here. About the horrific secret she hurled at me the
last time I saw her. No way I'm waiting around to find out
if that's "friend" or "foe" following me through this stupid,
stupid shortcut I've taken. My father must be spinning in his
grave. He taught me better than this—better than to get myself alone in an isolated place.

I think the person is speaking to me, but I can't make out
what they're saying over the whooshing sound in my ears as
I scramble over a small pile of lath and plaster in an attempt
to avoid the piece of the floor that's missing. Not likely there's
a basement—it's probably just a foot or two deep into the
ground below, but I can't really see, and I'm not stopping
long enough to pull out my phone and fumble with the flash-
light function. There's only about ten feet separating me from
my exit point, much dimmer than it was five minutes ago, so
I go up and over the debris. And then my heel catches on a bit
of electrical wire, and I go down. Hard.

By the time I manage to get myself—scraped and bleeding—
right-side-up again, he's right there, standing over me.

"Ow!" I wince sometime later, stretching the exclamation
across two syllables, sounding like I did when I was about
twelve.

"Didn't anyone ever tell you not to go snooping around in
condemned buildings?" David Raña asks as he squirts hand
sanitizer on one of my multiple cuts and scrapes.

"Didn't anyone ever tell *you* not to go sneaking around in
condemned buildings? I mean, seriously, stalk much, Raña?"

His response is an extra-large squirt of the alcohol-based
disinfectant onto my left knee.

"Ouch! You did that on purpose!" I howl. "Do that again
and you might end up singing soprano in the policemen's
choir."

Was that the hint of a smile tugging at the detective's lips?

"Almost done," he murmurs, unwrapping a Hulk Band-Aid to go along with the Spider-Man and Iron Man ones he'd already applied to my lacerations.

As luck would have it, the Raña family was here in La Perla for a basketball tournament when he caught sight of me—and decided to see what I was up to. I was so busy thinking that I never even noticed him trailing me . . . nor did I hear him calling me. If I had, I wouldn't have been so freaked out that I did a header in the rubble of that old house.

Fortunately his wife, Hilary—a petite blonde with big, green eyes and the hint of a soft American Southern drawl—carries a pharmacy in her purse for just such occasions. She has since left to take their two ridiculously cute boys home for dinner, leaving her husband to tape me up and tell me how stupid I am. Over and over and over again. I don't need to be told—I'm well aware of how dangerous what I did was. I'm just too embarrassed and stubborn to admit it.

Raña assesses his handiwork, nods approvingly, and then joins me on the bench overlooking the water. It's dark now, but the walkway is well-lit, and there's plenty of activity coming from the handful of bars and food stands in the immediate vicinity. It's just another balmy January evening in Puerto Rico.

"Why did you duck into the building? Didn't you hear me calling you? And why on earth did you try to run like that?"

"I was trapped, and I freaked out, okay?"

He scoffs. "Trapped? Please! You were on a small, dead-end block. All you had to do was turn around and walk out the way you came in," he says, making a twirling gesture with his fingers to illustrate his point. "But no, you said to yourself, 'Hey, look! This rickety old house might collapse at any second! What a great place to use as a shortcut!'"

I glare. "Really?"

He holds his palms skyward. "All I'm saying is you could have broken your leg. Or worse."

The truth is, I was never more relieved to see anyone in my life than I was when I realized it was the detective standing over me, and not some crazed junkie/rapist/ax murderer.

"I get it, Detective," I assure him begrudgingly. "I just . . . it was getting dark, and then I heard someone shuffling around in the shadows . . . I don't know, I guess my imagination just went into overdrive."

He shakes his head but doesn't bother to reproach me again. So we just sit like that for a good minute or two, taking in the crashing sound and salty smell of the waves somewhere in the darkness ahead of us.

"My God, this must be an amazing place to live," I observe, more to myself than to him. But he agrees.

"I know, right? I was away for a while—at school on the mainland. That's where I met my wife. When the kids came, we decided we wanted to raise them here so they can experience the culture and grow up bilingual."

I'm surprised he's giving me this kind of personal information. Prior to this, he's seemed so . . . buttoned-up and close-mouthed.

"Are they happy here?" I find myself asking.

He nods.

"They are. They'd like if their father worked a little less, but they understand. And they're used to it."

"Is that because you enjoy your work?" I ask, trying to figure what part of murder, kidnapping, and sexual assaults might bring one job satisfaction.

"I don't know if *enjoy* is the right word. I just . . . I take it very seriously," he replies carefully. "It's hard. And sometimes it's ugly—really ugly. You end up living, breathing, and sleeping this shit. But it's worth it if I can close a case. The work I do impacts people's lives. I try to bring them some closure and, if I'm really lucky, some justice. So, yeah, it can be rewarding, but I can't really say I enjoy the process. What about you?"

"What about me?"

"Do you enjoy being a writer—a reporter?"

"I don't know that I'm a reporter, exactly," I admit. "I think more than anything, I'm a storyteller. And if telling the story accurately means I have to do a little investigating in the process, then so be it."

"I'll bet a story like this could make your whole career."

There's a hint of accusation in the remark. One that I choose to ignore.

"Maybe," I reply with a noncommittal shrug.

Unfortunately, my disinterest isn't enough to keep him from taking another run at it.

"This is a long way from your home, your family and friends," he continues. "And it's a story that's been cold for twenty-five years. Do you really think you'll uncover something that was missed the first time around? Or the second time? Or the third? Because we've been at this for a while now . . ."

Aha! So *that's* why this guy's had his panties in a twist since he met us.

I look the detective straight in the eye when I respond. "Listen, I'm not looking to criticize anyone or discredit the investigation," I assure him. "I just need to know what's fact and what's fable after all these years. Besides, it's like you just said. It might be too late for justice, but wouldn't it be nice to give Isabella some closure?"

He seems to consider this for a moment, right before he rejects it.

"Yeah, I don't buy that," he tells me flatly. "Quite frankly, Miss Mack, I find what you're doing to be rather tasteless. So don't hold yourself up as some Good Samaritan uncovering the answers we've been desperately searching for these last twenty-five years. All you're going to do is bring back a lot of bad memories for this community. Memories of a time when things were very different here in La Perla. And if the story gets national attention, what you're talking about could easily paint this place as a slum and these people as a bunch of drug-dealing, baby-stealing murderers."

I'm facing him fully now, trying to keep my expression impassive so he doesn't see how much the accusation stings.

Why do I even care?

More to the point, why does *he* care?

He's had this case for like five minutes.

"Detective Raña, you don't know me. You have no idea how I plan to tell this story. But I can assure you that, while it will be honest, it will be even-handed. The last thing I want to do is portray this community in the way you're suggesting." I feel my face warming as the red creeps up toward my hairline. "And, *quite frankly,* I find it rather insulting that you would presume I'd do something like that."

He considers me. I consider him. And then we both shift forward so we're looking out at the water.

"Tell me about Coquí," I say quietly.

If he's surprised by the question, there's no sign of it. "What about him?"

"Why didn't you tell us about his role in the case?"

"Because we don't know what his role was—or if he even had one. Not officially, anyway. We have our suspicions—but nothing we can prove. Maybe someday, something will turn up that connects all the dots for us. But it hasn't as of yet, and it's not likely it will. Too much time has passed."

"I understand he and the guy named Yeti left with the baby—and with orders from Santiago to kill her."

This gets his attention, his head swinging back around to face me.

"And just who gave you *that* information?" he asks.

I shrug, and a moment later, he appears to have an epiphany.

"Oh, of course!" he declares, snapping his fingers as it comes to him. "*You* were talking to El Viejo, weren't you? That's why you're down here in La Perla."

Okay, I'll give him that—but I'm not volunteering anything else to this guy.

"I was," I admit. "That man's seen a lot of change in this community over the years."

He shakes his head, mouth pursed in irritation.

"Listen, like I said, there's not enough proof—"

"Is that because of the fire?"

I expect him to scoff at the question, but he surprises me by answering it.

"The fire didn't help. But, yes, there were some items recovered there to indicate Marianna had been there . . . at some point. As had Coquí. Beyond that . . . the general assumption has always been that the child was killed."

"But a body was never recovered."

He shakes his head. "No, Marianna's body was never recovered."

"But this Coquí guy, you're sure it was him who died in the fire? Did you do dental records and DNA comparison . . . ?"

"You know what? I'm about done with this conversation. You go ahead and snoop around all you like, but I'm not commenting on this story one way or the other. If you quote anything I've said here, I'll deny it."

And here I thought we were playing nice at last.

I throw up my hands.

"I don't understand you! Why are you so determined to keep me from writing this story? I want to help you do your job. We both want to see this through to the end, I think."

"Do we? Because I don't recall telling you what my goal is with this case."

"You didn't have to. It's the nature of the job. It's the nature of your personality."

His gaze hardens, then he gets to his feet. "I need to get going. Do you need a lift somewhere?"

I shake my head. "No, I have a car parked out on the street where the staircase is."

"Come on, I'll walk you there."

Part of me wants to decline the offer, but the other part of me is still shaken from my earlier scare—even if he was the one who delivered it.

"Thank you," I say, rising up to join him.

We take a few steps when he stops and looks over his shoulder.

"Oh, hey, Gabby, I think you left your phone on the bench . . ."

"Did I?" I spin around, but the bench is empty. "I don't—"

I'm already turning back in his direction when it hits me. And when my eyes finally meet his again, I see the smug triumph there.

"You did hear me calling you earlier, you just didn't answer to the name Lucy Mack," he deduces. "Because it's not your name, and you weren't listening for it."

I continue to stare, wordlessly, refusing to comment one way or the other until I figure out what to say.

Raña takes a deep breath, then sighs it out with resignation. "What do you say I buy you some dinner and we can talk about all of this someplace a little more private?"

"Do I have a choice?" I ask.

He smiles. "Not really, no."

"*Muff-ahngo,*" I try, my nose wrinkling as I mangle the word . . . again. I have no idea why I'm having so much trouble with this one.

The detective shakes his head. "No, the vowels are long," he corrects, then repeats it again for me from across the tiny table.

We're in a little restaurant—modest but clean, the kind frequented by locals rather than tourists. My companion seems hell-bent on getting me to try his favorite local dish, but I'm reluctant, having never seen anything like this before.

"Think *mofo*," he suggests. "As in, 'he's a badass *mofo*'? So, when you say it fast, it comes out like mo-FONE-go. *Mofongo.*"

I chuckle. "Right . . . *mofongo*. Okay, now that I can say it, what *is* it?"

"You take green plantains, cut them into pieces, and deep-fry them. Then, you mash them in a *pilón* . . ."

"A pea who?" I interrupt.

"*Pilón*. It's a mortar and pestle, but it's made out of a local wood. So, you mash it in that, and maybe you add some bits of *chicharrón* . . ."

This one I know from reading about it. "Pork? Like pork rinds?"

"Exactly. You grind that up, too, and add it to the mash, along with some chicken broth maybe. Then you take that mash and press it against the inside of the bowl with a spoon—so you're lining it. Sort of like a pie crust? Then you bake it so it's crisp on the outside and last, you fill it . . ."

Just then our orders arrive, his bowl filled with a mixture of rice and pigeon peas with braised beef. Mine is more like a stew inside the mashed bowl—a rich broth with huge shrimp floating in it. I poke at an exposed bit of the plantain mash "bowl," with new appreciation for its construction. Then I dip my large spoon so I can sample the warm, salty broth with a hint of tomato and chunks of red and green pepper accompanying the shrimp.

"Oh, my God," I murmur appreciatively through a mouthful. I think my eyes might be rolling back inside my head right now with the food orgasm that's happening in my mouth.

"It's good, isn't it?" He shovels another spoonful into his mouth.

I nod, and we eat companionably for several minutes—the only sounds between us consisting of slurping, chewing, and appreciative groaning over the meld of flavors and juxtaposition of the two consistencies—the baked plantain exterior and warm, salty elixir that it holds. I groan my approval periodically. Then, after a bit, the detective puts down his spoon and peers at me across the table.

Here we go.

"So why the lie?" he asks.

"So why the background check?" I counter.

"You walked into my office with an interest in a cold case. And with one of the family members in tow, no less. When I showed you that pink sock, you went white as a sheet. I'm a detective. You really think none of that would pique my curiosity? And—by the way—you really need to do a better job with the whole 'fake identity' thing. All it took was a call to the hotel to get your name, address, phone, and credit card info. Then it was just a matter of Google."

I shrug, pretending to be nonchalant.

"Yeah, so? What did you find out?"

"That you're not a writer—not officially, anyway—but you're credited as a researcher for *Flux* magazine. You own a condo in Brooklyn; you're not married or divorced. You're mentioned in the obituaries for Lucy DiMarco and, later, Mack DiMarco—hence the Lucy Mack alias."

"Okay, and?" I challenge between sips of the mofongo—which is so good I'm not willing to abandon it, even in the midst of this exchange. "Not much of a smoking gun there, Detective."

"Maybe not, but you're not the only one who can run around Puerto Rico talking to people like Beatríz Rodriguez, El Viejo, and Miguel Alvarez," he says, shattering my illusion—or should I say delusion?—that Isabella and I have been so covert and stealthy in our little game of Clue.

Oh, but wait, there's more. He leans forward and drops

his voice even lower. Anyone catching sight of us through the window would think we were lovers, all cozied up and exchanging sweet nothings in the back corner of the intimate little restaurant.

"Gabby, just stop, okay? I know you and Isabella submitted DNA for testing earlier in the week and that you're waiting on the results to come back. Now *that*, I would say, could be a smoking gun."

He's right. With an almost imperceptible sigh, I set my spoon down on the napkin next to my bowl and meet his dark stare full-on. I see him, then, as if it's the first time. I've glanced, and glared, and glowered at the man since the day we met, but this is the first time I've really taken the time to look at him—to really *see* him. And I have to admit I'm a little taken aback by what I find there.

Sometimes when I look into Isabella's eyes, I feel as if I'm standing at the edge of a tempest—fighting against the pull of her tumultuous emotions. But right here, right now, with David Raña, there's something on a whole other level going on between us. It's like there's something in him telepathically transmitting to something in me, as if he speaks a language I'd forgotten I ever knew.

I can't really find the words to describe the sense of well-being that washes over me as we consider each other across our plates, across our table, across our lives. Hidden behind the cold, hard veneer of those dark eyes lies a calm, quiet strength. This is a man who has seen the worst this world has to offer, yet refuses to abandon the well of kindness, compassion, and faith that runs to his very core.

This is a good man, an honorable man. This is a safe man. I don't know how I know . . . I just do.

And so, with a rush of relief that nearly brings me to tears, I tell him everything there is to tell.

CHAPTER 45

ISABELLA

Today

I walk in the front door at roughly the same time I'm usually walking out of it for work. Covered in paint spatter, dried sweat, and tears, I feel both exhausted and exhilarated. Every part of my body aches, and the only thing keeping me upright is the thought of soaking in a hot bath, then sleeping in a soft bed.

All of that disappears the moment I find my husband waiting for me as soon as I step across the threshold.

And my God, does he look pissed. Or is he scared?

Both.

"Matéo?"

The single word is all I can get out before I'm swept up in an embrace so tight it threatens to crack my ribs.

"Oh, thank God!" he gasps into my hair. "Isabella, where have you been? I've been worried sick about you! I was just about to call the police!"

I push his chest, so he'll loosen his grip and step back a foot or two.

"What? How long have you been home?" I ask. "I thought you were going to go from your parents' house straight to work . . ."

He shakes his head. "I couldn't do it. I couldn't sleep without you next to me. Not after the way we left things yesterday. So I came home in the middle of the night, and you weren't here . . . but your phone was. And you don't go anywhere without your phone. So I began to worry that something had happened to you. That you'd . . . or that someone had . . ."

He can't even finish whatever dark thoughts have been running through his head all night. Not that I can't guess a few of them.

I put a palm to his sweet face and look deep into his eyes.

"I had a few demons to face."

He leans forward, until his forehead is touching mine.

"From now on, we face them together, okay?"

"Yeah . . . though I have to tell you, I've been doing a pretty good job of it on my own."

He straightens up and cocks his head. "Oh, yeah?"

I nod and smile, feeling myself come to life again in his arms. "In fact, if you give me ten minutes for a quick shower, I'll let you take me to breakfast so I can tell you all about it."

"I'd like that," he murmurs, a second before his lips brush against mine.

CHAPTER 46

GABBY

Today

When I feel the hint of sea breeze on my face, I close my eyes and welcome it, inhaling until my lungs are filled to capacity. I don't know exactly when I'm getting onto a plane headed back to the bleak New York City winter, but it won't be much longer now.

Now that I'm finished.

Something woke me that night in my apartment—the night I realized I had to come here to Puerto Rico. Was that really only a week ago? Something—or someone—was trying to show that to me. God, maybe, or the universe? Possibly Mack and Lucy from beyond the grave? For that matter, it might have been my own subconscious. Well, whatever it was, it was absolutely right. So when I woke this morning before dawn with that same niggling sensation—that feeling that there was something I needed to do—you bet I listened. And I waited. It didn't take long for the thoughts to come to me—as if they'd been sitting there, just on the edge of my awareness all this time.

It was still dark when I took my laptop out onto the balcony and started to write. Without stopping to think too much about it, I just let my fingers fly across the keyboard, occasionally looking up long enough to catch a little of the retreating moon on the water. I lost myself in the words, letting them flow from somewhere deep inside me directly to my fingers, totally bypassing that stupid, brutal, soulless filter of insecurity that lives somewhere above the heart and below the brain.

I'm not sure how I did it, but I managed to miss the sunrise altogether, only noticing the sun once it had cleared the horizon of dawn and was starting its climb upward for the day. By the time I'd finished, four hours and four thousand words had flown by. I stopped, stretched my arms upward, and glanced down at the pages. I didn't need to reread them; I already knew they were good.

Very good, actually.

Because sometimes you just know. It's not vanity or hubris, it is simply . . . fact.

Now, I attach the pages to an email, and without a single moment's hesitation, I hit send and go to take a hot shower, leaving my words to make the journey through the ether, across the ocean, up the eastern seaboard and into his inbox. Once I'm out, I barely have time to throw on a robe and wrap my hair up in a towel when my phone starts to vibrate on the coffee table. I stand over it, looking down at Max's face on the screen.

"Hello?" I ask cautiously.

"Gabby?"

"Hi, Max."

"Gabby, this is—you wrote this?"

"No, Max, I paid little elves to do it for me while I was sleeping," I snark. "Yes, of *course* I wrote it!"

"I'm sorry, I just didn't expect . . ."

"What, that it would be any good?" I supply caustically.

"That it would be *this* good," he counters without missing a beat. "And the pictures . . . my God. I want this. I want to run this."

"I know."

"How could you have possibly known?"

"Because it's the right story. And you *always* know the right story when you see it."

He's quiet for a second, clearly trying to decide how to couch the question he really wants to ask. So I provide the answer for him.

"It's not the story we talked about—"

"No, it's not—but Gabby, you've given me something I didn't even know I wanted."

I give a silent fist pump on my side of the Atlantic.

"Well, I appreciate that, thank you." I work hard to keep my tone cool and even—professionally distant. "As for the original story, I still don't know what's going on with the DNA results, or what's going to happen with Isabella . . ."

"No, no . . . this is . . . for now, this is perfect. See how the rest of it all plays out for the two of you, and then you can decide how to proceed. Once you have all the facts. That is, assuming you want to come back to *Flux* . . ."

Okay, here we go. Time to stand my ground.

"Depends on what you're offering. Would I be a staff writer? Like officially?"

"Well . . . you'd be a junior staff writer—at first, anyway—working in tandem with Jay. Oh, and I'd need you to cover fact-checking part-time, just until we find your replacement. But, since you'll recognize the best candidate far faster than I would, I'd like you to run that search. So, really, as quickly as you can fill your old position, you'll be off that desk altogether. Then it's just a matter of you getting your sea legs. But, yeah, once we get all that squared away, it shouldn't be very long before you're up for full staff writer."

My mouth opens to accept but—for once—the filter in my brain catches the words before they can actually cross the threshold of my lips.

I hear Franny's voice in my head . . .

"The people who get ahead in this world are the ones who actively go after what they want."

And Isabella's . . .

"You don't owe him a damn thing," she informs me. *"That man doesn't want you as a writer . . . but he wants you to pick up after them?"*

And Mack's . . .

"People can only do to you what you allow them to do to you."

A week ago, I'd have jumped at this opportunity. Hell, a week ago, I was pretty much begging for this opportunity! But then, a week ago, I didn't think of myself as a writer . . . a *real* writer. And that lapse in self-confidence came, in large part, *because* of Max. And, while I have no doubt he'll honor his word and eventually name me a staff writer, there are these nagging, niggling questions . . .

"Okay, so what's your best estimate of how long it'll take? For me to make full staff writer."

He lets out a surprised whoosh of air, as if he was expecting me to accept on the spot.

"Oh . . . um, well . . . conservatively speaking . . . eighteen months to two years?"

Uh-huh.

"And this story about me . . . and Isabella?"

"What about it?" he asks, and I feel like giving him a dope slap on the back of his perfectly tousled head.

"Who does it?"

The single beat he takes gives me his answer before he can even reply.

"Gabby—"

"Max, I really appreciate the offer, but I'm afraid I'm going to have to pass."

"I—wait, I'm sorry—you're going to pass? I give you everything you asked for, and you're going to *pass*?" he sputters, emphasizing the last word as if it were the name of some filthy disease.

"I deserve better. My work deserves better. No, I think I'm going to try my hand at freelance for a while. You're certainly welcome to make me an offer on the story I sent you—and any others I write—but just so you know, I'll be shopping them to other magazines, as well. And . . . just so you know? You lost me at 'fact-checker.' That part of my career is done. I'm done being the girl who worries so much about covering everyone else's asses that she forgets to cover her own."

"Fine, I'll take that off the table, but—" he flounders, but when there's a knock at my hotel room door, I seize the opportunity to ditch this conversation.

"Oh, hey, listen, Max," I interrupt quickly, "I think housekeeping is here. Let's finish this discussion later, okay?"

I don't give him time to say another word before disconnecting the call.

"Just a second!" I call out to the closed door when the person on the other side knocks a second time.

I rush over and pull it open to find myself face-to-face with Detective David Raña. Again.

"Miss DiMarco," he says a little stiffly. "I'm sorry, I should have called first," he mutters, making a point of looking the other way as he enters the suite.

That's when I remember I'm in a robe with a towel turban.

"No, no, it's fine. Just give me a minute to get dressed," I suggest, holding up my index finger.

In less than two minutes, I manage to throw on some jeans and a white T-shirt, giving my wet hair a quick brushout before twisting it up into a bun atop my head.

"There, that's better," I say when I exit the bedroom back into the main portion of the suite.

Detective Raña is standing out on the balcony, taking in the same view I had only a few minutes ago. He turns around, looking much more comfortable now that I'm fully clad.

"What can I do for you, Detective?" I ask him pleasantly.

"I need to speak with you . . ."

"Okay—"

"And Miss Ruíz."

"Hmm . . . well, I'd be willing, but I doubt you can convince her."

His brows pull in. "What, are you two *still* not speaking?"

"No, afraid not."

He nods. "Right. That's okay. I can make it work," he assures me as he pulls his phone out of his pocket.

CHAPTER 47

ISABELLA

Today

Retired Detective Miguel Alvarez is waiting for me in the parking lot of the café when I arrive, stepping out of his car and striding in my direction before I've even had a chance to shift mine into park.

"You're late," he declares with a pointed glance down at his watch.

"No, actually, I'm right on time, considering you called me like five minutes ago," I counter, closing the car door and locking it with my key fob. "Now, you wanna tell me what was so important that I had to close up shop to come out and meet you?"

"Huh. You know, funny thing, I seem to recall more than a few times I dropped everything to be there for you. Like when you got arrested for defacing public property—three times. Then there was the night you were stuck out in the middle of nowhere, half-stoned, half-drunk with no way to get home . . . Oh, and that shoplifting charge that I got dropped . . ." He stops and looks at me, gauging whether or not he needs to continue.

He doesn't. Message received.

"You're right, I apologize. What can I do for you?"

I'm not one who offers up apologies easily, and this one has obviously taken him by surprise.

"Apology accepted," he says at last. "Let's go inside, and we can talk over a cup of coffee."

"Okay, well, all you had to do was tell me you were in town and wanted to get a cup. You didn't need to—"

He shakes his head. "No, Isabella. This is . . . It's not a social visit. There are some important things we need to discuss."

"Okay . . ." I agree, my voice trailing off in a way that lets him know I think he's acting strangely.

He leads the way to the front entrance, opening the door and then stepping aside so I can enter ahead of him. It doesn't even occur to me that this is anything other than a polite gesture . . . until I spot the couple seated at a table in the back of the café—Detective David Raña and Miss Gabriella DiMarco. Miguel must have anticipated my reaction, because he's ready for me when I spin back around, nearly knocking him over in my attempt to get out the way I just came in.

"What the hell *is* this?" I whisper/hiss at him.

"Come and sit, Isabella. Just for a little while," he coaxes quietly, putting a hand on my upper arm. "Please . . . it's important."

It must be, if Gabby is here. I haven't spoken to her since I stormed out of our hotel room the other day. It's not that I'm angry with her—the opposite, actually. I'm ashamed of myself—my behavior—and I haven't quite worked out a way to apologize.

Oh, who am I kidding? That's bullshit. This has nothing to do with the words.

I'm not afraid of the apology itself—I'm afraid of the possibility she won't even give me the chance to make it. Or, worse, she'll let me spit it out and decide she still doesn't want anything more to do with me. In other words, I've been paralyzed by the fear that I've come this far, just to screw it up beyond repair.

But at least she doesn't look away as I approach the table where Raña now stands to greet us, so I guess that's a good sign.

"Miss Ruíz," he says with a curt nod to me before extending a hand to Alvarez, who shakes it. "Miguel, thank you for coming."

I take the seat across from Gabby, taking more time than is necessary to situate myself and my purse before finally looking up. Her deep blue eyes are cool as she peers at me . . . but not totally frosted over.

"Hey," I murmur so softly.

"Hi," she replies. "How are you?"

I shrug. "Okay. You?"

She nods. "Yeah, I'm fine, thanks."

Before we can cycle through any more of the usual pleasantries, her attention is redirected to Raña, who has a hand on Miguel's shoulder.

"Miss Gabriella DiMarco, I'd like you to meet Detective Miguel Alvarez," he says, gesturing between the two of them.

For a second, I think maybe I've misheard. Did he just call her . . . ?

"Did I just call her by her name?" Raña reads my mind or, at least, my expression. "Her *real* name? Yes, I did."

I look to Gabby, who's already shaking her head.

"I didn't tell him," she says, holding up her hands. "He figured it out on his own. But it's okay, really. He's a good guy . . ."

"Is he now?" I ask, feeling a little less guilty and a little more defensive. "So you've spent some quality time together, then?"

"Let's just say we ran into each other," the detective says. "And we had some time to talk about who she is—and who you two think she might be."

I gape first at him, then at her.

"You *told* him?"

She opens her mouth to respond, but he beats her to it.

"More like I had a hunch—which Miss DiMarco confirmed for me on her little after-dark field trip to La Perla."

"Wait, you went back to La Perla? Alone? And at night? Why would you do that after I told you how dangerous it can be there?"

Gabby shrugs. "I needed to speak with El Viejo—about Coquí," she explains. "I didn't mean to stay there so late. And then I got a little lost . . . Detective Raña happened to be there with his family, and he helped me out."

I find her indifference infuriating—a feeling that hits me fast and out of nowhere. For the first time in as long as I can remember, something churns in my gut—a mixture of anger, and fear, and concern. It's an overwhelming sense of worry for what *might* have happened, and relief over what didn't.

Jesus, is this how Matéo feels every time I'm off the rails? I make a mental note to apologize to him when I get home tonight.

"What were you *thinking*?"

I don't mean for the question to come out as harshly as it does, but I can't bring myself to walk it back, either.

Gabby tilts her head to the side slightly, considering me for a few long seconds.

"I'll tell you what I was thinking," she begins coolly. "I was thinking that one of us needed to follow up on the Coquí lead. And since you took off for God-only-knows-where, leaving me high and dry on the other side of the island, it had to be me." When she leans forward across the table towards me, I see that something has changed in her eyes—that deep, warm ocean of color turns icy cold and hard. "But you know what I'm thinking *now*, Isabella? I'm thinking that I'm tired of you treating me like a child. You're not my mother. You're not even my sister. So how about you spare me the lecture?"

"Well, maybe if you didn't act like a child—" I reply, but

Miguel jumps in to shut down the spat before it can become any more heated.

"Okay! Okay," he interrupts, holding up his palms in a gesture of peace. "However we got here, we're here now. So yes, to answer your earlier question, Isabella, we are aware that 'Lucy Mack' is actually Gabriella DiMarco, who is actually Marianna Ruíz."

"*Might* be Marianna," I remind him. "We haven't gotten the DNA test results back, so we don't know for sure."

"You do now," Raña says flatly, sliding an envelope out onto the table between her and me.

Gabby and I look down at the envelope in unison.

"You—have the results?" Gabby asks, her anger completely evaporated in an instant. "But how did you even know we'd taken the test?"

"Did you really think I wouldn't hear about your little 'investigation'? You just said it yourself, Miss DiMarco—'the Coquí lead.' I know you two have been running around the island, interviewing people and collecting your little clues, a couple of Nancy Drews. If you'd just come to either of us in the first place—if you'd just told us your suspicions, we could have saved you a lot of trouble."

I want to clap back at him but, like Gabby, I can't take my eyes off the envelope.

"Go ahead, look inside," Miguel coaxes from next to me with a gentle nudge of his elbow.

So I reach for it. The flap isn't sealed, and the single sheet slips out easily. I unfold it and scan the results. The test concludes with 99.979% certainty that we are full-blood sisters. Funny how I've been telling myself—and anyone else who will listen—that I never had a doubt about this outcome. But now that it's here, in black and white, I realize I must have been lying to myself. Otherwise, why would I feel so . . . relieved? Had I really, truly been sure, this would just feel like confirmation. Wouldn't it?

Keeping my mixed emotions to myself, I pass the document across to Gabby so she can have a look at it.

"My God," she murmurs, a hand flying up to cover her mouth. "Oh, my God . . ."

She's looking a little chalky all of a sudden, and her hands are shaking as she stares down at the paper they're holding.

"Are you okay?" I ask.

She nods and, after a few more seconds, refolds it, slips it back into the envelope, and pushes it to the middle of the table again.

"So . . . it's true. It's really true, then . . ." she murmurs, more to herself than the rest of us.

"Well, that piece of it is," Miguel assures her. "David and I have spent the last couple of days going back over every bit of the case. We also ran some more advanced DNA tests that weren't available to us twenty-five years ago. And we think we've finally worked out what happened—more or less—to get us to this point."

Oh, wow. He's saying they know how Gabby came to be . . . well . . . Gabby. I glance at my newly minted sister, who's chewing on her lower lip and squeezing the edge of the table so hard her knuckles are turning white. This is the moment of truth for her more than anyone else. She already knows her life has been a lie. This is where she finds out just how much of a lie it's been.

I realize now, watching her from across the table, that I started to care for this woman long before our connection was one of her indisputable "facts." I wonder if she feels it, too?

I've no sooner thought the question than Gabby reaches across the table, her palm opened upward. For me. Her eyes lock onto mine, and she tells me, without a word, that everything is forgiven—all is forgotten. The harsh words and the rash actions are behind us. I agree with a single short nod, clasping her hand in mine and giving it a squeeze.

"Okay, let's have it," I say. "We're ready."

The two detectives exchange glances, and I can tell there's something else.

"Before we get into all that, we're wondering what you ladies intend to do with this information," Raña asks.

"What do you mean 'do with' it?" Gabby asks, her brows furrowing.

"I mean, are you going to go to the press with this—like *20/20* or *Oprah*? Do you intend to write a tell-all book, or sell the story to Hollywood . . . or what?"

With a slight shrug, I defer to the woman across from me. My sister.

She lets out a puff of air as she considers the question. "Uh, well, I honestly don't know," she admits. "I suppose it depends on what you're going to tell us about the case. And even then, we'd have to discuss it—Isabella and I. This is her life—*her* story as much as it's mine."

I'm surprised to feel the pressure of tears behind my lids, and I have to work hard to blink them back.

My God, I've behaved so badly, and here she is taking my feelings into consideration. It's kind and it's gracious—like the woman herself, I've come to learn.

"Fair enough," the detective says with a decisive nod. "We'll come back to that. Now, there's another document you should see, Miss DiMarco," he says, producing a second envelope and handing it to her. She lets go of my hand to open it while he continues. "We've done a bit of reverse engineering backwards from Gabby's birth certificate." He thrusts his chin in the direction of the paper she's reading. "One of them, anyway."

Frowning, she hands it across to me for a look. I have her original birth certificate—the one with our parents' names on it. The one that declares her to be Marianna Crucita Ruíz. This one, on the other hand, might as well belong to a stranger—with the name Gabriella Grace, and parents Mack and Lucy DiMarco. But there's one other detail that gets my attention.

"Why does this give her place of birth as the Dominican Republic?" I ask, using my index finger to point to the line in question.

"Miguel?" Raña hands it off. "You were the one who was there, I think you should be the one to untangle this all for us."

The older man nods from next to me and then begins. "Okay, clearly you are aware of the events that started everything. How Alberto owed Santiago money. Money which Yeti was sent to collect. I believe Beatríz gave you some insight into what happened after that—how Yeti saw an opportunity to get on his boss's good side by beating the man unconscious and taking his baby. I think you're also aware of the fact that Santiago wanted nothing to do with any of it, and he instructed Yeti to 'make the baby disappear.' Are you both with me so far?" he confirms, scrutinizing our faces.

Gabby and I both nod, hanging on his every word.

"Yes, well, apparently, they walked several miles to an abandoned shack where, we presume, they intended to carry out their . . . business. But something happened there—which we only discovered when the shack burned down and investigators found evidence that Marianna—you, Miss DiMarco—had been there. So I was called to the scene, where they found skeletal remains of a man in the rubble."

"Who was it?" I blurt, before I can help myself.

"Well, we weren't sure at the time. But we did find a medal of St. Christopher. There wasn't much we could tell about it at the time, but it was logged into evidence. Now with the advances in DNA testing, David and I have been able to confirm that it belonged to a young man named Jacinto Nuñez—also known as Coquí . . ."

Gabby and I look at each other. Here, at last, is the Coquí in question. The one who was with Beatríz and Yeti that day.

"He became a member of *Los Soldados Salvajes*," Gabby says, taking all of us by surprise. She looks at me. "El Viejo told me that his stepfather murdered his mother, leaving Coquí an orphan, and he ended up in the gang. He was really young."

"That's right, Miss DiMarco," Raña agrees. "So we now believe he was murdered in that shack by Yeti, who then doused the place in gasoline and set it on fire to cover his tracks and destroy evidence . . ."

"But why?" I want to know. "From everything you've said so far, he was in on the kidnapping. So why would Yeti turn on him like that at the shack?"

It's Gabby who figures it out first.

"Because he didn't want to go through with it," she whispers.

Raña nods in agreement. "Right again. Jacinto—Coquí—hadn't been with the gang very long and, as you just said, he was very young. We think Yeti was supposed to kill the baby—you, Miss DiMarco—at that shack . . . but that Coquí tried to stop him . . . and ended up losing his own life in the process."

Gabby looks at me. "He died trying to save me . . ."

I take her hand again and squeeze it. Hard.

Good thing she's got some money, because she's gonna need a really good therapist to work through this shitshow. We both are.

Raña shifts, I think a little uncomfortable with the emotional impact of the story he's telling. Without comment, he clears his throat and continues.

"Yeah, so once he set the shack on fire, Yeti made his way to the ferry between Puerto Rico and the Dominican Republic. We know this because we've got some grainy security film of him. Now, at first we thought Marianna had been killed in that shack as well, but there wasn't any sign of . . . you know . . . they never found any proof of that at the scene.

That's when we went back to that footage again and we noticed Yeti was carrying what looks to be a duffel bag." Raña looks at Gabby. "It is our belief that you were inside that bag, Miss DiMarco."

"But why drag a crying, hungry, cranky baby all that way?" she asks. "I mean, I'm glad he did, obviously, but it doesn't make any sense. It was super risky."

I nod in agreement, listening as Miguel fields this question.

"Yes, it was, but Yeti would have seen it as an opportunity to make some money. Enough money that it was worth the risk—and worth defying Santiago for. Sadly, it is not unusual for children to be sexually exploited in the Dominican Republic, even today. Yeti probably believed if he could transport the baby there, he could sell her on the open market. But then something interesting happened . . ."

"Right, because everything else up to this point has been so dull," I mutter snarkily and am surprised when Raña gives me a half-shrug/half-smirk.

It's the least uptight thing the guy's done since we first met. Maybe there's hope for Detective David Raña, after all.

"Yes, well, believe it or not, things get even more interesting from there," he assures us. "Within twenty-four hours of that ferry arriving in the D.R., a man fitting Yeti's description was killed in a bar fight. We think maybe he went there asking about where he might be able to find someone in the market for what he had to sell. The fact that it was a baby could have easily angered even the criminal element there, but that's just speculation. Whatever it was that he said or did, it got him a one-way ticket to the morgue, where he was logged as a John Doe and his body was cremated sometime later."

"Wait, wait, wait," Gabby says, pulling her hand out of mine so she can rub her temples with her index fingers. "So, he *didn't* sell her—me—the baby?"

"We don't think he ever had the opportunity," Miguel

says. "Our theory is that someone discovered you in that duffel bag—either there at the bar, or somewhere else where he'd left you while he went to the bar. However it happened, we know for certain that someone took that baby out of the duffel bag and brought her—you—directly to the nuns at the Catholic foundling home. The records show that a few weeks later, an American couple named Mack and Lucy DiMarco arrived as part of a missionary trip to build a school for the children . . ."

"Oh, my God!" Gabby interjects excitedly. "That was them? That was *then*? I've seen those pictures! My parents—they used to joke about how that's where I was conceived . . ."

Miguel smiles at this. "They might not have been telling you the exact truth . . . but it was close enough. For them, anyway. And, as you obviously know now, Mack and Lucy DiMarco chose to keep the adoption a secret from you."

"And the birth certificate?" I ask. "How did she not ever see that one?" I ask, nodding my chin toward the paper sitting in front of Gabby.

"She would have been issued a new birth certificate upon adoption, and when that happens, it usually reflects the adoptive parents' state of residence rather than actual location of the child's birth," Raña explains. "That's why the official copy lists the U.S. as her birthplace, while there is also one on file in the D.R.—from where she was adopted. And, of course, there's Marianna's birth certificate. But at that point, nobody put the two together. The nuns believed the little girl to have been left by an unwed teen or perhaps a sex worker. It never occurred to anyone there that she had been kidnapped from Puerto Rico."

Raña sighs and raises his palms slightly.

"So that's the story, ladies. Your story—*both* of your stories, actually. And, as such, you are free to do whatever you wish with this information. But there are a couple of things you should consider before you decide whether or not to go public with all of this—then you can weigh out whether or not it's worth it."

"Okay, we're listening," I announce for the both of us.

"It's possible—likely, actually—that, should you go public, this will all become sensationalized overnight. You think you'll be able to control the narrative here, but trust me, you won't. It's just too big, and the story of Marianna's disappearance has become something of folklore around here. It will make national—maybe even international—headlines. And when that happens, everything will be out there. Every dirty little detail. People will pick it apart. They'll judge you, they'll judge your family, they'll judge the police. They'll make accusations and assumptions. And while many people will be endeared by your story, just as many will call you frauds, or decide the DiMarcos were criminals. Miss Ruíz, they'll dredge up Alberto's past and everything that's happened to you since Marianna disappeared. Your privacy will be gone as long as it's a story of interest to the public."

That last one is enough to make my blood turn icy in my veins. He can't mean *everything*, can he? I look to Gabby, whose concerned expression mirrors my own.

"Are you okay?" I ask.

"Yes." She nods. And then she shakes her head. "No— actually, not really. You?"

"No, not really," I agree.

"I can't—" she says.

"I don't think—" I say at exactly the same moment.

It's just like our meeting at the resort. God, was that really only a week ago?

"Isabella," she says, "I—I can't do that to them. To my parents. They protected my privacy all these years. I can't let them—let our life become some cheesy Lifetime movie."

Raña speaks up then, and he's looking directly at me.

"I know he won't say it, Miss Ruíz, but I will," he begins, with a nod toward Miguel next to me. "This could easily be twisted into something ugly—something that makes Detective Alvarez here look as if he was incompetent during this investigation. Some might even call for a review of his conduct during that time. Even all these years later, it could tarnish the stellar reputation of an exceptional cop . . . and an exceptional man."

I'm struck by the sincerity in Raña's voice. It's the kind that can't be manufactured. The kind of sincerity that tells me he holds Alvarez in the same kind of esteem that I do. And that's saying something. When I glance at Miguel, he's staring at his hands, which are folded neatly on the table in front of him.

There is no decision here for me.

"Miguel, I owe you my life in more ways than one," I tell him softly, putting a hand on his forearm. "I swear to you, I won't say anything to anyone," I tell him. Then to Gabby, "And you're absolutely okay with this? Keeping it all a secret, I mean? This is supposed to be your big chance—your hook. What are you going to tell Max?"

She picks up the DNA report and tears it in half, and then into smaller pieces from there. "As far as I'm concerned, the original results were a mistake—a transposed number or misplaced decimal point or something. No long-lost sisters. No missing baby back from the dead. No skeletons in anyone's closet. No story to tell."

Gabby delivers this declaration with a smile so devious, it makes my heart swell with pride. She's grown some claws, this little kitten!

Raña nods in agreement, then gestures to Miguel. "I have to say, I think that's the best course of action. But if you should ever change your minds—either of you—please reach out to me first. That way, I can help you get your ducks in a row before you go public. Maybe help you figure out how much to disclose . . ."

"That won't be necessary," I inform him. "Neither of

us will be changing our minds. There's too much riding on this—too many people who could get hurt. Including us." I see his face soften in relief and the corners of his mouth twitch up—just a bit. "You know, Detective," I say, "you really should smile more often. You definitely look like less of a dick when you do."

Now he offers an actual, honest-to-God smile, and it's like I'm looking at an entirely different man.

"Yeah, my wife tells me that all the time."

CHAPTER 48

GABBY

Today

After the detectives leave the restaurant, Isabella and I are left looking at one another speculatively.

"So . . . you were right all along," I say. "We really are sisters."

She tilts her head to the side slightly and shrugs with one shoulder.

"Yeah, well, I have to admit—there *were* a few moments there when I wasn't so sure. The way this story kept taking those crazy turns . . ."

"I know, right?" I jump in, understanding exactly what she's talking about. "One minute I'd be crying because I thought I was Baby Marianna, and the next I'd be crying because I wasn't. What an emotional roller coaster!"

"Speaking of emotional roller coasters, what's going on with you and Max?"

"Nothing," I tell her, echoing her earlier pronouncement about my relationship with my former boss. "We're not colleagues, we're not friends, and we're sure as hell not lovers. But he did offer me a job as a junior staff writer—which I declined."

"You declined?" She gapes. "But isn't that what you've been dreaming about all this time?"

I nod slowly, trying to think of the best way to explain the decision I've come to only in the last day or so.

"It is. But this thing with Max—the way he's handled it—handled *me*—from the beginning has kind of soured me on working for him—or doing anything else with him, for that matter. I mean, he's sweet, and charming, and there's a lot I could learn from him. Not to mention the fact that he's ridiculously handsome . . ."

"But?" she coaxes when I leave the thought dangling.

I consider the best way to phrase this.

"Okay, so, this is probably going to sound immature, but I just can't seem to get past the fact that he didn't have any faith in me. And I know myself; it'll just keep niggling at me."

"I don't think there's anything immature about that," Isabella tells me sincerely. "Listen, Gabby, you're not the only one. There are times when believing in myself takes every bit of energy I have . . . and it's still not enough."

"Seriously? You always seem so confident. I can't even imagine you having any self-esteem issues!"

She scoffs and smiles a little. "Oh, I've got them all right. I think we all do at some point in our lives."

"Okay, so what do *you* do when that happens?"

She shrugs. "Those are the times when I have to turn to someone I trust—like Matéo. For you it might be your friend Franny or—"

"Or you," I interject, reaching to put my hand on hers.

Isabella's face flushes.

"Yeah," she agrees quietly but firmly, "or me. Anytime, you got it? Because those are the times when you need someone you *know* has your back. Someone to boost your confidence . . . not undermine it."

"So not Max," I state more for myself than for her.

She gives my hand a squeeze and when she speaks again it's with a tone of resignation. "I think, no matter how much you like Max or respect Max, part of you is always going to be wondering, *what does Max* really *think about this?* Do you see how it adds this whole other layer of insecurity that you have to overcome? Just one more hurdle."

Her insights are spot-on, and part of me wonders if the fact that we share DNA has anything to do with it. Is it possible this woman gets me in a way that no one else does—or could? I suppose it's one of those mysteries that will unfold over time.

Time.

The thought of it fills me with a warmth I haven't felt in so long. Not the hours themselves, but the idea that I get to spend them getting to know Isabella—and the rest of my family.

I'm not alone anymore, and that makes me stronger, bolder, braver. Because, fail or succeed, there'll always be someone who has my back.

"You're absolutely right about that, Isabella," I announce firmly enough that she looks a little surprised.

"Um . . . okay. Yeah, that's great . . ."

"I'm done trying to prove myself. No more trying to convince Max of how good I am. If he, or anyone else, for that matter, wants one of my stories, *they're* going to have to convince *me* of how much they want it."

I jump when Isabella slaps the table between us excitedly. "Holy shit, mama! I am proud of you!"

"Thanks?"

She flashes a huge grin. "Okay—so if not Max and *Flux,* then what?"

"Well," I start slowly, taking my newfound confidence for a test drive, "I figure if Max thinks my story is great, then other editors will, too. So . . . I was thinking maybe I'd try to shop it to other magazines, see who else might be interested in running it—"

Now she claps her hands together, throwing her head back and laughing.

"Ooo! That Maximilian What's-his-face is gonna be pissed!" she exclaims.

And just as I thought, her support buoys me, giving me the courage to speak my dreams out loud. "I'm thinking I might be a freelance writer for a while. You know, take the stories I want, when I want. Maybe . . . maybe relocate . . ."

Isabella's smile fades, and she straightens up. When she speaks again, all traces of amusement are gone. She's very serious now.

"Relocate to . . . where?" she asks.

"Um . . . well . . . I thought maybe here. At least part of the time. I own the place in Brooklyn, so I could go between or just sublet it for . . . I don't know . . . six months?" I throw the number out tentatively and then go one further. "Maybe . . . a year?"

"A year." She seems to ponder this. "You'll need at least that to get immersed in the language. And you have some family to meet, remember . . ."

"Oh, I do."

We're quiet for a few seconds, and it's just long enough for the elephant in the room to trumpet. It will not be ignored. I decide to be the one to call it out.

"Listen, I—I'm sorry about the way things went the other day," I tell her softly. "I didn't mean to say all those things I said . . . I was just . . . I was really pissed at you—the way you came after me like that."

"I know," she agrees with a somber nod. "I'm so sorry, Gabby. I was . . . I freaked out. I just panicked, and I said whatever I had to say to get you to hate me."

"But Isabella, why?" I ask, hearing a hint of heartache filter into my words. I don't think I realized just how much our altercation hurt . . . until now. Now that I know who she is . . . what she is.

Isabella considers the question for a few seconds, studying

her hands, which are now folded on the table in front of her. She doesn't look up when she starts speaking again. "I have spent my entire life looking for you, hoping to find you, *praying* to find you."

It's not nearly enough.

"Yeah, okay . . . again, why?" I repeat more strongly. "Why would you go through all this only to push me away— like this never happened, like we never met? It makes no sense . . ."

Her eyes finally connect with mine.

"I can't . . . you don't understand—"

"Then make me understand!" I say, more harshly than I meant to.

"Maybe I felt responsible!"

The force with which she blurts out the words takes us both by surprise.

"Responsible for what?"

She closes her eyes, as if steeling herself for whatever it is that comes next. Whatever deep, dark, unforgivable thing she's about to reveal. At last, she opens them again, and the words come slowly, softly.

"For you disappearing . . . for you being kidnapped. For putting into motion everything that sent you away from here—from us."

I blink a few times, feeling my brows furrow inward as I try to make sense of her statement.

"I'm sorry, but I don't understand. You were barely five years old. What could you have possibly done—"

"I wished you away," she cuts me off, hissing the confession. "I wished you'd never been born, because I thought if you'd never been born, then my mother would still be alive."

"Isabella—"

"No! Just . . . please, let me say this, Gabby. I *have* to say this, or I'll never be free of it . . ."

I nod slowly and wait for her to finish.

"I grew up thinking—believing—I had something to do with your disappearance. I knew it was irrational and ridiculous, but I could never shake the feeling that it was my fault. That every bad thing that happened to me was a direct result of that wish . . . like penance. At some point, I got this notion . . . this crazy idea that if I could just find you and bring you home, then I'd be forgiven . . ."

The guilt is written across her face as clearly as if someone had taken a Sharpie and printed the word in bold, black letters on her forehead.

When I speak again, my tone is different—more calm, comforting, and reassuring. A tone more appropriate to address the heartbroken five-year-old who's been living inside of this grown woman for decades. I put my hand over hers and squeeze it tight.

"Isabella, listen to me carefully. You were a child. There was absolutely nothing you could have done, or said, or wished that would have changed what happened that day. There is *nothing* for you to feel guilty about . . ."

She shakes her head as big, fat tears well in her eyes and spill down onto her cheeks. This is the most vulnerable I've seen her in our long but brief history.

"I forgive you."

I don't know where the words come from. There isn't a single cell in my body that thinks she has done anything wrong. But somehow, I know this is what she needs to hear. Isabella will never have a day's peace until she believes she has been absolved of her perceived sins. So that's what I have to give her.

"I forgive you," I repeat, but she just shakes her head again, waving away the sentiment with her hand. But I'm not having it. "No. No. I will *not* let you wave this away—it's too damn important."

We're attracting a few curious glances from around the

place, but I just don't give a shit about anybody but the woman sitting in front of me in agony. My sister.

I get up and move to her side of the table, crowding in as close to her as I can get. She needs to hear this from me. She needs to see this in me.

"I. Forgive. You," I repeat, this time more firmly and louder.

"You . . . you *can't* forgive me! You were just a baby . . ." she rasps.

I almost laugh. "That's ridiculous! Of course I can! Consider yourself forgiven, Isabella."

She doesn't shake her head this time, just stares at me, blinking through the tears streaming until they reach the point of her chin, dripping off and hitting her blouse in big droplets. She doesn't bother to wipe them away.

Then it happens. Isabella Ruíz flings herself at me so hard and so fast that she nearly knocks me right out of the booth and onto the floor. Her arms lock around me, and then she's crying—sobbing like the little girl she must have been the last time she saw Marianna . . . as Marianna.

I really do forgive her, but for what, I'm not sure. And just don't care.

When she's calmed down—and used up every napkin in a three-table radius—I smooth back her hair and wipe away the mascara that's trailed down her cheeks.

"Isabella, when we left the hotel, you told me . . . about what happened to you. I don't want you to think I didn't hear that—that I don't think it's important enough to address. So if and when you ever want to talk about it, I'm here," I tell her gently.

She stares at me for a long moment, her brown eyes searching my face from chin to hairline, ear to ear, as if she's looking for something there.

"About that . . ." she begins softly. "There's something I want to show you."

* * *

I'm not sure what to expect as she leads me out the rear entrance of the coffee shop, onto the freshly blacktopped parking lot. I take a sip of the iced frappé-mocha-something in my hand and immediately scowl. This is easily the worst coffee I've ever had in my life. I'm about to tell Isabella as much, but when I look at her, she just uses her chin to direct my attention to one of the walls that borders the lot.

It takes my eyes a moment to travel upward from the ground to the roof. And then it takes another moment to process what I'm seeing. But when I do, it takes my breath away.

Painted on the wall is a woman around my age. Long, dark curls tumble around her face and onto bare, delicate shoulders. Her neck is long and lean, her face soft and slightly rounded. She's wearing lipstick—a vintage shade of red that makes me think of the 1940s. But it's her eyes that draw me in—painted as a progression of blues starting with teal at the center, blending to sky blue, morphing to denim, a fine ring of dark cobalt encircling the outermost rim.

She's looking down at a little girl in her arms—a miniature of the woman with a headful of those same dark curls, the same sweetly curved mouth—minus the lipstick—and those arresting eyes. The two gaze at each other with a love—an adoration—so palpable that it transcends the two-dimensional likeness. Behind the two figures, a soft golden halo radiates upward around their heads, transforming this scene from a portrait of mother and baby to a modern take on the Madonna and Child.

Adding to this impression is the technique used to create it. Despite the size and scale of the image, it's been made to resemble one of the priceless paintings in the Louvre. To look at it, you'd think the brilliant colors had been created with the richest of oils, applied with the finest of brushes. The strokes, the shadow, the light . . . this bit of street art could easily look right at home next to a Rembrandt or Vermeer.

I have no idea how much time has gone by before my eyes have finally devoured every square inch of it—but when I turn to Isabella, I find her watching me anxiously, chewing on her lower lip, brows furrowed in the middle of her forehead.

She's afraid I won't like it.

"Oh . . . Isabella . . ." I whisper.

They are the only words I can find, but she understands, and her expression relaxes immediately.

"You . . . like it?" she asks so tentatively that I walk to her, nodding, and take her hand in mine.

"It's . . . I can't believe you . . . you did all this yourself? With spray paint?"

She nods, smiling. "It's this technique I read about, and I've been wanting to try for a long time."

"Well, you should have started using it sooner, because it's unbelievable!" I gasp, glancing up at it for a second. But when I turn back to her, the lip is tucked under her teeth again, the smile gone. "What? Did I say something? What is it?"

She looks up at her artwork, then at me, then down to the ground.

"Isabella?" I prod gently.

Her eyes swing up to mine, and she takes a quick breath, as if she's got to get the words out fast before they fail her. And then it all comes tumbling out.

"It happened here. What happened to me that night—it happened here. I was working on a different painting. I've been coming here all these years, just sitting in this parking lot and staring up at it as it faded to almost nothing."

"Oh! Oh, my God. Here? And this . . . this is where you wanted to put this?"

She nods. "I needed to face it and turn it into something else. Something beautiful. So . . . I made it a memorial for my mother, Rosaria. And . . . for Marianna."

I stare at her, uncomprehending.

"But . . . but I'm Marianna . . ."

"No," Isabella says, shaking her head. "No. The way I see it now, Marianna died the day she disappeared. And . . . and that was the day that Gabriella was born."

"I don't understand . . ."

She gives me a wan smile now. "Gabby, you're not Marianna—you never were. You never could be. And it's not fair of me to keep pretending you are. The little girl I knew for those seven months is never coming back. And that was hard for me to see for a very long time . . . until you. You're not the sister I was looking for, but you're the sister I was meant to have."

Before I can stop myself, I've pulled her into my arms with so much force that both our coffees are sent flying. We cling together like that, in the middle of the parking lot, in front of the most beautiful piece of art I've ever seen.

"*Te amo*," I whisper in her ear, and she pulls me even tighter than I would have thought possible.

"I love you, too."

I push back a little, holding her at arm's length so I can see her face clearly.

"There's something I need you to do for me . . ."

CHAPTER 49

MIGUEL

That Day

Now everyone knew everything. All the facts were out on the table, and they—each of them—were about to step past the point of no return.

"The baby has to get off the island," Miguel said.

Now that he had uttered the words, he knew there was no turning back.

"They must both go," Blanca said firmly. "The baby, *and* Coquí, must both leave the island."

Miguel looked to Mack and Lucy. "Just to be clear—if the father agrees, you *will* take the child?"

The couple exchanged glances once more, and it was he who spoke for both of them. "Yes. Yes, but only if the father agrees."

Alvarez nodded his approval. "All right then, Beatríz, you track down Alberto and bring him here. But you *cannot* let anyone see you. I mean no cops, no gang members, no one. Understood?"

She raised an eyebrow at him.

"Right, stupid question. Sorry," he muttered, while lifting his palms in an *I surrender* gesture.

"I can have him here within the hour," she assured him. "Though, I can't guarantee what condition he'll be in once I do . . ."

Next, they turned their attention to Coquí. His situation was just as dire as the child's was, but Miguel wasn't totally comfortable with the idea of just handing the kid a wad of cash and a ticket somewhere. He'd been through a lot. He would need some support.

"Have you got *any* family outside of Puerto Rico?" he asked.

Coquí nodded that he did.

"I have an uncle—in Texas, I think—named Guillermo. Guillermo Torres. The brother of my mother."

Miguel frowned. He wanted to know why, if he had an uncle in Texas, the boy hadn't just gone to him after his mother's death.

Coquí's response was simple enough—he didn't know how to find the man. And apparently no one from Social Services had tried. Miguel wanted to be angry, but he knew from experience that this kind of thing just happened sometimes. The department was woefully understaffed with nowhere near the resources necessary to help the children who needed their assistance most.

"I can find him," Mack declared, surprising them all. "Give me a phone. If he's alive and in the U.S., I can track him down."

"Come, I have one upstairs," the nun said, already moving toward the door at the back of the sanctuary, Mack on her heels.

"But what about the baby's papers?" Lucy asked. "Once we get back home, won't they know it's a fake birth certificate?"

"No," Miguel explained, shaking his head. "Because it's not a fake—well, the document itself isn't, anyway. We have a tremendous problem with identity theft here because of the way birth certificates are distributed. The government intends to recall them all and issue new birth certificates in the next couple of years. But for now, the one you have should be more than enough to allow for a new one to be issued in your home state."

"Got it," Mack said, triumphantly, when he returned less than ten minutes later. "I have a name, address, and one number for Guillermo Torres of Austin, Texas. I made a preliminary call to confirm he has a nephew named Jacinto Nuñez. He's eager to speak with him . . . but I didn't tell him anything about the mother. I figured it best to let Coquí do that himself."

Blanca translated for Coquí, who seemed concerned, suddenly.

"What are you worried about?" she asked.

"*Santiago. Él puede encontrarme en Texas.*"

"He's right," Beatríz agreed, grimly turning to Alvarez. "Santiago *can* find him in Texas. He can find him anywhere. Because he knows people everywhere."

Miguel took a quick mental inventory, considering all the facts he'd collected up to this point. His team had managed to turn up several clues in the first hours of this investigation, but it had been right here, in this room, that the majority of the blanks had been filled in. For instance, the only reason he knew the body in the shack was Yeti's was because both Beatríz and the boy had *just* told him so. God only knows how long it would have taken them to have DNA and dental records searched—if there even were any DNA samples or dental records on file to use for comparison. Aside from that, there was only one other item found in the charred remains of the shack that could be used to identify the dead man—or his killer, for that matter.

Miguel looked at Coquí thoughtfully, tilting his head to one side as he considered which of them it belonged to. Not likely it had been Yeti's. Which meant . . .

"Coquí, do you own a San Cristóbal medal?" he asked, and watched as the young man's hand went to his throat automatically.

"I did. It was my mother's. But it was lost somewhere in the shack . . . before the fire."

And there, Miguel had his answer.

The medal could be linked to this kid—especially if he made an after-hours trip to the evidence room and swabbed a little of his DNA on it. DNA that he could collect right here, right now. He might even be able to find a way to link that DNA to a file in the database. A file that he would create himself that very night—so his team could discover it in the morning and come to the conclusion that he wanted them to come to. If he played his cards right, the body in the morgue—Yeti's body—would never be identified as such, because all evidence would point to the young man standing in front of him at this moment.

Miguel took a quick moral inventory, considering all of the rules—all of the *laws*—he was about to break. But in less time than it took for his heart to beat, he knew that the means, no matter how risky they might be, justified the ends.

"*Coquí, Santiago no te buscará si cree que ya estás muerto,*" he explained to the young man.

Santiago won't look for you if he thinks you're already dead.

CHAPTER 50

ISABELLA

Today

Corozál isn't very far from San Juan—maybe a forty-minute drive. But today, it feels more like forty hours as I navigate the steep twists and turns through the mountainous area. It's been a long time since I've made this trip to my father's house, and I sure wouldn't be making it now if Gabby hadn't insisted she wanted to meet Alberto.

"I don't want you to get your hopes up, okay?" I warn. "And be prepared; he might be drunk. Or high. Or both . . ."

"I know," she says from the passenger seat, not bothering to look up from her phone.

"And he probably won't recognize you. Hell, I'm not even sure he'll remember he ever had two kids . . ."

"Yup."

I give her a sideways glance. "I wish you'd take this more seriously . . ."

Now she looks up. "I am taking it seriously. But I'm having a hard time taking *you* seriously. We've been over this a dozen times already. I'm a big girl, Isabella. I can handle whatever happens today."

I sigh. "Here's the thing, Gabby. Alberto is a disappointment—to say the least. He's not your . . . he's not Mack."

"I understand. Really, I do. Just stop worrying so much."

But I am worried, because there's one more thing I need to tell her, and I've been dreading it for days now.

"I have to tell you something," I begin slowly. "When I told you I didn't mean to make you think he was dead? I was lying. I did it on purpose. I was just so afraid that you'd take one look at him and be relieved that you didn't have to grow up here. I was afraid you'd be so ashamed of him that you'd be ashamed of me, by extension."

She's staring at me when I sneak a peek to my right, but I don't see any traces of outrage, thankfully.

"I know," she says simply.

"You know . . . ?"

She nods.

"I know you lied. And I could guess why. But Isabella, you're not responsible for him. And I could never judge you by the kind of man he is."

"You say that now," I mutter, shaking my head. "But once you meet him—"

"Once I meet him, what? You think I'm going to go running for the first Uber I can find and hop a plane back to New York?"

I roll my eyes. "Pfft. Yeah, good luck getting an Uber outside of San Juan . . ."

"You know, for such a bad-ass bitch, you're a real pussy," she tells me matter-of-factly.

I'm so stunned that I almost drive off the side of the road. "What did you just call me?"

She shrugs. "Pussy. Oh, maybe you need a translation in Spanish? How about *pelele*—that means wimp, doesn't it? Or maybe *pendejo* . . ."

When I look at her, she's got a big, goofy grin.

"Hey! Stop that! Stop smiling at me!"

"You," she tells me, her tone growing grave again, "need to stop punishing yourself for things that aren't your fault. The bad things in life—the disappointments and the failures, and, yes, even the tragedies—are *not* some kind of penance for something you've done. They're just the same old shit that happens to everyone else on any given day. So, for God's sake, get over yourself already and let's go meet this deadbeat dad of mine, okay?"

I shrug. "Just remember you asked for this."

"I will," she assures me.

Fifteen minutes later, we're parked in front of my father's very modest home, a tiny structure that leans more to the side of *shack* than *bungalow*.

She's opening her door before I've even set the parking brake.

"Alrighty, then, I guess we're doing this," I mutter.

We use the front walkway—not a real walkway, so much as a dirt path where the grass has been worn away by constant foot traffic—to scale the steep lawn to the concrete slab that serves as a front porch. A grungy resin lawn chair sits there, an empty ashtray next to it on the ground and an old transistor radio we used to have in the kitchen when I was growing up. I can just picture him perched out here in the evening with a cigarette and a beer, watching the world go by as he listens to the Gipsy Kings.

I'm surprised by how nostalgic the thought makes me feel. And a little alarmed, too. I haven't got the energy left to waste on Alberto. Better to just get this part over with and go back to forgetting I even have a father.

I rap on the unpainted wooden door with the back of my knuckles. You can do that here—go right up to a person's front door, unlike the houses in Levittown and other suburbs of San Juan, where bars keep the more dangerous element at a safe distance from your home. Crime isn't nearly as big an issue in a rural area like this. And, seriously, what self-respecting thief would waste the effort on a place like this? What could Alberto possibly have in there that's worth stealing, anyway?

"Papi?" I call out as I knock a second time. He may be sleeping off a hangover.

It's also possible that he's just working up to one. Or maybe he's gotten himself some of the "good stuff" that the woman down the block sells him. The stuff that leaves him passed out on his shitty couch, surrounded by his piles of crap.

"Papi!" I call again louder, with the idea of trying to jolt him out of his stupor. *"¡Papi, despiértate!"*

Gabby and I startle when his response comes from outside the house, on the path behind us.

"Oye, Isabellita. ¿Por qué estás gritando?"

"I'm yelling because you never answer me," I mutter, even as we're turning to face him.

I don't know what I was expecting to find . . . no, actually, that's bullshit. I know exactly what I was expecting to find— and the man standing in front of me isn't it. Rather than being holed up inside, "sleeping it off" in a darkened, stale-smelling room, he's standing here outside in the fresh air.

"Papi, te ve bien," I observe, unable to disguise the astonishment in my voice. Because he *does* look good! Better than I've seen him look in . . . well, in decades.

He's wearing clean clothes—including a white T-shirt, which is surprising, because it's not always a given that he'll bother with a shirt—let alone a clean one. Along with that, he's wearing khaki shorts and a well-worn but serviceable pair of running shoes. He's carrying plastic bags from the grocery store located a mile and a half away. I don't see a car anywhere, so he must have walked it. Or maybe he found his way to a bus?

But perhaps the most unexpected thing about Alberto's appearance is that he looks . . . sober. He's not swaying or grinning stupidly. No cackling or blubbering. His eyes look normal—not even bloodshot. I'll be damned if the sonofa-bitch *isn't* sober! My father looks like any other middle-aged

Puerto Rican man. And I'm having trouble getting my head around it.

"Gracias, mija. Ha pasado mucho tiempo. ¿Cómo estás?"

He's right; it has been a long time. Two years? Three, maybe?

"Estoy bien, gracias. Papi, quiero que conozcas a alguien . . ." I start to introduce Gabby, touching her lightly on the shoulder as I do.

He registers I'm not alone for the first time, his gaze flickering to the young woman standing next to me. He stops. We all do. Everything stops when their eyes meet. The sound of the wind is gone—and the nearby traffic noise. Even the birds have stopped singing as the world comes to a screeching halt and time stands still.

It's the only way I can describe what's happening at this moment. It's as if the three of us are in suspended animation—me staring at him staring at her. No ticking clock. No beating heart. Not so much as a breath passes between us for what feels like an eternity; then, as abruptly as it started, it ends, and all the sounds come rushing back at once, with so much force that I feel the earth shift under my feet.

Alberto drops the bags where he stands, then takes a few slow steps toward us—carefully, as if he's approaching a potentially dangerous creature. Which, in a way, I suppose he is. I'm just not sure which of us poses a more significant threat to him: me, or Gabby.

For her part, Gabby shifts uncomfortably under his stare.

"What's . . . what's wrong?" she whispers.

"I don't . . . I'm not sure . . ." I whisper back. "Papi?" The single word is packed with more concern for him than I've felt in a very long time.

His eyes never leave Gabby's as he takes a few more steps forward. It's like she and I are rooted where we stand, pinned by the intensity of his gaze upon her.

He's looking at her the same way my grandmother was, unable to look away as he comes closer to us. I don't think he's even blinked in the last thirty feet. When, at last, he's standing directly in front of her, I see the tears in his eyes.

"*Mija . . .*" he murmurs. "My daughter."

I'm stunned by his use of English. Since when does he speak English? I'm even more stunned when his tear-filled gaze swings to me, and he speaks again.

"*Mijas,*" he says. My daughters. "*Mis hijas han vuelto a mí.*"

I sense, rather than see, Gabby angle herself toward me, because I just can't take my eyes off Alberto. But I know what she wants.

"My daughters have returned to me," I translate in a voice barely above a whisper. "He . . . he knows exactly who you are."

And then the most bizarre thing happens . . . it's as if we are a couple of minor planets orbiting the sun. There is no fighting the pull toward him we are both experiencing right now—no matter how hard we try. Not that either of us is trying. We're just too mesmerized by him—by this bizarre, mystical experience that appears to be transpiring around us.

He reaches out and takes both of Gabby's hands in his.

"Marianna."

I am mesmerized as he touches her cheek with a warm hand.

"My sweet Marianna," he says in English.

I feel myself stiffen and suck in a shocked breath simultaneously.

"*¿Hablas inglés?*" I demand incredulously.

His response is to smile warmly as he nods toward the front door. "Come," he says to her. Then, to me, "*Ven, mi amor, ven.*"

Come, my love. Come.

And I do.

CHAPTER 51

GABBY

Today

When he takes my hand, I'm struck by a sense of déjà vu so strong that it nearly drops me to my knees. And, for just an instant, I'm paralyzed by the overwhelming feeling of familiarity—not with this place or these actions, but with these feelings. Alberto's touch sparks a memory from somewhere so far away. I'm struck dumb by it—not that I could find the words to describe it even if I could speak.

"You okay?" Isabella asks from behind me.

The only thing I can do is nod.

We follow him up onto the porch and into his house, where he lets go of my hand and gestures toward a small, sheet-covered couch against one wall.

"Please, you sit. I make us some coffee," he says, disappearing into his kitchen.

I do as he instructs, but Isabella walks to the middle of the room and spins around slowly, taking in the entire space, which, I gather, isn't the beer can–littered, trash-strewn pigsty she was expecting. I don't think the sober, amiable, neat man in the kitchen is what she was expecting, either. She looks so perplexed that I feel sorry for her—not that I dare express that. Or what just happened between me and Alberto. I'm afraid she wouldn't get it, and I'd end up feeling stupid. So I keep it to myself.

From the couch, I can see into the little kitchen—more of an alcove than an actual room. There's about three feet of countertop—just enough to accommodate a two-burner hot plate, cutting board, and small dish rack. Adjoining it is a narrow sink and miniature refrigerator with a microwave on top. Just enough for a single man.

I allow my eyes to roam the space, trying to get a sense of who this man is—if not the broken, wretched creature Isabella described. The floor and walls are made of concrete, and sunlight pours in from the jalousie windows, making the space feel bright and airy. Aside from the kitchen, I make note of a couple of partially open doors against the back wall—one looks to be a bathroom, the other a bedroom. There isn't much in the way of furnishings. Aside from the sheet-clad couch we're sitting on, there are a couple of folding chairs, and directly in front of us is a makeshift coffee table, constructed from a repurposed door on cinder blocks. Atop it are a battered Spanish bible and newspaper, as well as a neatly arranged game of solitaire in progress. There's also a small flat-screen TV sitting on stacked milk crates that double as a bookcase. I try to make out some of the titles, but they're all in Spanish.

And still, Isabella stands, scouring every square inch of the place as if the drunkard junkie she remembers might be hiding somewhere, just waiting for her to leave so he could pop out.

"*Papi, ¿qué pasó aquí?*" she calls out to her father.

"English, Isabellita," Alberto replies over his shoulder from inside the kitchen. "Your sister does no speak Spanish."

"Does *not*," she corrects him.

"*Hablo un poco,*" I correct *her*.

She quirks an eyebrow at me. "Really? What, are you going to tell *him* you're horny, too?"

Before I can shoot back a response, Alberto comes out with a cutting board-turned-serving tray, and carrying a French press, some mismatched mugs, sugar, and milk. He sets it all down on the door/table.

"Here we have the coffee," he declares with a smile, and I can't help but notice he's missing a few teeth. "You like the coffee, Marianna?" he asks, genuinely curious.

"Yes, I do," I reply softly, and he pours me a mug.

"Gabriella," Isabella says, a little too harshly, as she joins me on the couch. "She goes by Gabby." When I nudge her with my knee, she glares at me. "What?" she demands. "It's your name, isn't it?"

I give her a *knock it off* stare, which she throws right back at me, but not before I catch something behind her irritation. Oh, God, she's as rattled as I am by all this. Isabella doesn't know this man any more than I do. Not this version of him, anyway, and she doesn't know what to make of it. Of him. Of us.

"Gabriella," Alberto says, rolling my name around in his mouth as he fills Isabella's cup. When he's handed it to her, he pulls up one of the folding chairs and sits, leaning forward, hands clasped in front of him as he looks at us intently. "Gabby. I like this name," he says with a smile. "Tell me, Gabby, you have the husband?" Then, a little more tentatively: "Or . . . the wife?"

I smile at his attempt to be inclusive. "No, it's just me," I explain, and go on to give him a few more details so he doesn't have to ask for every single scrap of information. "I live in New York City, and I . . . I'm a writer." The words feel good coming out of my mouth. "I write for magazines."

Alberto claps his hands together, smiling broadly. "¡Que bueno! How wonderful this is! A writer in New York City! I know this," he declares, pointing at me. "I always know you would be important!"

"Oh, I'm not import—"

"Really? You knew all along?" Isabella cuts me off mid-sentence, the question dripping with sarcasm. "And how's that, Papi? Hmm? Was *that* in the bottom of your gin bottle? Did it come to you in a vision after you shot up? Tell me, Alberto, because I'd love to know what all-knowing entity told you."

He looks up at her and tilts his head slightly as he considers his daughter. His other daughter.

"*Mija*, you told me," he replies, unfazed.

She looks taken aback for a moment.

"What? What are you talking about?"

He sighs and offers her a half-smile.

"Isabellita, you never stop looking for your sister. There was no one who tell you she is alive. You just . . . you *know* because this in your heart. Yes?" Alberto asks, touching a hand to his chest, above where his heart is. "It took time, but I finally hear what you say, *mija*. I finally listen to what you are telling me all these years. *This* is when I knew I must stop with the drinking and the drugs. Because I know then you would find her—you would find our Marianna and bring her home."

"She's not Marianna," she replies coolly, for the second time.

Alberto sighs, nods, leaning forward to pour himself a cup of coffee.

"Yes, you are right. She is not. Our Marianna—she is gone. But we have a beautiful Gabriella," he says, in an echo of his daughter's earlier sentiment . . .

"*The way I see it now, Marianna died the day she dis-appeared. And . . . and that was the day that Gabriella was born.*"

He sits back, takes a sip from his cup, and faces me again. "Gabriella . . . you . . ." He pauses, searching for the words. Not the words in English. Just . . . the words. Period. "You have the happy life, *mi amor?*"

I'm not prepared for the question, and it takes a second for me to gather my thoughts and answer. I nod. "Um . . . yes . . . very happy. I had everything I could have ever wanted . . ."

"And love? You have the love in your house?"

He's asking if my parents—my *other* parents—loved me.

"I had *so much* love," I tell him, my voice now hoarse with emotion. "I was loved every minute of every day of my life."

Alberto sets his cup on the door/table so he can use both hands to wipe away the tears that have started to slide down his bronze-skinned cheeks.

"*Bueno.* It's good. And now . . . now you find your way back to us!" he says excitedly through the tears.

"Oh, no," I say. I shake my head and glance at Isabella. "She found me . . ."

He turns his attention to her now, too.

"Isabellita, *por favor mi amor—dime.* Please, tell me. Tell me how you have finally brought our Marianna—our *Gabriella*—home."

His tone is so gentle—so much an homage to his elder daughter and the impossible feat she's accomplished, that it seems to knock the nasty, suspicious chip right off her shoulder. She looks down into her own cup for a few seconds, and when she looks up again, she turns in my direction.

"I'm going to tell him in Spanish—just to be sure he understands everything. Okay?"

I nod. Then I sit, silently, listening to the long, fluid lines of Isabella's speech pattern. He watches her, transfixed, nodding and occasionally asking a brief question. I don't catch much of what she's saying, but I get the gist of it—after all, I do know this story by heart. Except for the ending, that is.

None of us knows how this story is going to end.

When she's finished relating everything up until this point, Alberto shifts forward, resting his elbows on his knees. His hands rub his jawline as he processes everything he's just heard. He looks both sad and happy—the epitome of bittersweet. Somehow, I know with absolute certainty that he's thinking of everything he missed—mourning the little girl he lost. But that sentiment, strong as it is, is no match for the gratitude he has in this moment. I see it all; I feel it all. It's like I'm in his head.

I stand up abruptly, needing to take a few minutes away from the intensity of this reunion.

"May I—May I use the bathroom?"

"*Sí, sí*. Yes, of course," he responds, pointing toward one of the doors along the wall.

Following his direction, I lock myself in the small beige bathroom and splash some water on my face. When I glance up in the mirror, I do a double take. An hour ago, the only face I'd ever seen in the mirror was mine—Gabby's. But now that I've spent some time with Alberto, now that I've memorized every curve and dip and line, I suddenly recognize some of him in me. It rattles me to my core, and I have to grab the edge of the sink to steady myself. This is going to take some getting used to. A *lot* of getting used to.

I take a deep breath and step out of the bathroom, and they're speaking in Spanish, something about Isabella's aunt, Annamaria. Maybe she's telling him about the *quinceañera*? I'm about to return to the couch when I catch a glimpse through the open crack of the bedroom door. I only intend to push it open another inch or two, just to get a look inside, but as the room starts to expose itself to me I can't stop until it's all been revealed. The room itself matches the rest of Alberto's abode. It's in miniature—a bed that couldn't be more than a double taking up most of the space, a three-drawer dresser the rest of it. There's just enough room for him to maneuver between the two. He could probably touch both walls if he stretched his arms out to either side.

But what's caught my attention isn't so much what's between the walls, as what's *on* them. There are photographs—dozens of colorful images captured, printed, and framed. I recognize one immediately—the Mona Lisa draped in the Puerto Rican flag. And the faux garden at the nursing home. And while I may not have laid eyes upon the others myself, there's no mistaking the creator of the artwork I'm looking at.

"Isabella?" I call out to her from where I stand, staring at the kaleidoscope of images—one brighter than the next. When she doesn't immediately answer, I call again. "Isabella!"

"What? What is it? You get lost on your way back or some—" her snark stops mid-sentence when she turns the corner and sees what I'm seeing. "Oh . . . my God," she mutters to herself as her gaze moves from frame to frame, cataloging each of her own works.

"They are all yours," Alberto says quietly from behind us.

Isabella spins around, eyes narrowed and suspicious.

"When did you do this?" she demands.

He shrugs. "Long time. Years. It take time to find them all. Some are gone now . . ."

"You're lying," she hisses. "You did this to try and butter me up!"

"Em . . . butter up?" He looks to me. "What is this 'butter up'?"

She doesn't give me time to explain.

"You did this so I would see it and think you actually gave a damn."

"Isabella!" I whisper sharply. "Think about it—how could he have? He had no idea we were coming here!"

She opens her mouth, prepared to spew some searing condemnation of her father, but then stops as what I'm telling her sinks in. This isn't some elaborate plan on Alberto's part to curry favor with her. It's nothing more than a display of a father's pride. She stares at him, as if the answer to whatever it is that she needs to know will be there, written in his expression.

Alberto smiles, comes forward, and wraps an arm around each of our shoulders, pulling us close to his chest.

When I was a kid—maybe seven or eight—I stuck a fork in a toaster that was still plugged in. The jolt lasted only a fraction of a second, but it seemed to touch every molecule of my body with a searing sting that sent me stumbling across the kitchen, landing flat on my butt on the linoleum. I was totally dazed—but okay. Later on, I learned just how lucky I was. The electrical voltage could have just as easily run a circuit through me . . . and stopped my heart. Just like that. Dead on the floor.

I haven't thought about that day in years, but it comes to mind the second Isabella and I are connected to each other by Alberto. It's that feeling—but so, so much more.

In the time it takes to blink, a white-hot jolt rips through me—as if a live current is ripping through my body on its way to closing a circuit I didn't realize was open. A circuit I didn't even realize I had.

I gasp raggedly as my blood thrums and sings.

It is as if, at last, all is right in my world.

CHAPTER 52

ALBERTO

Today

Once the girls leave, Alberto fumbles around in the tiny linen closet until he finds what he is looking for—the old shoebox on the top shelf. It's been so long since he opened it that it's migrated back against the wall, displaced by towels, shampoo bottles, and toilet-paper rolls. When he finally manages to grip the thing, it comes down in a cloud of dust, some of the particles catching in his throat, making him gag, sputter, and cough. In the kitchen, he uses a damp paper towel to remove the rest of the debris from the outside of the box before bringing it to the small table where he takes his meals. Once he sits down, he stares at it for a long time.

Years ago—before the girls, before Rosaria, he'd been a punk kid looking for a bit of cash and some excitement. That was when he and his brother had left the unbearably quiet town of Corozál for the lights and action of San Juan. It didn't take long for them to hook up with a small-time drug dealer in La Perla named Lorenzo. It was easy cash and easy access to product. But, while Alberto was perfectly content to stay in the lower tier of distribution, his brother had other ideas. He gained Lorenzo's trust, moving up the ladder quickly—all the while, undermining the man's authority with the other dealers. When the time came, his brother pushed

Lorenzo out, slipping into his place easily—expanding the reach and breadth of their operation. For his part, Lorenzo hadn't taken it well. Perhaps if he'd simply accepted the coup, things would have been different, but the man had gone on a crusade to bring down the man who'd ousted him.

He was dead two weeks later.

Alberto didn't want to believe that the boy he'd grown up with could do something so heartless, but he must've known on some level, because he never found the nerve to ask him about it directly. The name *Santiago* became a dark threat murmured on the streets—building his empire one city block at a time, absorbing his competition where it was advantageous, eliminating it where it wasn't.

That's how Alberto ended up killing the kid. He was just supposed to scare him—beat the shit out of him because he was late with a payment. But instead of taking his punishment like a man, the kid had to act like a tough guy—pulling a knife. And when they tussled on the street, Alberto ended up putting that knife through the kid's gut. And he was a *kid*—not quite seventeen years old. Alberto would never forget the way his face had turned chalky as the blood seeped out of him, forming a river that ran down the street, through the grout lines of the cobblestones.

That was it for him. He was out. He would never do anything to hurt his brother, but he was done helping him. The decision couldn't have come at a worse time. After spending so much time undercutting his competition, Santiago became paranoid about loyalty—obsessed with this idea of "saving face." You didn't screw with Santiago. Ever.

Alberto knew his brother wouldn't kill him. But he was also well aware that there were worse things than death—and that Santiago was a man who held a grudge. His brother allowed him to live in peace so long as he kept his head down and stayed out of his business. Alberto complied happily—falling in love with Rosaria, having Isabella. But then came the new baby and the death of his beloved wife. He was a mess—unable to care for his children, desperate for the blissful oblivion of drugs and booze.

Out of work, he'd been forced to turn to Santiago for help. And he *had* helped him, but at a cost. If there was anyone who could not be seen as receiving favors, it was Santiago's own brother. So, while Alberto was only supposed to receive a beatdown that night in the alley, that little shit Yeti got ballsy and snatched up Marianna. It's not that Santiago wanted to kill his own niece—or any child, for that matter—he just couldn't see any way out that didn't make him look weak in the eyes of his men . . . and his enemies.

That was how Alberto came to see the last twenty-five years as his punishment—his penance for murder. He lost his wife; he lost his baby. Even his older daughter had lost all faith in him as a father and as a human being. Giving Marianna to Mack and Lucy had been the hardest thing he'd ever had to do . . . but he knew it was the right thing. And for that single, brief moment when he *wasn't* sure, he had only to recall the morning he came to in the alley behind El Gallo Rojo. He would never, for as long as he lived, forget how it had felt when the realization struck him—the certainty that his child was either dead . . . or soon would be. And he had no one to blame but himself.

Alberto learned in that instant that helplessness—mixed with equal parts regret, shame, anger, and fear—was enough to drive a person totally and completely mad. It was a sensation he'd never even imagined, let alone experienced, until then. Not even the death of his wife had been enough to propel him into the kind of violent, maddening desperation that made him want to claw the skin from his own face. So relieved was he when Beatríz had told him Marianna was alive and presented him with their plan to keep it that way, he immediately agreed. It was the only way.

He only wished he could have done better by Isabellita,

as well. But she was too old—she would remember him. She would remember everything. And if their plan was to work, everyone had to believe Marianna was gone for good. Including her own big sister. Still, what he wouldn't have given to have spared her what she endured that night when she was a teenager. If only he'd been home as he promised he would be. If only he'd paid attention, listened, watched . . . if only he'd stayed clean and sober long enough to keep his child out of harm's way.

She had no idea he'd been there, watching her sleep. She had no idea that he even knew what had happened to her. And she had no idea what he'd done to avenge her—how he had called on the one man with the power to do something. Santiago had not disappointed. They would never speak of Isabella, or Marianna—or anything else, ever again. And now Santiago was dead, taking his secrets, his sins, and his lethal pride with him all the way to hell. Alberto didn't lose a single night's sleep over the state of his brother's soul. They had all made their choices over the years. And they had all had to live with them—or die with them, as the case may be.

Now he takes the lid from the shoebox and pulls out the thick stack of sealed envelopes. He flips the pile over so as to start at the bottom . . . and he does what he has longed to do for more than two decades—he opens it. Inside is a handwritten letter in beautiful, straight, looping script on creamy blue paper. Tucked away within the pages are pictures of a stunning child with silky dark hair and the bluest eyes he has ever seen—her mother's eyes. She's in a highchair, a small cake with a single candle lit in front of her. The child was caught mid-reach as she stuffed a fistful of fluffy white frosting into her mouth.

He feels the tears as they stream down his face.

With his baby brought safely back to him and his Isabellita, they can finally be a family again. There was no denying the electricity that ran through the three of them when they touched—like some kind of magic current connecting them. In that moment, he had known his penance was finally complete, his sins forgiven at long last.

Looking at the letter in his hand, he knows this is just the beginning. There are dozens more that have remained unopened all these years—dozens of birthdays and Christmases, school plays, and vacations and graduations. They have been here, waiting for him—waiting for a time when he was clean and sober. A time when he was humble and genuinely repentant. It was a time only God could determine.

And now He had.

Alberto puts on his reading glasses and begins the slow process of deciphering each of Lucy's letters in English—which he has spent the last several years learning for precisely this moment. The moment he finally gets to know his own daughter. They have a lot of time to make up for.

And it begins right now.

CHAPTER 53

RAÑA

Today

It's late by the time he finishes up all the paperwork and stretches until his chair tips backward. Standing, he gathers all the documents together, taps them on the desktop until they form a uniform pile. They go into the manila folder and then into the very back of their designated cardboard file box. He takes one last long look inside before securing the top. His colleagues often joked that you could construct a small wall with the number of identical cardboard boxes stacked on his office floor.

His days are filled with the San Juan PD's ongoing cases, but after hours, off the clock—with sleeves rolled up and tie loosened, he digs into these boxes—each representing an unsolved case from years gone by. Without adequate resources or manpower, the "cold" cases have been collecting dust—neglected and forgotten. Until he arrived.

They are the cases that stalk his dreams, waking him from his restless sleep, drenched in sweat and shaking. Hilary reaches for him then, pulling his head to her breast so she can stroke his hair and murmur soothing words until his heart stops racing. She never complains about the nights she's left alone to get the kids tucked in on her own, leaving a supper plate for him in the microwave. She never questions where he's been or what he's been doing. Because she knows as well as he does that every clue he uncovers, every lead he finds, buys him a few more minutes of peace. Eventually, he hopes that they will add up to a whole night's sleep.

He picks up the box marked: R-22583 RUÍZ, M., balancing it on his thigh as he closes his office door, locking it behind him. He takes the little-used stairway to the basement archives, flipping the switch that brings the flickering, buzzing fluorescents to life. Industrial metal shelving reaches from floor to ceiling, each stacked with hundreds of file boxes like the one he is holding.

He walks the narrow aisles, head tilted up and then down again as he scans case numbers and names until he finds the spot where this box now belongs amongst the closed cases. There will be no further investigation into the disappearance of Marianna Ruíz, and after twenty-five years, that suits him just fine.

So much has happened in that time—Mack and Lucy are gone now, as is Santiago. Sister Blanca has found her peace in God's work, while Beatríz has found hers in family. Alvarez has finally retired—but only after ensuring the position he vacated went to him—the only man he trusted to put it all to bed once and for all. And he's done it—but only because not a single one of them has broken the pact they'd made that night so long ago.

They couldn't have known back then that the child, Isabella, would prove to be the biggest threat to their secret. Refusing to give up hope, she never stopped searching for Marianna. She questioned everyone and trusted no one. Her instincts rejected all of their manufactured evidence, even if she didn't know why. He was certain that Isabella herself could not explain the source of her obsession.

But he can.

It's the blood they shared. The distance doesn't matter, nor do the years that have passed, or the incongruous, simultaneous lives they have lived. Something deep within them calls out for the other—causing a deep, inexplicable longing that is often mistaken for depression. Even if they had never found each other, Isabella would have known for the rest of her days that Marianna was alive . . . until she wasn't. Just as he knew the day, the hour—the *moment* his mother had left this earth, her spirit taking up residence in his heart. She'd guided him, showed him the path, protected him. She brought him back home to the island he'd always loved; to this place—right here, right now.

Once he gets the box situated, Raña reaches out and runs his fingers over the name one last time. He won't open it again—because he won't have to. It is now well and truly closed, their vows fulfilled.

The baby Marianna has grown up safely, wrapped in the love of the parents who cherished her—and who had waited so long for her. She will never know the sacrifices that had been made to ensure her safety. She will never know that he had been the one to choose the name with which she was reborn—Gabriella—for his beloved mother. She will never know the hopes and dreams that have been pinned on her survival.

For their part, Mack and Lucy had spent every moment from that night on joyous and grateful for the gift of the child they'd dreamed of for so long.

Miguel, Beatríz, and Sister Blanca carried on with their lives, knowing they had been instruments of God, or fate, or the universe—depending on the person and the day.

In finding her long-lost sister, Isabella has also come to understand the nature of her father, Alberto's, demons. It wasn't that he didn't love her—it was that he was unable to accept her love—or anyone else's. The solitude has been his penance for setting the events that transpired that day into motion. Whether or not the three will ever be a family again remains to be seen.

As for himself, he can relax, knowing that with the closing of this file, their fabrication became fact. Jacinto "Coquí" Nuñez has been laid to rest once and for all. It was his body that was found in the burnt-out shack that day; at least, that's what the official report reads. It also concluded that the man known only as Yeti had murdered Coquí before fleeing to the Dominican Republic with the kidnapped child. It was there that he had apparently attempted to sell the little girl on the black market before getting himself killed. And, by a miracle of timing, cash, and connections, the child had ended up in the arms of the New York couple who'd been waiting so very long to adopt their own child. The child who would go on to become the woman, Gabriella DiMarco.

Detective Raña turns out the lights but stands there for a long moment, staring into the darkness, as a few rogue tears slip past his defenses and down his face. Finally, he closes and locks the door to the archives, saying a last, silent goodbye to the child who'd been dubbed "Coquí" by his mother so many years ago.

May he rest in peace.

EPILOGUE

Today

"Come on!" Gabby called out over her shoulder. "Come on, slowpoke!"

Isabella ignored her sister, refusing to walk any faster. "It's not like it's going anywhere."

Gabby rolled her eyes, stopping so her sister could catch up with her. "Can't you at least be a little excited about this? For me? Pleeeeease?"

"MOMA I was excited about. Broadway I was excited about. Hell, I even got excited about riding in the subway. But a newsstand? Not so much."

"You haven't seen half the things I want to show you," Gabby informed her. "And wait till you see where Franny and I are taking you for dinner tonight—it's supposed to have the best mofongo anywhere north of Puerto Rico."

Isabella snorted. "And that sounds like a good thing to you?"

Gabby was used to the whole jaded, snarky thing by now—it was a protective shell Isabella pulled out whenever she was uncomfortable or afraid. Both of which she was right then. She grabbed Isabella's hand tight, and they walked like that, following a throng of tourists, construction workers, dog walkers, and hundreds of other people having their own New York City experience that day.

When they reached the little red shack dripping with magazines and newspapers from all over the world, it was all Gabby could do to keep from jumping up and down excitedly. She held tight to Isabella's hand, only letting go long enough to point to one of the covers up in the corner.

"That one!" she told the old man behind the counter. "*Art in America.*"

He obliged by grabbing it down and handing it to her. She slipped him a five and held the item close to her chest with one hand, pulling Isabella along with the other. Finally, once they were seated in the Starbucks with their *cafés con leche,* she put the glossy-covered magazine on the table between them.

They gasped in tandem.

"Holy shit," Isabella muttered, reaching out to touch it gingerly.

"Holy shit," Gabby echoed with equal parts reverence and awe. Her heart was so full, she felt as if it might just burst right there inside her chest at any time.

There on the cover was a perfect image of the Mona Lisa draped in a Puerto Rican flag. Written in big letters on the bottom was the main coverline:

Beauty Amidst the Rubble:
How Puerto Rico's street artists have brought hope
and pride back to their home

With wet cheeks, Gabby glanced at Isabella. There were tears running down her cheeks, too. But these tears were different than all the others they'd cried together and separately. These were not tears of loss, or fear, or loneliness, or abandonment. These were the kind of tears that came on the best of days—the most special of occasions. These were the tears that overflowed from your heart when there simply was no more room to hold the gratitude or the happiness.

With a shaking hand, Isabella flipped the cover open. Then they huddled close together, devouring the pages as the big, salty tears came, falling to the ground and baptizing the world in their joy.

ACKNOWLEDGMENTS

To say I'm an optimist would be a gross understatement. I'm one of those obnoxious people who believe they can do whatever they set their mind to. I have complete faith that, even as I write this, there is a complicated confluence of events underway which will—somehow—get me where I want to be. I don't worry about how I'll get there . . . I just know that I will. And a huge part of that is the people who cross my path—some of whom I've known for a lifetime, while there are others I've never met.

There are way too many of these folks to name, so I'm just going to give a shoutout to a few . . .

To my amazing agent, Jill Marsal, who never gave up on me. She has stuck with me, encouraged me, and showed me what is possible. I am a better writer because of Jill, and there's no one in this industry who I trust more.

To the folks at Kensington Books Publishing, especially Liz May, Elizabeth Trout, and the rest of the editorial/acquisitions team who read this manuscript and immediately "got it." I'm so grateful for the care you've shown me, and *Familia* and I look forward to sharing many more projects with you.

Now, on to the more personal thanks . . .

To my husband, Tom, who's suffered more take-out meals than I can count. Even as the house was falling down around our ears—laundry piled to the ceiling and every surface covered with bits of paper—he encouraged me to skip the domestic tasks and take the time I needed to get this story written. I promise to get a house cleaner for the next one, honey!

I'm so very grateful for the love and support of my friends including Jannet, Jeannie, Jen, Nika, Patti, and Patty, as well as my beloved cousin and friend, Liz Penney.

The dedicatees of this book are my grandparents, Mike and Crucita, who showed me who I was and who I could be. Because of David, Kim, Jeremiah, Nathan, Josh, Hannah, Laura, Michelle, and Bonnie, I can sleep at night knowing they're safe and cared for.

To my family for all their support and love and encouragement, but especially Vanessa, Janet, Kwaku, Michael, Karen, Jessica, Cheryl, Kathy, and Melissa.

To my parents, Gregory and Marie, and my paternal grandparents, Carol and Mario Rico. I wish they'd lived to see this moment. Though, I suspect they might have had a little something to do with the words that bubble out of my soul and onto the page. I miss you so much.

Familia Book Club Discussion Questions

1. The themes of penance and redemption are present in the lives of several of the characters: Isabella, Coquí, Alberto, and Beatríz. In your opinion, is redemption truly possible? Or do our actions define us for the entirety of our lives? How does this book, and its characters' experiences, support that argument?

2. The role and definition of family varies for the characters in this book. How did Coquí, Lucy and Mack, and Isabella come to find "family" outside of blood relations? Were there particular moments that you found real life parallels to?

3. Some of the characters were forced into actions they never would have considered under normal circumstances, and the motto of 'ends justifying the means' was a rationale for some characters' actions. How did the ends justify the means for Coquí, Beatríz, and Alberto? What would you have done differently in any of their shoes? Have you ever felt forced to make a decision you would be uncomfortable with under any other circumstances?

4. Familial DNA testing has become increasingly popular in recent years. Have you or someone you know used a service like this? If you are willing to share, was that person surprised by the results, or was a long-lost relative unearthed through the process? Are there any ethical complications to consider as a result of DNA matching?

5. Several of the characters put themselves at risk or made major sacrifices to keep baby Marianna safe. Who do you think had the most to lose by their actions and why? Has

there ever been a time when you or someone you know has made a big sacrifice for another family member?

6. Cross cultural adoption is a common practice in America, but less common in many other countries. Sometimes the adopted child may wonder about the circumstances surrounding their birth, or the culture they might have been raised in, had they not been adopted. In what ways did this book address those issues? Were you, or someone you know, adopted from another culture? Was it important for that person to learn more about their birth, or connect with the culture of the country they were born into?

7. How important was the setting, Puerto Rico, in this book? Did you feel this was a story that could have taken place anywhere, or was the setting an integral part of the story? Did the book make you want to visit Puerto Rico?

8. In what ways did Gabby and Isabella grow or change by the end of the book? Despite being raised apart, what similarities did they have? Were they more similar by the end of the book than at the start? Did the characters offer any insight into the timeless question of nature versus nurture?